Lucky at Love

Also by Cynthia Hamilton

NOVELS

Alligators in the Trees

Golden State

Spouse Trap (1st Madeline Dawkins Mystery)

A High Price to Pay (2nd Madeline Mystery)
Girl Trap (3rd Madeline Dawkins Mystery)

MEMOIR

Once Upon a Lyme… A Tale of Two Journeys

Finding Ruth

To learn more about the author,
please visit cynthiahamiltonbooks.com

Lucky at Love

Some guys just never give up...

Cynthia Hamilton

First Published 2006
Woodstock Press

ISBN: 978-0-9776278-0-6
Library of Congress Control Number: 206900631

Editing by Gail Prather
Cover design and formatting by Six Penny Graphics

For my mother, Ruth
In loving memory of Elena

say if his awkwardness was due to sadness over our friction or if it was merely due to the fact that he had nothing more to say to me.

"So, the awards banquet is tonight, then?" he asked, clearly struggling to keep the conversation afloat.

"Yep, in a couple of hours. Judith called right before you. Her flight was diverted to Chicago. She won't be able to get here at all."

"Really? Oh no. I wonder if you're going to have problems flying out on Monday," he said. Even over the phone, I could feel his relief at having sidestepped this potential aggravation.

"I guess we'll have to wait and see," I said.

"Well, good luck tonight," he said, evidently forgetting that the winners had already been decided. How did I ever marry such a dope?

"Thanks," I replied dryly. I started to hang up, but his voice stopped me.

"Allison?"

"Yes?"

"Be sure to stay warm." Not only did I not love Elliott anymore, I found his single-minded rigidity unbearable.

"Goodbye, Elliott," I said and hung up the phone.

From the moment I stepped out of the elevator and into the lobby, I could sense something more than the standard holiday excitement. Those rushing in from the snow were obviously giddy at having escaped the elements. Guests and employees streamed through the lobby and passageways, packing bars and restaurants, while exchanging greetings and weather updates.

I was fortunate enough to have my limo waiting directly in front of the awning, and all I had to show for my brush with nature was a dusting of snowflakes on my head and shoulders.

In another attempt to reward me for my success, Judith had arranged for a bottle of champagne on ice waiting for me as I slid into the back. As we crept the dozen or so blocks to The Waldorf, I tried not to let the absurdity of the full bottle of champagne and excessively spacious limousine mock me.

I peeled back the foil and loosened the cork as quickly as I could for the maximum pop, sending it ricocheting off the ceiling. I poured a glass and toasted myself. "Like anyone cares," I said, and tossed back the champagne.

I had a nice little buzz going by the time the chauffeur opened the door for me to emerge from my cozy cocoon. I wrapped my coat tightly around me with one hand and held onto his arm with the other as he escorted me under his umbrella to the entrance. I followed the directions to the ballroom reserved for the Prescott honorees and was fine until I entered the room.

I was fifteen minutes late and I was surprised to find that the room was barely half-full. Everyone was spread out in tidy cliques and I searched vainly for familiar faces.

Since I had been in this racket for over thirteen years, I had more than a passing acquaintance with many people whom I expected to encounter that evening. With the exception of an editor from *Avant Garde* and a writer for *The Washington Herald-Sentinel,* I knew no one.

The buzz around the room was that several of the most prominent figures for the evening's ceremony had been delayed due to the beastly weather, including one of the evening's recipients. If I hadn't already been checked in and tagged, I would've headed to the nearest exit and let them believe that I had been one of the unlucky travelers.

But not only had I been marked, the MC for the evening had introduced himself to me after we collided in my haste to find the ladies' room. I was trapped and beginning to hate Judith for having nominated me for this damn thing to begin with.

After waiting entirely too long for the stragglers to arrive, the pomp and circumstance finally got under way. The one and only good thing about the whole affair was that I was no longer pathologically nervous about delivering my acceptance speech. I was three glasses of wine removed from all fear at that point.

In fact, I could scarcely remember anything from the time I was called to the podium to the time I determined it was safe to cut out, except for making some wisecrack that luckily generated an appreciable amount of laughter. But I do recall how wonderful it felt to break out of the insufferably stuffy lobby and into the head-clearing cold of the night, inspecting the long line of limousines as I looked for my driver.

If it had been on my tab, I would have instructed him to cruise the city streets till dawn, while I sat snug as a bug watching the snow blow in wafts across the wide avenues. The traffic moved at a snail's pace due to the treacherous conditions of the roads, so at least the thrill was prolonged as long as possible.

I was almost tempted to walk a few blocks, but that was absolutely out of the question. One step outside the awning's protective path and my foot nearly took off without me. So I returned to my room, deflated and semi-drunk.

So disheartened was I that I initially failed to notice two striking additions to my room. It wasn't until I leaned against the desk chair to remove my shoes that I spotted the massive crystal vase with three dozen white roses and another bottle of champagne, which sat chilling on the table by the window. Confused by their sudden appearance, I cautiously removed the card attached to the bouquet.

"Congratulations and best wishes to my favorite interrogator," signed, "Yours faithfully, Jake."

I clutched the card to my chest and marveled at his ability to cheer me. It really wouldn't have taken much effort for my own husband to make such a gesture, and I suppose the fact that Jake was a relatively new friend touched me even more in light of Elliott's oversight.

I laughed at his closing and reread the message. "Yours faithfully." I had to admit I loved his ability to lampoon himself. But there was a postscript I had missed the first time—"If you have trouble drinking the whole bottle by yourself, dial room 786."

I stared at this cryptic message, not daring to believe its implication. After a moment's hesitation, I picked up the phone, pounding out the numbers and waiting impatiently for the line to connect.

"Yes?"

"I can't believe you're here!" I said incredulously.

"You can believe it, it's true," Jake replied mildly.

"But how did you get here? I heard the airport's virtually shut down."

"I flew in yesterday." I was momentarily speechless.

"Yesterday?" He flew in the same day I did? "But…what are you doing here?" I asked, thoroughly puzzled.

"Oh, I'm just here in case you need a little moral support."

I laughed in disbelief. "You came all the way to New York, in a snowstorm, to offer me moral support, without even knowing if I needed it?"

"It was just a hunch," Jake replied. "Call it men's intuition."

"This is incredible," I said, hand to my cheek, still not certain if I could trust my ears.

"So, do you need some help?"

"Help?"

"Drinking that outrageously expensive champagne."

"I do."

"Well…we can drink it at your place or mine. I don't know what your room is like, but I've got a view of St. Patrick's Cathedral that'll knock your socks off."

"I'll be there in five," I said.

A clean-shaven, tuxedo-clad Jake stood grinning slyly at me as I tried to convince myself he wasn't merely a wishful hallucination.

"You can't imagine how glad I am to see you," I said belatedly, as he held the door to let me in. "I thought you were allergic to wearing penguin suits," I said as passed.

"Yeah, well, this is a special occasion, isn't it?" I rolled my eyes and snorted.

"I've just endured the most insufferably boring awards dinner of all time, and my own editor wasn't even there to back me up."

"Was he supposed to be?"

"She, and yes. But they shanghaied her flight and rerouted it to Chicago. This thing was all her doing, anyway. I'm not going to let her nominate me next year, I can tell you that," I groused.

"I thought winning the Prescott Award was all you journalists cared about," he said, relieving me of the dripping wet bottle.

"I don't care about anything anymore," I replied petulantly. "Oh, my God, what a sight!" I cried out as I walked into the living room of Jake's suite. The cathedral, which stood smack in front of our hotel, could not have looked more dramatic.

From our height on the seventh floor, we had the most phenomenal vantage point, allowing us to gaze straight into the most striking features of the Neo-gothic design. And with the perfect coating of snow on the spires and rooflines, the massive structure was positively glowing in the reflected light.

"I told you it was spectacular," he said as he silently removed the cork and poured me a glass. "Now do things seem a little brighter?" he asked as he raised his glass to mine.

"Much. Thank you." We clinked our glasses and stared at the unearthly sight before us.

"The only thing missing is a fireplace," Jake said.

"That's about the only thing," I agreed as I took in his elegant digs. "Wow, this must have cost a medium-size fortune," I estimated, wandering from living room to dining room to powder room to the bedrooms.

"Two bedrooms? A little big for one mule breeder, isn't it?" I asked suspiciously, half expecting a new girlfriend to burst from some unseen quarters.

"It's all they had available besides the regular rooms, which I refuse to stay in if I'm going to come all the way to New York."

"Not bad, if you can afford it," I said, wondering for the first time just how wealthy he really was.

"When you're finished with the tour, why don't you come and have a seat," he called out. I was marveling over the size of his bathroom, amazed by the excessive amount of plumbing fixtures and granite. His toiletry bag was the only sign that he had actually occupied these rooms. I drifted back to the living room, a big, goofy smile on my face.

"What's so funny?" he asked. He had made himself comfortable on the sofa facing the window, one foot propped up on the other knee.

"This place—it's crazy."

"It'll do."

"I never knew you had such a flamboyant side. When I think of you, I think of barns and mules and country picnics."

"That's the country side of me. This is the city side."

I sat down next to him and laughed. "Well, this isn't so bad," I said as I leaned back against the down-filled cushions.

"Here, let me give you a topper, and you can tell me all about your problems."

I held my hand over my glass. "You already know about my problems. Anyway, they're boring."

"Nothing about you is boring."

I snorted. "Yeah, right. I still can't get over the fact that you're here. I'll tell you, if I ever needed a friend to materialize out of thin air, this was the time." I tapped my glass against his. "Thank you."

"You already thanked me," he said.

"Well, I really mean it." I sat thoughtfully for a moment. "Why are you here, anyway?"

"I had some business to attend to."

"Then why didn't you tell me you were coming to New York the same day I was? We could have flown in together." Even in my semi-inebriated state, I could tell that something didn't add up.

"It was a spur of the moment decision. Looks like you need a refill," he offered again.

"No, I'm fine. I'm already half-looped as it is. Besides, don't change the subject. So, after I left yesterday morning—God, was that really only yesterday?—it seems like a lifetime ago. Anyway, after I left, you suddenly decided that you had to come to New York on business?" I asked skeptically. "And did you take care of business?"

"Not yet, but I will before I leave." I gave him a dubious look. "You apparently didn't like my original answer, so I figured you wanted to hear something different."

"What was your original answer?"

"That I came to lend you moral support, in the event you should need it," he answered.

"Did you really come all that way for me?" I asked. I couldn't imagine why he would do such a thing.

"No, actually, I just felt like doing some Christmas shopping," he said snidely.

"Jake, nobody's ever done anything like this for me before," I said, touched by his incredible gesture.

"I can see why—you don't know how to appreciate it." I could tell he was only ribbing me, so I let his remark slide. "Feel like hearing some music?" he asked.

"Sure."

He disappeared into one of the other rooms, just as there was a knock at the door. "Can you get that?" he called out. "It's probably room service." I went to the door and let the waiter in.

"Good evening, madam. Where would you like me to set this up?"

"Uh, the living room, I guess." I followed behind and watched as he set up the table and uncovered plates of delectable morsels. Jake returned in time to sign the bill.

"This is quite a spread," I said.

"I ordered up a few nibbly things, in case you were still hungry after your banquet fare."

I examined the smoked salmon, smoked trout, pâté, caviar, all with the appropriate condiments, plus a large platter of French fries. "French fries?" I inquired as I sampled one.

"I don't know where I picked it up, but I love caviar on French fries."

"It would take a lot of caviar to cover all these fries," I commented, sticking a fry into the caviar bowl and trying out this odd concept.

"We can always order more," he replied.

"Boy, you really do know how to live it up, don't you?" I said, impressed by both the combination of flavors and his ability to afford such extravagances.

One

I followed Judith Paige into her office, the promise of yet another brilliant idea my ticket to an audience with the editor-in-chief. It would be a bit much to classify this idea as brilliant, though I hadn't let that stop me from advertising it as such.

"Let's hear it," she said as she closed the door behind me. I waited to speak until she had taken her seat, my loosely knit idea requiring her full attention lest I start rambling on in a disjointed, incoherent manner. I was hoping once I started putting it into words, a whole, cohesive storyline would emerge, thus satisfying Judith and easing my anxiety over what I wanted to embark on.

"It's a take on the notion of being addicted to love." As soon as I saw Judith's reaction, I knew I was out on a limb. I didn't want to give her the impression this was to be a soppy, romantic, swept-off-one's-feet piece. True, I did intend the story to be about love, or what passed for love in some people's minds.

But it was the downside of romance that I was really angling for. I wanted to explore the hypothesis that some people are actually obsessed with falling in love, literally hooked on the thrill of new romance. I cleared my throat and pressed on.

"I met this guy—at a wedding, of all places—who has been married and divorced seven times." Judith's jaw dropped, but I could tell she was intrigued by the notion.

"*Seven times?* You think his story's legit?" she asked.

"It was backed up by the bride's siblings. They had a gay old time teasing him about his numerous nuptials. I wish I'd had a tape recorder with me. It was quite a lively conversation on the subject of marriage and divorce—and rather irreverent, considering where we were. In addition to the seven brides, there've been countless live-in girlfriends."

"So, what are you proposing? Writing a piece about one man's obsession with marriage?"

"That, but break it down—find out what it was that attracted him to each of these women, and what compelled him to jump from one failed marriage to another, especially when there are men out there mortally afraid of getting married even once. I'd like to know why he thinks the relationships failed, and really, this is the angle that first caught my curiosity, what makes a woman take a chance on a guy who's been married four, five, six times before. You'd think they'd see a pattern there." I took a breath and gauged Judith's interest level.

"It seems to me there is some kind of mystique attached to a person who has been married so often," I continued, sensing I had caught her attention. "Maybe it presents some kind of challenge to a woman, you know, '*if he only found the right person, he would be happy.*'"

The beginnings of a smile appeared on Judith's otherwise placid face.

"One woman volunteered to be wife number eight right in front of own her husband. Needless to say, her husband was not amused. It just made me wonder what his many wives found so irresistible."

Judith studied me for a moment. "Are you thinking of interviewing some of these ex-wives as well?"

At this point I couldn't tell if I had pushed the idea too far. I donned my best poker face and nodded.

"So, just how in-depth do you see this thing being? I mean, it is an interesting topic, but what is the real crux of your story? Is it this 'Lover Man' angle, or is it the man-woman attraction thing? I can see either having potential, but so far the way you're describing your concept is a little too…nebulous."

This was precisely my own worry. I smiled confidently and started tap dancing.

"The way I see it, the piece is twofold: it's about one man's choices and the motivation behind them. You can't really tackle his particular situation without taking a hard look at the man himself. And I don't think it's possible to accurately portray this Jake Sorenson character without the balancing perspective from the women who have shared his life for a while. His point of view versus theirs."

Judith mulled over the concept.

What I needed at this juncture was more proof of Jake's larger-than-life personality. But unfortunately, the photo I had of this wild and wooly frontier man just wouldn't cast the right spell. "I've got to tell you, Judith, this Jake is something else. You just wouldn't believe he was a Don Juan if you saw him."

"Why? Is he one of those shy, helpless guys that women feel sorry for?" she asked, already losing her taste for the piece.

"Oh God, no—just the opposite! He's like a brick wall of a man—massively built, with swagger galore. Not handsome per se, but he's got this irrepressible charm about him. Not the Cary Grant or Pierce Brosnan class of charm—more like raw animal magnetism." I had Judith's attention now.

"On top of being a ladies' man, he's also a decorated Vietnam vet. And he's been a nightclub owner, a Hollywood stuntman, antiques dealer, South American furniture importer—the list goes on. Now he's living on a sixteen hundred-acre ranch in eastern Oregon where he breeds and trains mules…*mules,* for God's sake!"

Judith laughed. "What the hell does he do with them?"

I knew I had her now. "He sells them for as much as a good quarter horse," I informed her, with a derisive snort.

"No kidding."

"No kidding. He claims they're a better ride than a horse—smoother." I let my eyebrows punctuate this remark. Judith swiveled back and forth in her chair. I could tell she was going to give me the go-ahead. She stood and I stood.

"Jake Sorenson," Judith said, savoring the sound of it. "I like the name. Rugged sounding. I assume you wouldn't be here if you hadn't already set up an interview with him."

I smiled vaguely. "He's ready, willing, and able."

"How old a guy is he?" she asked as we walked toward her door, apparently tallying the countless women who had marked time in his life.

"Somewhere in his fifties, I'd say. But you'd never know it." I knew for a fact he was sixty-two, but for some reason I felt compelled to lie.

"Okay, you get the goods on this Renaissance Romeo. Settle the age-old conundrum of what attracts people to one another. But don't let this thing get too far-flung. Email me a detailed memo, with story outline and estimated travel expenses. I assume you plan to visit this man, and maybe an ex-wife or two?" she said, eyeing me deliberately. "I want to see a rough draft no later than the end of October."

I nodded obediently. This gave me just shy of a month to make something out of this cockamamie, half-baked idea. Now all I had to do was inform my husband of my imminent travel plans, a chore I never looked forward to.

Two

"So I went ahead and booked a reservation on an 8 a.m. flight to Boise. His ranch is about a four-hour drive south of there. Boise is actually closer than Portland, so that gives you an idea how remote he is," I said to Elliott the night before my departure, as I dished out the salad and handed him the plates.

I had just related his specially tailored version of my current project and the necessity of traveling to eastern Oregon to interview the rogue mule breeder we had met at our friend's wedding.

In his customary distracted state, the project as I had outlined it so far had produced little more than the occasional assenting murmur. I had managed to give the plain, almost clinical essence of the piece, identifying what causes the insane optimism that leads some people into a string of disastrous relationships. In Jake's case, I was assuming they were disastrous as not a single one had survived.

Despite my careful phrasing, I could tell my husband hadn't listened to a word I'd said. As Elliott is a man consumed by modern technology and its inner workings, the trivial aspects of human caprices go largely unnoticed by him.

My articles tend to focus almost entirely on what makes people tick, so I am accustomed to his less than enthusiastic response to my writing inspirations. He is supportive of my work, in the abstract. But his aloofness aside, something had apparently caught his attention, for he was now focused on the fact that I was headed out of town again.

"You're going to Oregon?" he asked as the information belatedly registered.

"Yeah, to interview Miriam's brother," I reiterated patiently. "You know, the guy who has a mule farm, or whatever he called it." The light of recognition finally dawned in Elliott's eyes. Unfortunately, the light was quickly clouded over by confusion.

"Are you writing a piece about mules?" he asked. I gave him the long-suffering look of a woman whose husband doesn't fully appreciate her career.

"Honey, you haven't heard anything I've been telling you for the last ten minutes."

Elliott paused in the middle of pouring our waters, offended by my accusation, mostly because it was true. "Of course I have," he said hastily, "but I just don't see the connection between that old coot and…and…um, relationships," he said, triumphant in the fact that he had managed to recall another pertinent fact of what I had been telling him.

"You don't see the connection between relationships and a guy who has been married and divorced *seven times?*" I asked accusingly. Elliott looked sheepishly at me for a moment, then recovered.

"Oh, so you're focusing on the *failed* relationship angle."

Nice try, I thought, barely able to keep the smile off my face. It didn't matter to me one whit that he was blasé about my writing, or in this project in particular. All I wanted was to take my little excursion without any static from him. In spite of his seemingly cold nature, he is surprisingly dependent on my company.

Judging by his current level of guilt at having been caught ignoring my conversation once again, I didn't anticipate a whole lot of protest on his part. I sighed pointedly and handed him a bowl of pasta.

"I'll just let you read it when it's finished," I told him. I picked up my bowl and water glass and headed to our tiny dining table, its only highpoint being the view of the Bay Bridge.

This last statement generated a contrite appeal for more in-depth information. After a certain amount of obligatory pleading on his part, I relented and began to elaborate on the finer points I hoped to explore with our much-married acquaintance.

True to form, Elliott quickly lost the thread of what I was saying, presumably more interested in his own professional challenges. Out of sheer orneriness, I continued my monologue, using this unique forum to think out loud and further hone my idea.

I knew I would have plenty of time on the plane to outline my questions, but as I saw much potential in the topic of frenzied attraction resulting in repeated marriage and divorce, it helped enormously to bat the idea around in the open air.

The more I indulged in this stream of consciousness, the more remote Elliott became, lulled into productive thought by my endless drone. Just out of spite, because I knew he wasn't listening, I told him I wasn't sure how long I would be gone; maybe a day, maybe three or four. The ticket was open-ended.

This disclaimer produced not a sound out of him. Well, I had told him, and if my extended absence came as a shock to him later, I could truthfully say he had been advised of my uncertain plans.

Goaded into an even feistier mood by his indifference, I told him that in addition to mules, Jake Sorenson also raised prize-winning elephants that he sold to the Chinese government to patrol the Great Wall, to which he responded with a pleasant "I see."

I sighed and took a long sip of my water. It was a damn good thing I'm the independent type, I consoled myself, or else I would be writing about failed marriages from firsthand experience.

Elliott snapped back to reality as soon as I stopped speaking. He complimented me on the fettuccine, which he had gobbled down, and cleared the table except for my glass. As I listened to the sounds of Elliott washing the dishes, I figured I was pretty lucky, all things considered, as undoubtedly there had to be a lot worse husbands out there than him.

Three

I reread the directions I had printed from the Internet, wondering where exactly I had gone wrong. I had pulled off to the side of a sleepy country road, in the middle of softly rolling hills that stretched out in every direction. The last road marker I had passed announced that I was headed west on State Route 74, yet by my reckoning, I should have been going south on Route 207. My vast experience of negotiating subways and airport terminals was of little good out in the middle of nowhere.

I was starting to feel vaguely panicky, for even though I was ready to admit defeat, there was no one within miles to whom I could surrender. I didn't want to start the interview process with a Mayday call, for my confidence was already flagging and I was loath to give that particularly intimidating man any whiff of uncertainty. But as I sat in my economy size rental car, four hours outside of Boise, Idaho, I wondered if perhaps I had let my caprices get the better of me this time.

In addition to doubting the validity of this particular concept, I was also shouldering a fair amount of guilt for the way I had championed it. I had been less than forthcoming in my motivation for wanting to tackle the subject of romantic attraction via this wild and evidently untamable man.

Let's face it, finding seven different women willing to marry the same man in one lifetime is no mean feat, and realizing this had spawned my theory that perhaps some of us actually find that dubious achievement tantalizing, as though those successive marriages were an endorsement and not a deterrent. As contrary as this was to my own levelheaded way of thinking, I found myself susceptible to the same wicked allure, though purely out of professional curiosity.

But there was another cause for my unease, one that nearly had me driving straight back to Boise. The main reason for my trepidation was the fact that after a brief four-hour acquaintance, this indiscriminant womanizer proclaimed he'd marry me in a second if I ever left my husband. I had dismissed this outrageous proclamation at the time, not only because I discounted the sincerity of the remark, but also because I was already intent on writing a story about this man.

As awkward as his apparent attraction to me could end up being, it did come in handy when I called and proposed writing a piece about him. True, I hadn't come out and told him exactly the angle I was after, though I did say I wanted to ask him about his long and active love life. Somehow I think he got the impression I intended to do a piece that chronicled his complete life and times, an homage to his incredibly hedonistic lifestyle.

I wasn't particularly worried about the distinction, as a great deal of his life has been spent shuttling from one woman to the next, and therefore would be encompassed in his colorful oral history. I planned to simply listen to everything he wanted to tell me and extrapolate what I needed for my piece. I would, however, have to watch him closely to make sure he didn't start getting the wrong idea about my clinical interest in him.

As I sat staring at the map, flashes of the charismatic, slightly oafish giant clouded my vision. I realize this characterization is less than complimentary, but that's what made this guy so fascinating to me. It wasn't that he was homely, but I had come away with the idea that keeping up his physical appearance was not high on his agenda.

He was big—six foot two and built like a linebacker or a lumberjack. As his name would suggest, he was of Scandinavian descent. His hair was an almost clownish spray of blond-turning-to-grey curls, and most of his face was obscured by an unruly beard. He was *not* GQ material, if you get my drift.

Yet, he had this smile, a great big, disarming smile with perfect white teeth— apparently the only area he devoted any personal hygiene to—and when he used it, it could be dazzling. When he favored you with one of those smiles, you could actually see life sparkle in those pale blue-grey eyes of his.

At this point, I caught myself. What the hell was I doing out here? Had I lost my mind? I had been so wrapped up in the topic of sexual attraction, the fly-on-the-wall journalist in pursuit of answers to my enormous curiosity, I had completely overlooked the precarious position I was willing to put myself into just to get the goods. How else could it possibly appear to this man, me traveling seven hundred miles out to his desolate ranch to "interview" him about his love life? Especially when you considered his offer of marriage, harmless or not. Jesus, what was I thinking?

I turned my map upside down, executed a quick one-eighty and headed my subcompact back toward Boise. I'd call him from the airport and give him some BS story as to why I would not be coming out to see him after all. I'd find another way to explore my theories on why people are attracted to each other when they ought to know better.

Maybe I'd run an ad in the *San Francisco Chronicle* advertising for those unfortunate souls thrice or more divorced, pick their brains, figure out what the heck compelled them to jump all willy-nilly into one doomed marriage after another. Yeah, I thought, that was a much safer approach.

Satisfied that I had regained my senses and had not sacrificed my integrity, or worse, I was now able to enjoy my bucolic surroundings. As my mood calmed, my paced slowed and I studied the passing sights. I had retraced my tracks for about twenty minutes when I came upon a very picturesque property that I had somehow missed my first time through.

I slowed past the impressive gated entrance, admiring the fancy ironwork depicting a spirited equine and its hapless rider. It was one of those sights you can't help but smile at. As my eye followed the handiwork down, I read the sign for the Buckin' J Ranch.

"Well, I'll be damned," I thought, as I pulled the car onto the shoulder and stared down the long gravel driveway. How was that for luck? As soon as I decided against this assignation, I had no problem locating Jake Sorenson's rural hideaway.

Behind the gatepost, an avenue of sycamores lined the drive, bending in a gentle arc and obscuring the view of what lie beyond. Even though the signpost confirmed my whereabouts, it didn't give any clue about the man I came to interview. I still had difficulty imagining that the flamboyant character I had met in San Francisco resided in such a remote and tranquil setting.

I cut the engine and wrestled with my better judgment. Now that I was there, I found it harder to justify dropping Jake from the story. After traveling all that distance and seeing where he lived, could I really be satisfied with not knowing the reasons behind seven failed marriages? Did I really want to let that big unknown niggle at my subconscious forever? Would I concoct some lie for Elliott and Judith, or would I admit I lost my nerve after all the trouble I had taken to pursue this angle?

Had I never found the place, I would have faced those dilemmas and dealt with them. But the circumstances were different now and my natural instincts would not let me back away from this challenge. I had never been cowardly when it came to delving into another's psyche, and I wasn't going to let a redneck, mule-breeding ladies' man intimidate me this time. I backed the car up and headed down the gravel drive, an ominous cloud of dust trailing behind me.

Once I made my way around the curve in the drive, several outbuildings came into view. I idled past what I took to be housing for the ranch hands, looking for any signs of life. Finding no one, I continued on past a copse of tall trees to a barn flanked by two large arenas. Several pickup trucks of varying vintages were parked helter-skelter in front of the far arena.

I aligned my rental car with the last of these, hoping not to generate too much attention from the group of wranglers arranged alongside the fence. I was almost too successful. Once I had reached the spectators, I had a little trouble making my presence known.

I finally tapped the shoulder of an old, weathered man and asked him where I might find the proprietor. His blue eyes surveyed me curiously, then he tipped his head toward what he and the others had been watching so intently.

Cautiously, I hoisted one leg up onto the split-rail fence in order to get a better look. There, on one of the most powerfully built animals I had ever laid eyes on, was Jake Sorenson engaged in, and apparently winning, a battle of the wills.

"He took that wild mare on a bet," my neighbor advised me as I watched Jake momentarily struggle with what I assumed to be a mule. I'm your average city chick when it comes to country life and customs, but I did know enough about the animal kingdom to know that mare meant female.

"She sure is big," I ventured.

"Big, and ornery as hell," the ranch hand replied. "Jake bet the owner he could tame her in a week."

I watched as the mare reared her head briefly, then submitted to Jake's command. "How's it going?"

The cowboy looked at me and grinned. "She's good as broke. Jake had her reigned by the second day and neck-reigned by the third. He's just teaching her tricks now to pass the time."

"I take it that's an impressive feat, breaking a mule in less than a week," I said.

He squinted over at me skeptically. "Downright miraculous, I'd say. The damn bitch kicked a hole clean through a steel trailer on the way over."

I raised my eyebrows, suitably impressed. "What was the wager?"

"He breaks her, he gets to keep her." The cowhand suddenly regarded me suspiciously, as if he'd just realized there was a foreigner in their midst.

"You've got business with Mr. Sorenson?" he asked.

"Yes, he's expecting me. I'm a little late. I got lost on my way out here." He looked back at Jake and waited until he had finished executing a series of spins, first clockwise, then counter. I was getting dizzy just watching.

"Hey Jake, you've got company," he called out. Jake looked in our direction for the first time since I'd been there. Either he was very intent on what he was doing, or he was accustomed to being the center of attention. In any case, he barely acknowledged that he saw me, but he switched maneuvers and began a routine of what I later learned are called side passes.

The mule, appropriately named Jezebel, edged closer to my side of the fence, prettily crossing one front leg over the other until she and Jake were directly aligned with me. Jake gave a gentle signal with a flick of the reigns and Jezebel backed up, then lowered herself on her front legs as if she were curtseying for me. It was such an unexpected gesture; it just about took my breath away. Jake apparently got the reaction he was looking for. He was sitting atop his now docile mule, grinning like a jackass.

"I see you finally found us. I was afraid we were going to have to send out a search party to find any wayward journalists," he said, releasing the mare from her servile posture and bringing her to rest. He dismounted with a lightness that belied his size, though he seemed perfectly in scale when compared to his new mare, like Paul Bunyan and his big blue ox.

He praised Jezebel and patted her face roughly, then stroked the inside of her ears in a way that seemed both pleasurable and uncomfortable for her. He whispered something to her, an intimate act that suggested a strong bond had already formed between animal and master.

One of his ranch hands hopped over the fence and took Jezebel by the reins and led her away. Jake watched her retreat, not nearly as cooperative as she had been with him. This sight evidently pleased Jake. He laughed out loud.

"That's one feisty female," he said as he approached me from the other side of the fence. "But I haven't met one yet I couldn't get the best of." He crossed his arms over the top of the fencepost, looking me directly in the eye. I couldn't help thinking there was a message for me in that statement.

Cocky son-of-a-bitch, I thought, though it was hard to take offense when he was wearing that contagious grin. I smiled in spite of myself and stepped down from the fence, preferring to keep a safe distance between us.

"Congratulations on your latest acquisition," I said.

Jake nodded his acknowledgment and began walking toward the gate. My reporter's instincts kicking in, I fell into step as I formulated questions in my mind that would put the focus on him and give me a more advantageous position.

I was already feeling as though he had the upper hand in this interview, and of course he did. I was on his home turf and he was the master at breaking stubborn mules. Maybe it was the same desire to tame a wild creature that attracted so many women to him. I hid behind my journalistic shield and started the interview process benignly enough with the topic of mules.

"I hear you tamed her in just three days," I said.

"I got her cooperation in three days. I don't know that you ever really tame them. They just let you think you have," he said.

"How many mules do you own right now?" I asked.

"I've got twenty-six mules at the moment—twenty-seven, counting Jezebel—four horses, and three donkeys, but I think I've got three of the mules sold."

"So, that's what you do then, train them and sell them?" Jake emerged from the corral and leaned back over the fence to watch one of his men try to put Jezebel through her paces.

"And breed them. That's my main focus these days. Breaking mules is challenging and I like it, but my goal is to breed the perfect mule."

Somehow this didn't surprise me. Suddenly, I remembered one of the few facts I know about animal husbandry. "I always thought that mules couldn't reproduce."

"They can't," Jake replied. I began to suspect he was having me on.

"Exactly how do you breed them, then?" This seemed a reasonable enough question to me, though I could tell that Jake was tickled by my ignorance. For a minute I thought he was going to let me continue to labor under the delusion that the stork brought baby mules into the world.

He turned to me and patiently clued me in on the mating complexities that result in mule birth. "It takes a horse and a donkey to make a mule," he began, sparking something in my memory long forgotten.

"Of course, I knew that," I thought out loud, feeling hopelessly stupid. If Jake sensed my embarrassment, he didn't let on. Nor was this the end of my lesson.

"The reason mules usually can't reproduce is because they are lacking a chromosome. They have only sixty-three—thirty-one from the sire and thirty-two from the dam. You with me so far?"

I nodded my head feebly.

"In extremely rare cases, a mare mule can foal, but a male mule has never sired a foal. Now, a female horse—a mare—and a male donkey—a stallion or a jack—make a mule. If the mother is a jenny donkey and the father is a stallion horse, the foal will be a hinny. The male offspring is called a John and the female is a Molly."

Now I thought for sure he was putting me on. I was reminded of the Dr. Seuss stories I read as a kid. I was immediately lost and I wondered if I should be taking notes. I stood there, completely bewildered, while Jake turned his attention back to the arena.

"So, how do you know if you've got a jenny or a hinny if you don't know the parentage of the mule?" I asked, desperately trying to assimilate this confusing new information. Jake turned around and grinned.

"You don't, and it doesn't matter a damn bit, one way or the other." A strong gust of wind swept out of nowhere, adding a chill to the overcast day. "Come on, let's go inside and get some coffee," he said in answer to my shivering.

We walked past my car and I stopped briefly to grab my bag and briefcase, then scurried to catch up with him. His gait was as strong and purposeful as a conquering Viking's as he traversed the gravel path that led down to the main house.

I was grateful I'd had the foresight to wear my most sensible footwear, though I suppose my shoes betrayed my ineptitude in rural surroundings. As if he were reading my thoughts, Jake glanced back as I picked my way down the path to the modest, low profile ranch house.

"We need to get you into a proper pair of boots," he said. "We'll get you a pair of riding boots and put you on top of Jezebel," he teased as he lightly ascended the steps of his wrap-around porch and held the back door open for me. We entered through the mudroom where Jake traded his dirt-caked Ariats for a pair of sheepskin boots.

I busied myself looking at the photos that covered the walls, most of which depicted Jake and his mules, past and present. "How long have you owned this ranch?" I asked as he led the way into the kitchen. After the authentic ranchiness of the mudroom, it was something of a shock to see the sleek elegance now before me. The white walls and custom-built cabinets, the granite countertops and the gleaming stainless steel appliances were hardly my expectation of how a working ranch kitchen would look. Nor was I prepared for the spaciousness of the room. It was so large that at first I didn't notice the compact Hispanic woman working at the sink at the far end.

"I've owned it for ten years now, but it's been my main residence for the last seven," he answered before addressing his housekeeper. "You got any coffee left, Rosalinda?"

"There is half a pot left from lunchtime, Señor Jake. I think it is still hot," she said. She took down two coffee mugs and placed them on the large island counter that bisected the room, giving me a brief once-over. I started to place my bags on the counter when Jake amended the plan.

"I think we'll be more comfortable at the table," he said as he casually strolled over to the breakfast table and pulled out a chair for me. I hauled my bags over and resettled myself, grateful that I had props to play with, for I had suddenly become very self-conscious. I suspected that maddening smile of his was the cause of my unease.

I pretended not to notice the way he was looking at me as I pulled out my pad and pens and recorder and arranged them purposefully in front of me. This was a charade, for I almost never employ these aids. I'm blessed with quite a reliable memory. Only in rare instances do I need to jot down a name or date.

The recorder is almost solely used as a sort of intimidation tactic; only in cases where the interviewee is particularly cagey do I tape record our conversation. If someone knew how to read me, they'd immediately figure out I was posturing to create a subtle barrier between the subject and myself.

In this case, I was nervous enough to warrant donning my useless spectacles, psychologically my most effective armor. Okay, I thought, I'm as prepared as I'll ever be. I crossed my arms on the tabletop and studiously turned my attention to Jake.

"This is fun," he said, his goofy smile making a mockery of the interview process.

"I'm glad you think so," I replied.

"Honey, if you'd come all the way up here to give me an appendectomy without benefit of anesthesia, I would've thought it was fun. I'd have agreed to almost anything for the chance to see you again," he said, leaning in toward me as he delivered this unabashed compliment.

I knew I blushed this time, for I could feel my face grow hot. I should have listened to my better judgment and stayed on the road. I didn't know why in the world I had thought I was any kind of match for this guy. He was going to control the process from beginning to end.

"Shall we get started?" I asked. Rosalinda appeared and placed a cup of coffee in front of each of us, distracting me once again.

"Thanks, Rosie. Hey, are you hungry? Rosalinda can throw something together for you real quick."

"Oh, no thanks, I'm fine," I said to the wary housekeeper. She returned my smile rather perfunctorily and went about her business. I waited for Jake to pick up my last cue, not wanting to repeat myself.

After grinning at me abstractly for a minute or so, he got with the program. "Okay, I'm all yours now," he said. "Tell me again—what is it you're writing about?"

Oh brother, I thought. He really is going to put me through my paces. Just like that mule.

"I'm doing a piece for our magazine about what it is exactly that makes men and women fall in love and marry repeatedly. Seeing as how you have had ample experience in this arena, I thought you could give me your insights into what makes people take the plunge, even when they've had less than storybook results."

He mulled this over for a moment. "Hmm…this is not particularly flattering for me, is it? I'll look like a seven-time loser. Or is that why you chose me in the first place, to illustrate how stupid some guys can be when it comes to love?" Fortunately, his smirk was more playful than his words, but there was no doubt I had to put the right spin on what my intentions were, or he might tell me to forget the whole thing.

I laughed lightly to convey the notion that he had gotten me all wrong. "I certainly didn't come away with the impression that you've ever been on the losing end of any of your marriages," I said. "In fact, I suspect you've left quite a trail of broken hearts in your wake." I couldn't tell by his expression if I'd helped or hindered my case with this assertion.

"So, you want me to confess my trade secrets to you, let you see what goes on in the mind of a womanizer?"

There was a note of challenge in his voice, but I didn't want to back off again or the entire interview process would be lost. Instead, I grabbed my pad as I studied him closely.

"Is that how you see yourself?" I asked, poised to make notes as he spoke.

"Isn't that how you see me?"

I paused to consider this. "I have to say I haven't thought of you that way either. I think 'womanizer' is a rather harsh term to use in your case."

Jake sat back, arms crossed in front of him, obviously trying to penetrate my thoughts with his stare. "Well, that's awful nice of you to give me the benefit of the doubt and all, but why do you think I've been with so many women and never been able to stay with just one, if I'm not a loser and I'm not a womanizer?"

"I don't know. I was hoping you'd tell me," I said. I refrained from telling him that I was there to ask the questions, not the other way around. I was beginning to suspect our tête-à-tête would consist of one nonstop skirmish. Jake offered the sugar bowl to me, which I declined.

He then poured an almost sickening amount of sugar into his cup and stirred it thoughtfully. "I like my coffee sweet, like my women," he said.

This remark made me wonder if he saw the endless parade of women through his life as nothing more than aids to his pleasure.

"So is that what initially attracts you to a woman—sweetness?"

"I can't say that there's any one thing. I guess there've been as many different things that caught my eye as there've been women. I couldn't say, really. I've never given it any thought."

This came as a surprise to me. "Really, you don't know what it is you're attracted to?"

"Oh, I know it when I see it. I'm just saying there's no one special thing that gets my attention, except for a curious mind," he said for my benefit.

I smiled tersely and tried to continue.

"Those glasses don't look too strong," he interrupted me, peering at my eyes closely. With unexpected swiftness, he reached across the table and removed them from my face.

"You don't really need these things, do you?" he said, putting them on and testing his vision as he scanned the room and looked back at me.

Damn. I felt as ineffectual as a novice animal trainer in a room full of ill-behaved chimpanzees. "They help me concentrate," I replied lamely as I extracted the pair from his large hands. At this point, I was just grateful he didn't start laughing.

"Oh, I see," he said. Whether the pun was intentional or not, I couldn't tell. I stowed the instrument of my humiliation back in my briefcase and cleared my throat pointedly.

"Okay, if there isn't any one characteristic that you look for," I said, picking up where I'd left off, "could you tell me what attracted you to each of your wives?"

Jake exhaled roughly, as if this session had already become tiresome to him.

"You really want to hear the whole gory history of my love life?"

I nodded while he took a long, meditative sip of his coffee. "Jake, if this is too uncomfortable, we can stop. You're not obligated to go through with this interview. After all, it's your life—you don't have to share it with me or our readers."

Rosalinda, apparently annoyed or embarrassed by the conversation taking place in her kitchen, stopped what she was doing and went to find work in some other part of the house. Jake seemed to relax a bit after her departure.

"Now, don't get all worked up. I said I'd help you out and I will. You just have to understand that despite the fact that it's my life, I've never analyzed it at all."

I let him take a moment to gather his thoughts. Out of sheer hopefulness, I marked the numbers one through seven on my notepad. It belatedly occurred to me that if he were to start cooperating, I would, fantastic memory aside, need some sort of scorecard to keep his matrimonial record straight.

"Well now, if you take Marissa—wife number one—for example, there wasn't anything about her that attracted me to her."

"What do you mean?" I asked.

Jake shrugged. "I couldn't stand her from the moment I laid eyes on her."

I gave him a look of puzzlement to spur him on.

"I had just returned to Ann Arbor from two tours in Vietnam. It was the summer of '69. I was twenty-four, a decorated war hero, and I couldn't find work. The country had gone crazy in my absence—war protesters and sit-ins, free love, hippies, and drugs. I felt as out of place in Michigan as I had in 'Nam. I finally took a job as a lifeguard at the Belvedere Country Club.

"Oddly enough, I had no trouble fitting into that world, where the rich were happy to accept you into their environment, so long as you did their bidding and kept your answers polite.

"To tell you the truth, after the less than hospitable welcome home I received from my contemporaries, it was kind of a nice switch to be treated with respect by the club members. The men would always shake my hand heartily, after a few highballs of course, and tell me how much they appreciated my service to our country. The women would give me proud, approving looks, most of them, but their daughters were all over me. I was a hog in heaven, I'll have to admit that," Jake said with a fond laugh, evidently enjoying this trip down memory lane.

"Anyway, the chicks there were something else, with their tanned bodies and their teeny bikinis. The other lifeguards and I had very little actual work to do. Most the time we sat up in our chairs, pretending to do our duty while surreptitiously flirting with all the sweet young things.

"Once in a while, the general manager busted our chops for one thing or another, but for the most part it was a dream job, while it lasted. I got along with everyone there, except for one snotty deb who seemed to think I'd been put on this planet solely to bow and scrape to her. Everything else there was so good, I decided I wasn't going to let her bother me. When she ragged on me about too much chlorine in the pool or not enough towels in the changing rooms, or her car not being parked in the shade—which wasn't my responsibility, anyway—I would basically ignore her.

"Eventually, it became a battle of wills with her. Then one day she accused me of taking money out of her purse while I was on my break. It caused a real pain in the ass for the GM but everyone believed I hadn't taken that hoity-toity bitch's money. I got a halfhearted lecture on being polite to the guests at all times, and the GM took twenty bucks out of his own pocket to pacify the spoiled brat. But from that moment on, it was open warfare between Marissa Sue Parsons and me."

Jake paused to take a sip of his coffee, while I anxiously awaited the details of how Marissa Sue became the first Mrs. Jake Sorenson. Jake leaned back in his chair, obviously warming to this new game of kiss and tell.

"So, for the next several weeks, Miss Parsons, only child of Mr. and Mrs. Ambrose Parsons, and the only heir to a fabulous car dealership fortune, did her level best to piss me off. Then one day, she went too far. I don't know if you've caught on yet, but I did not come from the right neighborhood of Ann Arbor, Michigan. I was the son of immigrant parents who worked like devils to make a good life for us in the land of plenty.

"When I returned from the service, none of that had changed. I had to be very careful with every buck I could lay my hands on. So one day, as a big thrill for myself, I had decided not to bring the customary bag lunch, but to splurge instead on a cheeseburger from the snack bar, with all the fixings.

"I had just arranged my lunch on one of the employee tables, which sat behind a wall off the main kitchen, separated from the pool area. I was about to take my first bite when Marissa saunters in wearing nothing but a bright yellow bikini and sunglasses, smoking a cigarette through a filter like she's some kind of movie star. She had no business being back there, but the members could do as they pleased. She blew smoke in my face and then helped herself to one of my French fries.

"Now, I've just returned from three years of jungle warfare in 'Nam, where a man would get killed for less insulting gestures, and there was no way in hell I was going to sit there and take that kind of crap from this candy-assed twit, job or no job. So, I grabbed her by the wrist and looked her straight in the eye.

"'You ever do anything like that again, I'll turn you over my knee and give you the spanking you should have gotten years ago,' I told her calmly. She glared at me, her bottom lip protruding like she was about to drown me in crocodile tears. I let go of her wrist and watched her while I ate one of my fries, knowing I'd probably be thrown out of there before I had a chance to finish my lunch. When she didn't run off right away to get me fired, I figured she was too shocked by my actions to make a move.

"Feeling like maybe I'd taught her the first lesson in discipline of her life, I began to smugly eat my burger. It was then that Marissa put her cigarette out in my soda. The look on her face filled me with a red-hot hatred of her and her kind. I threw her over my knee so fast, her sunglasses went flying across the patio. I don't know how I kept from spanking her bloody, but I managed to limit myself to three or four good smacks. I stood up when I was through, launching her backward. It was funny to see how all the rage I had been feeling had now been transferred to her.

"She was so mad, at first she couldn't speak. Then she found her tongue and just let loose on me. She called me every name she could think of and all I could do was laugh. Of course, that made her all the madder. If she'd had a gun, I'd have been a dead man. Instead, she came at me with her fists up and flailing. She landed a couple blows on me before I grabbed her by the arms and held her still. It was then, with her squirming and spewing, that I pulled her close and kissed her.

"I honestly don't know why I did it. Maybe I'd seen it in a movie once. But it had a powerful effect on both of us. We pulled apart, stunned by what had just taken place, not quite sure what to do next. We both stood there panting, staring at each other. I could see the conflicting emotions flit across her face.

"It's funny how I've never forgotten it. I think that moment softened me toward her. Anyway, all of a sudden, she raised her arm as if to strike me again. But she didn't. This time when we kissed, it was much sweeter, but still fiery.

"Of course, we were both young and dumb, or else we'd have realized that kind of passion wears off real quick, and we'd have had the sense not to rush into marriage the way we did. But we were caught up in the moment and so were her folks. Surprisingly, they didn't object to a short engagement, though her mother had to move heaven and earth to arrange everything in five weeks.

"I can't remember what the big rush was. I think we must have thought if being together was so marvelous, living together had to be even better. It wasn't, of course.

I think it became boring for me on the honeymoon, to some degree, but it all went to pieces once we moved into the brand-new home her folks had bought for us.

"Looking back, I believe Marissa probably would've been happy to fall into a carbon-copy of her parents' lifestyle—me working for her dad at one of his dealerships, her sitting around the pool at the country club all day, dinner and bridge at their house or ours."

Jake shook his head, a grim expression on his face. "Jesus, it gives me the willies just thinking about it. We fought constantly once we fell into our preordained routine. I swear it was all that I could do to keep from strangling her. I can see now that it wasn't really her I was mad at. It was my fault for getting into that situation in the first place. So, I turned into the big asshole, with Marissa running home to mother at least once a week.

"Finally, one day when I woke up alone for the fourth or fifth time, I threw my meager belongings into the Cadillac convertible—another wedding gift from her parents—pointed it west, and didn't stop until I'd hit California." Jake reached for his coffee cup and took another sip while he judged my reaction to this sudden flood of information.

It took me a second or two to realize I had been totally mesmerized by Jake's account of marriage number one. I closed my mouth, cleared my throat and tried to put myself back into the role of interviewer.

"How long did that marriage last?" I asked.

"Less than two months, I think." I made a notation on my pad of paper after the number one, quickly trying to assimilate all the pertinent points of his fascinating tale.

After the tug-of-war that preceded this revelation, I was caught a little off guard by his sudden candor. I would have liked to have put the scene on pause for a minute or two to gather my thoughts. I was racking my brain for a question that would spawn similar disclosures when Rosalinda reentered the kitchen and set about preparing the evening meal. The distraction gave me the reprieve I was looking for, but it also seemed to break whatever mood had loosened Jake's tongue.

As soon as she reappeared, the ranch hands began to shuffle in, their spirited conversation further dislocating our separate trains of thought. They took turns washing up in the mud room, four of them altogether, then one by one they went back outside and arranged themselves on the porch furniture directly outside the breakfast room windows. One of them had retrieved a six-pack of beer from the cooler and passed it around. It was the end of their workday and it was clear even to me that they would pass the time there until their supper was served.

"Feel like taking a tour of the property?" Jake asked, clearly peeved at having his forum disrupted.

"Sure," I said, stowing my paraphernalia back in my bags.

"But first we need to fix you up with the proper footwear for stomping around a ranch." He got up and walked toward the mudroom. "What are you—'bout a six and a half?"

"Seven," I said as I joined him. He picked through a large selection of cowboy boots stowed under the bench that ran the length of one wall, the colorful pairs apparently the women's. It was odd to view this collection of female footgear, trying to imagine the women they had once belonged to, or still did.

"Jake, I guess it never came up in our previous conversations, but I don't know if you're currently involved with someone," I said, suddenly feeling as though I was poaching on somebody else's territory. My interest in Jake was strictly professional, but it might not look that way to an uninformed girlfriend.

"I see a couple of ladies occasionally—nothing serious. Here, try these on for size," he said as he handed me a pair of red and black boots with a trail of flowers up the sides. His answer didn't clarify whether I should expect an impediment to our work. I doubted very much I would get the same straight answers out of Jake if girlfriend number fifty-seven were there to censor every word.

"These look pretty fancy for mucking around on a ranch," I said, sitting down to exchange my practical city shoes for the flamboyant cowgirl boots.

"Yeah, I can't remember who those belonged to, but they'll work," Jake said as he watched me stand up and give the pair a test drive. They fit me fine in the length, but it was very foreign to encase my feet in such rigid construction. Something about the heel and the curve of the toe made me walk differently. I felt like an ungainly duck.

"Hey, those look great on you," he said admiringly. "How do they fit you?"

"Fine, I guess."

Jake consulted his watch. "We've got about an hour before dinner. In the interest of time, we'll ride and then walk. How's that?"

"Great," I said. "I think I'd better pop into the restroom first."

"Oh sure, let me show you where it is."

We passed out of the kitchen doorway that led to the dining room with a long, country-style table big enough to seat twelve. This room was more like what I had expected to find, though it still had an understated elegance about it. We turned left in the hallway and passed the entrance hall on the right and the large living room on the left.

Again I was struck by the sophistication of the furnishings. It was haute country living, with none of the usual kitschy affectations. Large, solid leather sofas and saddle blanket-upholstered chairs were grouped around a mammoth fireplace. Stunning Navajo rugs graced the glossy Mexican pavers, and a game table, liquor cabinet and a grand piano rounded out the ensemble. Arrestingly beautiful oils of mostly pastoral scenes studded the white plaster walls.

"Very nice room," I commented, as I slowed to take a better look. "Do you play the piano, or is that another leftover from one of your various women?" The question had more acid in it than either one of us had expected. Jake looked at me askance and I tried to lighten my query with a belated titter.

"I've been known to tickle the ivories from time to time," he replied placidly as he opened a door that gave onto a spacious powder room.

"I'll be just a minute," I told him.

"Take your time. I'll pull the Jeep out front." I closed the door and stood staring at my reflection. Despite my progress—one wife down and only six to go—I felt rather irked at myself. It was a comfort to know that with my main subject's volubility I would surely collect enough material to weave into a reasonably cohesive hypothesis of the singed moth hell-bent on the flame.

But my reactions to Jake and his surroundings puzzled me. Why, for instance, did I make that last crack about his "various women?" I sounded like a jealous lover, or at the very least like I was mocking his life, not the sort of message to send if I wanted his continued cooperation.

I glanced down at the borrowed boots, the interior contours of which so differed from my own, and I wondered whose shoes I had stepped into. I thought of Dorothy and the ruby slippers and all the trouble that came along with them.

It was a peculiar feeling to be wearing the boots of one of Jake's former lovers, a sensation I wasn't all that comfortable with. It was funny how nonchalant he had been about me trying on the personal possessions of someone who he had presumably been close to at one time. Not only that, but he couldn't even remember whose they were. Maybe that showed how interchangeable one female was with another—if the boots fit…

On the other hand, it must be hard to keep seven wives and countless other live-in girlfriends straight. Could he really have had that many relationships, I wondered. There seemed no way to verify that. I certainly didn't plan to make a career out of hunting down all of Jake Sorenson's former love interests, so I would just have to look for other proofs of his multiple conquests. But judging by everything I had witnessed about him so far, I seriously doubted he had shed many tears over failed romances.

I was snapped out of this contemplation by the sound of a vehicle pulling up outside the front door. I looked out the window and saw Jake behind the wheel of an ancient army Jeep. I hurriedly set about my purpose for being there and let myself out the front door, only to find the vehicle abandoned and no sign of Jake.

I was glad to have had a moment of reflection, for now I was refocused on the essence of the story: finding out Jake's mindset as he flitted from woman to woman. I would need to remind myself of this from time to time to avoid being drawn too far off course by his colorful commentaries. I was sure there was enough in this man's past to fill ten volumes—mules, et al—but I didn't want to get so bogged down in information that it would take months to assemble only what was pertinent to my piece.

While waiting for Jake's return, I took in the sights immediately surrounding the house. It was tucked into a protected setting, secluded from the working part of the ranch by a border of tall trees that curved alongside the gravel drive. From where I was standing, I couldn't see past the arc of trees that led away from the house.

When we were seated in the kitchen, I could see beautiful rolling hills dotted with a variety of trees visible from the back side of the house, stretching far off into the horizon. It was a magnificent view that highlighted the remoteness of this spot. There were no other dwellings visible outside that window as far as the eye could see. I was curious to see just how much of this land Jake's property encompassed.

I heard the heavy footfalls of my host and tour guide as he returned from the far side of the house and slung a small thermal pack into the back of the Jeep. I crunched my way over the gravel drive to the passenger's side and hoisted myself in.

"All set?" he asked, and fired up the engine. It clunked hesitantly a few times, then fell into a loud, rhythmic purr. He shifted into first and I clutched the top of the door as we lurched forward. Jake grinned in his devilish way, the mischievous, overgrown boy who never tired of unsettling people.

The thought crossed my mind that perhaps Jake's long line of relationships stemmed from his desire for fresh new minds to dazzle. Maybe once someone got a line on what made him tick, he felt compelled to search for a new audience.

We bounced along the path that followed the line of sycamores away from the house and meandered gradually down to an old wooden bridge that crossed a creek bed, merely a trickle of water coursing over the rocky bottom. We chugged up the treacherously steep embankment, the bumpiness and the incline threatening to eject me from the vehicle. It was all I could do to refrain from grabbing Jake's arm to help root me to my seat.

Finally, we crested the slope and found ourselves on a more accommodating path. From then on, it was pretty smooth going. We drove for about ten more minutes, winding up and down and around until we came to a clearing that jutted out over the countryside below. I had been impressed with the view from the breakfast room, but it paled when compared to the panorama now before us.

"Wow," was all I managed to say as I pulled myself from the tattered leather seat and went to take a better look at the valley beneath us. Jake led me down a footpath that cut down the side of the hilltop. We walked about a hundred yards till we reached a bench seat cut out of a fallen cedar. We rested on it while we took in the sight below. There was enough height in our position to make it look like the whole world stretched out in front of us.

Jake took a cold beer from his compact cooler and handed it to me after courteously unscrewing the cap. He did the same for himself and clanked bottles with me. Not wanting to seem an ungrateful guest, I took a cautious sip. I couldn't remember the last time I had a beer, probably not since my college days. It had a bitter bite to it, but it was oddly satisfying in those rural surroundings. I took another couple of sips, and right away I could feel the tension go out of my legs and my frame of mind shift to one of greater acceptance.

"This is one gorgeous view," I said, my rosier outlook further enhancing the scenery. "How far does your property go?"

"Can you see that line of pine trees over to the right there? That's my northern border. I don't know if you can see it, but there's a fence that runs straight across, just below that rise."

I followed the movement of his hand along the horizon, though I couldn't see the landmark he was talking about. I feigned comprehension, nonetheless.

"That runs to the water tank in the left corner. Just to the other side of that is the western border. If you come straight back toward us and all the way to the road where you came in today, that's the south side and the highway is my eastern border."

"Sixteen-hundred acres sure is a lot of land," I said. Having spent my entire life as a city girl, I found it almost inconceivable that one person could have so much space. There was no hint that another soul lived within miles of where we stood. All I could see were green rolling hills that gradually descended and then rose again on the other side of his land, dotted here and there with trees. It reminded me of countryside I had seen in movies set in Europe. It was awe inspiring and incredibly soothing.

"Yeah, this is the one place on the ranch where you can see just about all of it, half on this side and half back over where we parked. But as far as land in these parts goes, mine is downright small. Jenkins, on the other side of the fence, owns six thousand acres. Same with the people to the right of me. The parcel to the left and mine were split off from the parcel on the other side of my neighbor."

"Wow, you've got all this land over here that you don't even use," I remarked, staggered by the thought of such excess.

"We ride over here, but all the living quarters and out buildings are over on the other side." He tilted his bottle back, finishing the last half of his beer in one swig. "You ever ride?" he asked, giving a sidelong appraisal of my physical attributes.

"Not since I was a kid," I said, casting my mind back to those infrequent and uncomfortable Saturday morning rides I had taken as a teenager. I can't say they were my fondest memories.

"We'll have to get you on top of an animal and take a ride over here. You get a real nice perspective of the land when you're sitting in a saddle." I smiled politely, but had trouble imagining enjoying the view while desperately trying to remain in the mount.

"Better get going," Jake said as he stowed his empty bottle back in the small cooler. He regarded my half-full bottle with a challenging look to drink up. I took two big gulps and choked with the effort of trying to kill it like a man. I wiped my mouth with the back of my hand and Jake laughed.

"I guess we're going to have to teach you how to ride and drink like a proper cowgirl," he teased. I extended my bottle to him, but he waved it away.

"Take your time—there's no rush. Let me show you the view from the other side." We walked back up the path, Jake charging and me trudging, my whole body now loose and wobbly. I kept wondering if I were in higher altitude than I was accustomed to; I couldn't remember ever getting intoxicated so easily.

The view from where we'd parked the Jeep was equally impressive, maybe even a little more interesting with the tops of Jake's various outbuildings visible from our height. It might have been the beer's euphoric haze, but the scene struck me as incomparably beautiful. It hit me that Jake would have no problem attracting women with bait like this.

"Jake, how many wives or girlfriends have lived at this ranch?" I asked as I came up alongside him to peer down to where we had started out. My borrowed boot slipped on the loose dirt and Jake had to grab hold of me to keep me from pinwheeling down the embankment.

"Easy, there. You'd better give me that until we're on solid ground again," he said, relieving me of my nearly empty beer bottle. "I don't think I've ever seen someone get so much out of one measly beer before."

If I hadn't felt so good about life just then, I might have been offended at being called a lightweight. But I was more intent on getting an answer to my question. "How many of your wives have lived here?" I repeated.

"You really are the diehard reporter, aren't you?"

"Journalist," I clarified.

"Okay, *journalist*. I bought the place right after my marriage to Marlena was annulled. That means I had it when I was married to Darla, Nikki and Connie, but I never spent any time here with Darla. So, your answer, Ms. Journalist, is two.

"Oh," I replied, strangely disappointed. Just a short while earlier I had the unsettling feeling of treading in the footsteps of the ghosts of too many failed romances, and suddenly I missed the chance of picking up their individual traces.

"But there have been a few others who've left their boots in my closet," Jake added playfully. He left me to ponder this as he headed back toward the Jeep. I watched as he tipped back the bottle and drank the last of my beer.

"How many girlfriends have lived here?" I called out as I attempted to catch up with him. He shot me a look I had seen many times in my thirteen years of dogging others for the truth about their lives.

"Hell, I don't know," he said, seemingly pained by my insistence, "it's not like I've had them sign a guest book when they've moved in," he said in an effort to shut me up.

"In light of how things turned out, it might not have been a bad idea," I replied, that oddly accusing tone resurfacing again.

Jake stopped and regarded me, his expression softening and breaking into a broad grin. He turned his back on me and stashed my empty bottle with his. "You coming with me?" he called out, as he hopped into the driver's seat. I barely got myself planted in the seat before we began our perilous descent back to the ranch. Only the din of the engine prevented me from pursuing that unanswered question.

Four

Jake chose a different road for our return trip, one that took us past the corrals, bunkhouses, and barns. I craned my neck as we bumped past the corrals, the largest of which now held over a dozen of his prize beasts. Seeing my interest, Jake executed a sharp U-turn and pulled up along the fence.

"Want to take a closer look?" he asked, already climbing out of the driver's seat before I could answer.

"Sure, I've never seen so many mules in one spot before," I said, though to be honest, I couldn't say for certain if I'd ever seen a single mule prior to that afternoon.

All the animals were intent on devouring every last straw of their evening meal, and only a handful even raised their heads as we approached. But once we reached the fence, we did garner the attention of two curious mules, both of which now vied for Jake's affection. He rubbed and stroked their ears, cooing to them in a tone I never expected to hear coming out of a man of his size and disposition.

It was obvious he was as fond of his oversize pets as they were of him. I hung back a little and watched, pinpricks of envy needling my subconscious, though I had difficulty determining why I should be experiencing this vague sense of longing.

I have always felt uncomfortable around horses, and in my book there was no significant difference between horses and mules. Both are big and strong and I had the sneaking suspicion their massive heads belied the actual size of their brains.

"So, you don't like to ride?" Jake asked me over his shoulder.

"When I was a teenager I rode a few times, but I never really had an affinity for it," I said. I edged closer, wanting to join in the love-fest, but still too wary. I've always held this unfounded fear of those great big teeth sinking into my hand and biting it clear through.

"You can get closer—they're not going to bite you," he teased, as if reading my thoughts. "Just hold your hand out so they can get a whiff of you, make sure you're not some kind of monster." I moved in closer and did as he said and eventually one of the mules decided to give me the once-over.

"What do you call this one?" I asked, as I nervously watched the mule's nostrils flare and contract over my outstretched hand.

"That's Baby Jane. She's about three years old now. I raised her and Rufus here since they were born. Two sweeter, gentler mules you couldn't find. They were imprinted when they were a day old, that's why they're so friendly to humans."

"I saw a program once about geese that had imprinted with humans. Is that the kind of thing you mean?"

"Well, I don't know about geese," Jake said, a slight shift in his tone, something I would come to recognize as the preamble to a speech on one of his well-considered opinions. "But imprinting with horses or mules means you make physical contact with them right from the beginning.

"Traditionally, it was always assumed that it was better to leave the foal to the mother's care, which is what the mare would prefer. But some people feel that bonding with the animal right from the get-go makes for an animal that's a whole lot easier to train when the time comes. That's been my experience, anyway. But imprinted or not, I've still never come across one I couldn't get to see things my way, eventually."

"I guess Jezebel is a good case in point, then," I said, alluding to what the ranch hand had told me. Jake threw me an arrogant glance and snorted.

"Jezebel's only problem was that half-wit who used to own her," he said contemptuously. "Ninety-nine times out of a hundred, a difficult animal can be brought around if the owners or trainers know what they're doing."

Seeing how the mention of Jezebel's previous owner had ruffled Jake's feathers, I turned my attention back to Baby Jane. Having apparently passed the sniff test, I was able to run my hand up and down the side of the mule's long face. Her coat was coarse yet soft, the nap of her fur lying in different directions as it ran above her nose, up her jaw line and around her eyes.

After proving my intentions were harmless, I let my hand work its way to her ears. I attempted to emulate Jake's movements, which had the other mule wriggling with delight. But as I tried it, my mule snorted and balked, stepping quickly away. After a moment's hesitation, she cautiously approached me again.

"Stroke the outside of her ear first, see how she likes that," Jake coached me. I patted her face softly, then gently reached for her long ear and massaged it. The fur on her ears was surprisingly soft and silky. Within seconds, she was leaning toward me, clearly enjoying the sensation and offering to let me go further.

"Now rub your fingers back and forth right inside there like this." Jake demonstrated his technique and I followed suit. As if by magic, Baby Jane laid the weight of her large head against my arm and let me scratch her ear to my heart's content.

It brought about in me a feeling I don't think I had experienced since I was a child; it was that rare occurrence of feeling unconditional love and trust from another being. It hit me hard enough on an emotional level that I had the instantaneous desire to turn my back on journalism, say goodbye to the city, and sign up as a loyal and devoted ranch hand, pay or no pay. At the risk of sounding hopelessly corny, I would have to call it a genuinely heartwarming moment.

While I was busy enrapturing my newfound friend, Jake had let himself into the corral and began inspecting some of his other livestock. Despite the fact that they were all the same breed, mules, they were of a wide assortment of colors and patterns, just as you might find in any random group of horses, only more colorful and varied.

Because I knew that donkeys were involved in the breeding process, I had figured that the offspring would look like the classic donkey, only larger, as was the case with Jezebel with her markings of a burro. Jake had in his possession brown, grey, black, white and fawn mules, as well as spotted mules, paints and appaloosas. There was even a buckskin mule with dark zebra stripes running up his legs like fancy socks.

In all this mule variety, there was one that stood out from all the others, both in physique and in attitude, and that was Jezebel. I watched as Jake slowly wound his way to where she was standing in the back, away from all the others, her disdain for her comrades a palpable thing. But as her new master drew closer, Jezebel began pawing skittishly, her head rolling in anticipation of Jake's visit, though from my limited experience it was hard to tell if she was happy to see him or afraid.

Once abreast of her, Jake seized her oil-can head in a maneuver reminiscent of Greco-Roman wrestling. Yet, as soon as Jake had her firmly in his grasp, Jezebel's body went perfectly still, as if she had fallen into a trance. He spoke softly to her as he stroked her chest, running his hands the length of her body and flanks. Having completed his inspection, he held her big head in his arms and kissed her right between the eyes.

If Jake could charm a wild beast like Jezebel, it was a cinch he had the same sort of talent with women. It would undoubtedly be worth my while to observe how he approached a new animal—if given the opportunity—for surely there would be some sort of clues that would help me figure out what made him so fascinating and irresistible to the fairer sex of the human species.

Once we were back in the Jeep, Jake took a side path that led away from the main house. He cut the engine in front of what I had assumed was another hay storage barn. It was painted and finished the same as the two other buildings we had passed, both of which I could see were used to house farm equipment and animal feed. But as we approached, it became apparent that this one served some other purpose.

"A tour of the property would not be complete without seeing where I keep my toys," Jake said as he removed the padlock and pushed the barn door aside far enough to let us and a stream of daylight enter. As my eyes adjusted to the darkened interior, I could discern the shapes of several motorcycles lined up in a perfect row, making me wonder if Jake was host to a Hell's Angels refuge.

"Besides wives, I've always had a fondness for collecting bikes," he said sarcastically as we ambled along the impressive assortment of high-priced playthings. Every motorcycle was in pristine condition, chrome and leather gleaming in a way that caused me to suspect that one of Rosalinda's many chores was to keep them all free from dust, not an especially easy task on a mule ranch. I counted twelve bikes in all.

"Do you ride them, or are they strictly for show?" I asked as we halted at the last bike in the lineup.

"I ride most of them, when I find the time, but a couple of these are very old and rare. I don't ever take them out, though I imagine they'd run just fine." I surveyed the collection again and almost laughed. So, I had a compulsive collector on my hands. Mules, women, and motorcycles. Maybe that was the whole story with this guy; maybe he had to possess everything that pleased or challenged him.

"Come over here, I want to show you something else." We walked back in the direction of the entrance to a rather nondescript door. Jake opened it and again I was thrown by what I saw, not because it was an entirely unfamiliar sight, but because its existence was so well concealed.

There, in a space that was roughly twenty by fifty feet was the quintessential male paradise. On the far wall ran a bar about twelve feet long, with half a dozen stools lined up in front of it. A pair of handsome pool tables flanked either side of the bar.

At the end of the room, to the right, was a large fireplace made from what appeared to be river rocks, surrounded by two Chesterfield sofas and a couple of wingback chairs. At the other end of the room was a similar setup, the focal point being a big-screen TV. Pine paneling and the heads of various unfortunate animals adorned the walls, along with paintings and photographs of man in his element. A more masculine place could not have existed.

"This is my little hideaway," Jake said as he surveyed his pride and joy.

"Looks like you could accommodate half the county here," I said.

"I do entertain a few of the locals occasionally," he said modestly. "It's just something I do for fun. It can feel kind of isolated out here at times."

He gave the room one last look and then ushered me toward the door. "Don't want to be late for dinner," he said. "It puts Rosalinda in a sour mood when her food gets cold."

I glanced down at my watch once we were back outside. It was still light out, but the clouds would mean an early nightfall. "Yeah, it's getting late. I better get on the road," I said, thinking of the long drive to the town sixty miles away where I had motel reservations for the evening. I probably wouldn't find anywhere to eat there, and I was not thrilled with the prospect of getting lost in the pitch dark.

"You're not thinking of driving anywhere tonight," Jake asserted matter-of-factly.

"Well, I didn't expect to arrive so late. I'm afraid it threw my timing off."

"Look, we've only made it through one wife—I've still got six more to go!"

I had to laugh at his candor. "I realize that, and I'd like to come back tomorrow, if it's all right with you."

"Of course it's all right with me. You could stay and grill me every day for a month, if you wanted to," he said.

It really did amaze me that he could slide so fluidly from gruff cocksure cowboy to incurable flirt without missing a beat. That had to be part of what had attracted so many women to him; no matter how insincere his overtures might be, I got the sense almost any woman would feel flattered if caught in the right frame of mind.

"So is that how you've brought so many females to their knees—persistent, undeserved flattery?"

"Hey, I'm just saying it like it is. I happen to like your company. Something wrong with that?"

Again I wished for that freeze-frame feature to stop the dialog and peruse it at my leisure. There were many clues to his character in these last few sentences, and all I could do was try to preserve them in my mind until I could dissect them and commit them to black and white. "No," I answered him, my brain working in two different directions. "I'm grateful that you do, or else I wouldn't have the opportunity to put your life under a microscope and try to figure out what makes people fall in love so often," I told him.

For reasons I couldn't understand, I found it terribly easy to tell Jake whatever was on my mind, quite the opposite of my usual MO, wherein tact and diplomacy ruled my tongue. Jake gave me one of those skeptical sidelong glances and barked out a short, harsh laugh, leaving me to wonder if I'd hurt his feelings.

"See there," he said, raising a finger at me, "I'm nothing more than a science experiment to you. You have no idea how much seeing your gorgeous face brightens my day." There was such sincerity in his tone and his eyes, I had to pause to regain my equilibrium.

"Okay, I appreciate the demonstration of your considerable charms, really I do. But you don't have to feel compelled to win me over. I'm a journalist, and a married woman. Flattering me is only a waste of your talents," I said.

"So you think I'm just compulsively flirtatious, is that it? Like I've got some sort of disorder or something? Like I'm some romance-addicted freak?"

We had stopped our slow shuffle toward the Jeep and we now stood facing each other, his head a good foot higher than mine. It crossed my mind that I had offended him this time, but oddly enough it didn't bother me.

"I never said that," I replied calmly.

"Not in so many words, but your attitude says it loud and clear." It was my turn to snort derisively.

"I honestly don't think you've got a disorder, and I don't see you as a science experiment. And you're certainly no freak. Freaks don't end up with seven wives and umpteen live-in lovers."

Jake eyed me coolly but I could tell my words appeased him somewhat.

"Look, I'm sorry that my profession requires me to act so impersonal and calculating. I truly find you and your history with women fascinating, and I think there is a good story at the root of it. Like I told you on the phone, I'm not here to get names, dates, and places out of you so I can publish a tell-all exposé of your love life. I would like to see if I can find out what has motivated you to take the plunge so often. My reasons for being here are strictly professional, and aren't born out of any desire to ridicule you."

This apparently smoothed the waters, for Jake nodded his head ever so slightly and then flashed me one of those infectious smiles.

"So, you'll stay here tonight, and if you find our hospitality lacking, you can check into whatever motel you've managed to uncover on the Internet," Jake said, his arm wrapped lightly around my shoulder as he escorted me back to the jeep.

"And how did you manage to come to that conclusion?" I asked. "The last thing I remember saying about the subject was that I would like to come back in the morning. I can't come back if I haven't left."

Jake laughed. "That's what I like about you—you're just so doggone quick. Assertive, too. Equal to any man, I reckon," he teased, putting up his dukes in a mocking imitation of my inherent bossiness. I felt the sting of grade school taunts, but I supposed that's what I was in for if I planned to go toe-to-toe with a woman-izing mule-breeder.

I let the remark slide, but I was more than a little irritated that he had made me smile in spite of my resolve. We took our respective seats and headed back toward the house. We passed by my rental car and I motioned for him to stop. He cut the engine so that we could converse without yelling.

"You're not really going to drive to Dustin tonight?" he asked plaintively. "I can guarantee you'll be stuck making dinner out of whatever the Gas 'n Go has to offer. And I've got the sneaking suspicion a tiny thing like you eats like a stevedore."

I hated to admit he was right, but my stomach was already in the process of eating itself. That was probably why I had gotten halfway looped on one bottle of beer. I knew Jake was right on all counts, but I didn't want to concede to him that easily.

My list of faults is as long as the next person's, and always having to prove my point and have the last say is chief among them. But was I going to be so pigheaded this time that I would spend a miserable night in a shoddy motel, trying to make a meal out of V-8 and Funions? Jake closed in on my weakening resolve.

"Stay and have some of Rosalinda's wonderful cooking, and we'll put you up in the nicest guest room in the house. You'll be perfectly safe, scout's honor," he said, holding up three fingers and crossing his heart.

"C'mon, let's get your bag," he said when I put up no argument to his tempt-ing proposal. We both got out of the Jeep to retrieve my bag, only to discover that I had locked the car and left the keys in my purse.

"I'll send one of the hands over to fetch it. But we'd better go, or Rosie'll be madder than a wet hen." We drove the short distance back to the main house, the enticing aromas greeting us from a hundred yards away.

Five

While I waited for one of the ranch hands to fetch my suitcase and computer bag out of my car, I inspected the guest quarters Jake had assigned to me for the evening.

True to his word, the room and adjoining bathroom were very nice; comfortable and as tasteful as the rest of the house. It was simple, in that the walls were the same white plaster as the other rooms, and there weren't a lot of fussy decorative touches; just a queen-size bed, side tables, a pine dresser and a writing desk, and a comfortably overstuffed chair positioned to take advantage of the same view visible from the breakfast room.

The heavy green velvet draperies that framed the window, the iron hardware on the doors and windows, and the beautiful hardwood floor gave the room a cozy elegance. The bathroom was reminiscent of the charming haciendas I had stayed at in Mexico, with hand-painted tiles in the shower, on the floor, and as wainscoting running halfway up the walls on all sides. A hammered-silver mirror over the pedestal sink and a small mesquite cabinet added to the *Colonia* look.

I had been warned that dinner would be on the table in ten minutes, so I used the time to evaluate and repair my appearance. As usual, I had become so absorbed with my latest subject I had become completely unaware of myself.

One look in the mirror and I had to laugh; besides the windblown hair and the rumpled outfit, my eyes and cockeyed grin gave me the goofy look of semi-intoxication. No wonder Jake argued against my venturing off into the sunset to find a town so small, it barely showed up on the map.

As compromised as I felt by his hospitality, I was grateful I hadn't spent my night driving in large, desolate circles. And with the smells emanating from Rosalinda's kitchen, I knew I would not go hungry tonight, which was definitely another plus. The only immediate challenge was to make myself presentable by chow time.

There wasn't a whole lot I could do about my travel-weary clothes until my bag arrived, so I did what I could with the tools at hand. I took my handbag into the bathroom and fished out my hairbrush. My hair was so tangled from the Jeep ride that it took me a good three or four minutes to smooth it out. During that time, my reflection queried me on several points, the main one being the nagging suspicion I was chasing after a story that didn't really exist.

I can't say I've never taken on a topic that fizzled during the research phase, but those occasions were few and mainly in the distant past. I realized then I had been smugly confident each new idea that passed the initial internal debate phase would result in an article I could be proud of. But as I studied myself in the mirror, I wondered if perhaps I had allowed something other than journalistic interest to influence my judgment this time.

To combat this doubt, I marshaled all the reasons I had outlined for Judith, Elliot, and yours truly when trying to sell this concept. Okay, I told myself, I'm interested in finding out what it is that makes some people habitually attracted to others again and again and again. *Character flaw* was the first answer that popped into my head, though that was hardly helpful, as it didn't support the necessity of traveling to the backwoods to interview one man in particular.

No, the angle I was going for was more on the order of an irresistible force that simultaneously made an individual attractive to and *attracted to* another. Yes, that was it; the hypothesis I had been germinating was that being attracted to a person became itself an attraction for the admired. That was good, I congratulated myself, and it tied in nicely with what I had observed of Jake so far.

I wished that I had my computer hooked up so I could get some of these thoughts down. I knew I would have to wait until after dinner anyway, as I certainly had no desire to offend the cook, so I jumped to the next step in my restoration.

I located my emergency toothbrush and toothpaste and hastily scoured the stale beer and coffee breath from my mouth. I suddenly felt a sense of urgency to get back to our interview. It was a relief to have one solid premise to build on, and my uncertainty was now replaced by the keen curiosity I've always relied on in the past.

A knock sounded at the door and I abruptly abandoned my oral hygiene. A tall, lanky cowhand presented me with my two bags, tipped his hat in an uncertain show of respect, and informed me that supper was just about on the table. The seriousness of his delivery spurred me into high gear.

Though I was craving to wash the grime of the day from my face, I had to make do with a quick powdering and a fresh layer of lipstick. I tore through my bag and found the only article of clothing that wasn't hopelessly wrinkled. I ripped off my shirt, then sat down to struggle with the cowboy boots, not the easiest things to take off in a hurry.

Once free of my travel clothes, I wriggled into the long-sleeve, black knit dress and grabbed the heels I wear with it. As soon as I slipped them on, I knew I was probably overdressed for the occasion, but there was really no alternative at that point. I smoothed down my dress, took a deep breath, and headed down the hallway to the dining room.

Despite my efforts to hurry, the dinner was already being served when I arrived at the table. My five male dinner companions rose out of their seats as I approached, coaxed into this action by my host, who was appraising me with a look of unabashed pleasure.

Rosalinda was laying the last two dishes on the table. She shot me another one of her steely looks that only I could see and interpret, then straightened and politely asked me if I wanted ice tea, coffee, or water with my meal.

"Water," I said, as I started to pull out the remaining chair at the end of the table. The man I had spoken to earlier that day beat me to it, and graciously helped me into my seat.

"Rosie, I bet you our guest would probably love a glass of that designer bubble water," Jake added, pegging me in that annoyingly uncanny way of his.

"Yes, that would be great—if it's not too much trouble," I said, though Rosalinda made it clear my being there was trouble from her point of view. Conceding this telepathic statement, I averted my eyes and busied myself with my napkin.

"Well, aren't you a vision in black," Jake said admiringly from the head of the table. I don't know why this comment embarrassed me so much; perhaps it was because I was picking up on the unease of those around me. I shyly glanced at the four other men, all of whom were dividing their attention between their empty plates and surreptitious peeks at me.

"Sorry I'm late. I hope I didn't hold dinner up," I said to the table at large.

"You're right on time," Jake said. "It's hard to hold these heathen savages back when there's food anywhere in sight. Men, this is Allison Tyler-Wilcox, our guest for the evening. I guess you've already met Lowell," he said, indicating the man to my left who I had spoken to at the arena.

"This fellow to my right is Billy. Dieter is on my left, and the hombre to your right is Pico." The five of us nodded and murmured our "nice to meet you's" respectively as Jake raced through the perfunctory introductions. He picked up the platter in front of him and dished a generous portion of meat onto three corn tortillas.

"You're in for a real treat tonight. Rosalinda's carnitas are the best I've ever tasted," he said, as he passed the platter to his left. Dieter helped himself to the meat while Pico heaped a pile of stewed chili peppers onto his plate and handed the bowl to me.

"Why've you got two last names?" Billy, the youngest of the ranch hands asked me as he ineptly dished the salad onto his side dish.

"It's a hyphenated name," Lowell said in a way that led me to believe furthering this young man's education was his never-ending duty.

"Hyphenated? You mean like rail-road or base-ball?" he asked naively. Dieter, whose name and accent were clearly German, sniggered coldly at Billy's inadequate grasp of the English language. Even Pico seemed to find this exchange amusing, though it was hard to tell if it was due to linguistic superiority or if he just enjoyed seeing his coworkers having a go at one another.

"Railroad and baseball are compound words, not hyphenated," Lowell explained patiently to Billy, who looked as though he were about to leap over the table and give Dieter a nose-bleed.

"Allison has two last names because she didn't want to give up her maiden name when she got married. She tacked her husband's name to her own with a hyphen so that people would still recognize her name. Successful women in big cities do it all the time," Jake said with a finality that indicated the subject was now closed. He shot a warning look to his right then his left, and then regarded me with an expression that conveyed the difficulties of living in the country with a pack of yokels.

"So what, if I may ask, brings you out to our neck of the woods?" Lowell inquired as he ladled salsa onto his dinner.

"Allison is writing a piece for her trendy, upscale magazine about mules, so city folk will be able tell the difference between a jackass and a racehorse," Jake said sarcastically, generating snorts of laughter from his hired hands.

I couldn't blame him for wanting to keep the true nature of my story secret from his workers; no man likes to have the intimate details of his love life broadcast about, unless of course, he's the one doing the blabbing. But hospitality aside, I didn't exactly take to the idea of having my profession or my magazine mocked so blatantly.

"Actually, Lowell," I said, "if it were just facts about mules I was after, I could have gone online and gotten all the information I needed to help us 'city folk' distinguish the various equine characteristics. I'm really more interested in finding out what makes a man take on the somewhat suspect task of mule breeding, especially a man that is, shall we say, rather past his physical prime."

That got everyone's attention. All action stopped; platters remained aloft and all eyes were turned to me. Even Billy grasped the fact that his boss had just been slighted. The only one who didn't appear shocked was Jake, who chuckled when I questioned his virility, and now sat beaming at me as if I'd just performed a particularly pleasing trick.

"One thing I can tell you, Missy, age doesn't have a thing in the world to do with training animals," Lowell said in hasty defense of his employer. "In fact, you take the biggest, strongest buck and put him next to Jake, and I guarantee you that Jake would make him look like a helpless girl out there in the arena. Intellect and instinct—that's what it takes to train mules," Lowell concluded, indignation replacing his earlier friendliness.

"It's okay, Lowell—Allison was just getting back at me for that crack about ignorant city folk," Jake said.

I was going to end up the villain here if we kept up this line of conversation. Jake and I sat locked in a stare-down, a sort of checkmate brought about by his desire to deceive his employees. It took a moment, but Lowell evidently recognized the innuendo and significant glances that he had no doubt witnessed with Jake many times before.

As Lowell relaxed and returned his focus to dinner, so did the others. Jake and I abandoned the snide remarks, however harmless, and gave ourselves over to the truly exceptional dinner that Rosalinda had prepared.

The rest of the meal passed in amiable chitchat, mostly about livestock, farm equipment, and feed supply, which was fine with me. Jake had made it clear that the nature of my visit would have to remain undisclosed, so any more prying into his past would have to wait until later. That was no problem; now that I was ensconced in his guest room, I'd have all evening to delve into his psyche, if he'd let me.

I discovered ranch hands work up a powerful appetite and eat with amazing alacrity. I had barely consumed one carnitas taco by the time the others had polished off everything on the table. And typical of men accustomed to all-male company at mealtime, Pico, Billy, Dieter, and finally Lowell each excused himself to take up a more comfortable position on the porch. Jake ate more slowly than the others, but I think that was out of deference to me.

Fortunately, I had overloaded my plate, lost as I was in the other stimuli before me. I had taken enough to feed two of me, but I ended up devouring every last scrap. When Rosalinda reappeared to clear away the last remaining plates, I looked at her with sincere gratitude. I didn't care if this woman snarled every time she saw me; she was a marvel in my eyes.

"That was absolutely delicious," I said as she removed my plate. My thoroughly clean plate threw her, for she had undoubtedly noted the excessive quantity of food I had absently heaped upon my plate.

"You were very hungry," she surmised, a benevolent smile replacing her earlier scowl.

"I was hungry, but honestly, that was one of the best meals I've ever had. Thank you."

"Thank you, señora," she said graciously as she exited.

"Well, looks like you got yourself on Rosie's good side," Jake commented admiringly.

"It never hurts to be friendly with someone who can cook like that," I said, idly fingering my water glass, suddenly in the mood for something stronger than mineral water.

"Feel like an after-dinner drink?" my host asked, again reading my mind.

"Sounds good," I said. We were just pulling away from the dining table when Rosalinda returned with a tray laden with coffee and an impossibly rich-looking chocolate cake.

"What a nice treat, Rosie. Take that to the Great Room—we're going to have a drink. You follow Rosalinda," he said to me, "I've got to get something."

As Jake pushed through the kitchen doors, I got a glimpse of Pico, beer in hand, leaning against the counter, helping himself to the leftovers. I followed Rosalinda to the living room, where she laid out the coffees, which she had made with sweetened cream, and cut two slices of the chocolate cake. I was grateful she took the rest of the dessert with her when she left the room, for I didn't trust myself alone with it, even as stuffed as I was.

Jake entered as she left, carrying a pipe and a pouch of tobacco. "You don't mind if I smoke, do you?" Judging by his earlier comments and the way he posed this question, I got the impression Jake had me pegged as some ultra-left-wing, semi-militant feminist with the sensibilities of a former commune member.

Just because I make San Francisco my home doesn't mean I fall into line with the overall mindset of that town. True, for all intents and purposes I am a vegetarian, though it is mostly due to Elliott's habits than my own.

Still, I would have rather been hog-tied and strung up than make that known at the dinner table this evening. It had been a good ten or twelve years since I had eaten pork—which is probably one reason the carnitas tasted so good to me—and I had to wonder what effect that fabulous meal was going to have on my system.

But hell would have to freeze over before I'd admit my dietetic preferences to Jake. I could just hear him howl with laughter if he ever found out I had eaten a plate full of pork just to conceal my quasi-vegetarianism from him.

Now that the topic of pipe smoking had arisen, I smiled pleasantly and told him that I loved the smell of pipe smoke and how it always made me think of my father—a lie on both counts. Whether he believed me or not, I couldn't tell, for even though he lit up without hesitation, he regarded me with an infuriating grin on his face.

"What's your poison?" he asked as he opened an armoire to reveal a well-stocked bar. Just about every high-dollar liquor was on display, from fine anejo tequilas to fifteen-year-old singlemalt scotches. He had a bottle of my favorite scotch—Lagavulin, but I wasn't sure how that peat-smoke flavor would taste with coffee and chocolate cake. I spotted a reasonable substitute hidden in the back.

"I'll take some of that Armagnac, if that's all right with you," I said. Jake didn't flinch as he reached for the bottle of the twenty-five-year-old spirits, though I had remembered seeing it offered on a restaurant wine list for seventy-five dollars a glass. As if to prove a point, Jake filled a snifter half-full and handed it to me.

"Think I'll join you," he said, though the shot he poured himself was much smaller. I carried my heavy glass over to the sofa and set it down next to my coffee.

"Rosie makes the best desserts I've ever had in my life, not that I'm much of a sweets eater." Typical of most people who make this claim, Jake polished off his slice before I had my second forkful.

He was right about the cake, though—it was heaven on a plate. I ate about half of it and washed it down with the coffee. I knew I was doomed to a sleepless night, but that would give me time to go over the little gems of insight I had gathered so far.

I leaned back on the sofa and nursed my drink. With the amount of food I had just ingested, the first couple of sips had no effect on me, but the third and fourth did. Now I was in a pleasant cloud of satiation, impervious to just about anything. I looked over and caught Jake studying me over his snifter.

"Is Pico Rosalinda's son?" I asked. Jake shook his head.

"Nope, no relation. They seem to think of each other as surrogate family, though, since they're both foreigners and speak the same tongue."

"I guess there aren't a whole lot of Latinos in this neck of the woods," I said.

"No, that's why Pico and Rosie stick together."

"Rosalinda sure is a treasure. I imagine you were pretty lucky to have found someone like her out here."

"Actually, I brought her with me when I left Venezuela—or Lowell did, technically. Lowell married her in order to bring her into the country, though as it turned out, it wasn't only a marriage of convenience." Jake noticed the perplexed look on my face and elaborated.

"Rosalinda was our housekeeper when I was married to wife number four." Jake laughed and shook his head. "If ever there was a marriage that should have cured me of taking those vows again, you would think that one would've done it."

Reflexively, I reached for the pen and pad of paper that weren't there. I didn't dare ask for a time-out to retrieve the tools of my trade for fear I would break the mood. That had already happened once, and I had a feeling I was about to hear a pretty colorful tale. Wife number four already; I would have preferred chronological order, but I guess that was too much to ask. It would be a miracle if I could keep all these wives straight.

Jake stared down into his glass before continuing, employing that pregnant pause good storytellers use to keep their listener's attention.

"Yeah, Marlena was the one woman that nearly brought me down. And it just goes to prove that whatever it is I suffer from, I've got it bad. I mean, it was no mystery why I fell for her. She was the most beautiful woman I've ever seen. Absolutely flawless complexion, perfect features, the body of a centerfold.

"But Jesus Christ, what trouble. It's funny, too, when I think about it. Here I was, this American importer, buying stuff all over Central and South America, kind of swaggering my way across the continent, and then I met this goddess at a nightclub in Caracas.

"Of course, I fell for her like a ton of bricks—nothing new there. I remember thinking this one was out of my reach. Those Latina women—especially the young ones—they come on like firecrackers. But underneath it all, they're very Catholic and very much into family and babies. You spend the night with them and you'd better be prepared to walk down the aisle. So I generally stuck to harmless flirtations when in that part of the world. Window-shopping, I called it. I could look all I wanted too, but I didn't dare touch.

"But Marlena was different. She came after me with such directness, it was like she claimed me and I wasn't going to have any say in the matter. I did, of course, but I'm a red-blooded man, and when a gorgeous woman like that singles you out, you don't question fate.

"So, like a fool, I went with her, knowing I could wake up with some half-crazed brother trying to slit my throat. I figured at least I'd go happy. Not only did I survive the night, I woke up to another round of… never mind, I won't go into that. But suffice it to say Marlena wasn't your average Catholic girl. From that night on, she made it perfectly clear that a wild love affair was all she was after.

"In the beginning, I guess I was impressed by the fact that she didn't give a damn about what people expected of her. She flaunted me everywhere, made a show of having an older American man for a lover—she was twenty-five and I was forty-seven. She had wealthy parents who had spoiled her rotten and had completely lost control over her by the time she started boarding school. She was flashy and flamboyant and a hell of a good time. Being with her reminded me of what I had been like at her age. So, we lived the high life, flitting here and there all over the globe; anywhere there was fun to be had, that's where we went.

"This was the mid-eighties, '85, '86. In addition to my import-export business, I had three nightclubs—one in New York, one in Miami, and one in Los Angeles. I've never done anything smarter financially than getting in the bar business. I figured that out right away when I opened my first hole-in-the-wall joint off Sunset, but that was over thirty years ago and I don't mean to digress. I guess I kind of jumped ahead of the order when I started talking about Marlena. Do you want me to back up to wife number two?" he asked.

"No, no—this is fine. I don't want you to lose your momentum. I'll sort them out later," I hoped.

"Hey, you don't even have anything to make notes with. Let me get you something," he offered as he started to rise from his chair.

"It's not necessary," I said, motioning for him to remain seated. "I'm sure I'll be able to remember everything you've said."

"Okay, if you're sure. So, where was I?"

"Three nightclubs—New York, Miami…

"That's right. Marlena fit right into the groove. That kind of scene was right up her alley. So, we bounced back and forth from Caracas, Miami, New York, wherever—happy as two lusty teenagers. Then out of the blue, things changed. Looking back, I have to wonder if that was her plan all along, but at the time it just seemed a minor irritation." Jake picked up the Armagnac bottle and offered me some more. I covered my glass and shook my head. He topped up his own glass and continued.

"We had flown into Miami from Caracas and were going through customs, just like we'd done a half-dozen times in the past. But that night we ended up with some overzealous customs official who probably thought we fit the profile of big-time drug traffickers. He went through every single item in our luggage, tore all of Marlena's makeup apart, and just made a goddamn exhibition of the search. Pretty soon, his cohorts joined in, going through everything all over again.

"By this time Marlena was ready to kill someone. Ordinarily, she didn't put up with any kind of crap from anyone, but I think she was on her best behavior for my sake. She figured silence was the best policy when dealing with American customs officials.

"Anyway, she had all she was going to take and she let loose on them. All of a sudden, they start taking a closer look at her, asking her a lot of personal questions, such as were we married. She said no. Then the one with the bug up his ass tells us that it is a federal offense for two unmarried people to combine their personal belongings in one bag. I had never heard such B.S. and I told him so. He whips out his handy customs handbook and points out the federal code and the possible sentencing time for such an offense.

"Now, I think the guy's trying to cover his ass for having so needlessly ripped our bags apart—it probably didn't help matters that Marlena was threatening to sue every one of those bastards who had fondled her lingerie. Anyway, the whole thing turned into one big pissing contest, the upshot being that we agreed not to sue if the customs office overlooked our ignorance of the law this one time.

"Ugly scene, but end of story, right?" Jake scoffed. "Only the beginning. Once we climbed into the limo, Marlena threw a fit that lasted for days and ended with her storming back to Caracas without me."

"Did she think you should have known that quirky rule about luggage? I personally have never heard of it before."

"No, she didn't blame me for not knowing better. But her justification for her tantrum and alienation of affection was the fact that she had been humiliated publicly solely because I hadn't the decency to marry her."

I had to smile at that one; I had a feeling at the onset of this interview that I would learn of some fairly crafty methods for snaring a husband.

"What's so funny?" Jake demanded.

"Nothing. It sounds like you had a real live one there, is all."

He groaned and rubbed his eye. "Oh, you have no idea." Jake sipped his drink, lost in thought.

"Well…you called her 'wife number four,'" I prompted.

"Yep, I caved in. Not at first, though. I was back in the States then, and I sort of drifted back into the relationship I had dumped when Marlena and I got together. And for a couple of months everything was cool. Then I passed through Venezuela on another buying trip. I wasn't even going to stay in Caracas, but I don't know—there was some business meeting or something.

"Anyway, I ran into Marlena and it was all over except for the rice throwing. We just fit, there was no denying that. And she had some kind of spell on me. That girl could be so sweet, your head would spin. We ran off to Vegas—using separate luggage—and had a quickie wedding. Then we rented a small Greek island for the honeymoon, which was great while it lasted.

"On Marlena's insistence, we set up house outside of Caracas right away. All of a sudden, Miss Jet-Set goes domestic on me. I didn't really mind. We'd done more than our fair share of traveling, so it was kind of fun to have a swanky villa with all the trimmings, being treated like a king and having a stone fox for a wife. It worked for me. But not for very long, I'm afraid." Jake stood up and stretched, a big grizzly bear kind of a stretch.

"Feel like getting some air?" he suggested. It sounded like a good plan to me. His storytelling and the Armagnac were having a soporific effect on me, lulling me into a tranquil, dream-like state where everything he said made perfect sense.

I used the excuse of getting a jacket to grab a small notepad and pen and tape recorder, all of which I stashed in my pockets. I also took a quick check of my teeth for food and touched up my lipstick. I joined Jake on the front porch and he suggested we take a stroll.

The porch light illuminated the gravel walk until we rounded the corner, then everything was pitch black. Jake held the flashlight out in front of us for my benefit, but I still had to fight the urge to grab hold of his sleeve for guidance. Once we broke into the clearing, the night sky stretched before us, littered with ten million stars. I had never felt so close to the heavens before.

"Wow!" was all I could manage to say, as I slowly turned to take it all in. The sky was so crowded with stars and planets, they gave the impression they were about to crash down around us. The sensation of having so much suspended over my head made me hunker involuntarily. I wobbled as I tried to follow alongside Jake, my attention riveted to the spectacle above us.

"There's a bench up here, if you'd like to have a seat," he said. I nodded my head mutely and he led the way. I felt much more grounded once we had sat down with our backs to the side of the barn. Not only did it allow me a chance to get a better look without losing my balance, but it effectively eliminated half the sky, cutting the scope and breadth of the stars to a more reasonable size.

For a long moment I was too awestruck to think of anything other than the few minor facts I could still remember from my summer astronomy class back in high school. The Milky Way, Venus, and the Dog Star, Sirius, were the only astral features I could name with any certainty.

"We don't get to see this kind of thing in the city," I told Jake once I had overcome my amazement. "This is truly incredible."

"Yeah, I know. It's not a sight you can ever become bored with," he replied. I tried to imagine such a thing.

"Do you think boredom is one of the reasons you've gone through so many women?" It was hardly the most eloquent way to pose the question, and I immediately regretted my choice of words. What was it that made me blurt out such things to him? Jake reared away from me with exaggerated alarm.

"That's what I like about you, girl. You just say whatever's on your mind."

It hit me that this line of questioning—if I could get him to respond to the question and not the phrasing—might lead to some insightful answers. Because I couldn't very well make notes in the dark, I shifted slightly to hide my movements and reached into my pocket to turn on the recorder. I'd had mixed results when taping in a concealed manner such as this, but I usually ended up with at least some salvageable dialog. It was worth a shot.

"Let me rephrase that—do you find that you tend to get bored in your relationships with women?"

"I'd say I've become bored with certain traits or habits or maybe attitudes, but I don't think I left any of my wives out of boredom. Now, it's true in most cases, with girlfriends as well as wives, that my eye wandered, but not because I had tired of whoever I was with."

"What was it that caused your eye to wander?" Jake shrugged.

"A beautiful face, the way a woman handles herself, a certain sparkle in her eye that made me want to find out more. I don't know—just the classic reasons that make anyone stray." I considered this.

"When you entered each of these successive relationships, did you start out thinking, 'this was the one?'"

"Oh sure, at least two or three times. It's not like I've ever gone into a marriage thinking 'this will last for a year or two, then I'll move on.' But yeah, I've definitely fallen hard for a woman and thought I'd be with her forever, but then, I'm basically a diehard romantic."

I don't know why this struck me as preposterously funny.

"Why do you find that so amusing?" he asked. I grunted inarticulately then turned my palms up helplessly.

"You just don't strike me as being a 'romantic.'"

"Oh really? Why not?"

"When I think of hopeless romantics, I think of people who charge blindly into a relationship with stars in their eyes and notions of bliss that can never be fulfilled, and who virtually always end up with their hearts broken. I can't see you fitting that profile in any way."

"I didn't say that I was a 'hopeless romantic,' only a romantic," he clarified.

"Okay," I said grudgingly, "what's the difference?"

"I think of myself as a romantic because it is so easy for me to imagine being with nearly every attractive female I meet. I see her, I look into her eyes, and I immediately find myself thinking, 'I want to know this person.' Next thing I know, I'm trying to win her over, even if I've got a wife or girlfriend waiting for me at home. I can't help it—I'm just fascinated by women. It's like a curse, almost."

I laughed out loud. "A curse? You're cursed because you are unavoidably susceptible to every pretty face that comes along? Oh, that's a good one!" In the pale light of the stars, I could just make out Jake's wry smirk.

"You make a good show of being The Ice Princess, but my guess is you've had your share of weak moments when your libido got the best of you."

"How did you come to that conclusion?" I asked, flabbergasted that he could presume to know the first thing about what made me—or my libido—tick.

Jake laughed at my indignation. "You don't much care for it when the tables are turned, do you?"

I didn't say anything for a moment while I mulled over this observation. It certainly wasn't the first time an interviewee took issue with the imbalance of prying questions. Because of this, I've sometimes used the old technique of revealing my thoughts or secrets in furtherance of extracting similar disclosures from the subject. It's also true that if my life experiences didn't include the same type of relevant material, I've simply made something up. I don't believe that I violate any journalistic ethics with this tactic, as my confessions are never put into print, but I admit that it is sneaky. Underhanded or not, I thought this was probably one occasion I would have to play the game.

"So, you're suggesting that my momentary lapses are no different than yours, yet you've actually ended marriages over mere temptations, and I'd never do that."

"Then you do know what it's like to be hit by a thunderbolt of lust."

"I don't know about a 'thunderbolt of lust,' but yes, I know what it's like to meet someone and wonder what it would be like to be in his world. But I think it's different for you."

"How so?" he asked, leaning forward, elbows on knees, as though he were deeply curious to find out my theory of what causes his compulsive behavior.

"People don't go around marrying everyone they're attracted to," I said, stating the obvious.

"Neither do I! There have been dozens of women I could have married if I wanted to," he reminded me. No matter how many times he'd tell me this incredible statistic, I couldn't swallow the idea that he'd found dozens of women willing to shack up with him.

"Then why didn't you?"

The question made him sit back and reflect. "I don't know. I guess after living with them a while, I figured out we weren't right together, or I'd meet someone else. I'm not obsessed with marriage."

I could tell I had hit a nerve. I heard an uncharacteristic note of defensiveness in his voice. "You're just not afraid to take the plunge if your heart tells you to?"

"Yeah, that's right."

I let that simmer for a minute. "Why do you think that you've been so susceptible to the opposite sex, whereas most people have only a handful of relationships throughout the course of their lives?"

"Hell, I don't know. Maybe because I'm so irresistible." I gave him a sidelong, doubtful glance. "I'm just not like other people, what can I say?" He stood up suddenly. "Look, all these questions are making me thirsty. How about another drink?"

"Okay," I said. "But I need to visit a restroom first." Standing up had made me acutely aware of the fact that I should have seized the opportunity before we left the house.

"You can pop in here, if you want," he said, indicating the barn behind us.

"Is this your pleasure barn?" I asked, having not recognized it in the dark. Jake fiddled with the lock and pulled back the massive door to let me in. I followed him to the door that led to his sanctuary. He switched on the lights and adjusted them to accommodate our eyes. The room had a very inviting quality to it in that more mellow lighting.

"The little girl's room is just past the TV screen, on the right."

I ambled off in that direction at once.

"What do you want to drink?" Jake asked just before I slipped around the corner.

"I'm fine right now," I answered.

"How 'bout a beer?"

"Okay," I relented, and ducked inside his swanky girls' lounge.

I guess all those years of owning nightclubs had ingrained in him a certain level of hospitality that he couldn't shake, even in his private quarters. It made me wonder as I let myself into one of the two stalls exactly what the shindigs at his rural hideaway were like.

I imagined tough country cowgirls in boots like I had worn that day, with skintight jeans and competitive attitudes, vying for male affections—most probably Jake's—and slinking off to duke it out in this elegant environment. It made me want to be a fly on the wall, just once, just to see Jake in command of his lair. What a character, I thought. What a great big rogue of a man.

When I rejoined Jake, he was racking the balls on one of his pool tables, my beer thoughtfully poured in a pilsner glass resting on the rail.

"You play?" he asked as he gave the balls one last shake and removed the rack.

"A little," I replied. Fortunately for me, I had older brothers who taught me how to shoot pool when I was growing up, and though I seldom played anymore, I still had confidence in my ability. I'm not tournament material, by any means, but I'm no slouch either. Jake handed me a cue stick and a cube of chalk.

"Ladies first," he said and stood aside to let me break. It was a decent break, yielding me the eleven ball in the right side pocket. Jake grinned broadly and took a swig of his beer.

"Stripes," I claimed, and set about knocking off one ball after the next.

"How did I know you'd be good at this?" Jake asked rhetorically. I allowed myself one small smile of triumph, then sank another one.

"You going to let me play, or is this just an exhibition game?" he asked. Like a jinx, I missed the next shot.

"All righty, let me show you how it's done." I stood back and watched as he put away two balls in one shot. It was hard not to appreciate his talent, even if he showed no modesty about his skill. After watching him sink several balls, I was feeling grateful that he had let me break or I would have never stood a chance.

Just when I thought he was going to run the table, he scratched. Jake cursed as he removed the two balls, placed the three ball on the mark, and rolled the cue ball back to me. It was not surprising that he didn't take losing lightly, and it made me wonder if he had ever been the loser in his ongoing game of love.

"Have you ever been dumped by a woman, or have you always been the one to initiate the breakup?" I asked as I sank the twelve ball and set my sights on number ten. Jake stood watching me, resting his hands on his cue stick like a staff.

"Well, I am impressed. Even when facing a sound thrashing, you still have your reporter's mind firing on all cylinders."

I crossed to his side of the table for a better look at my shot. It was rather distracting to have him hovering at my elbow as I tried to concentrate. I threw him a look over my shoulder, and he grinned with amusement as he relocated himself to the other side and let me take my shot.

"Nice touch," he complimented me. The ball glanced off the left side and glided straight into the corner pocket. It was beautiful, and if I'd ever wanted to yank down my arm in a self-congratulatory *Yes!* this was the time. But I kept my cool and went courting the eight ball.

Typical of the male ego, Jake found it difficult not to kibitz while I strategized my final shot. Instead of ignoring him, I turned the focus back to him.

"You never answered my question," I reminded him.

"What question?"

"Have you ever had your heart handed to you on a platter?" I bent and measured my shot one last time. I really wanted to make this shot, probably more than I had ever wanted to make any shot. But I had been too cavalier, dividing my attention between winning and keeping Jake on his toes. The eight ball bounded blindly from bank to bank, landing in the worst possible position for me.

Jake nodded his head, keeping time with the music, broad grin on his face. All I could do was hope he would miss, but I knew that was a waste of time. Instead, Jake humiliated me in the most disgraceful fashion, chasing in the three ball with the eight ball fast in its wake. The most irritating part was that Jake took his success far too jovially. I took a long draft of my now warmish beer and let the bitterness of it linger on my tongue.

"Good shot," I finally managed to say while Jake pranced around in step with Johnny Cash. The only thing that got my goat more than his victory was the fact that I was feeling like a sore loser. I had never really considered myself competitive, but something about Jake's cockiness had fueled my desire to win. Jake danced himself to the other side of the bar and surveyed his stock.

"That was a dandy finale, one that calls for a celebratory drink," he said as he hunted for exactly the right liquor for the occasion.

"It's getting late," I said looking at my watch.

"Hell, it's only 11:15. There's plenty of night left."

"I've been traveling a good part of the day, and I still have some writing to do," I insisted. My defeat had turned me into a real stick-in-the-mud.

"Oh, don't go all prissy on me. One drink—you can manage that." I studied him from across the pool table and grudgingly relented.

"All right, one drink, but only if you answer the question I've asked you twice already." Jake screwed up his features in a look of consternation. "What was that question again?"

More likely than not, he knew exactly what I was talking about. He just got a kick out of putting me through my paces, like one of his trained mules.

"Have any of your wives, girlfriends, lovers, concubines, ever given you your walking papers?" I asked. I was getting bored with the inquiry myself. I think Jake sensed my growing disinterest, for he now gave me his undivided attention. He probably didn't want to lose his only playmate for the evening.

"Once," he admitted solemnly.

"Was it one of your wives?" I prompted, after no embellishment seemed forthcoming.

"No, this girl was too smart to make that mistake. Annalise was her name. I tried to get her to marry me for five years, but she didn't trust my track record. She would have been the fourth Mrs. Jake Sorenson, but she had more sense than that. She made the right decision, I reckon. She ended up marrying a dentist. They're still married. Last I heard they had a couple of kids in college, so I guess everything turned out all right." Jake turned his attention back to the bar. "Okay, what'll it be? I've got some killer fourteen-year-old tequila…"

"No tequila for me."

"*No problema*. We've got just about every alcoholic beverage on the planet, so take your pick." I moved in closer and scanned the shelves behind him.

"How about a shot of Ricard with some water," I decided on a reckless whim. Jake nodded at me approvingly and took down the pastis and a couple of glasses.

"That doesn't sound like a bad idea. Think I'll join you." He poured a generous shot into both glasses, and searching under the front bar, pulled out a water carafe and filled it with water from the tap.

"Just like the high-class joints," he said, setting it on a bar napkin in front of me. I poured in as much water as the glass would accommodate and watched as the clear yellow turned milky-white. Jake did the same, though he used less water.

"*Salud*!" he said, lifting his glass in a toast and knocking it back in one gulp. I stared at him in disbelief. I had never seen anyone do shooters of pastis before.

"Ahh,*"* he sighed, wiping his mouth with the back of his hand, and reaching for the bottle of Ricard again. He looked at my untouched glass with concern.

"What are you going to do, sit and stare at that all night? Drink up," he commanded. He watched as I took a cautious sip and set my glass back on the bar. "C'mon, bottoms up!" he coaxed. I shook my head.

"Sorry. Where I come from, we sip our psychotropic beverages with care," I said, crossing my arms in front of me. Jake raised his eyebrows in mock reproach.

"Okay, have it your way, but you're guaranteed of having a great night's sleep if you knock back of couple of these babies. Gives you some freakin' awesome dreams."

I took a bigger sip, and no sooner had I set my glass down, I began to feel the potent Pastis take effect. Jake splashed a jigger of water into his second drink and raised his glass again, this time offering a proper toast.

"To love and marriage," he said, clinking his glass against mine. He was struck by the hilarity of his words, his laughter coming in fits and starts as he tried to lift the glass to his lips without spilling its contents. His laughter was contagious, and I had to fight to swallow my mouthful without choking on it.

"Do you think you'll ever get married again?" I asked after I had regained my composure. Jake leaned over the bar top, his half-full glass in his hand, and regarded me semi-seriously.

"I'm really not a good one to ask. I've found myself to be wholly unreliable when it comes to that subject."

I could tell that the drink was starting to work on him as well, for his eyes now had a glassy sheen to them.

"Let's sit over there," he said, indicating the seating arrangement around the fireplace. I slid rather ungracefully off the barstool and ambled over to one of the wingback chairs.

"Want a fire?" he asked. I shook my head.

"It's getting late," I reminded him. We sat down in our respective chairs, both of us practically glowing with contentment. I was going to find it very difficult to pry myself out of the blissfully comfortable seat. I took another sip of my drink and set it on the table between us.

"So, you didn't exactly answer my question," I said.

Jake, who was sitting with his eyes closed, head and hand keeping time with some country western tune, opened one eye and regarded me cautiously. "Jesus, you never give up, do you?" He closed his eye and let his head fall back against the chair and began to croon along with the singer with an exaggerated hillbilly twang. I was feeling far too relaxed to be put off by his noncompliance. I let my body sink further into the leather and took in the manly décor. I was on the verge of nodding off when he suddenly answered me.

"After my third marriage, I swore to myself and every woman I met that there was no way in hell I would ever get my neck in the noose again. I don't know if anybody ever believed me, except for *moi*. If anything, it might have made snagging me more of a challenge. It's kind of funny when you think about it, you know, the psychology of that kind of declaration.

"I was with a lot of women before I met Annalise, and I guess the women who probably hate me the most are the ones I told up front I would never marry them. Without exception, those breakups were the ugliest. But Annalise was the exact opposite. She was totally fine living with me without benefit of a marriage license. Like I said, she didn't think I had any business getting hitched again with my poor judgment.

"And here's the weird thing—when I figured out she really had no interest whatsoever in marrying me, it was all I could think about. It was like I had become obsessed with getting her to say yes. I worked on that girl for nearly five years, until she finally left me. Said she couldn't take the pressure anymore. Now, how is that for funny?" Jake asked with an ironic snort. "The same weapon I had used to keep all those other girlfriends at bay had turned around and bitten me on the ass."

His quip had just given me a very interesting insight, and I took a moment to ponder it.

"Do you feel women have been more drawn to you when you've been in a relationship than when you've been single?"

"It's hard to say. Seems like I've always been involved with someone." Jake stared thoughtfully into space, as if running a mental check of any and all of his bachelor periods. "I really couldn't say. Why do you ask?"

"What you said about the girlfriends you warned of your boycott on marriage. I was just wondering how much our desires are shaped by the knowledge that what we want is unattainable. You know, always wanting what we can't have. Maybe that's part of the reason you've had such an amazing number of romances. Maybe they were so caught up in winning you away from another woman, they didn't realize what they had set themselves up for." I let this thought hang in the air for a moment.

"We've all heard the story a hundred times about a mistress clinging to the hope that her unfaithful lover will leave his wife for her, and you know how that story usually goes. Maybe your inordinate number of marriages has more to do with the irrational thinking of the women you've encountered than any weird compulsion on your part," I mused.

Jake grinned at me, his eyes lowered to half-mast, clearly amused by the fact that I was so interested in dissecting his love life. "Yeah, maybe that's it," he said. "Except that in most cases, I've been the one who introduced the idea of marriage in the first place, and in most cases I really did leave my wives for the other woman."

"Really? Why?"

Jake shrugged. "I told you, I'm an incurable romantic."

"So what, you have some old fashioned notion that true love requires marriage?"

"No. I guess I've always just gotten caught up in the spirit of new romance and taken it to the hilt." Jake, distracted, reached for his drink without looking and drained it. He looked at the empty glass with mild disappointment and hefted himself out of his chair to refill it.

"Ready for another one?" he asked. I glanced at my half-full glass and declined.

"So…would you say the relationships became anti-climatic once you were married?" I asked over my shoulder. I could hear Jake clanking around behind the bar as he fixed himself another pastis and water. He didn't respond right away and I wasn't sure if he'd heard me or not. I turned around in my chair and was about to pose the question again, when I discovered that Jake had moved to the far end of the room, where he was changing the CD.

I've never been a fan of country western music, so it was quite a relief—as well as a surprise—to have my ears treated to the sultry, urbane sound of what I mistook as an accordion and later learned was a *bandoneon*, playing a vaguely tango-esque piece.

Jake, glass braced close to his chest, tangoed back toward me. It was an amazing sight to behold that bearded, wild-haired mountain man mincing around his high-macho sanctuary in his cowboy boots to this sophisticated sound from another part of the world. One thing I could say for certain, you just never knew what to expect next with this guy.

"I like this—what is it?" I asked, barely suppressing my urge to laugh out loud at the spectacle he presented.

"Astor Piazzolla," he replied, as if it were plainly obvious. I nodded my head uncertainly to the rhythm as Jake drew closer. "This drink put me in a Parisian frame of mind," he said, as if that explained why an unsentimental hulk of a man should suddenly start dancing about à la Fred Astaire. Before I knew what was happening, Jake pulled me out of my chair and began dragging me around with him.

"I don't know how to tango," I protested, trying unsuccessfully to disengage myself from his commanding grasp.

"Nothing to it," he claimed, impervious to my lack of interest. "I'll have you floating along with me in no time."

"I seriously doubt that," I said, breaking away from his lead. Dancing had always been one of those activities I only relented to at social occasions where an appearance on the dance floor was mandatory. I was only sufficiently proficient where the foxtrot and swing were concerned. Tangoing had never been my forte.

Jake eyed me coolly, unperturbed by my reaction. "You telling me you're going to be a quitter, just 'cause you don't know how to do something?" I crossed my arms and glared at him.

"I don't feel like taking a dance lesson right at the moment," I said flatly. Out of nervousness, I guess, I reached for my drink and reflexively drank nearly all that remained.

Jake smiled broadly. "That's the spirit," he said. "Now picture yourself in the Latin Quarter of Paris, the scent of garlic and strong coffee and this music wafting through the air," he instructed, with arms held out to guide me through the steps. I warily took his hand and braced myself. Before we began, Jake decided a little tutoring was in order.

"Now, this music is meant for the Argentine tango versus the ballroom glide that most people think of. In Argentine tango, partners hold each other tight, at the hips, and the steps are smaller and cover less ground. The main thing the woman has to keep in mind is her footwork, which is like a figure eight, with one foot passing in front of the other like so."

Jake gave a brief demonstration, which flew right past me, and then resumed our stance. Apparently deciding that was adequate instruction, Jake pulled me toward him and braced my right thigh against his. As if it didn't feel awkward enough to suddenly find myself in this compromising position with the man I was supposed to be interviewing, there was the added mismatch of stature to make me feel foolish.

"Okay, let the weight of your body settle against me, and let me do the leading." Jake waited for the right moment to fall in line with the tempo. With little warning, he began to propel me forward and back. I was stiff with trepidation and I knew it, but slowly I managed to let go of all need for control and allowed Jake to pilot me through a series of twists and turns that I was too unsure of to appreciate.

We moved, we danced all right, and I did try to keep my mind on my footwork, though I goofed up several times. I suppose all in all, it was a moderate success. At least Jake treated it as such. When the song ended, we stopped with a flourish, and upon releasing me, Jake commended my efforts.

"See how easy that was? You did great!"

I wasn't so convinced. I polished off the dregs of my drink, wishing I had a fresh one. The music started up again and Jake attempted to coax me into an encore performance. I begged off, citing my empty glass as the reason.

"I need another drink," I confessed bluntly. Jake was more than happy to oblige me. "I need a glass of water, too," I amended, and followed him over to the bar.

I took a seat on one of the stools and tried to assimilate what had just taken place. Jake was whistling along with the music, as pleased as he could be. Beaming, he placed both of my beverages on the bar top and leaned over in his gracious barkeep mode.

"That was fun, wasn't it?" he asked, almost giddy with happiness. At that point, I couldn't tell if what had transpired was fun or not. I might have enjoyed it if I hadn't been so confused by it.

"Do you dance like that often?" I asked.

Jake stood up and rested one foot on a shelf under the bar. "Nah, I don't get the chance much out here. When there is dancing, it's mostly the two-step. I used to dance a lot when I lived in L.A."

"Then what brought about this sudden urge to tango?" I asked, wondering if he had inflicted that bit of shenanigans on me out of pure orneriness.

Jake held up his glass. "T'was the drink that did it," he said in a heavy Irish brogue.

"Funny, Ricard doesn't have that effect on me," I said.

"Yeah, well, I guess I have a lot of fond memories attached to this drink," he said rather wistfully.

"Don't tell me one of your wives was French," I said sarcastically.

"No, but I spent one of my honeymoons in France," he replied.

"One of your honeymoons," I echoed. "I don't know how you keep everything straight." I had let bitchiness enter my voice again, even though I knew it was counterproductive. Apparently, the subconscious thoughts I usually kept to myself had found a way to bypass my brain and head straight out my mouth. I supposed the liquor wasn't helping matters. Jake smirked at the last remark, but didn't reply.

"So, tell me—which honeymoon was it, then?" I asked in a more conciliatory tone.

"That was wife number…three," Jake said, holding up his fingers as he mocked the effort of having to remember exactly which wife was which. "Pami—nee Pamela Westerly. We took a three-month honeymoon, how do you like that?"

I laughed. "Maybe you're in it for the honeymoons," I suggested, only half in jest. Jake didn't bother to respond to that theory.

"We spent a whole month in Paris, and we toyed with the idea of setting up house there, but we didn't."

Jake thoughtfully washed out his glass, then reached into the cooler for another beer. I didn't know how the guy could put away so much booze and remain fairly sober in appearance. My second pastis was still half-full and I could already tell that I would be paying for this extravagance in the morning. I pushed it away and tried to refocus my attention.

"Tell me about Pamela—Pami," I said. Jake carried his beer bottle around the bar and pulled up a stool next to mine.

"Pami was a pretty nice girl. She and I were married for about three years."

"Was that long compared to the others?" I interrupted.

"Well, I guess it was about average. It seemed long in retrospect, since we were always fighting. She was a very suspicious woman, always accusing me of cheating on her."

"Was she right?"

"Sometimes. But I was going to be dogged with that kind of behavior even if I had been faithful to her through the whole marriage."

"Why was that? Did she have a jealous nature?"

"Well, she entered into the relationship with the knowledge that I was less than a saint when it came to fidelity. She was the best friend of my second wife, Kate."

I controlled my reaction this time and held my tongue, but mentally I was writing this man off as a scoundrel. *His second wife's best friend.* The guy was contemptible. I began to have serious doubts about my instincts on this one. Maybe there wouldn't be any useful insights gained by probing into his past; maybe I would muck about in all his sordid episodic marriages and come away thoroughly disgusted with no story worth printing.

I was beginning to suspect this man and his successive marriages were an anomaly, and his tale would not provide any practicable understanding of human nature. I grabbed my water and drank it down as I pondered my exit strategy.

"It's late. We should save wives two and three for tomorrow," I said as I started to climb off my barstool. Jake grabbed hold of my arm and held me in place.

"I don't want to leave the story there," he said earnestly. I wriggled my arm free but remained where I stood. "Have a seat—this is going to take a couple of minutes."

I perched tentatively on the stool and waited.

"I realize it sounds terrible to admit I was cheating on my wife with her best friend, but I did it and I'm not proud of hurting Katherine that way. Pami hated herself, too, for sneaking around behind her girlfriend's back like that, but neither of us could help ourselves."

This explanation was doing little to change my opinion of him. I could feel my eyebrows arch, but that was the only comment I made.

"Katherine was a gorgeous, gorgeous lady. I met her at one of my clubs in L.A. She was a newscaster for a local station. She was college educated, career minded, but kind of a late bloomer socially. She came into one of my clubs one night—The Riptide—to see Pami, who was one of my waitresses.

"Right away, I was awestruck. Now, you have to remember that my first marriage was something I just fell into—a lark, really. So when I met Katherine, I felt I was really on to something. This was the first time I actually thought about marrying someone and being with her for life. I had lived with a few other girls since I moved to L.A., but that was mostly for the sake of convenience. But with Kate, I felt she was the real deal." He paused for a moment to take a swig of his beer.

"On the face of it, we were a pretty odd couple. Katherine was intelligent and beautiful and refined, and for her the biggest challenge in life was having fun and fitting in like a normal person.

"Then there was me. I was not refined, not a college graduate, didn't look like a museum piece, but I was a successful business man and I was confident—or arrogant, depending on how you looked at it. And I was well liked. So, in this case, I guess you could say that we were attracted to each other because what one lacked the other possessed. And for a while, our differences added flavor to our marriage.

"You know how they say that after some time, you get to be like the person you're married to? Well, that didn't happen to us. Kate never became more relaxed or self-assured, and I never became more well-behaved or refined. After three years of marriage, I was still the same hard-edged bar owner with a wandering eye.

"To be absolutely honest with you, I tried very hard to remain faithful to Katherine. I think that was the reason Pami and I fell into a fling. It was the proximity that caused me to weaken and give in to adultery." Jake looked up at the back bar, lost in contemplation of his love triangle. He turned his attention back to me and resumed.

"After we'd been married about six months, we both realized that having other people around eased the friction between us. We had Pami over to our place every other night, it seemed like. She'd quit the club and was working as a secretary at one of the big Hollywood studios. Anyway, we often had a foursome, but sometimes it'd just be the three of us.

"The point is she became very intimately involved in our lives. She could see after being with us so often how much we depended on having a neutral party around to counteract the strain of our dissimilarities. We'd go to Palm Springs for a long weekend, and Pami and a date would come along. We'd spend a week down in Puerta Vallarta—same thing.

"Then sometime after our second anniversary, Pami started coming over more often by herself. It got to the point where she'd find herself having to listen to Kate's tales of cruelty and aloofness, then turn around and administer to my feelings of alienation and frustration. The whole situation was bad—none of us should have tried to function under that set of circumstances. I know that now, Katherine knows that now, and so does Pami. And here's something that you might find of interest for your article—the three of us are still in contact with each other. We're still friends, if you can believe that," Jake said with an unexpected laugh. He looked over at me and playfully elbowed my arm. "Weren't ready for that one, were you?" he teased.

I wasn't. But I also wasn't ready to believe that the fact they had become one big happy legion of ex-spouses made his actions commendable. I reached past my water glass and took a sip of Ricard. Apparently encouraged by my silence, Jake began to hum along with the music again.

"If you're still on friendly terms with wives two and three, do you think they would be willing to share their perspectives of their marriages to you?" I asked. Despite my earlier misgivings, the thought of hearing these women's stories piqued my curiosity. Jake laughed.

"You're really something, I'll tell you. You're like a machine—whir, whir, whir, all the time, your brain just keeps spinning." He leaned over his beer and chuckled to himself. I didn't care if he made fun of me, as long as he put me in touch with Katherine and Pamela.

"Are you threatened by the thought of those women telling me their side of the story?" I taunted him causally.

"Hell, no—be my guest," he said. "I'll call them in the morning and let them know you're on a quest to unearth the reason why I've failed to become a monogamous creature."

"That'd be great," I replied, and both of us fell quiet while we digested the idea.

"You ready to turn in for the night?" Jake asked as he got up and began to restore his playroom to its proper order. "I've got a mule ranch to run," he said. "I can't be out all night kickin' up my heels with every pretty reporter that comes my way." I grabbed my jacket and hid my smile.

"Not to mention that we're both missing out on our beauty sleep," I added.

"Darling, I could sleep for a month and it wouldn't help me a bit, and you're already beautiful," he said as he held the door open for me.

He was a compulsive flirt, that's all there was to it.

Six

I awoke suddenly from a deep, debilitating sleep. I had been too restless to go to bed once I had finally gotten back to my room, and I had spent nearly three hours making and reviewing notes on my computer. I didn't hit the sheets until sometime around 4 a.m.

It had been my plan, after realizing my night's rest wasn't going to amount to much, to sleep a couple of hours, then jumpstart my day with an invigorating run around Jake's ranch. It was an old trick spawned during my college years that I occasionally fell back on when I found myself burning the candle at both ends.

Good intentions aside, it was hard to imagine extracting my tired carcass from the comfy bed, let alone propelling myself over the rugged terrain of Eastern Oregon. I mustered enough strength to reach for my watch and was horrified to discover that it was already half past nine.

I fell back onto the pillow and groaned at my pathetic condition. I had been relying on the promise of increased mental and physical stamina to get me through this day, and now that I'd overslept and blown the only chance I had of being one up on my host and interviewee, I had to rethink my day's strategy. As I lay there, I reviewed my progress of the previous day. Now that I'd had the opportunity to digest my many hours of conversations with Jake Sorenson, notorious lady-killer, I no longer felt the same sense of repulsion that had come over me the night before. Sure, it was still difficult to think of his multitude of conquests without feeling a twinge of disdain regarding his natural infidelity.

Upon reflection, I was able to view him in the same manner I had when I first met him. On balance, there was an aspect to his admitted womanizing that made his antics acceptable. The flashy, devil-may-care attitude was probably partly responsible for attracting so many women to him in the first place.

Admirable or not, Jake Sorenson was one of those likable characters who was a breed apart from the average Joe; he had a certain charm underneath his brusque exterior that persuaded one his deeds were in reality harmless and all in good fun. He was one of those rare individuals who could get away with almost anything.

One other thing I had sorted out in the wee hours of the morning was the viability of this story. I had come to the conclusion that there was enough real meat to this angle to make further investigation worthwhile. The fact there were two former Mrs. Sorensons who would likely divulge their versions of what it was like to marry then divorce this incorrigible "romantic" revived my interest. This prospect alone had solidified my resolve and inspired me to put my thoughts in order.

As there was nothing more to be gained by lying in bed, I forcibly hauled myself up and managed to perform the few tasks necessary if I were going to venture out of my quarters and into the half-spent morning.

I put on jeans and a sweater, and crept down the hallway toward the kitchen, gratefully encountering no one along the way. I slithered into the spotless kitchen intent on finding some leftover coffee, once again unaware of Rosalinda's presence until I nearly collided with her as I lurched for the coffee pot.

"Good morning, señora," she greeted me, startling me half out of my wits.

"Good morning," I answered when I got my breath back.

"I save some breakfast for you. It might not be so good now," she said, removing a foil-covered plate from the oven. "The boys knocked on your door, but you did not answer. You must have been very tired from your travel." She took a clean mug from the cupboard and filled it with coffee.

"Actually, your employer kept me up half the night," I said, not realizing until too late how provocative that statement sounded. "The interview, I mean. We were up past midnight talking. Once I got him going, it was hard to get him to stop," I laughed awkwardly. I was aware of sounding like a babbling fool, but that formidable little woman unnerved me with her steely calm.

"I was awake till four in the morning working at my computer," I confessed for no good reason. Rosalinda's stern countenance revealed nothing.

"Si, señora," she replied cryptically. "You like some juice with breakfast?" I told her I would love some.

"You are writing a story about *mulas?*" she asked as she set a plate of scrambled eggs, sausage, and biscuits in front of me. There was enough skepticism in her tone to tell me that she didn't buy Jake's cover up.

"Actually," I said, "I'm writing a piece about love and marriage."

"Oh, then you have picked a good man to talk to," she said with a chuckle. "Señor Jake knows a lot about that." I shared in her joke.

"That's why I chose him for the interview. I figure a man that's been married seven times must have learned something about the subject."

"Yes, but I don't think he learn enough yet. He always want to make the same mistakes again and again."

I thoughtfully chewed a forkful of eggs. I couldn't understand how three-hour-old eggs could still taste so good.

"I guess you've seen Jake with a lot of different women while you've worked for him." Rosalinda snorted and wagged her head disapprovingly. "What do you make of him being married so many times?" Rosalinda wiped the meticulously clean countertop while she considered this question.

"He want a person that don't exist," she concluded. "I see all the time, he bring home many women, and sometimes they stay for a long time, sometimes only a short time. Now I know right away which ones won't last long," she said, finger to her nose, as if she had developed a sixth sense where Jake's affairs were concerned.

"So, Jake's been married to four different women since you've been with him?" I asked. Rosalinda nodded solemnly. "Has it surprised you that he's been willing to take the risk after so many failed attempts?"

She studied me silently for a moment, perhaps debating whether or not to share her feelings with me. When she turned her back on me, I felt certain I had pushed the envelope too far. I upbraided myself for having spoiled such a valuable contact so early in the game. It was not uncommon to lose cooperation from a source when the questioning got too close to the truth for comfort. But I had barely begun to tap this fountain of knowledge.

I was toying with a half-eaten sausage when, to my astonishment, Rosalinda pulled up a chair across from me. She took a sip of her coffee before sharing her insights with me.

"I am with Señor Jake since Venezuela," she began. "The señora hired me to take care of their house. Oh, it was a beautiful big house—so many rooms! It was a lot of work, but it was good. The Senores were very happy in the beginning. But after a few months, I could see that it was no good. I think, they need a *bebe*, then everything work out fine. I wait, I look for signs, but the señora no get *embarasada*.

"Then, one night I wake up to hear terrible fighting. The señor and the señora are screaming at each other. I hear things breaking all over the house, but I am too afraid to leave my room. Then I hear Manuel the gardener try to stop the fight.

"I sneak into the hallway and I see Señor Jake throw the señora's bags out the door. Then he grab the señora by the hair and he throw her out the door, too. She beat on the door, screaming and cursing at the señor, but he don't listen. He tell us all to go back to bed, the señora don't live here no more."

I waited as patiently as possible while Rosalinda took another sip of her coffee. But instead of continuing, she merely shrugged, as if that had explained everything.

"Did you ever find out why he threw Marlena out of the house?" I asked.

Rosalinda consulted her coffee cup a long time before answering. "I know the señora was a bad woman. When Señor Jake went away, the señora would have her lover to the house. She say he was her brother, but I see them together one day, by accident. I try to sneak away before they see me, but he tell me that if I say a word to Señor Jake, he will kill me. He is a very bad man. He have an evil look in his eye. I believe him. I say nothing to Señor Jake, but he found out another way."

I had not been prepared for this type of revelation. It occurred to me that Jake had ended his account of wife number four rather abruptly the night before. Now I understood why. I could also see why Rosalinda, after what she had witnessed in her capacity as housekeeper, had seemed so leery of my appearance at first.

"Did you stay in Venezuela long after they split up?"

"No, Señor Jake say that it take a long time to get rid of Señora Marlena, but he no want to stay in that country anymore. I beg him to take me back to America with him. I no tell him, but I fear the bad man will think I tell Señor Jake about him and the señora. I think he will kill me because I tell on him."

She paused for a moment, holding my gaze as if to assess my comprehension. "Señor Jake is very rich man. The señora and her lover no want to lose the house and all the money. I think they plan to harm Señor Jake and take his money," she confided in a whisper. She leaned back, evidently satisfied to have this secret off her chest. Fifteen years was a long time to keep a disturbing suspicion like that to herself.

"What were Jake's other wives like, the ones you've known?" I asked, hoping to keep the flood of information flowing. Rosalinda made a face that indicated she wasn't particularly fond of any of the wives she had had the duty of serving.

"Señor Jake don't know how to pick a good wife," she said sourly. "He always like the ones with the pretty face, but the inside is more important."

I happen to subscribe to that philosophy myself, but her opinion shed very little light on the dynamics of these three marriages. I was formulating my next line of questioning when we heard a vehicle pull up out front. Rosalinda cocked her head as she strained to identify the footfalls as they approached the house. Without notice, she sprang to her feet and stationed herself in front of the sink, just as a young woman burst into the kitchen.

"Where's Jake?" she demanded of the housekeeper without preamble. Rosalinda was telling her that her boss went into town when the intruder became aware of my presence.

"Who are you?" she blurted out suspiciously.

"My name is Allison Tyler-Wilcox," I said as I stood up and extended my hand. She glared at me, the heavy dark eye shadow conveying the full menace of her demeanor. I let my hand fall to my side as I abandoned the hope of making friends with this twenty-something tart in full Western regalia.

"What are you doing here?" she asked, folding her arms across her well-formed chest.

"I'm a journalist with *Savoir-Faire* Magazine," I said. "I'm here to interview Mr. Sorenson for an article I'm working on." To show my indifference to her antagonistic welcome, I reseated myself and took a sip of coffee, which had grown cold while I listened to Rosalinda's tale.

"Give me a cup of coffee, Rosie," she commanded as she pulled out the chair the housekeeper had just vacated.

"He never told me about no reporter comin' out here to do no article," she challenged me, as if I had fabricated that reason out of thin air in order to hide my real motives.

I smiled blandly, making no effort to justify this breach of communication. She'd have to take that up with Jake himself, a chore I was certain she'd jump to at the first opportunity. Though I realized I would stand almost no chance of deriving information out of this chick, her hostility toward me didn't bother me. To the contrary, she nearly had me laughing out loud.

What on earth did Jake see in this one, besides the fact that she was more than thirty years his junior? I guess the argument could be made that she was attractive, if you could wipe off all the make-up and hairspray and start fresh.

She had colored and streaked her hair to the point that it now resembled a loosely thatched broom, which she had curled at the ends, topped off with a curious spray of hair framing her face like a stiff halo. Her makeup looked as if she had put it on in a closet, without the benefit of adequate lighting, resulting in a garish array of unnatural hues.

There was no denying that she possessed a knockout figure underneath her embroidered shirt and skintight jeans. But still it made me wonder about the veracity of Jake's claims that both wives two and four had been drop-dead gorgeous. After seeing this girl, I had to question his taste. Some men's heads are easily turned.

Rosalinda returned without a word and thrust a coffee mug in front of my inquisitor, pouring a stream of scalding hot coffee into it. She shifted the pot in my direction and I nodded for her to warm mine. A flicker of solidarity passed between us, then she was gone, leaving me with my morning's entertainment.

"What kind of article you writin'?" the girl asked as she heaped sugar into her coffee. "What kind of magazine is Sav..Sav…whatever you said?"

"*Savoir-Faire*," I repeated. "I'm sorry, I didn't get your name."

"I'm Jaylynn, Jake's girlfriend. I live here," she said haughtily. I discreetly scanned the kitchen looking for some sort of confirmation from my new pal, but Rosalinda had her back turned to us. Jaylynn took the inference anyway and qualified her claim with "part of the time."

"I see. You live here part-time. Do you live close by the rest of the time?" I asked.

"I live in Denton, outside of Portland," she said.

"You come out here on the weekends?"

"I come out whenever I feel like it," she shot back, apparently figuring out that all the questions were now coming from me rather than her. "Why are you here if Jake isn't?" she asked hotly.

"Jake had already left for town by the time I woke up," I said, knowing full well the reaction this would elicit from Little Miss Possessive. She did not disappoint me.

"What the hell are you sayin'—that you spent the night here? Will somebody tell me what the hell's goin' on here?" she howled in Rosalinda's direction, as if she were somehow culpable in this matter. Rosalinda remained at her post, though she now regarded us openly.

Jaylynn sat with her mouth agape, dumbfounded that no one would answer her. She quickly recovered her wits and dug through her massive satchel for her cell phone. I could only guess who was being summoned. Her agitation grew as the phone rang unanswered for several seconds. Finally, Jake's voice boomed loud and clear through the receiver.

"Where the hell are you?" Jaylynn asked accusingly.

"I'm right here," he said as he walked through the mudroom entrance, a bag of groceries in one hand and his cell phone in the other. There was an aloofness to his manner that suggested this wasn't the first tantrum Jaylynn had treated him to, nor was he moved to contrition by her anger.

"I got you everything on the list, Rosie, except for the black beans. They were out, so I got pintos instead," he said as he handed the bag to her. "Hey, sleepyhead," he said jovially to me as he approached the table and placed his hands on the back of the chair that separated me from his jealous girlfriend.

"I was afraid you'd gone into hibernation. I see you've met Jaylynn." I had to smile at his cool temperament. Even Jaylynn got the message that a fit at this moment would not be tolerated. She watched the two of us for a moment and adjusted her tone.

"Hi sugar," she said, standing up to wrap her arms around his neck seductively. Jake gave her a perfunctory hug and a peck on the cheek before patting her on the butt dismissively. Jaylynn did her best to hide her discomfort, opting for a bright, sunshiny attitude.

"So, what have you two ladies been up to?" he asked.

"Oh, nothing," I said. "We've just been having a friendly chat."

Jaylynn glared at me then laughed coquettishly. "Yeah, she was just tellin' me about the article she's writin' about you," she sang out sweetly. "You didn't tell me you had a reporter comin' out to see you, darlin'." She had so much syrup in her voice, it made me long for the she-devil side she had originally shown me.

"Why should I? It's none of your business," he said rather harshly. Jaylynn pretended not to be offended by his tone. "Guess it's time to get down to business," he said with a meaningful look in my direction. "What are you doing here?" he asked Jaylynn as an afterthought.

"Well, I just came by to cheer you up," she offered optimistically. Jake's apparent lack of interest put the kibosh on that hopeful scenario.

"Sorry darlin', I don't have time for fun and games today. You should have called first. Besides, I really don't need cheering up." Jaylynn squirmed desperately as she tried to win Jake's attention.

"I know, but I just thought it would be a nice surprise," she said softly as she cozied up to him. This scene was becoming too painful to watch, even for a hard-boiled student of human nature.

"Jake, I'm going to get a few things out of my room. Should I meet you somewhere?"

"Yeah, why don't you meet me out front in about ten minutes. I'd like to take you over to see the mules and show you the rest of the operation," he said. "And be sure to wear your boots."

"Will do," I said, gathering up my plate and glass and coffee mug to take to Rosalinda. I nodded cordially at Jaylynn before departing.

As I walked through the dining room, I could hear Jaylynn say, "Is she really staying here?" in a most aggrieved tone of voice. I didn't want to hear another word, for the whole episode had left me vaguely disturbed.

The impression I had formed of Jake did not jibe with what I had just witnessed, and it made me wonder if Jake had gone soft in his old age, taking up with the likes of Jaylynn just for the sake of female companionship. I packed a few working essentials into my pockets and went outside to wait for him.

Seven

When I walked out the front door, Jake was already waiting for me. He had his leg cocked up on the Jeep bumper, and a distracted look on his face that lifted as soon as he saw me.

"There you are. Let's get this day started, already. Nothing like getting out at the crack of noon to lengthen your day."

"It's not even eleven yet," I corrected him after consulting my watch. "Hey, I had every intention of being up before sunrise, but I stayed up half the night trying to sort out your love life," I said as we ambled off in the direction of the corrals.

"Speaking of which, I realized you never finished telling me about your marriage to Marlena. Last you spoke of it, you had both settled into domestic bliss. What happened to break up your wedded idyll?"

"Nothing really happened," he said, "we just began to drift apart after awhile, that's all."

"How long did that marriage last?" I asked as I trotted alongside him. I don't know if it was my imagination or not, but Jake's pace seemed to have increased dramatically once I brought up the subject of wife number four.

"The marriage part lasted about a year, but that was because it took a good six months to get it annulled. We were together—happily, that is—for about a year and a half. But technically speaking, my total involvement with her lasted only a couple of years. Does that finish off that chapter of my love chronicles for you?"

"I guess so…I mean you still haven't told me what precipitated the break up. Even if a couple grows tired of one another, there is usually an event or outside circumstance that brings about the end, you know, like a third party's sudden involvement," I said, baiting him to reveal a story similar to Rosalinda's. Instead, he gave me a sharp sidelong glance.

"Sounds to me like you and my housekeeper have been putting your heads together," he said flatly.

"I was just curious to hear her perspective, seeing as how she has been witness to four out of the seven marriages," I said.

"Then you already know what happened between Marlena and me, so why are you asking?"

"All Rosalinda told me is that you physically threw her out of the house one night, bag and baggage, and that was the end of it as far as she knew."

Jake's agitated gait slowed to a halt. "That's it in a nutshell," he said, deliberately side-stepping the issue. I decided I probably wouldn't get him to admit his wife had been unfaithful to him in his own home, so I let the subject drop.

It was telling enough to discover that a man of his philandering ways harbored a wound too painful to admit. Perhaps his skirt-chasing was inspired by something more than pure lust; maybe he had spent the last several years trying to pave over his hurt with constant validation of his appeal to a never-ending stream of admirers. For the first time, I started viewing Jake's repeated failures in a more sympathetic light.

Having acknowledged his final word on the topic, we resumed our pace. Jake seemed a little edgy still, but the closer we got to the corrals, the more animated he became. He had picked up the mule lesson where we had left off the day before, with more fascinating equine facts and in-depth descriptions of his facility and what went on where.

We passed the large arena where Lowell was instructing Dieter and Billy as they put two mules through their paces. We paused while the boss gave his input. It was clear Jake was a hard man to please when it came to his business. This didn't surprise me, as it went along with his gruff exterior.

What did continue to puzzle me was his ability to constantly attract female attention, especially from one as young as Jaylynn. As tacky and unworldly as she appeared to me, she still possessed something that older men often find hard to resist: relative youth. And though I was ready to chalk it up to another one of Jake's character flaws, I had to remember that this weakness was hardly unique.

In his case, as well as in many others, I had to wonder how these older men found a way to mercifully overlook their own aging bodies when cast beside those of their nubile young counterparts. To my way of thinking, the comparison would strike me as unbearably unfavorable, no matter how energized I might feel sleeping with someone so much younger.

But then again, I'm a woman—a woman in her thirties, for that matter—and I have absolutely no idea what propels middle-aged men toward the pursuit of girls as young as their own daughters, or granddaughters, in this case.

After consulting with his hands, Jake led me around the arena, past a series of corrals, empty now, to a vast tree-shaded pasture where the mules roamed at will. Jake held open the gate and we wandered in among them. It was interesting to observe the distinctly different personalities of these semi-domesticated beasts when they were allowed to congregate and mingle, and I couldn't help but feeling like an uninvited guest.

Although several of the mules flocked to Jake, their lord and master, a few paid us no mind whatsoever; they just went about their business, contentedly chewing every blade of grass within reach.

Of the ones that came to greet us, two in particular took an interest in me. As luck would have it, they happened to be the largest in the pack, and both seemed intent on eating my hair. I suppose a horse or mule-savvy person would have shooed them away and stood her ground, but I was flustered by the size of them.

As Jake socialized with his lap mules, I was forced to navigate in a tight circle around the trainer and his brood to avoid my pursuers' massive teeth. Finally, one got wise to me and doubled back, bringing me face to face with both of them, leaving me no option but to flee for the gate.

"Hey, where are you headed?" Jake called out as I made a beeline for safety.

"I'll just wait out here for you," I said as I wrestled with the stubborn latch. It gave me little comfort to discover the two were still close on my heels.

"Back off, you darn varmints," Jake hollered to my admirers. Somehow they understood him and sulkily gave up the chase.

"Looks like you've made some friends already," he said, looping a lead rope around the neck of one of the mules he had been examining. He led that one, a beautiful dun colored mule, in the direction of one of the colossal bay Jacks that had me on the run. He deftly slipped a rope over the second mule's head and led both of them toward the gate.

I reopened it and stood out of the way until Jake and his charges passed through. I secured the gate and followed them at a respectful distance to the nearest hitching post. Jake disappeared into the barn and returned with a saddle that he placed on the dun mule. As I watched his retreating figure a second time, it occurred to me he had some plan up his sleeve.

"I don't suppose you're going to demonstrate how to ride two mules simultaneously," I said once he returned. He didn't bother to answer me. I guessed his advise to wear boots had been my only warning that I was expected to ride. I could already imagine how sore my butt was going to be by evening time. Jake, alerted by my unusual silence, turned around to regard me.

"You're okay with taking a ride, aren't you?" he asked.

"Oh sure, no problem," I lied.

"I thought I'd take you on a little tour of the neighborhood. Rosie's packing a lunch for us right now."

"Sounds lovely. You'll have to give me a refresher course on how to operate one of these things," I said. "It's been twenty years since I've been on a horse, and I've never even been this close to a mule before."

"You'll be fine. You just follow my lead. Sabrina will do all the work. She's an excellent trail animal, aren't you, sweetheart?" Jake patted her roughly on the rump and tightened her cinch. He looked over at me, judged the length of my legs and adjusted the stirrups. After saddling Jeb, the Goliath he was going to ride, Jake ducked back into the barn and returned with an assortment of cowboy hats. The first one he placed on my head swallowed my eyes and ears.

"Didn't think that one would work," he said with a chuckle. "Let's try this one." He slipped the first one off and replaced it with a white straw model, which was a much better fit, but still not quite right.

"Okay, Goldilocks, third time's the charm." The tan felt hat fit like it was made for me. I had the boots and the hat—I was all set. All I needed now was to Velcro my jeans to the saddle so I could stay on the damn thing and make it back in one piece.

Jake had untied Sabrina and was backing her up when, out of the blue, Jaylynn rode up on a magnificent pure black horse. I had to admit she looked much more fetching in this environment. In fact, the fineness of horse and rider made the mules and their riders look positively shabby by comparison. Jaylynn brought her horse to an abrupt stop, kicking up a spray of gravel and dust for effect. I heard Jake release a chest full of air like an exasperated parent.

"I thought you'd left by now," he said curtly.

"Decided I'd stick around and ride along with you."

"Sorry, Jaylynn. Allison and I have work to do. I told you that before." Turning to me, he said, "Okay, little lady—up and over."

Just what I didn't need, an audience to watch me sail right over the top of this animal. Jake steadied Sabrina and motioned for me to hop on board. I grabbed hold of the saddle horn, slipped my left foot into the stirrup and was just about to hoist myself up when Jaylynn chimed in again.

"Oh Jake, I promise I won't be in the way. You won't hear a peep out of me, I swear."

"That's right, I won't, because you won't be coming with us. Okay, up and over," he directed me a second time.

Despite Jaylynn's continued wheedling, I actually managed to fling my right leg over the saddle and was now on top, exhilarated, but still nervous. My heart was pounding, but not so much that I couldn't keep my cool in front of Jaylynn.

"Jake, it's not fair that I should drive all the way out here to see you and you won't even—"

"Jaylynn, that's enough. You'll have to take a ride on your own, and then be on your way. You okay up there?" he asked me. I nodded and Jake handed me the reins and went to mount Jeb. My mule, which was hardly a small animal, seemed like a dwarf next to Jake's. Just as on the ground, Jake towered above me. We were just setting off when Dieter appeared with a basket filled with goodies from Rosalinda's kitchen.

"Good thing you showed up, Dieter. I almost forgot about lunch." Jake took the basket and emptied the contents into his saddlebags. When he ran out of room, he stashed the rest in mine. He handed the basket back to Dieter, who had been waiting uncomfortably for Jake to relieve him of his duty.

I couldn't help but notice that his gaze kept straying to Jaylynn. This didn't go unnoticed by her, either. *Interesting*, I thought, as she postured for his benefit, acting unaware of his attentions. Jake made a clicking sound to set Jeb in motion. Without any direction on my part, Sabrina followed in his wake.

"Jake," Jaylynn implored once more as we neared her. I have to say that I almost felt sorry for her. Almost.

"See you, Jaylynn."

"Some kind of funny work you're doin' that you need to take a picnic with you," she accused shrilly. Jake wouldn't even give her the satisfaction of a reply. With a yell of the scorned, Jaylynn spurred her horse into action. At the risk of losing my balance, I turned around and watched as horse and rider sped off in the opposite direction.

Dieter, who was left to eat her dust, stared after her with a mixture of lust, awe and dust in his eyes. After we had ridden far enough to be out of earshot, I inquired about his unlikely ranch hand.

"It seems quite an anomaly to find a young German on a mule ranch in rural Oregon," I said. "He doesn't really strike me as the ranching type. How did you ever find him?" Jake slowed his pace until I was even with him.

"Dieter found me. And yeah, he's an anomaly anywhere you put him. He's an odd duck and next to useless with the mules, but I can't get rid of the guy."

"What do you mean?"

"I've tried to let him go, cut his pay, give him crummy jobs to do, but he won't leave. This job is the only thing he's got going and it's the only thing he wants to do." Jake shook his head in bewilderment.

"Go figure—the guy works like a devil to save enough money to leave Germany and travel around the States until he can find a ranch that will take him on. All his life, that's all he's dreamed about, living the life of a cowboy. I was so amused by the concept, I took the guy on. But damn, he's an odd sort. He's always getting up Billy's nose and always pissing Lowell off. He doesn't have any friends. The guy's got no life! But he wouldn't give up being 'a cowboy' for anything in the world. I don't even think the dude's gotten himself laid since he's been here."

"I noticed he seemed captivated by Jaylynn," I said.

"Good, they'd make a perfect pair," Jake said with a callous laugh.

Even though Jaylynn rubbed me the wrong way, I was slightly taken aback by Jake's attitude toward her. "That's an odd thing to say about your girlfriend," I admonished him.

"She's not my girlfriend," he said.

"I think someone forgot to tell her that."

"She's just a kid," Jake shot back. "Just because I gave the girl a horse doesn't mean she's my girlfriend.'

"Well, imagine her getting the wrong idea about that," I mocked. "According to her, she lives here."

"She said that?"

"Yep, and the way she bossed Rosalinda around seemed to give credence to her claim."

"I'm going to have to have another chat with that girl," Jake said, hunkering down in his saddle to avoid a tree limb. "I guess it was a mistake to let her keep her animal here," he mused out loud.

"Awfully magnanimous of you to buy a beautiful horse for a girl you're not involved with," I said.

"Yeah, well I'm just a magnanimous kind of guy," he replied testily.

I suppose he was sending me a message to drop the subject, but his reply did not deter me. We rode on in silence for a moment before I tried another tack. "Do you think if you ignore her long enough, Jaylynn will just go away?"

"She will," Jake said confidently.

"Oh, I wouldn't be so sure about that," I said, sticking my big nose where it didn't belong. I couldn't decide if I was hammering away on this topic because of Jaylynn's hostile attitude toward me, or because I felt compelled to needle Jake about his lousy taste in women. "In fact, I wouldn't be surprised if Jaylynn was expecting to be made the next Mrs. Sorenson." He looked at me askance, clearly not amused by my allegation.

"Well, I wouldn't know where she got an idea like that, if what you're saying was true, and it's not."

"Think about it, Jake—a simple country girl meets a wealthy older man who buys her a horse and lets her come and go from his house as she pleases. Does she know your marital history?"

"Yeah, I told her."

"So, knowing you've had seven wives, wouldn't it be only natural to assume you were up for number eight? Even if you have given her that up-front disclaimer about never wanting to get married again, don't you think it would be impossible for her to not harbor the hope that you'd change your mind? After all, you told me last night the women in your life who resented you the most were the ones you warned off in the beginning," I reminded him.

"I'm really starting to believe that a string of failed marriages is like an irresistible challenge to some people, and I wouldn't be surprised if your friend Jaylynn is just another example," I concluded. Jake was wearing a painful wince when I glanced over to judge the effect of my observation.

"Okay, you've got a point," he finally admitted. "But I honestly didn't plant any kind of seed in her head about being anything more than an occasional lover." Though I had imagined their relationship was of a sexual nature, I found his free admission of this fact somewhat disconcerting. But not as much as what he then told me.

"Believe me, Jaylynn would not be the one I'd be marrying if I was stupid enough to stick my neck out again." Jake had made mention of seeing a couple of women these days, but the reality had seemed too abstract and insignificant as it pertained to my story.

In that dismissive frame of mind, Jaylynn's appearance had come as a rude eye-opener. Now the prospect of another, more serious love interest in this man's life made me reevaluate my focus. The trail narrowed and I gratefully fell in behind my guide as I mulled over the importance of witnessing Jake in action firsthand.

I had been so absorbed in our conversation that I hadn't even appreciated how effortless it was being on the back of this well-trained mule. Sabrina took her cues from the animal in front of her, and if I was inadvertently sending her any signals of what to do, she was deftly ignoring them.

The path that we were on began to climb. I found the jerky forward motion as we chugged upward a tad unsettling, as though the ground beneath us was unstable and unpredictable. But the animals seemed unfazed. Finally, we made it to the top of the ridge, where we were rewarded with one of those magnificent views, though we didn't stop to enjoy it. After the arduous trip upward, I felt a well-deserved breather was in order, at least for the animals' sake.

Whether still irritated with me or intent on keeping to an agenda, Jake seemed determined to press on. Right away we began our descent, traveling down the uneven trail closely bordered by tall trees on both sides. The downhill portion of our ride took nearly twice as long as the climb, and when at last we left the shade-darkened trail and broke into the bright blue day, we came into a lush green valley so beautiful, it took my breath away.

"This is absolutely stunning," I said, as my mule came abreast of Jake's. "It's like stepping inside a painting. It's so perfect, the lighting and everything."

"It's a special spot, all right. And it's completely private. You can't see it from any-where else on the property," he informed me as our mules rocked us smoothly along.

I couldn't have imagined a more idyllic spot to consume one of Rosalinda's tasty meals, and I assumed that any second we'd stop and make ourselves comfort-able. The whole while we passed through the hidden valley I looked forward to this imminent respite and I commended myself on my first successful mule ride.

Heck, I thought, this wasn't so bad; we'd been riding approximately forty minutes and my rear end wasn't even the slightest bit sore yet. We'd have our lovely picnic and head back and the time spent in the saddle would be less than an hour and a half. That seemed perfectly reasonable and acceptable to me.

I held on to these pleasant thoughts until we hit another trail head and it became painfully obvious Jake did not share my desire to stop. How he would have scoffed if I'd mentioned my readiness to stand on my own two feet again.

Now that I had to adjust my level of resolution and tolerance, I became acutely aware of the soreness spreading up my legs and back. It would have done no good to dwell on my discomfort, and once we started our ascent of the rugged hillside, the only thoughts I had were about staying on my animal. I was so terrified at two passages in particular, I actually thought my heart had stopped. It was all I could do to keep my eyes open, though fear kept me from lifting them above Sabrina's head.

Oh, how I wished I had asked Jake to stop back there in paradise. It was too horrible to consider that we hadn't even come to the halfway point yet, and already I was prepared to get off the mule and take my chances getting back on foot.

"How you doing back there?" Jake yelled out over his shoulder.

"Uhhhh," was all I managed to reply.

"Just a little bit farther, then we'll be back on level ground," he assured me.

Praise the Lord, hallelujah! As soon as we hit flat land again, I'll hop off this thing and walk the rest of the way, I promised myself. It was probably my imagination, but I swear that even Sabrina was relieved when we'd cleared our last rocky obstacle. Jake was waiting for us as the trail abruptly ended and gave way to tall, thick grass, as soothing and peaceful as a calm sea.

"You did good, girl," Jake said. "I was afraid you'd chicken out on me and I'd have to haul you out on my back."

"Believe me, if I'd known it was an option, I would have taken you up on it. Why the hell didn't you tell me you were taking me on a death march?"

"Because you'd have worried and fretted and backed out on me, that's why. People are capable of getting through a lot more if they don't know what's in store for them, especially women."

Oh fine; my duty as a quasi-feminist demanded I make a stand and coerce him into amending that statement. But frankly, I was too wrung out to get my back up about anything just then. Besides, I couldn't let every minor slight get to me; with Jake I'd have to pick only the battles that were worth fighting.

"Just so you know, I'm walking when we go back through there," I said, slouching over my saddle horn in fatigue. I couldn't believe Jake had the nerve to laugh at my distress.

"Don't worry, you've passed your test. You've proved you've got as much gumption as any cowgirl in the state. We'll be taking a different route back, so relax.

You're doing great," he said with a great big smile of approval. "C'mon, we've only got a little way to go before we get to the picnic spot."

As long as we remained on level land, I was appeased. I realized I was too shaky to get off my mule yet, and it was calming to sit in the saddle and let Sabrina ferry me along. Soon we came to a gate that Jake opened without dismounting, and when we passed through it, we were now on his neighbor's six-thousand acres.

Just as when you cross over certain state lines, the terrain abruptly changed. His neighbor's property had more trees and seemed relatively flat. Even when we descended to the creek, the grassy turf stayed smooth and easy to traverse. Evidently finding the spot he had in mind, Jake swung off his mule and tethered him to a nearby tree. He led my mule to another one, and securing her, helped me out of the saddle.

I couldn't account for the feeling of pure joy I had as my feet hit the ground again; it wasn't entirely due to the fact I didn't need to worry about falling off my mount for the time being. In retrospect, I believe I was giddy from the experience of riding an animal through challenging terrain and coming away unscathed.

My chest swelled in appreciation of that mule for having saved me from peril. If I wasn't mistaken, I think I had also developed an appreciation of Jake's foresight at putting me through such an experience. Even though I was galled that he'd cavalierly put me in harm's way, I couldn't deny the sense of accomplishment it had given me. Beaming from ear to ear, I knelt down and watched Jake as he laid out our picnic spread.

"Let's see here, what did Rosalinda put together for us?" he said as he opened containers and bags and arranged it all in front of me. "Looks like we've got some pickled quail's eggs, some chicken and cucumber sandwiches—no crusts—ooh, a couple of artichokes and a nice sauce, some radishes and celery sticks, a nice hunk of Shropshire cheese and some biscuits, rice pudding with raisins, and freshly made ginger cookies."

I stared at the food before me in astonishment. I had been expecting *tamales* or *chili rellenos* or leftover *carnitas*. If I weren't seeing all this with my own eyes, I would have thought Jake was having me on.

"Did you pick all this up at the market in town?" I asked, baffled.

"Heck no. You're lucky if you find aged Velveeta at Hendrey's," he said. "Rosalinda made all this for us." Seeing my look of complete incomprehension, Jake enlightened me.

"It's Lowell's influence," he said. "You can't hear it in his voice at all anymore, but Lowell Sutherland is as English as the Queen Mum. And you know what those English are like—no matter how good the local food is, they'll move heaven and earth to keep themselves stocked with their favorite treats, Crumble bars and Bovril and all that crap.

"I don't mind it from time to time, especially for picnics. You can say whatever you want about the Brits, but they've got it all over the Mexicans when it comes to picnics," he said as he helped himself to a quail egg. "Hey, I almost forgot the most important thing," he said as he rose to his feet and went to retrieve something from my saddlebag. He returned with two bottles of Woodpecker cider.

"This wouldn't be a proper English picnic without the cider," he said as he opened a bottle and handed it to me. "Cheers," he said, "To your maiden voyage, muleback." I drank to that. Jake watched me for a moment then passed me the wrapper of sandwiches.

"You'd better eat something before you down that whole bottle," he advised. "We don't want you on your lips so soon in the day. We've still got a good bit of distance to cover yet." I took a sandwich quarter and chewed it gratefully.

"But not as far as we've come," I said, seeking reassurance through a mouthful of food.

"No, we've got most of the ride behind us at this point," he agreed. "And it'll be much easier from here on out."

"Thank God," I said as I took another swig of the warmish brew. I'd never had hard cider before and I'd been drinking it purely out of thirst and nerves. The taste took some getting used to, but I liked the instant kick of it. Within two minutes of the first sip I could feel a wave of relaxation wash over me. I leaned back onto my elbows and stared up at the pure, unblemished sky, so bright blue, it almost hurt my eyes to look at it. There wasn't a thing in this world that could have perturbed me at that moment.

"This is fun," I said, sitting up to take the napkin loaded with goodies Jake held out for me.

"Yep, it ain't a half bad way to spend your day," he said, popping another quail egg into his mouth. I followed his example, another first for me.

"Um," I said appreciatively. "So, is this a typical day in the life of a mule breeder?" I asked.

"No, I don't do this kind of thing too often. Twenty-plus mules take a lot of time."

"What got you started in this business? Seems like such a departure from your other occupations." I plucked an artichoke leaf and dredged it through the sauce.

"It's kind of funny how I stumbled into it. It was just a fluke, really. When I left Venezuela, I decided that a nice, out of the way hideout was in order. I don't know how much Rosalinda told you—I'm not even sure what all she knows, but my breakup with Marlena was a costly and difficult affair. It got pretty ugly there for a while.

"But the long and short of it is I managed to get the marriage annulled. You know how Catholics feel about divorce, so that was out of the question. Marlena became fairly reasonable once I promised her a healthy chunk of change for her cooperation. But the longer I waited around to free myself of her, the more disagreeable details I learned. By the time I left Caracas, I wasn't in the mood to be so generous with ex-wife number four." Jake paused as he ate two sandwich quarters in rapid succession.

"So," he resumed after a slug of cider, "my plan was to lay low long enough for Marlena to lose my trail. I picked a few remote states where I might've liked to take up residence and started looking for property. I was actually just about to go into escrow on a big spread up in Montana when I found out about this place. The weather's more hospitable here and I like the fact that it's closer to California—I still have interests there. It's very remote here, but not as isolated as the other place was.

"The only catch to it was this ranch was for sale, mules and all. The man who had owned it—Hank Ridgeway—had died and his widow couldn't be bothered to dispose of the livestock, so it was an all-or-nothing kind of a deal.

"Once I saw the place, I fell in love. I won't even tell you the asking price because you wouldn't believe it. I offered all cash and a quick close and figured I'd sort out the mule issue later. What I hadn't bargained for was developing a fondness for these darn beasts. After going through all the machinations of trying to sell the whole lot wholesale, I decided to keep them, what the hell. And as you can see for yourself, it's turned into a fairly organized business. I'm not saying I can live off what I generate here, but I derive more out of this venture than monetary satisfaction."

"What made you think you could train mules? You hadn't ever done anything like that in the past, had you?" I asked.

"No, but there was something about their nature I could relate to. That whole episode with Marlena had left me pretty disgusted and antisocial. Being out there in an arena with an animal that has his or her own views about life was just the challenge I needed to bring my head back into focus."

"But how did you know how to go about it? It doesn't seem like the type of endeavor the uninitiated would have much success at," I said.

"There was an old caretaker living here minding the place when I bought it. I kept him employed while I tried to relocate the mules, and then when I decided to try my hand at the mule-making business, I gave Chester a generous raise to stay on and teach Lowell and me the ropes.

"Chester Hornsby had been Hank Ridgeway's right-hand man for twenty-something years and there wasn't anything about mules and breeding he hadn't seen. That old guy was good as gold. He taught us a wealth of knowledge in the three years we had him. I owe all my success here to him," Jake said, an uncharacteristic hint of emotion creeping into his voice.

"Where is he now?" I asked as I sat upright and tackled the rest of my artichoke.

"He's buried on the ranch," he said. Not exactly the answer I had expected. "Close to the pond. We've got a small burial ground over there, just a few dogs and Chester. I guess I haven't taken you over to see that part of the property yet. Anyway, he died of emphysema a few years back. He didn't have any family—the mules were his whole life. So we thought it was best to keep him here, among his friends and his beloved animals."

"I don't think I've ever known anyone who had a body buried in his yard before. I guess it's not the typical method of disposing of the dead—not in the city, at least," I said.

"Hell, nobody gives a damn about stuff like that out here. We buried him properly. Besides, where else would we put him? This was his home." Jake sat forward and stared off down the creek.

"Something you said has been niggling at me…"

"What is it?" he asked as he turned around to face me.

"I guess subconsciously I had been expecting a pack of dogs to be swarming the place when I arrived. I kept thinking something was missing, and it finally hit me when you mentioned that you've got a few dogs buried on the property. Are you not a dog man anymore?" I asked.

"Let's just say I'm between dogs right now—between dogs and wives, as it happens."

"Ah," I said. "How long has it been?"

"What—since my last dog or my last wife?"

"Both."

"Two years on the wife and eight months on the dog."

"I guess I shouldn't ask which loss hurt the most," I said.

"No, you shouldn't," Jake said flatly. "Bob was the best ranch dog we've had out here. He got stepped on by a mule, so badly he had to be put down. I don't know if you've ever had to put an animal to sleep, but it's never fun. And neither is getting divorced. Just because I've done it so many times doesn't mean I'm used to it. And it never gets any easier."

"So, how come you keep putting yourself through it, again and again?"

"I told you, I'm an incurable romantic. I fall in love and I become wildly optimistic that this is *the one*, and next thing you know, I've got another wife." I couldn't tell if he was sincere or if he was clowning with me.

"Oh come on, it can't be as simple as that."

"How do you know?" he said defiantly. "It just so happens I've got a very susceptible nature, that's all. Sure, I can understand why you'd think I'd certainly know better by now, and I really should, but then I meet someone new and boom, I'm in love like it's the first time." Jake shrugged and helped himself to the cheese. There was something about his offhand manner that struck a wrong chord with me.

"That sounds like the made-for-Hollywood version," I told him.

He shot me an indignant look over his sunglasses. "What do you mean by that?"

"Well, you're trying to give me the impression—once again—that you're a helpless soul who lets his heart lead him into one misadventure after another."

"Yeah…?"

"Jake, you just don't strike me as a man who is ever out of control of his life or his emotions." He didn't say anything right away, which surprised me. He picked at the cheese with his pocketknife and handed me a sliver on a cracker. I took it, but I was more interested in his response than food at the moment. Instead of answering me, he arranged his saddlebag behind him and laid against it, hands folded across his chest in an attitude of total disinterest.

"Well?" I prodded him.

"Well what? You seem to have it all figured out. What good is my opinion?" he said in a slightly petulant tone. I merely laughed at his claim.

"I'm probing for the truth, that's all. I've heard enough bogus tales by this point in my career to know one when I hear it." I waited for a reaction to this but didn't get one. "I have a hard time not picturing you as the aggressor in a new romance. I just don't believe that it's the woman that always comes on to you," I said.

"I never said that I wasn't the aggressor," he stated mildly, as he raised himself on one elbow to confront me better. "I'm almost always the one who makes the first move. I guess what you're missing here is that, sure, I initiate the relationship, but it's because I can't help myself. I'm a goner before the woman ever notices me, usually." He laid back and resumed his feigned indifference.

"Okay," I said, willing to let that answer suffice for now, "What happened to marriage number seven, to…Connie?"

"The love died. It happens," he said. "Look, I think I've had enough time in the hot seat. It's your turn to do some talking, spill your guts for a change," he challenged me as he sat up and gave me his full attention. "Go ahead—tell me your life story."

"There's nothing to tell," I said, which elicited a censorious bark from Jake.

"Sorry, I'm not buying that. You're a journalist, you're thirty…something, you're married. You've got a life—let's hear about it."

"It'll bore you," I said. There was honestly nothing in my thirty-six-year history that could compare with anything Jake had done in his sixty-odd years of swinging life by the tail.

"Let me be the judge of that. Go on, tell me all about yourself."

"What do you want to know?" I asked, stalling.

"You know, for a person who's spent the last twenty-four hours poking her nose into every detail of my life, you're not being very cooperative."

He had a point, but I still found it intolerably uncomfortable to have him prying into my own personal life. "Well," I began reluctantly, "I've been poking my nose into other peoples' lives—as you call it—for almost fourteen years now. I started writing for various publications straight out of college, and I've been on staff at *Savoir-Faire* for seven years now. Occasionally my uninvited probing earns me an award or two, so I've come to enjoy the status of a first-rate nosy-body."

"Sounds exciting," Jake said with a sarcastic yawn. "Tell me something more interesting, like how many lovers you've had."

"My life is very dull compared with yours, Jake. My career is about the only remarkable part of it."

Jake gave me a look of pure disbelief. "Oh come on, you weren't raised in a nunnery, were you? I mean, look at you—you're gorgeous!" It was my turn to scoff. "You can't convince me that you haven't been chased and hounded by men all your life," he said.

"I haven't," I said truthfully. "I know this comes as a shock, Jake, but not all men run around trying to see how many women they can bed or wed in one lifetime."

"I think you're being naïve, darlin', if you believe that. I think you see me as some sort of oddity, like I'm some Don Juan on steroids or something. But the truth is I'm really no different than any other red-blooded man out there."

"Hah!" I said, flat-out dismissing this comparison. "You seem to lose sight of the fact that the vast majority of men get married once, maybe twice in the course of their lives. You've got seven marriages under your belt and you still haven't ever come out and told me that you'll never do it again. You might end up married and divorced ten times before you're finished. So come on, don't be trying to pass yourself off as the average Joe."

"I'm like all other heterosexual men. I'm just luckier, that's all," he said nonchalantly, as he took a gingersnap and passed the bag to me. I waved it away as I was still holding the cracker he'd given me. I had become far too caught up in this discussion to be interested in food. All these bold-faced admissions and posturings had to be pulled apart to get at the real substance hidden behind his swashbuckling façade.

"You really consider yourself lucky to have a string of *seven* failed marriages to your credit?"

"I don't know why you insist on calling them 'failed' marriages. What makes you so sure that they were all failures?"

"Because they *ended*. The whole idea behind getting married to one person is to spend the rest of your life with him or her. Remember the line about 'until death do us part'? You should, you've heard it often enough," I said, my zealousness to stick up for this institution startling even me. Jake just laughed.

"You really do get all worked up over this topic, don't you? I had assumed you were investigating this subject for purely journalistic reasons, but now I can see you have a personal interest in it."

"No I don't," I protested. "My interest in the subject is solely professional. I was intrigued by the concept of a serial husband, and it made me curious as to why people would continue to trust their judgment if they'd made multiple bad marriages. It also made me wonder about the mystique or allure attached to the often divorced. Aside from that, the subject of marriage is not particularly perplexing or compelling to me," I said with finality.

I could tell Jake was licking his chops, relishing this ongoing debate. It probably wasn't too often that he got to trot out his outlandish philosophies and go head-to-head with someone as opinionated as himself, stuck out here in the boonies as he was.

"Unlike you, I don't see my marriages as failures. I don't happen to subscribe to the provincial dogma that a union between two people is of no worth if it doesn't last a lifetime. With the exceptions of marriages one and four, I'd say that I've been married rather successfully. So they didn't last forever—maybe some marriages aren't meant to. But that doesn't mean that they were a total loss.

"You know," he went on, finger pointed and wagging at me, "I'm glad you're doing this piece on marriage because I think there's too much pressure on people to make marriages last longer than they're supposed to. You hear people toss around the claim that fifty percent of all marriages end in divorce, which of course is interpreted to mean that we're a bunch of losers because we didn't make the wrong marriages last.

"Think about it," he said as I shook my head, "if there wasn't all this emphasis on mating for life, I think we'd find ourselves living in a much happier society. There wouldn't be any reason to track how many marriages ended in divorce because it wouldn't have any significance. So your marriage ends—big deal. You just go out and find yourself another spouse, if you want to. People wouldn't have to tiptoe around the recently divorced, careful not to offend them with their own wedded bliss. Marriage would be a chapter in one's life, not the whole book. It would allow folks to experience much more variety in their otherwise humdrum lives. See, I like the idea of baring my soul for the benefit of mankind," he said graciously.

"Oh really," I said tucking my legs under me, positioning myself for the rebuttal. "You don't honestly believe any of that hogwash, do you? You want to change the wedding vows to read 'to love and cherish until either of you gets bored?' What would you say to all the couples out there who've managed to make a go of it for thirty, forty, fifty years?"

"That they've missed out on a lot of living," Jake interjected.

"You just don't get it, do you? There are many more people who want to make a good choice and build a marriage that will last a lifetime than those who share your blasé standards. There is a depth of satisfaction and love that comes from decades of living and growing with another human being. *That* is what most people are looking for in marriage. Very few say their vows without the expectation of making it work, despite your convenient opinion that a marriage is as disposable as a diaper."

"Crude analogy aside, I think you're missing the bigger picture here," he said as he stretched out on his side and propped himself up on his elbow. "None of us can possibly know if our choice of husband or wife is the right one from the onset. All I'm saying is that it's not the end of the world if they turn out to be mismatched. It's ludicrous to expect two people who don't work well together to spend the rest of their lives chained to each other, hoping in vain they will be rewarded for their obstinate, misguided stoicism. What is the point of that?"

I had no immediate answer, and as I consulted my cider bottle for possible retorts, I found it already empty. As I dejectedly tossed it aside, Jake, always prepared, produced a hip flask and handed it to me. I had to laugh, for at that moment it struck me that Jake was the devil himself, selling me a one-way ticket to perdition, and I, the cocky journalist, was only too happy to buy it.

I accepted the outstretched silver flask and took one harsh swig of the tepid whiskey and handed it back. Jake grinned and followed my example. Oh what the hell, I thought; I was doomed to ruination now, anyway. In the span of one day, I had allowed myself to become embroiled in philosophical debates instead of mining significant nuggets of truth out of my subject, thereby forfeiting my journalistic integrity.

Drinking whiskey and hard cider in the middle of the day was merely an outward manifestation of my loss of control. Here I was, pursuing a story I suspected was ill-conceived from the start, quite possibly lacking in any journalistic merit, slinging out opinions I only halfway supported, to a man who was morally bankrupt and therefore impossible to best.

What exactly did I expect to accomplish, I asked myself, staring out into the bright blue sky overhead. On a whim, I decided it no longer mattered; I'd allow myself to be amused by this larger-than-life mule breeder/womanizer, ditch the angle I was after and reevaluate the topic altogether. I'd treat this trip to Nowhere, Oregon, as a vacation, a much needed break, take advantage of Jake's hospitality, and chalk it up as an idea that just didn't pan out.

Now that I had freed myself of my obligation, I was in the frame of mind to banter with Jake to his heart's desire; after all, I was going to have the last laugh here, for I had no intention of letting him know I was no longer interested in his life and times for professional reasons.

I'd have to make up some sort of story for him and my editor of why I dropped the piece, but I didn't think anyone would really mind, least of all Jake. Like he'd said when I arrived, he would have welcomed my visit on any pretext. I was a lively diversion for a man who required constant new stimulation. I lay back languidly and smiled up at the sky.

"You look like the cat that swallowed the canary," Jake observed. "What are you so smug about?"

"Nothing. I was just thinking about something you said."

"What?"

"About how every time you fall in love, it feels like the first time."

"Yeah…?"

"I don't know, I just find that hard to believe," I said.

"Why?" Jake asked, his curiosity and indignation aroused.

"Surely by the fourth, fifth, sixth time around it'd be hard to work up the same enthusiasm for the whole experience."

"Not for me," Jake said confidently.

"Really?"

"Really. When I meet someone new, I can tell straight away if she's got that certain mix of qualities I can't resist. And when she's got it, I go through the same thing every time—butterflies in the pit of my stomach, this swelling sensation in my heart, this overpowering physical craving to be with her."

"So, it's basically a lust thing, then?" I said, rolling over onto my side to observe his reaction. Jake tilted his head thoughtfully before admitting that was probably the case. I wasn't surprised.

"Do you think if you'd been looking for something other than sex you might have stumbled onto a marriage that had a better foundation and half a chance of lasting?" I asked.

"I don't see how any relationship could last without a strong sexual attraction," he said doubtfully. "Unless, of course, you're telling me your own situation is a case in point," he speculated, trying to bait me.

"My relationship with my husband is fine on every level, thank you," I replied pleasantly.

"*Fine!*—your love life is just *fine?* Sounds pretty lukewarm to me," he said, in an obvious attempt to rile me.

"So it's got to be fireworks all the time for you? When that ceases, and it always will, you're done—you go off and look for someone else who brings back the butterflies?" I asked, a sarcastic smirk on my face.

Instead of taking offense, Jake laughed. "You know, you might be overlooking another important fact here," he said.

"Do tell."

"I get the impression you see me as some kind of shark, lusting after every good looking woman I see." I lifted my eyebrows, daring him to prove the contrary. "I'm going to let you in on a little secret," he said confidentially. "There are many different things that attract me to a woman besides a beautiful face and a killer body."

"No!" I exclaimed as I sat up in mock surprise. "You mean you really are like all the rest of us? I find that hard to imagine." Jake's calm attitude slightly unnerved me, but I sure wasn't ready for his next remark.

"In fact, I don't think there's anything sexier in the whole world than someone who's so confident, she comes at me with both barrels blazing, regardless of the fact she doesn't have a clue what she's talking about. There's just something irresistible about that kind of spunk," he said, looking straight into my eyes.

I was so caught off guard by his words, I couldn't speak. Seemingly content with the effect his confession had on me, Jake lay back against his saddlebags, his hands behind his head, leaving me to wonder if this remark was directed to me personally, or if he'd said it only to be provocative.

I resettled myself in the grass and pondered this backhanded compliment—if such a comment even rated that high—until drowsiness overcame me and I fell fast asleep.

Eight

I was abruptly torn from my impromptu nap by a persistent jiggling of my right foot. Jake stood over me, one foot resting lightly on the top of my boot, wearing his customary self-satisfied grin.

"I'm afraid you might have caught some kind of sleeping sickness," he teased me as I sat bolt upright, disoriented and parched. When I finally figured out where I was, I became acutely embarrassed at having conked out cold in the middle of the day.

"It must have been that cider," I speculated as I struggled to my feet. I looked in vain for a bottle of water or anything that would wet my whistle, but all remnants of our feast had been repacked in our saddlebags and reloaded onto the mules, which stood at the ready.

Jake, anticipating my thirst, handed me his canteen. I sipped cautiously at first, not sure what I'd find in it. To my relief, it was only water—warm, but still very welcome.

"That's okay, I almost dozed off myself," he admitted. "I watched you snooze instead. You're pretty nice when you're asleep. You make this cute little wheezing noise—not quite a snore—softer." He then demonstrated the sound I supposedly made, which was not the least bit flattering. I replaced the cap and thrust the canteen back at him.

"I don't make any such noise," I protested as I brushed leaves and dead grass from my backside.

"Oh yes you do—you just don't know it 'cause you're asleep when you do it."

"I've lived with Elliott for almost nine years and he's never once told me that I snore," I rationalized.

"He probably didn't want to hurt your feelings," Jake said, clearly enjoying this charade of his. I was reminded of being in grade school, where a boy let you know that he liked you by picking on you. Apparently some men never get the little boy out of their systems.

"I think you did fall asleep and you only dreamt that I snore," I said, playing along with his game. Jake laughed and placed my borrowed hat back on my head.

"Ready to hit the road? The day's getting away from us," he informed me.

I was shocked to find that it was already a quarter to three. "Oh my gosh, I had no idea that it was so late! You should have gotten me up sooner. I'm sorry I wasted your whole afternoon like that. I just need to make a pit stop in the bushes before we head back."

"Be my guest," Jake said with a grand wave of his hand that indicated the best spot for relieving one's self. While I squatted in the thick brush, careful to stay out of Jake's line of vision, I thought about what he had said before I had so unceremoniously passed out, the vague intimation that he found my combative nature sexy.

I was feeling quite puzzled by his remark at first, though examining it now I found it to be a harmless, throwaway line. One of those insignificant pieces of bait he habitually threw out on the off chance he'd hit a nerve. There was no point in looking for hidden meaning in it because there wasn't any. Jake lived for getting a rise out of people; he was a consummate mind-twister.

As I walked to where Jake waited to help me remount, I also remembered my hasty decision to give up on this story. It actually took me a moment to recall what it was that had so offended me I wanted to scrap the whole ball of wax.

In retrospect, my reason for wanting to abandon the story seemed silly and not at all like me. I was sure it would tickle Jake to no end if he knew that I had nearly thrown in the towel because I couldn't get a handle on his outlandish personality.

I shook my head in wonder; in all the intense and explosive topics I had tackled over the years, never had I been as intimidated as I was by this wily mule trainer. My repeated visits to a death row inmate hadn't caused my convictions to falter; yet one day with Jake Sorenson and I was ready to pack it in. As Jake turned around to greet me, I wondered if that had been his intention all along.

"All set?" he asked as he steadied Sabrina for me. I nodded and hopped up into the saddle as if I did it every day of my life. Jake smiled broadly and gave me the reins. As soon as he mounted Jeb, we were on our way.

Whereas the first leg of our ride had been a trial by fire, the way home was calm and downright pleasant by comparison. My butt was sore, but in a way that felt good and healthy, as when you exercise long neglected muscles. I had gotten so used to the rhythmic side-to-side jostle of Sabrina's stride that once I dismounted, it took me awhile to get used to my own two-legged gait. I was stiff, tired and ravenous, and deeply soothed by my outing in the countryside.

It was late in the afternoon when we returned to the ranch, and as I had not made any practical decisions regarding my imminent plans, I fell into the same predicament as the previous day. It was too late to venture out into the unknown in search of food and lodging, so I had to once again avail myself of Jake's welcome hospitality.

It was fortunate that he pretty much insisted on my staying, because I seriously doubted I would've gotten very far on my own steam. I promised myself I'd have a departure plan in place before I retired for the evening, as I really did need to get down to brass tacks, get the foundation of this story settled and get myself back home.

I made a mental note to call Elliott as soon as I got back to the room. I wasn't sure what I could tell him at this point, but I had been remiss in not contacting him, and had purposefully turned off my cell phone as soon as I had gotten there. I was sure to find several voicemail messages, most of them from Elliott, but I couldn't put off dealing with them any longer without seriously alarming my worrywart husband.

"How do you feel?" Jake asked as we left the corrals. We had just handed over our mounts to Billy and Dieter, who were feeding the mules when we returned.

"Good. Kind of sore in my sit-down muscles, but otherwise, I feel great. I enjoyed every minute of it."

"I had a feeling you'd take to it. I think if you gave yourself a chance, you'd be a pretty decent rider in no time."

"Yeah, well, I don't know about that. I'm just grateful I didn't embarrass myself too badly out there," I said.

"Naw, you were terrific. You're a natural born rider, I'd say."

This was extravagant praise, but I took it in the spirit in which it was given. In any event, I felt like I was stumbling along on a cloud all the way back to the house.

As we came around the hedge on the front walkway, we noticed a vehicle parked out front that hadn't been there when we left. In the same spot where Jaylynn's pickup truck had been parked now stood a sleek late model Jaguar with Washington plates.

"Aw, Christ," Jake said under his breath. At the same instant, I noticed the figure seated on the porch bench, reading a book. She looked up when she heard our footfalls crunching across the gravel drive.

"Is this another non-girlfriend?" I asked facetiously, low enough that the woman couldn't hear me.

"No, this would be the real thing," Jake said. I don't know why this news disturbed me so, but as soon as the woman stood up to greet us, I felt an unexpected surge of disappointment, unease, bewilderment?—I couldn't say what.

"Looks like you got Jaylynn out of here just in the nick of time," I said blithely, despite my misgivings.

"Tell me about it," Jake whispered back, then, in the same breath, he welcomed the comely woman now standing on the steps. "Well, hello there," he said, adroitly covering his initial reaction. "This is a surprise."

The woman, who was wearing a beautiful cashmere cardigan that came almost to her knees, over a matching skirt cut slightly shorter, at first had her eyes riveted on Jake. It wasn't until after Jake and she had kissed and embraced that she seemed to become aware of my presence.

"Lavinia Houtz, this is Allison Tyler-Wilcox. She's interrogating me for a piece she's writing—"

"I prefer to call it interviewing," I said, extending my hand to the newcomer.

Lavinia laughed. "It's a pleasure to meet you, Allison. You're a writer?" she inquired with polite distraction.

"Yes, I'm on staff with *Savoir-Faire* Magazine—"

"Oh really? I've been a subscriber for years! I read that publication cover to cover every month. Allison…?"

"Tyler-Wilcox," I supplied.

"Of course—your last piece was about that woman who had AIDS, and two of her three children had it as well," she said enthusiastically. "It was *so* touching, it just about broke my heart!"

"Yeah, it was a tough story to write," I said.

"Oh, but you did a fabulous job. I hear that it's up for some sort of award…"

"The Prescott Award," I said.

"Isn't that wonderful!" she exclaimed, turning to Jake who had been observing our spirited exchange with mild surprise.

"Darling, what a privilege to have such an accomplished writer do a story about you! What type of piece is it, exactly?" she asked, suddenly puzzled by this prospect. It was my turn to go mute. I looked to Jake for guidance on this one. Our eyes locked for a moment as we tried to divine what the other was thinking.

"Allison wants to crack open my skull and find out what makes me compulsively drawn to women," he said bluntly, leaving Lavinia to titter prettily and me to shift nervously on my feet.

"Really?" Lavinia asked once she realized that Jake wasn't kidding.

"Jake's been kind enough to share his marital experiences with me to aid in the research I'm doing on male/female attraction," I said. I wasn't altogether comfortable having the true purpose disclosed to this rather formidable woman, especially because I hadn't had an opportunity to properly size her up yet. I could see a woman in her position taking offense at this proposal and putting the brakes on the whole idea. In a show of friendliness, I blathered on, hoping to portray my concept in a non-threatening light.

"I became curious—at a wedding we both attended, funnily enough—about what makes certain individuals attracted to a man or woman who has been married and divorce numerous times. I've been working on a theory that some people naturally gravitate to the often-divorced as though it were some sort of stamp of approval, or a…"

"A challenge," Lavinia said, the light of comprehension beaming in her eyes.

"Yes, exactly," I said, curious at her response. Lavinia turned to Jake, a mysterious smirk twisting her perfectly painted lips.

"This is going to be one long weekend," he said, taking off his hat and wiping his brow with exaggerated annoyance. Lavinia laughed and I remained clueless until Jake took pity and enlightened me.

"Lavinia is a psychologist. She's been trying to find out what makes me tick for two years now," Jake said.

"Is that right?" I asked, looking from Lavinia to Jake and back again. "That's a bit of luck for me, then," I said. "You must have some valuable insights."

Lavinia laughed and took Jake by the arm. "I'm afraid he's still an unsolved riddle to me. Maybe the two of us can put our heads together, see if we can't use our combined wisdom to sort out what makes a seven-time loser such a woman magnet." Lavinia dropped Jake's arm and linked her arm in mine. "Come on, Jake. It's almost cocktail time," she said as she led me toward the door.

I craned my head around for one last look at Jake, seeking reassurance of some kind. He merely stared at our retreating figures as though he was watching two trains about to collide. His expression gave me pause, for I couldn't tell if I'd just found a new best friend or if I'd stumbled into *Who's Afraid of Virginia Woolf?*

I smiled warily at Lavinia, who was holding the door open for me to enter. Her eyes were dancing with merriment, yet I still couldn't determine if she was ecstatic about finding a kindred spirit with whom she could share her most personal observations, or if she was relishing this opportunity to flay Jake—or perhaps me—for the affront that my presence caused. I truly hoped for the former scenario, but my instincts were telling me otherwise.

Nine

"**Y**es, but San Francisco has more of a European influence, don't you agree?" I nodded dutifully while I took another bracing sip of my scotch and soda. Lavinia chattered on obliviously. The three of us were having a cocktail in the living room, all of us comporting ourselves as civilly as the situation would allow.

We had resorted to the harmless enough topic of Seattle—her hometown—and how many similarities it had to the town I call home. Lavinia was so glib there was no way for me to tell if our quirky threesome had the same unsettling effect on her as it apparently had on Jake. I certainly could've named a couple dozen things I would've rather been doing just then, like picking up garbage along the highway or having my tonsils removed, but I did my best to hide my discomfort.

The natural observer in me wanted to sit back and study this unlikely couple for clues as to what, besides sex, qualified them as sweethearts. But Lavinia was hell-bent on keeping the conversation flowing, whether out of professional habit, natural compulsion, or nervousness, I couldn't tell.

Her almost maniacal cadence left me little time to collect my thoughts or draw any conclusions, although it was plain her presence had had a marked effect on Jake. Though I had not known him long, I never guessed he possessed such a somber and aloof side. He tossed back the last of his bourbon and went to the liquor cabinet to replenish it.

"You should pace yourself, darling. It's going to be a long night," Lavinia said, interrupting herself in order to pass on this warning.

"You're telling me," Jake shot back as he splashed more whiskey into his glass. "Either of you ready for another one?"

"I'm fine," I said looking down into my nearly empty glass. Lavinia's cognac and soda sat largely untouched. She had been far too involved in her duty as hostess, controlling the scene with her ironclad cordiality, to indulge in social drinking.

"I'm sorry—what were we saying?" she asked, touching my knee lightly to imply a level of fondness and intimacy between us that had not yet been established. Jake swaggered back to his chair, his expression now one of acute boredom.

"You were droning on about the arts in San Francisco versus Seattle," he said. Lavinia eyed him as coolly as a Bette Davis character and swallowed the dig with studied aplomb.

"Yes, it is true that San Francisco has Seattle beat hands down culturally, but I believe that in ten years we will have a citywide arts program to rival any of the great American cities," she said with so much authority, there was no room for additional comment.

I watched Jake as he jangled the ice cubes in his drink, another hostile gesture intended to shake Lavinia's nerves. Instead, she merely laughed at his impudence and took a modest sip of her drink. There are occasions when the combustible chemistry between two mismatched lovers can generate a provocative and witty current that electrifies those around them. This was not one of those occasions. My parting excuse was just about to leave my lips when Lavinia turned and headed me off.

"So, the subject of male-female attraction—that's rather a departure for you, isn't it? And rather a broad topic, if you don't mind my saying so." She paused and fixed me with her stern gaze. "Do you feel qualified to present that topic in your usual perceptive fashion?"

"I wouldn't say I was any more qualified then the next person, but I do have my own theories and observations about attraction and its many complicated components."

"I'm intrigued. Do share some of your theories and observations with us," she said brightly, smoothly aligning herself with Jake.

I looked at Jake and wondered how he tolerated such a manipulator. It seemed so out of character and it made me suspicious of my previous conclusions about the man. But Jake held my look calmly, as if to say his allegiance at the moment lay with me, no matter how hard Lavinia tried to prove otherwise.

"Well, I think it's safe to say that we as human beings can allow some small curiosity to lead us into relationships that have no chance of making it," I said.

"What do you mean?" Lavinia asked, implying her professional superiority when it came to discussions of this kind.

"I mean it's easy to let yourself get lost in the concept of another person, no matter how ill-suited he or she might be for you. Think of all the situations where someone could be tempted to abandon his or her own world and jump straight into a stranger's life, with no thought of the practical matters of compatibility. Imagine all the times when a minor flirtation has turned into a life-altering experience, only to end abruptly when the dissimilarities become impossible to overlook anymore."

"Interesting," Lavinia said condescendingly, nose in the air.

"I'm sure you understand what I'm talking about—the guy behind the checkout counter who always smiles and makes small talk, or the bank teller whose face lights up when he sees you walk in. Or the handsome businessman who sits across the aisle from you on the plane and keeps looking at you as if you're the one woman he's been searching for all his life.

"I think we've all had moments when we've projected ourselves into a stranger's world, fantasizing about how life would be if we just walked away from what we hold dear in favor of taking up with a person we know almost nothing about. They can be tempting, those chance encounters, making us believe for a fleeting moment our lives might be richer or more fulfilling, or that perhaps we might be a different type of person under different circumstances.

"Most of us have built up a healthy distrust of these initial attractions and are wise enough to let the momentary impulses pass. But I believe some people can't resist that spark of new attraction, regardless of how many times they've been burned."

I'm sure that Lavinia had not bargained on me defending my position so vigorously; her challenge had been put to me with the intention of silencing me, hopefully causing me to demur and slink off to my room—or better yet, leave altogether.

But I was on a roll now, articulating thoughts that had never occurred to me in full form before. It was quite an edifying experience, for it gave a much-needed backbone to the story that had to this point remained in a vague, limp heap. I let my gaze wander off, my sudden detachment spurring Lavinia to contradict me.

"But you make it sound as if a person is completely without self-knowledge if they trust their instincts, even if their choice is totally out of the norm for them."

"If they make a habit of choosing someone who is all wrong for them, yes, I do believe that."

"So, you don't think it's possible for opposites to attract and hold for any length of time," Lavinia concluded.

"I never said that. In fact, I do think mismatched couples can have lasting relationships, though I don't believe it is ever easy for them."

By the look on Lavinia's face, it was evident she had taken my comments personally. If I had her savage lust for control, I would have seized the opportunity and gone for the jugular. Instead, I was happy to give her a little more line to tangle herself in. I sat back quietly in my chair, allowing her time to regroup. Jake was either asleep or wise enough to keep out of our antagonistic discourse. Lavinia didn't miss a beat.

"So, I would have to assume from what you said earlier that you consider our friend Jake Sorenson to be one of those poor dopes who is too impulsive for his own good." Jake apparently hadn't nodded off, for he now groaned and tipped his hat further down over his face.

"Leave me out of this," he said, crossing his arms over his chest. "I'm just going to snooze while you two wizards sort out the world's troubles."

"Of course," she continued on, unfazed, "it's to be expected he wouldn't care for your characterization, but there is no doubt you are correct. Some people cannot control their impulses and they react to every attraction that happens along. But you realize that even with the most hopeless cases, there is the possibility that one of these encounters could actually pay off with a lasting relationship."

It wasn't hard to figure out why she should champion this particular theory. "So, you wouldn't advise any of your patients with this particular compulsion to try to modify or curb their behavior?" I asked.

"It's not my job to advise," she said. "I simply point out the behavioral traits that continually lead to disappointing outcomes."

"I see."

"Besides, your supposition involves only one side of the story, taking into account only one person's motivation, and you know it takes two to tango," Lavinia said patiently.

At the mention of the word 'tango,' I had a sudden flash of the previous night's activities. I glanced over at Jake who wore a sly smile underneath his hat brim. Hard to fathom this rugged creature stepping so carefully with unexpected grace, guiding me along so adroitly that I had almost felt like Cyd Charisse to his Gene Kelly.

I looked back at Lavinia, her patronizing smile just begging me to stumble so she could preserve her standing as The Knower of All Human Foibles. Surprisingly, I could envision her and Jake in a sensuous embrace as they tangoed together, away from prying eyes. Maybe that was the level on which they connected, a level where Lavinia could discard her need for control and let herself be led.

Contrary to appearances, Jake was a cultured man beneath that gruff exterior. Perhaps Lavinia had been able to see through his rough outer layer to the man Jake managed to keep hidden from the rest of us. And it wasn't like she was a hideous shrew.

She may have had a penchant for power, but she was very attractive, with her luminous porcelain skin, which looked as though it had never been exposed to one harmful ray of sunlight, and her bewitching olive green eyes. She had a big city attractiveness; perfectly chosen clothes and makeup and expertly coifed hair, and assertiveness mixed with charm that would definitely appeal to some men.

But even with all these allowances, I just couldn't see these two together for any length of time. I reckoned my observation about stepping into a stranger's world might be dead on for either of them.

"Well, that brings up an interesting point, Lavinia. I hope you won't think me rude for saying this, but the unlikelihood of your relationship with Jake makes me wonder if, a: Jake was compulsively drawn to you, as he has been to so many others in the past, or b: you were tempted out of your usual circle by a crazy, spontaneous urge to try on another lifestyle, or c: that you were drawn to him out of purely professional interest." She blanched ever so slightly under her flawless foundation, but didn't lose a beat.

"I'd say d: all of the above," she replied with a lilting laugh. Jake grunted and raised his hat to give me the evil eye. I smiled blandly and plowed on.

"No really, I'm serious. You are a highly educated woman, with a background in psychology. Surely your better judgment would warn you away from getting involved with a man who has such an abysmal track record. Was it just professional curiosity that compelled you into a relationship with Jake?"

I asked the question nicely enough, but I could tell that my impertinence had rubbed her fine fur the wrong way. As I imagine her doing with her more tiresome patients, she took a deep breath and straightened her already perfect posture.

"Certainly you didn't draw such hasty conclusions on the other topics you have so brilliantly covered," she said by way of an answer. I tilted my empty glass and let a nearly melted cube slide into my mouth.

Here we were, two successful women who used our powers of observation to reach inside others and drag out truths about themselves that they may never admit to otherwise, now sizing up each other's vulnerable spots for the kill. I had to stifle my laugh, for I find situations like this impossibly diverting. Sure, I intended to stand my ground and argue against whatever she branded as true and correct, but I couldn't help but see the humor in our bitchy exchange.

"I'm not trying to ridicule you, Allison, but for the sake of accuracy, I'd like to help you understand the human mindset better before you compromise your quite capable writing with misinformation."

"I'm not drawing any conclusions yet, only looking for clues. In this case I'm fortunate enough to have a bona fide psychologist to give me her valuable insights. And it is handy for me that you know the subject so intimately."

Lavinia's smile told me loud and clear that she knew what I was up to. Mindful of the position I had backed her into, I sweetened my tone before continuing. "I'd be grateful to hear your take on why some people are so prone to falling in love."

"I'm not altogether sure people are addicted to love, to use the vernacular. I think the circumstances that surround each new encounter are in constant flux, thereby altering our perceptions of the people we meet. If you really look at it, it is difficult for us to compile lessons that can be applied to new situations, as every person presents an entirely new set of circumstances." Lavinia sat back and allowed herself another cautious sip of her drink, satisfied she had put the subject to bed.

"Not all of us go through a couple dozen serious romances in our time," I replied. "Why is it that some of us manage to differentiate between who is good for us and who isn't?"

Lavinia glared at me as if I were trying her patience. "You know, Allison, I do have to admire your tenacity in tackling such a complex subject, but I don't think you can cover all that ground in one casual conversation. Perhaps we can talk about your ideas at length some other time. In fact, I'd be more than happy to allow you to interview me for your piece, if you'd like."

"That's very generous of you, Lavinia. I appreciate the offer."

"It's not that I don't want to help you now—"

"Oh, I understand—"

"I just think that if we could meet one-on-one, as one professional to another, we could have a more…productive exchange of ideas."

"Of course," I agreed. "As it is now, I can't help but associate you with all the other women that Jake's been involved with. It's impossible for me to not be curious about what attracts you to him. To me it's no different than asking Jake about his past relationships, except that I have the unique opportunity to hear your side of the story personally. I can't tell you what a help this brief conversation has been for me."

Lavinia's smile tightened into a grimace. We had gone a few rounds without a clear victory for either side, but at least we stopped before we had drawn blood. We had merely sharpened our claws and shown our fangs and made our capabilities known. She might now view me as a conniving, backstabbing member of the press, whereas she had formerly regarded my writing with respect.

For my part, I had come away from our initial conversation suspicious not only of her academic acumen, but also of her knowledge of herself. I don't go in for psychobabble as a rule, but it was obvious to me that controlling Jake and those around him was crucial to her peace of mind. And I've always been leery of those who feel the need to control others.

Sensing a truce or a stalemate, Jake raised his hat and regarded us cautiously.

"Is it safe to come out now?" he asked sarcastically as he pushed himself slowly out of his chair, his muscles apparently stiff after our long ride. It was the first time I had seen him show his age. "I trust you two can behave yourselves while I go inform Rosalinda of the dinner arrangement," he said as he passed between us.

"I've already seen to it, darling," Lavinia said, unsuccessfully grabbing for his hand as he stepped past her. "I brought all the ingredients to make a special dinner, just for the two of us. I told her that we'd take dinner in our room tonight."

Jake stopped and looked at her, clearly incensed. "I suppose you thought Allison could just eat in the kitchen with the help."

"I'm sorry, dear—I didn't realize she was staying for dinner."

"She's staying the night, and the whole weekend, as a matter of fact."

"Oh."

"I really should go into town for the evening, give you two some time alone," I said, standing up, suddenly aware of my own aching body.

"You're not going anywhere," Jake said. "You came all this way to do an interview with me, and by God, we're going to do it. You're staying the weekend, I don't care what else happens."

"Well, Jake…" I'd never had any intention of staying that long. Jake ignored my attempt to protest; he was absorbed in a power struggle with his girlfriend, who at the moment looked more like a sulky child than a female bulldozer.

"I'd better go have a talk with Rosalinda and straighten things out," Jake said after some subliminal communication with Lavinia. I don't know what message he had sent her, but Lavinia stood and swept past us without another word.

"I seem to have picked a bad time to descend upon you," I said to Jake after Lavinia had vanished down the hallway.

"No, it's the other way around. Everyone else has picked a bad time to show up unannounced. Damn. I swear there's nothing that puts me off more than a woman who won't let me have my space. I never asked Lavinia to come out this weekend, and I made a point of telling her last weekend I wouldn't be able to join her in Seattle, either. So what does she do—she comes all the way out here just to keep tabs on me." Jake made a low noise like escaping steam and shook his head. "Sorry, I didn't mean to unload on you."

"That's all right, I understand. But I think since she is here, it might be better for me to get out of your hair for a while. I'll come back tomorrow, if you want to set aside some time—"

"You're not leaving, goddammit, and that's final!" The force of his words made me jump. "You're staying here for the weekend or however long it takes you to figure out what makes me such a goddamn fool. I'll throw a big shindig tomorrow night, invite all the locals. It'll be fun. That'll create enough of a distraction," he mused. "I was having a good time with you before we were so rudely interrupted and I want to continue to have a good time."

"All right, then," I said, not wanting to further inflame him. "I'll just go get cleaned up. Let me know what time dinner is going to be, and I'll be ready."

"Good girl. We'll find plenty of time to cut out so you can bombard me with questions, I promise. But in the meantime, I need to stop Rosie before she gets too far involved in whatever orders Lavinia gave her."

I watched Jake for a moment as he ambled toward the kitchen before heading off to my quarters. Suddenly, I felt overwhelmingly tired. The lengthy ride and then the unexpected battle of wits with yet another of Jake's lovers had wired me up with a burst of raw energy. But that was all over and now I felt thoroughly drained. And dirty, very dirty.

I stripped off my clothes, noticing as I did so how much they smelled of animals and earth. I would have to ask Rosalinda for laundry privileges if I was going to stay any longer, as I was already running short of things to wear.

I took a gander at myself in the mirror before I hopped into the shower and I had to laugh. My hair was matted with sweat, and my face was tinged with pink from the sun and coated with dirt. Lavinia probably took one look at me and marked me down as some insignificant local talent, undoubtedly trying to usurp her position in her absence. You had to be careful when you hung out with Jake; you never knew who might show up and take offense at your presence.

I was towel drying my freshly washed hair when I heard a knock on my door.

"Hi there," Jake said, as he leaned in to speak to me. "You look nice and clean and refreshed."

"I don't know about refreshed, but I can certainly say I'm a lot cleaner than I was earlier." I was using the door as my shield as I was dressed in only my skivvies.

"Well, I didn't mean to barge in on you—just wanted to let you know that dinner is going to be awhile. Rosie had to abort the complicated menu Lavinia had requested and start something else. So you have a good hour or more to rest before dinner."

"Okay, I think I will. That kind of ride can wear you out if you're not used to it," I said, gently massaging my sore gluteus maximus muscles.

"You did great, though. I want to get you back in the saddle again before the weekend's over. Okie-doke," he said with a wink, "I'm going to have a good long soak before dinner. See you about seven."

I closed the door and marveled over the change in Jake's mood. He seemed so much more relaxed and happy than he had been around Lavinia. Surely a person knows when their choice of mate has made them miserable, I speculated. I wondered if Jake spent half his time in relationships in denial about his poor choice. Was that the pattern with him? If that were the case, I figured it couldn't be much longer before he woke up and faced the truth about his current entanglement.

I brushed the tangles out of my hair and let myself drop onto the bed. Lying down felt so good, it hurt. I lay there and mused about Jake's lousy judgment until it dawned on me I still hadn't called Elliott yet. I had been gone a day and a half already and hadn't bothered to check in with him once. I was sure to get an earful about that. He wouldn't be much happier when I informed him that I would be up here another two days.

To be honest, I wasn't altogether sure I wanted to stay with Jake and his contentious know-it-all girlfriend for that long. It was true that I was enjoying Jake's company a lot more than I had expected to, but I couldn't say the same about Lavinia. It was too bad, too; having her around gave me the chance to observe Jake and get a better idea of what made him tick around women.

Well, as long as Jake was in my corner, I guessed I'd stick around. Being too lazy to get up, I reached over as far as I could and finally snagged my bag and fished around for my phone. Fortunately, I only had four messages to listen to, and three of them were from Elliott. They ranged from being mildly concerned to highly annoyed. I bit the bullet and dialed his cell phone. I could tell from all the background noise that he was on the freeway, making his nightly creep homeward.

"Hi, it's me," I said brightly.

"It's about time."

"Yeah, sorry about that. Things just got off to a running start and this is the first opportunity I've had to call."

"Sure," he replied stonily.

"Look, Elliott, you know I have to travel for my work—"

"I don't have any problem with the traveling part. I just wish you had the decency to let me know you made it there safely. Is that really too much to ask?"

I stared up at the ceiling, following the patterns in the knotty wood, feeling like a disobedient child. "You're right, Elliott. I should have made a point of calling you the moment I got here, but I got lost on the way out and it was so late when I finally got here…what?"

"I said forget about it. I don't feel like arguing long distance while I'm stuck in traffic. Where are you right now?"

"I'm at Jake's ranch."

"Still? I thought you'd be halfway home by now."

"Well, things are going really well, even though we've had a few disruptions. Anyway, I'm going to stay on another day or so, cover as much ground as I can because it's such a trek to get out here." Silence. "Are you still there?"

"Yeah, I'm here. So when do you plan to come home?"

"Tomorrow or the next day," I fudged. This was stupid and I knew it. It would be much better to prepare him for the worst so that we wouldn't have the same aggravating conversation all over again. But I hadn't decided when I would be leaving yet, so I opted for the answer that would sit best with my husband. I could hear him change the phone from one ear to the other, a sure sign of his annoyance.

"Anyway, sweetheart, I just wanted to check in. The work is going well and I have a lot to tell you about when I get back."

"You sound like you're rushing out."

"I'm afraid so—dinner's almost ready. I'd better go now."

"Alright," Elliott said resignedly. "Will you do me a big favor and let me know when I can expect you back?"

"Sure, I promise."

"Okay." Silence.

"Okay. I love you."

"I love you, too," he said and hung up. I turned off my phone and continued to stare at the ceiling.

I had a vague emptiness inside me, most likely due to the awkward conversation with Elliott and the bizarre confrontation with Lavinia. But the thing that struck me hardest while I lay there was my sadness at the thought of leaving this place.

It was weird; it wasn't like I had an affinity with mules or the great outdoors, though both were definitely starting to grow on me. As strange as it seemed, I had already felt like some sort of bond had begun to form between Jake and me, and the notion of leaving in a day or two and heading back to city life filled me with an unexpected dread.

Confused by my own feelings, I decided the best policy was to forget about my eventual departure and concentrate on making the most of my time there. I would use Lavinia's visit to my full advantage and see what telling clues I could pick up through Jake's interactions with her. I became thrilled at the prospect, and with renewed enthusiasm, my mind began to piece together all the peculiar tidbits I had assembled so far, creating a collage of facts and observations that left me with no clearer picture than I had started out with.

There had to be reasons behind Jake's deeds, some M.O. I was sure of it. That was the one great lesson I had learned in my life as a journalist: we could trace all our actions to decisions we've made, whether we're aware of them or not. All those decisions lie like buried artifacts in the depths of our subconscious, hidden until someone comes along and digs them up.

It's not always an easy task to unearth these telltale markers, but I was hell-bent on tapping into Jake's, with or without his help or consent. The trick would be sidestepping Lavinia's interference. But something told me Jake would come to my aid on that front. It was plain, even to me, that her charms were beginning to lose their effect.

Ten

That evening's dinner was a bizarre affair. I had managed to get to the table at the same time as the ranch hands, but the five of us had to wait nearly fifteen minutes for Jake and Lavinia to show up. Rosalinda wrapped foil over the serving dishes and stood sentry while we waited. I speculated silently that the delay was due to friction between the lovebirds, envisioning a scene with much yelling and cursing and a fair amount of flying objects.

But when they finally made their appearance, it was evident that the exact opposite was true. They entered the dining room with hands clasped together like a couple of teenagers, a smile on Lavinia's face to rival any bride's. She was attired beautifully enough to attend any wedding, in a low-cut, cream colored satin blouse with a single strand of pearls, and a sweeping wool skirt, at least six gore by the looks of it.

Her outfit was a strong and embarrassing contrast to my black T-shirt and jeans. Her radiance made me instantly feel like a lowly peasant. Jake shot me a fleeting but meaningful glance as he waited for Lavinia to settle into her seat, and turned dutifully away as he pushed in her chair.

"Sorry we're late, Rosie. You should have gone ahead and served everyone."

"We wanted to wait for you, boss," Lowell said as he took the platter of corn from Rosalinda, helping himself to two ears and passing it on to me.

"Fried chicken," Lavinia said, as she spied the massive heap of chicken parts. Rosalinda studiously ignored her as she handed the platter to Jake. Though Lavinia had smiled as she acknowledged this apparent change in menu, I think it was more for show than delight. Jake smiled back at her cordially, evidently enjoying her discomfort.

As I sat there and feasted on fresh peas, mashed potatoes, corn on the cob, and possibly the best fried chicken that has ever passed through my lips, I was grateful I had used my time-out to regroup and refocus on the challenge before me. Because I had adopted a policy of keeping my eyes and ears open and my mouth shut, I happily stuffed my face while Lavinia chattered on as carefree as a bird, dominating the conversation with suspicious gusto.

She talked about the weather, how fall-like and lovely it was there compared to the dismal, dreary weather they were having in Seattle. She talked about the drive over, how nice the ranch looked this time of year, the mules, and anything else that popped into her brain.

The oddest part of this performance was the effect it had on Jake. When he had entered the dining room, he seemed much more at ease, though I couldn't help sensing an undercurrent of discomfort on his part, shyness almost. It seemed he was definitely less annoyed with Lavinia's surprise visit than he had been earlier. I could only surmise their time together in Jake's private quarters had had a beneficial effect on both of them.

But as the dinner progressed, Jake fell silent and assumed the faraway expression of a man with many things on his mind. Lavinia took little notice as she turned her sights on me, picking up her earlier inquisition, though she didn't show her talons this time around. Lowell and the others observed us silently as they gnawed thoughtfully on fried chicken.

"So, how long have you been in journalism, Allison?" she asked as she chiseled ineffectually at a drumstick with her fork and knife.

"Thirteen years altogether, ever since I got out of college. I've been with *Savoir-Faire* exclusively for seven years now." Lavinia made the appropriate sounds of appreciation, but said nothing.

"How about you—was psychology your major?"

"Oh yes, it's been my life's work. I started out at one of the private hospitals in Seattle, and was there for several years. Then I opened my own practice, which I've had for fifteen years now, though I'm cutting back on the number of patients I see. I'm devoting more of my time to other interests—my radio spots, which have become so popular locally, they've moved into syndication. And on top of that, I've accepted a very promising book deal, which should be finalized by next weekend," she said, beaming at the mention of her accomplishments.

"Congratulations. That sounds very impressive."

"Thank you. Yes, I'm quite excited about the prospect," she said, looking at Jake for encouragement, "though I'm afraid I'll be busier than ever for the foreseeable future." It was my turn to nod and smile politely.

"But I like the change of pace. It can become a real drain on your own psyche to listen to people's problems incessantly, especially when the most you can do for them is point out their self-destructive behavior and coach them on ways to overcome it. But you can't *force* them to make changes, and that's the really frustrating side of my job.

"You would be astounded to learn how many people come to me week after week with the same complaints, the same pitiful stories, and I give them the same instructions and they act like they've never heard them before. Or they'll tell me that they've tried to do as I've told them, but it didn't work. Some actually act as though it's my fault their problems still exist! I'll tell you, it's not always easy to give people advice—"

"But you never let that stop you," Jake said derisively. His remark stopped Lavinia mid-sentence. She covered her humiliation by pretending not to have heard what he said. She looked down at her plate and pushed the plentiful remnants around with her fork, then dabbed at her lips daintily with her napkin.

"Well, that was delicious," she pronounced, leaning back in her chair as if she had just gorged herself.

"You hardly ate a thing," Jake said as he poured the last of the wine into his glass. "Rosie, can you bring the other bottle of wine?" he called out. Rosalinda appeared from the kitchen with the bottle and corkscrew in hand and began to clear the table. In a move that startled Rosalinda more than the rest of us, Lavinia rose and collected the dishes on her end of the table.

"I take care of that, señorita," Rosalinda protested softly.

"No, no—I'm happy to lend a hand. That was such a fabulous meal, Rosalinda—a much better choice than the one I had suggested. But perhaps you can make the salmon *en croute* tomorrow night."

"We're having a barbeque tomorrow," Jake informed her. "Boys, invite anyone you want. We're going to have an old fashioned hootenanny; bring the roof down. Pico, how 'bout you dig us one of those barbeque pits and we'll roast a pig, and maybe a goat. I'll call old man Kroger and see what he's got." While this bulletin was welcome news to the ranch hands, it made Lavinia's insincere smile freeze on her face.

"What a fun idea!" she said with false enthusiasm. When she swept gracefully out of the room with two serving bowls in her hands, Jake loosened up noticeably.

"Allison, pass your glass," he said, extending the bottle to refill it. Lavinia's radar must have gone off, for she returned immediately from the kitchen in order to monitor Jake's liquor consumption. She was openly relieved when she found his glass still full. For her benefit, he drank his wine in one long swallow and filled his glass promptly. I was dreading Lavinia's inevitable comment, fervently hoping that she'd resist making one. She didn't.

"Save some for me, darling," she said cheerfully.

"There's plenty more where this came from," he replied, as he topped up her glass. I suppose the strain of playing the indefatigably happy hostess had gotten to her. She drank her glass halfway down in one gulp.

"I really like this wine," I said in an effort to lighten the general mood. As soon as Rosalinda and Lavinia had begun to clear the table, all the ranch hands had excused themselves. It was now just the three of us, and I was afraid I was the only buffer against an all-out brawl.

"Yeah, it's a good one. It comes from your part of the world, as a matter of fact," he said, handing the Napa Valley cabernet to me so that I could read the label. I knew the wine only through its reputation. At a hundred-twenty-five dollars a bottle, it was way out of my league.

"Jake has the most phenomenal cellar," Lavinia said proudly.

"Oh yeah?"

"You wouldn't believe how much wine he has. How much do you have, darling? A couple hundred cases, at least."

"Closer to four," Jake said, standing up with his glass in hand. "I feel like a cigar."

"Well, you'll have to smoke it outside. You know how I feel about those filthy things."

"That's where I'm headed," he said. "Care to join me, Allison?"

"No, you go along. We'll stay in here like civilized human beings," Lavinia said.

"Actually, I wouldn't mind a little fresh air," I said, not relishing another one-on-one with that fiercely dominating woman.

I was curious what had attracted her to Jake, as I was with all of his previous women, but I seriously doubted I would come away with anything but her carefully worded, artistically packaged version of events that would vary dramatically from the truth. I would rather rely on Jake's former wives' perspectives than take the word of a Mrs. Sorenson wannabe, whose account would be as much PR as anything else.

I distrusted her every action now, seeing with my own eyes just how far she would go to keep Jake under her thumb, and it rather sickened me to watch her play at the subservient little woman, all the while trying to exercise her power over him.

"You won't find any fresh air out there once he lights up," she said in her superior tone.

"That's okay, I don't mind the smell of a good cigar," I said. Jake held the dining room door open for me and handed me his glass.

"I'll be right back," Jake said. I cut through the kitchen and out to the back porch, where the others had sought refuge. Through the dining room window, I could see Jake as he passed through on his way to the living room where he kept his humidor. I watched as Lavinia sprang to her feet as Jake strode down the hallway. I could see their animated exchange and it didn't look friendly. Jake disappeared from view and Lavinia stared after him.

I looked away as she turned in the direction of the window, not wanting her to know I had witnessed their encounter. When I looked back from a safe vantage point, I saw Lavinia kill the remainder of her wine and refill her glass. Jake passed through again and I took a seat on the porch with my back to the window, not wanting to see any more of their interaction.

Observing the two of them made me acutely aware of the volatility of relationships, with the kind of scenes that would cause almost anyone to lose their taste for voyeurism.

I was beginning to understand that most marriages wore a thin veneer of harmony that didn't welcome in-depth probing. What happened inside a relationship was generally better left to the individuals involved, as most of us find other folks' shortcomings less tolerable than our own.

"Join me in a stogie?" Jake asked Lowell as he presented him with a cigar.

"Don't mind if I do, boss," Lowell said as he gratefully accepted it. The two men carefully clipped the ends and within a couple of minutes the porch had all but vanished in a cloud of smoke. I had used that same false line about enjoying the smell of tobacco smoke, but any atmosphere was better than the one that hovered around Lavinia Houtz.

Before I started gasping for air, I moved over to where Billy and Dieter were engaged in a combative game of ping-pong. I took a seat next to Pico and watched their heated volleys.

"Keep the ball on the table, dummkopf," Dieter said snidely.

"Maybe if you knew how to *hit* the ball, Kraut-face," Billy fired back.

"If you *chicas* ever finish, I'll play the winner," Pico said as he picked at his fingernails. I think my presence made him a little uncomfortable, but it was the safest haven I could find. I sat back and tried to make myself as inconspicuous as possible.

"Ha!" cried Dieter as he pranced around victoriously. Billy swore under his breath as he passed the paddle to Pico and went off to sulk in the corner with his Budweiser. Pico gave Dieter as good as he got, the two being very well matched opponents. It was thrilling to watch them play, and I guess I got pretty caught up in the competition.

"Mexico versus Germany," Jake said as he planted himself next to me. I had to laugh. The way Pico and Dieter went at it, one would have thought the honor of two countries really was at stake. In the final round, it was Pico's turn to celebrate, although he took his victory in a more understated fashion than his rival had.

"You want to try me, boss?" Pico asked as he bounced the ball on the table.

"Let's let Allison take you on and I'll play the winner," Jake said.

"Oh no, I haven't played in years," I said.

"Yeah, that's what you said about riding, and look how well you did. Go on," he urged me. I reluctantly picked up the paddle and readied myself for the worst.

"You want to warm up first?" Pico asked.

"Yeah, that would be helpful."

He gently lobbed the ball over and I sent it back—not with finesse, but it made it over the net. We practiced for a couple of minutes, then Pico served it. I missed it by a mile.

"A lot of *picante* on that ball," I said as I chased after it. Pico chuckled as he caught the ball and served it back again. We managed a reasonable game, but only because he went easy on me. I wasn't a challenge, so he had nothing to worry about.

"This looks exciting. I like a rousing game of ping-pong. Who's winning?" Lavinia asked just as I raised the ball to serve. She startled me, as I hadn't seen her slink out to the porch.

"No kibitzing," Jake said. "Have a seat. I'm playing the winner." It didn't take much longer to eliminate me from the match. I passed the paddle to Jake, who was smiling broadly.

"You did good, kiddo." I grunted and went in search of my wine glass. I hung back and watched their game from a distance. I didn't know what exactly had brought about the marked change in Lavinia's mood, but I still figured it was wise to give her as wide a berth as possible. There was an unstable, frenetic quality to her behavior that made me nervous.

"You did a good job out there. Pico's a hard one to beat," Lowell said from the shadows. All I could see of him was the glow of his cigar.

"He was just being a gentleman. He could have creamed me in straight serves."

Lowell emerged from the darkened corner and stood by my side while we watched Jake ham it up for our benefit. He executed a series of fancy turns each time he hit the ball and it was amusing to watch Pico deliberately try to plant the ball where Jake couldn't return it. But Jake's clowning finally got to Pico and he missed the ball due to a fit of laughter.

"No fair, boss. You can't be dancing while you play," he joked.

"Ah, don't be a spoil-sport," Jake replied, acing one over on Pico.

"I hear you and Jake took a nice long ride today," Lowell said quietly.

"Yes, it was spectacular. I have to tell you I was scared stiff for a good part of the ride, but it really was fun, on the whole. Where we went was so beautiful—"

"Over on Jorgensen's spread?"

"Yeah, I think so. The property you get to if you ride along the ridge and dip down over in that direction?"

"Yep, that's it. There's a great picnic spot down by the creek—"

"That's exactly where we went," I confirmed.

"That parcel is a beaut. 'Course, so is this one. I just love it out in this part of the world." Lowell sighed and took another puff on his cigar.

"My turn!" Lavinia cried suddenly, popping out of her seat on unsteady legs.

"We're not finished yet," Jake said, serving the ball. Pico returned the serve, but he was afraid to take his eyes off Lavinia, who was lurching in his direction. The ball came back to him and he stopped it with his paddle, killing the play. He nodded to Lavinia and abandoned the table.

"For chrissakes, Lavinia—you hate ping-pong. You don't even know how to play," Jake said. It looked as if he was also going to quit playing, but something must have changed his mind. In all likelihood, he was probably trying to save Lavinia any further embarrassment. I imagine he hadn't bargained on her being as drunk as a sailor on shore leave. The first serve, however, was a dead giveaway.

"Jesus, Lavinia," Jake moaned, as the ball went whizzing past his ear. Lowell stopped it with his foot and tossed it back to Jake. "If you're going to play, try to keep it on the table."

"I'm sorry, darling. I guess I don't know my own strength," she giggled. Jake turned and pulled a face, then regarded his tipsy opponent.

"Okay, let's try that again," he said. I had to admire his patience, given the circumstances. This time the ball hit him square in the chest. For some reason, this struck Lavinia as hilariously funny.

"Ooh, hoo, hoo, hoo!" she laughed, bent over, holding her stomach as if it would burst. Jake stood stoically until she laughed herself out. She fanned herself with the paddle, belatedly realizing she was the only one who appreciated the humor in what she had done.

"She used to be such a nice lady," Lowell confided. "What a shame."

"This is your last chance," Jake warned her. "I'll serve."

"I think finding another woman staying under her man's roof must have unnerved her," I whispered back.

"Naw, I don't think it really has anything to do with you. She's had a few unseemly episodes over the last couple months. I'm not sure what exactly sets her off, but it has to be something between her and Jake."

"That's it." Jake laid down his paddle and walked away from the table, the ball rolling alongside him as he strode past us.

"Wait a sec, hon. You got to cut me some slack. So I'm not as good as your little journalist friend, I'm still pretty darn good." Her speech had become slurred and had lost its characteristic upper crust tone. She looked the classic example of a socialite who's gone slumming, only to find out she's way out of her element. Just as she fastened her hateful glare on me, she swooned and went down like a bag of rocks.

Pico, Dieter, and Billy looked up from their card game, shocked by the sight before them. Billy leapt to his feet and helped Lowell lift her off the ground. She was conscious, but just barely. Recognizing Lowell from the depths of her drunken stupor, she began to coo and clumsily caressed his face before momentarily blacking out again.

"Let's take her to the second guest room," he said to Billy. "I don't think it would do to put her in Jake's room tonight." The two men hoisted her as best they could. Lavinia was a tall woman but not heavy, though in her hyper-relaxed state, she was as difficult to maneuver as a full-grown marlin.

"Would you like some help getting her into bed?" I asked as I followed along.

"That would be much appreciated," Lowell answered, just before Lavinia flailed her arm and nearly knocked him off his feet.

"What's going on here?" she demanded. She tore herself away from her escorts and staggered through the kitchen doorway. She had almost made it into the hallway when she went down again, this time for good.

Lowell and Billy surveyed the inert figure and concluded it would be safer if Lowell grabbed her underneath her arms and Billy carried her by the ankles. They shuttled down the hallway to the room one down from mine. I opened the door and the two men casually launched Lavinia onto the bed like a sack of grain.

"See if you can make her more comfortable," Lowell said on exiting. He may have had a fondness for her at one time, but I reckoned too many experiences like this one had dampened his feelings for her. Apparently, the same was true for Jake, as well.

Lavinia had landed in an awkward position, halfway on her front and halfway on her side, with her right arm pinned beneath her. I removed her shoes and pushed her left shoulder so she now lay face up. I tried to assess what more I could do to make her guaranteed hangover less painful.

The only other thing I could think of—aside from undressing her, which I wasn't about to do—was to remove her pearl necklace and her large silver cuff and set them on the nightstand. I turned off the overhead light and turned on one of the bedside lamps, and closed the drapes. I found a glass in the bathroom medicine cabinet and filled it with water, setting it where she could find it when her tongue swelled from dehydration. The rest was up to her. I closed the door tightly and tiptoed down the hallway, lest I wake the sleeping ogre.

"Thanks for taking care of her." It took me a moment to figure out where Jake's voice was coming from. He was sitting in the darkened living room, in a high-back chair turned toward the unlit fireplace.

"No problem," I answered. I stood there for a moment, debating whether to skulk back down the hallway or rejoin the others.

"Come have a seat, I won't bite," he said. I saw the burning ember of his cigar glow as he inhaled on it. I stepped down into the living room and sat in a chair to his left.

"Do you think she's feeling insecure about me being here? After all, she had no idea she'd find another woman here."

"That's not what's turned her into a raging lunatic. Believe me, it's a lot deeper than that."

"Oh. Well, if you'd feel better if I left, I'd be happy to clear out and take a little pressure off the situation."

"I don't want you to go anywhere. I told you before, you're the only one who was actually invited this weekend, and you're staying because I want you here. As long as you're comfortable, I'd like you to stay."

"I'm honestly having a great time here, and I'd love to stay."

"Good. I don't want to hear anymore talk about it."

That being settled, I leaned back and relaxed. It was interesting how at ease I was when I was around Jake. Even with all his girl drama, I still felt oddly tranquil in his presence. It was as if we'd been old pals for years and knew one another well enough to overlook minor, inconsequential incidents. But it was largely conjecture on my part, for although I had learned many salient points about his history, I had shared relatively little about myself with him.

"You know, it's too gorgeous a night to be cooped up inside. Why don't you grab a jacket and we'll go on a wander. The moon's three-quarters full, and it would be a shame to waste all that lovely light. You up for it?"

"Sure. I'll be right back."

"Take your time. I have to get something. I'll meet you out front." On the way back to my room, I stopped to check on Lavinia. I don't know why I was so concerned about her welfare; maybe it was because she had been so complimentary of my work prior to going all to pieces. I guess I also felt a tad guilty for provoking her earlier in the evening. I had no idea then that she was so emotionally fragile.

She was lying exactly as I had left her. Her energetic snoring confirmed she was still among the living. I closed the door and crept into my own room. It would be eerie sleeping in the room adjacent to hers. My fertile imagination was already conjuring up images of her flying through my door, butcher knife poised above her head, murder in her heart. I would have to be sure to draw the bolt before retiring, maybe prop a chair underneath the doorknob. I was surely overreacting, but I feared her earlier meltdown was merely a preview of coming attractions.

I grabbed my leather jacket and met up with Jake out on the front porch.

"I love these mid-October nights, when summer is still barely winning the tug-of-war with fall. But you never know what to expect from one day to the next. We could wake up tomorrow and find frost on our windows."

"Really? It changes that fast?" I asked as Jake pushed away from the railing.

"Yep, it can shift from summer to fall overnight, literally. It's even stranger to see it change during the day, when a perfectly crystal blue sky can be suddenly overtaken by ominous grey clouds, and a fierce wind howls in from the north. I like it, that dramatic swing in weather, even though it can wreak havoc with farm life. I find it electrifying. It reminds you of the real force of nature and how pathetically inept we are at predicting or counteracting its moods." I leaned against the railing and looked out into the night, envisioning a scene straight out of *The Wizard of Oz*.

"I want to show you another one of my favorite hangouts," he said, as he hoisted a small knapsack over his shoulder. We headed off down the path, moonlight illuminating the way when the treetops permitted.

In the darkest patches I stuck close to Jake, bumping into him twice before he extended his hand to mine. It was a natural enough gesture, but I relinquished his helpful grasp as soon as we broke into the clearing, feeling uncomfortable with such an intimate act on the heels of Lavinia's sudden disappearance from the picture. I was sure that to Jake it had been an ordinary and logical response; still, it had made me self-conscious.

We wandered down the path that intersected the two large corrals, hearing the mules as they stirred in their separate confines, the distinct sounds of shuffling hooves and swishing tails and mules nuzzling each other sociably. As we passed, several curious animals raised their heads above the fence in an effort to greet their owner. Jake stroked and patted each one he passed, gracing all like a campaigning politician.

"Hey, whatcha doin'?" he asked as he paused in front of the majestic Jezebel. She alone had the ability to halt her master. He grabbed her head in his customary grasp, arresting any movement on her part. He kissed her on her forehead and rubbed the inside of her ears. I could see her almost melt under his touch.

"She's such a good girl, aren't you baby?" he cooed to her. I had my doubts about that.

"Come here," Jake coaxed me. "Give her a pat. She's not going to hurt you."

"Are you sure?" I asked as I slowly approached her. Even in the sparse moonlight, I could see the hostile glint in her eyes. "She looks like she'd sooner eat me than look at me. Doesn't it mean they're angry when they flatten their ears like that?"

"She's just wary of an unknown. Let her smell your hand." Cautiously, I extended my hand through the fencing to let her get a whiff of me, ready to withdraw it at the first hint of trouble.

"See, she's not so bad," Jake said as Jezebel's nostrils flared and contracted over my hand. "Now rub her ears—she loves that." Doing so would require that I get closer, which I wasn't crazy about. Apparently, Jezebel felt the same about me; as I advanced, she retreated.

"Come on, girlie," Jake told her softly. As she obeyed, he wrapped his hands around her massive oil can head and held her still. I moved my hand in and stroked her long, furry ears. The hard glint in her eyes seemed to soften as though she'd been enraptured. If I didn't know better, I'd have said we'd both fallen in love.

Leaving the company of mules, we rounded the far side of the corral and entered a barn I hadn't been in before. This one was an authentic working barn, with bales of hay stacked along one side and various farm implements stored throughout. Once Jake closed the door, we were thrown into complete darkness.

We crossed the barn guided only by the meager glow of Jake's lighter. He climbed up a ladder and bent down to light the way for me. He unlatched the shutters and pushed them outward, tethering them to the outside of the barn. We were now awash in moonlight. I looked around at our surroundings. Jake had made this hayloft his own private fort, every male's childhood dream. He opened two director's chairs and placed them in the portal. He then tipped a wooden crate on end for use as a makeshift table.

"How's this?" he asked, angling the chair so I could take a seat.

"Couldn't think of a better hideout," I said. Jake reached down into his knapsack and pulled out a large thermos and two flat discs, which he transformed into cups like a magician.

"I haven't seen one of these in years," I said as I picked one up to examine it.

"Pretty handy little devices," he said

"My grandmother always carried one of these in her purse. She would never let us drink out of the drinking fountain the normal way—she insisted we fill her little collapsible cup instead. I never knew why—either she was germaphobic or she considered the act of bending down with one's mouth open uncouth. Who knows?" I placed the cup back on the crate and Jake handed me the other, which he had filled from the thermos.

"What's this?" I asked as I took an experimental sip.

"It's one of my concoctions. Cognac, Kahlua, milk, and soda. It's supposed to be served over crushed ice. It's meant to be an after-dinner drink. What do you think?"

"It's delicious. It's like an adult fountain drink. Does it have a name?"

"It's called Midnight Fizz. Silly name, isn't it? I came up with the recipe spur of the moment for a contest and won hands down. That's one of the pitfalls of owning nightclubs. You're always getting suckered into these drink-inventing contests promoted by liquor companies to move more of their product. This one was sponsored by a cognac manufacturer. They built a whole ad campaign around it. Some overpaid ad exec came up with that brilliant name."

"Well, the name sort of fits, I guess." I looked up at the sky just as the moon slid behind a cloud. "What would you have called it?"

"Ass in a Sling."

I nearly lost my drink. "I like your name better. Cheers." I really felt like a kid drinking out of those midget glasses, holing up in my friend's fort, swigging booze, and hiding from disapproving adults. I was hoping the smallness of the portion would temper my consumption, but before I realized it, my thimble-size cup was empty. Jake instantly refilled it.

"I'm going to be a full-fledged alcoholic by the time I get home," I said, leaving my replenished cocktail where it sat.

"Nonsense. A moderate amount of alcohol is beneficial. It relaxes your muscles and lets the stress of everyday life drain from your body. It also frees the mind of bothersome details. I firmly believe it's the secret to a long, happy life. In fact, I'm leery of those who don't practice moderate drinking." Jake tipped his cup to illustrate his point, and sat back with a self-satisfied smirk. I could never tell for sure when he was putting me on.

"What's so funny?" he asked, glancing over his shoulder at me.

"Nothing. I was just thinking how your definition of moderate varies from my husband's. Elliott is one of those people who can't take a drink without calculating how many brain cells he's just wiped out."

"Your husband doesn't drink? Didn't I see him drinking at my sister's wedding?"

"Yeah, he drinks, but *moderately*. And he feels immense guilt with every sip he takes."

"Because of the brain cell thing?"

"Yes, that and because he tries so hard to regulate his world. I think it scares him whenever he feels like he's not in complete control."

"So, does that mean he monitors every drink you take?"

"I don't really drink much when I'm around him."

"Well, I hope you don't mind my saying so, but you've done a bang-up job since you've been here."

I couldn't help but laugh. "Yeah, well, I always try to blend in with the natives. When they lock me up in rehab, I'm going to have to rat you out as the main contributor to my downfall."

Jake chuckled. "Believe me, there's nothing wrong with you. You handle your booze like a perfect lady. Although, you did worry me with that first beer you had. It must have been an act."

"I wasn't faking it. I don't know what the deal was, but that did knock me for a loop. I think it was because I hadn't had much to eat yesterday. That certainly hasn't been a problem since then. I'll have to look for a combination rehab/fat farm when I get back to the city." I laughed and picked up my drink. "To chubby boozehounds," I said.

"Get out of town," he said, tapping his glass against mine. "You'll never be either. But that's more than I can say for some people." I assumed he was referring to the woman who lay passed out in his guest room. The thought of Lavinia's current condition caused me to set my glass back down.

"Well, now that we're finally alone, I guess it's time to get back to work. Where did we leave off, do you remember? Were we on wife number five or six?" When I didn't answer right away, Jake looked over at me. "Something wrong?" he asked.

"No..."

"What is it?"

"Nothing. I guess the more I get to know you, the harder it is for me to reconcile the fact that you've been married so many times. You seem so deliberate and self-aware. You just don't strike me as someone who would make so many wrong choices. I know that's not a very flattering thing to say—"

"The first part was okay."

"I'm sorry, it's still not possible for me to believe a person can be married that many times and come away not feeling like they made a few mistakes."

"It's because you still have it in your head that divorce means failure, and I'm never going to see it that way."

"So, after all the wives and girlfriends that have gone through your life, you don't ever say to yourself, 'What the hell was I thinking?' I mean, take Lavinia, for example. She is a very fine woman, I'm sure, despite her momentary lapses, but she hardly seems right for you."

"I thought she was at one time," Jake said, staring out into the night.

"So, which one of you changed?"

"I'm sure we both did," he said matter-of-factly. "Every one of us is in constant flux, or don't you believe that either?"

"I believe we change; I don't know about constantly. To me it seems more like a slow evolution. The trick is to find a mate that can grow in the same direction, at more or less the same speed."

Jake laughed hoarsely at this supposition. "As if any of us could possibly know that type of thing in advance! I guess if we did, there would be no more divorce. We would take our preprinted futures and mill around until we found a match."

"So do you think some of us are supremely fortunate to have stumbled on compatible mates? According to you, love is a series of romantic crapshoots—sometimes lucky, sometimes not. And even the lucky ones don't have the lifespan of a German shepherd. As far as you're concerned, getting hitched doesn't have anything to do with using your heart and your head to make the right decision."

"You're sounding awfully superior. You talk like someone who's been married for fifty years to the same person."

"I've had a strong, successful marriage for seven years now."

"*Ooohhh,* seven years! That's impressive. When you and what's-his-name celebrate your thirtieth, call me. If that makes you an expert, then I guess I'm an expert, too. I've been married a total of seventeen years, so I reckon that would make me at least twice as expert as you."

I glared at Jake, hotly resenting his out-of-hand dismissal of my marital accomplishment. Yet, at the same time, I realized how smug I had been. I had gone there to interview a man, convinced I would find a feckless, fickle heathen whose moral compass had long ago shattered. I knew I was far better than he, because I rightly believed in the notion of 'till death do us part.'

But he was right—seven years with no divorce meant virtually nothing. Somehow in my piety I had disregarded a very crucial point; we're all subject to change without notice. I should never consider my marriage or anything else as a guaranteed right. His words had a humbling effect, yet I wasn't anxious for him to know that.

Stung and bristling from each other's words, we both fell silent and observed the night. The window in the hay barn was perfectly situated to take in the moon's ascent. It was three-quarters full and bright enough to illuminate the corrals below us. There was a light breeze with enough chill in it to make me pull my jacket tighter around me.

"Cold?" Jake inquired. I detected a note of reconciliation in his voice.

"No, I'm fine. It's nice and refreshing. I suspect there won't be too many nights as pleasant as this before the weather changes."

"You're right about that. But even when it gets cold, I love to be out at night. I put on a few extra layers and go out for a moonlight ride."

"Really—you go riding in the dark?"

"Oh sure, there's nothing like it. My last wife, Connie, loved to go riding at night. Sometimes we would get a group together and take a long, three- or four-hour ride. In the summer months, it was especially fun 'cause we'd go down to the creek we rode to today, to a different spot, and we'd all go skinny-dipping."

Jake sighed at his fond recollection. I watched him as he smiled out into the evening, and I wondered if he regretted the breakup of his last marriage. There didn't appear to be any sign of remorse on his face, but I wondered how deep his philosophical attitude really ran.

"You sound like you miss those days."

Jake rubbed his chin reflectively. "I guess I miss certain things about my life with Connie. She truly loved this ranch. It's kind of funny, too, because I had met Connie in Florida when I was still married to Darla. Darla never cared for the idea of country living and flat-out refused to come out here, so we lived in L.A. most of the time.

"I'd come out here on my own every month or so to check up on the place. Lowell was in charge, so I didn't have anything to worry about. But I was always finding excuses to get away from home. That's why I decided to open a nightclub in Palm Beach—gave me another reason to travel. I met Connie when I hired her to do the interior of the Boom-Boom Room. Now here's the weird part—she and I didn't so much as look at each other during that time. It was Nikki who I fell in love with while I was married to Darla."

"Nikki?" He had completely lost me. There was no way that I should have tackled his long succession of women without some sort of tracking device.

"Nikki was wife number six, remember?" I shook my head. "We went over this the other day."

"Sorry. It's beyond me how you can keep them all straight. So, you were married to…Darla and you met…"

"Connie…"

"But you didn't fall in love with *her;* you fell in love with Nikki."

"That's right."

"Then you fell out of love with Nikki and in love with Connie."

"Yeah, over a period of years."

"Okay, I follow you, I guess. So, if I'm remembering this correctly, Nikki and Connie both lived here at the ranch."

"Connie did, Nikki didn't. Nikki would occasionally come out here with me, on holidays and such, but she worked in New York, where we lived while we were married."

"But you continued to come out here to the ranch, by yourself?"

"Yep, more and more toward the end. It was after we split up that I decided to live here permanently."

"And then you met Connie again?"

"You've got it. Since neither Nikki nor Darla had taken much of an interest in the place, it had remained virtually unchanged from the previous owners. So, once I decided to make this place home, I called up the designer who had done such a great job for me in Florida. She agreed to take on the project sight unseen, just for a change of pace. And then when she got here, I don't know, things just sort of clicked for us."

I nodded my head thoughtfully. Maybe there was something to his assertion that he was luckier than most. I've known many people who've gone for years without meeting even one person they've hit it off with, yet Jake connected with nearly every woman he met, on one level or another. It was truly fascinating, especially to look at this guy.

I think women find it easier to overlook men's physical shortcomings, but there must be a magnetism about him I simply couldn't appreciate. That's not to say I didn't thoroughly enjoy his company. I did, but I couldn't imagine myself falling head over heels for him. He reminded me at times of a woolly mammoth. Then, of course, he was getting a little long in the tooth, though it was irrelevant to our burgeoning friendship.

"Nothing happened between you in Florida, but as soon as she came out here, whammo?"

"Something like that."

"How long before you two got married?"

"About six months, I think."

"How old was she?"

"When she came out here? I don't know—forty, forty-two."

"How old is Lavinia, if you don't mind my asking."

"'Bout the same age, I guess. Are you getting at something here, or just being your nosy self?"

"I was only curious, that's all." I did the math on Connie and figured they had only been about ten years apart in age, which didn't exactly make him a serial cradle robber after all.

"Age has never mattered to me. It's as immaterial as the color of someone's eyes, as far as I'm concerned." This assertion struck me as a tad too diplomatic.

"I have a hard time picturing you with a seventy-year-old," I said.

"If I found one I was attracted to, I certainly wouldn't have a problem with her age."

"Ah, but that's it—seventy-year-old women don't attract you, do they?" Jake twisted around in his seat to look at me.

"You've got it all wrong if you think only nubile young things turn me on," he said. I wasn't even sure where I was headed with this line of questioning, so I conceded the point.

"I believe you," I said. "Lavinia would hardly be considered a spring chicken, but there is still a considerable age difference."

"Why don't you just come out and call me an old geezer," Jake said crossly.

I don't know why I felt so compelled to needle a man who'd bent over backward to accommodate me. Something about him caused me to be brutally frank around him. "Because you're not an old geezer. Even with all that scraggly hair, you still seem much younger than you really are."

"There you go again, shamelessly showering me with backhanded compliments."

"Really, Jake—a man that's been so 'lucky at love' hardly needs to be reassured of his attractiveness. Look at you—you're in your sixties and you still have to beat women off with a stick. I can't personally say I've been bowled off my feet by you, but I certainly can see how other women could be affected by your robust…charm."

Jake turned to face me full on. "Well, I guess I might as well end it all. How could I possibly go on, knowing that you find me an unattractive old goat? Here I was thinking you were The Love of My Life, and you toss me off like some old, used-up rag," he ranted theatrically, holding hand to chest as if my words had mortally wounded him.

"Oh, cut it out," I said, turning away from him. "You know I didn't mean for it to sound that way. Obviously, you're a virile, *attractive* man, in the prime of his life. All I was saying is fortunately for me, I was born with an immunity to your particular powers of persuasion."

Jake threw his head back and roared, startling me with his abrupt outburst. "Oh Ali, you kill me!" he said after he'd laughed himself out. "You make me almost sad that I'm not in love with you. You're one hell of a pistol!"

Jake had turned the tables on me and it was now my turn to feel slighted. What I felt was an odd mixture of insult, disappointment, and sadness. It touched me that he had referred to me as Ali; I hadn't been called that since college.

Yet, what had really thrown me was his unsolicited rejection of me. True, I had just done the exact same thing to him, but I couldn't see why he would mind my saying he wasn't my type.

But stranger still was the fact that it made me feel rather hollow to hear him imply I wasn't his kind of girl—like it mattered in the slightest to me.

Irritated by my own indulgent pride, I fumed in stony silence. But the evening was magical in its calming powers, and after a short while, I nearly dozed off. I was instantly brought back to myself when the chorus of nighttime noises was disrupted by a huge, bear-like yawn from my host. I wriggled to alertness, not wanting to be caught asleep in my chair. When I turned to Jake, he was grinning from ear to ear.

"You sound tired," I said, barely suppressing a yawn of my own.

"Not at all," he claimed. "I feel great. I find listening to the sounds of nature at night to be one of the most peaceful experiences you can have. It's almost Zen—being at one with the world, and all that crap." I cracked up at his sentiment. I was finding it impossible to stay mad at Jake for very long.

"Are you tired?" he asked.

"No, not really."

"That's funny, I thought you'd fallen asleep."

"No, I got pretty relaxed there for a minute."

"I could have sworn I heard you snoring."

"That wasn't me—that was one of your four-legged beasts down there. Like I told you before, I don't snore. But I'll tell you who does—that girlfriend of yours. I looked in on her just to make sure she was alright, and she was snoring as good as any man." Jake seemed to find this quite amusing.

"Yeah, she is a champion snorer, especially when she's pushed the fool button," he said.

"Does that happen often?" I asked.

"It seems to be a fairly regular occurrence these days." Jake didn't offer any more on the subject. I held my tongue for a few seconds, until my curiosity got the best of me. For the sake of propriety, I couched my question in an observation.

"That's a bit like the god with clay feet, isn't it? I thought psychologists and psychotherapists are supposed to have all the answers."

Jake scoffed. "To hear her talk, you'd think so. That's why she loves her radio show so much—she gets to broadcast her superior logic to thousands at once. I tuned in and listened to her show one time. She took call after call, dispensing perfect ironclad solutions just as quick as you please. Those poor saps take her advice like she's some sort of oracle."

"Did her advice make sense?"

"Yeah, in an over-the-counter, one-size-fits-all way. Platitudes, most of it. If those people only knew." Jake shook his head.

"'Physician, heal thyself'?"

"Yeah, that kind of thing." He sat back and stared out at the moon. "Want a wee topper?" he asked, holding up the thermos.

"A right wee," I said, extending my glass. A right wee was about all that would fit in one of those contraptions. "Does she have any demons in particular?" I asked, trying not to appear too interested.

"She's got a couple good ones."

I waited. I began racking my brain for ways to pry without prying. At length I just put it to him straight. "What are they, if you don't mind my asking."

"No, Miss Noseybody, I don't mind, though I probably should. Lavinia would have my head on a stick." He paused before he elaborated.

"It's the classic female conundrum: too much fun and not enough time to have a kid, then wham! It's all she can think about. And as you so astutely phrased it, she's no spring chicken, so she's desperate to get the ball rolling. Her clock's not about to go off, it's about to stop. Now, it's a matter of life or death to get married and knock out a couple of babies, preferably two at once."

"So, I guess the instant family plan is not on your agenda."

"Precisely. Referring again to your uncanny assessment of me, I'm too old for that sort of thing. Do you and what's-his-name have any kids?" he asked.

"No."

"I suppose one day in the not-too-distant future your little tick-tock is going to start growing louder," Jake said crassly.

"I don't think so. Elliott and I aren't especially anxious to alter our lifestyle just yet. We're both far too involved in our work to accommodate that big a responsibility."

"Yeah, but don't you think that'll change? Can't you see yourself passing a schoolyard one day and bursting into tears because you don't have one of those cute, cuddly, runny-nosed monsters of your own?"

I couldn't help but laugh. "No, as appealing as the prospect is, I just don't think it's for me. I like children, don't get me wrong. But I've got enough nieces and nephews to fill that corner of my life," I said. Jake eyed me askance, but apparently took me at my word. "How about you; do you have any children?"

"Oh yeah. With seven wives and umpteen girlfriends, it would be a little hard to avoid."

"Doesn't sound like fatherhood is your fondest ambition," I observed.

"Naw, I love my kids. I can't say having them was my idea, but they've been great."

"How many do you have?" I asked, picturing a passel of offspring to go with his harem-size collection of wives.

"Only two, remarkably enough."

"Did you raise either of them?"

"No. As a matter of fact, I didn't know about Ben or Eliza until they both were in their teens."

"Really?" I asked skeptically. That wasn't a very positive reflection on him that their mothers had kept his paternity unknown to him.

"Different wives, I assume."

"I was never married to either woman, actually. Had I been, they both would have taken me to the cleaners. I suppose it's rather ironic that the two most resentful and vindictive women I've ever been with would be the ones to bear my only children." Jake shook his head with a rueful laugh. "At least I had enough sense to not have married either one of them, though if I had, it might have curbed my enthusiasm for the sport." I could see Jake's grin in the pale moonlight. I could tell he enjoyed trying to shock me with his outlandish sensibilities.

"If that was the case, you'd think that they would have cashed in on their paternity right from the start," I speculated.

"Yeah, you'd think so, but I reckon both found it more palatable to go without financial aid than to have me involved in their kid's lives. But eventually both women came to the conclusion it was better for them to know who their father was, even if it was me."

"Did you have their paternity tested? It's easy enough to do, if that was an issue."

"I know, Ms. Smarty-pants. It's not important to have clinical proof. They're my kids, and even if I were to learn they weren't my natural progeny, I'd still love them all the same."

"That's very commendable," I said, "but isn't it an issue as far as your estate is concerned?"

"I don't give a damn about that. When I'm gone, they can all have at it, as far as I care. It's only money, and anyone who feels I owe them something is welcome to it." This unusually magnanimous notion raised my eyebrows.

"Are you serious? Don't you have a will or a living trust or something to stave off an all-out feud?"

"I've got a will of sorts," he replied cryptically.

"Humph," I mumbled, completely baffled by his complex philosophy. "You're a hard man to figure out, Mr. Sorenson." Jake leaned back in his director's chair, hands laced behind his head.

"I guess you're right, Ms. Two-Last-Names. I guess you're right."

Eleven

The next morning I surprised myself by actually waking up before the house came to life. Like a thief in the night, in sweats and running shoes, I stole down the hall and out the mudroom entrance. It was much chillier than I had expected, my breath creating clouds of steam as I chugged into cruising speed.

The combination of frosty air and complaining muscles made me wish I'd eschewed this high-minded burst of fitness and stayed beneath the eiderdown until the smells of coffee and breakfast lured me out. Nevertheless, I was up and wide awake now and it was the hope of getting warmed up that kept me moving.

My smug satisfaction grew as the sky lightened and dawn flared across the horizon. As I trotted along, I was treated to the symphonic sounds of assorted ranch animals as they began to wake and socialize. There were no lights on in the bunkhouses, and no lights visible in the main house by the time I huffed and puffed my way back into the kitchen. I filled a glass with water and drank it as I leaned against the sink for support. It wasn't until I turned around in search of the coffee maker that I discovered Jake sitting in the corner of the breakfast room.

"God, you scared me half to death! I didn't see you sitting there," I said, hand on chest to still the frantic thumping of my heart.

"I didn't think you did," Jake replied, the rising sun silhouetting him with a backlight of soft orange glow. "I made some coffee, if that's what you're looking for."

I found a mug in one of the cupboards and helped myself. I took a seat across from Jake that allowed a view of the sunrise through the back porch. "Looks like it's going to be another beautiful day," I said.

Jake looked over his shoulder and grunted. "Yep, it's going to be a fine day for a barbeque," he said.

I couldn't figure if he was not a morning person or if there was something on his mind. There had to be something to account for his uncharacteristically somber manner.

Whatever it was, Jake evidently wasn't in the frame of mind to disclose it. We drank our coffee in silence until Rosalinda entered the kitchen and began what would be a day of nonstop food preparation. As soon as she appeared, Jake's introspective mood lifted and he became his usual animated self again.

"Got the list together, Rosie? I'm going make an early run over to Pendleton to get everything we need."

"I have the list right here, but don't you want your breakfast first, Señor Jake?" Rosalinda asked as she retrieved a bowl of fresh eggs from the refrigerator.

"You bet. Can't start the day without your good cooking," he said with a wink in my direction. "Feel like taking a ride into town with me? You can help me with the shopping," he suggested.

"Sure, I'd be happy to."

We ate a hearty farmer's breakfast and made it out to Jake's truck just as Dieter and Pico came walking up the path to the kitchen.

"Dieter, I want you and Billy to give Pico a hand with the barbeque pit. You're going to have to get the chores done early. There's going to be a lot to do when I get back from the market."

"You got it boss," Pico replied, obviously feeling chipper at the prospect of a country fiesta.

The drive into Pendleton took a little over an hour. It was a pleasure trip all the way for me, taking in the bucolic scenery as we passed from brilliant, blinding sunlight into the cool, deep shade of the pine trees and back again. The radio reception faded in and out as we navigated the turns. Jake happily filled in the gaps with his hammy off-tune improvisations.

The shopping experience itself was an exercise in hyperbole. By the time we had marked off everything on Rosalinda's almost indecipherable list, we had three heaping carts between us.

"Okay, that has to be enough to keep our neighbors fat and happy," he said as he surveyed our carts one last time.

In addition to fifteen pounds of ground sirloin, eight packs of hot dogs, several packages of buns, ten racks of spare ribs, two sacks of potatoes, eight heads of cabbage, two five-pound bags of flour, four dozen eggs to augment what his chickens produced that morning, cases of soft drinks and beer, bottles and jars of ketchup, pickles, mayo and mustard, and various odds and ends, we also had a fully dressed pig, destined for Pico's barbeque pit.

"Looks like we're in business," Jake said, as he loaded the last crate of food into the back of his pickup and covered it with a tarp. "Now the real work begins."

"I bet the neighbors love you," I said, wondering if this type of hospitality was commonplace. "How many people are you expecting?"

"I imagine by night's end we'll have between seventy-five and a hundred people pass through our gates."

"That many? Wow. That will require a lot of work."

"Yeah, but it's fun. I let the hands invite anyone they want, and by now everyone around these parts knows that if I'm having a shindig, they're all invited. I left a message on Jaylynn's machine inviting her and her rowdy girlfriends to come."

"You must be crazy," I said, looking at him in disbelief.

"Aw, it'll add a certain spice to the evening, don't you think?" he said with a chuckle.

"Well, that's one way to put it." I could just about envision Lavinia and Jaylynn squaring off in front of a crowd of anxious onlookers, money passing hands as they backed their warrior. "I forgot to look in on Lavinia this morning," I said.

"She migrated to my room in the middle of the night. She woke me up so she could apologize profusely, then promptly vomited all over my bathroom. I never did get back to sleep."

"Is she all right?"

"She'll be fine once she sleeps it off."

"A party with a hundred of your closest neighbors and favorite chippies is probably just what she was hoping for."

"Too bad," Jake said flatly. "I never asked her here in the first place. Maybe she'll get the message to call before showing up out of the blue like that."

Somehow, I doubted she'd have such a sensible response to the situation. I had been looking forward to an old fashioned country hoedown, but I wasn't thrilled at the thought of witnessing another one of Lavinia's temper tantrums. I was getting the distinct impression that Jake thrived on fireworks, regardless of where the sparks flew.

We returned to the ranch at a quarter after ten. Immediately, everyone was assigned tasks, which we all jumped to at once. The one notable exception was Lavinia, who still hadn't made her appearance.

Rosalinda put Billy and Dieter on potato peeling and cabbage chopping duty, while I helped her make and frost eight dozen cupcakes. There were such enormous quantities of food scattered about, I felt like I was stationed in an army canteen. If I had been in charge of such an undertaking, I would have surely panicked, and most likely fled. But Rosalinda set to it with such organization and determination, one would have thought she handled that kind of extravaganza every week of the year.

The first wave of guests started arriving around one. Amazingly, the kitchen team had managed to prepare the coleslaw, potato salad, deviled eggs, and a cauldron of chili to go along with the hamburger patties, hot dogs, and ribs. I was thoroughly worn out by the time the picnic was in full swing, but also satisfied as I watched all our hard efforts appreciated.

Sometime during our mad frenzy in the kitchen, Lavinia appeared, looking rather sheepish, but amazingly good considering her recent alcohol intake. Only the tentativeness of her movements gave away her unstable condition. No one had time to pay much attention to her, and eventually she slithered out unnoticed.

I caught a glimpse of her later from the kitchen window, over by the barbeque grill with Jake. He apparently didn't have the time or inclination to dote on her, either. Next time I looked, he had put her to work rolling plastic utensils up in paper napkins, which she did with very little enthusiasm. If her pride survived this humiliating ordeal, I imagined she'd be well on her way to solidifying a future with Jake, rocky as it might be. Only a huge compromise on both sides could ever sustain this painful mismatch.

Around 3:00, after I had stuffed myself with assorted picnic goodies and the crowd had settled down to a post-gluttony lethargy, I stole off to my room to get some work done. There were a few choice observations of Jake I was anxious to get down before I lost his exact wording. I felt sure they would be useful for me when it came time to reassemble his multifaceted personality for purposes of stating my case, whatever that would be.

I still felt I had jumped into a raucous, turbulent river, no raft or rudder to support me, and only the vaguest sense of what I had hoped to achieve as I plunged along headfirst.

I worked for an hour or so until I became distracted by the gleeful squeals of children as they took turns bobbing for apples and other adolescent activities. Jake had told me that the first part of the day, which was family-oriented, would give way to more adult-style fun after the nighttime barbeque. I imagined this would entail the use of his clubroom and a fair amount of alcohol consumption.

It was funny to look back to my first impression when I used his multi-stalled ladies' room and how I had instantly pictured what the place would be like in full party mode. Soon enough I was going to experience it all firsthand. I had to chuckle at the thought of this country-style soiree; it would certainly be a new one on me.

But jaded city girl that I am, I have to admit that the genuine joy I had observed during the lunch portion of this feeding frenzy was contagious. It was such a refreshing change from the parties and events I usually attended, the literary mixers and the rendezvous with friends at the various watering holes, which more often than not deteriorated into inconsequential, high-spirited shenanigans or malignant, sugarcoated gossip fests.

Most of the talk I overheard seemed to pertain to the pluses and pitfalls of farm management and rural living. If the children could be classified as a tad awkward, they were also more pleasant and well behaved than most I have encountered in cities and suburbs.

Of course, the atmosphere was bound to change once the kiddies were sent home and the parents had a chance to kick up their heels. It made me simultaneously anxious and delighted as I envisioned Jaylynn and her posse from the Portland outskirts making their arrival. I was sure Jake was right about their appearance livening things up. It was almost a guarantee that fists would fly at some point during the evening. I just hoped for Jake's sake that none of them belonged to Lavinia.

Somewhere in my pleasant reverie, I dozed off. I was awakened by what sounded like urgent banging on my door. Groggy and disoriented, I opened the door to find my very relaxed host leaning against the doorframe once again.

"The way you were pounding, I thought the house was on fire," I said, smoothing back my bed-ruffled hair.

"I'd been by a couple of times already looking for you, and when I combed the ranch twice, I figured you had to be in here, either asleep or dead," he replied. I stepped back and he sauntered into my room, making himself comfortable in the chair by the window. Fortunately, my laptop was still on the bed, so I was able to plead intense concentration as my reason for not hearing him earlier.

"Now that's what I call being wrapped up in one's work," he said, though I wasn't sure if he was convinced. I caught a slight shift in his posture and guessed rightly, and just in the nick of time, that he was about to see for himself what I had been so involved in. I quickly saved my work and closed the document.

"Darn," he said as I snatched the computer out of his reach. "Aren't I entitled to a sneak preview, seeing as how I'm the main topic and all?"

"I never let anyone read my work until it's finished," I told him as I placed the laptop safely out of harm's way. "Why were you looking for me? The party's not over yet, is it?"

"Oh, not by a long shot. We'll have people crawling all over this place for another twelve hours. I just wanted to converse about something other than crops and rainfall totals." I had to smile at this, having heard plenty of those mundane statistics myself.

"I guess that's what you get when you invite all of rural Oregon for a hootenanny," I reminded him. "What exactly inspired this wild burst of hospitality, anyway?"

"I don't know. It was probably a knee-jerk reaction to Lavinia's ambush. I knew it would make her crazy, so that's why I've gone to so much trouble and expense. Kind of stupid of me, I reckon," he said, chewing on a hangnail.

"Don't rip that off with your teeth," I said, but it was too late. I could see the blood running down his finger. "Oh, God. I don't know why men have such an aversion to cutting hangnails off properly instead of making themselves bleed," I said as I brought him a dampened washcloth from the bathroom. Before I reached him, he had already located another problem nail and was about to repeat the same gory process.

"Don't even think of it," I threatened him as I searched my bag for my cuticle clippers. "Hold still," I ordered as I neatly snapped off the offending spur. "Man, these hands are a disaster," I said as I examined the rest for potential trouble.

"I don't know if you noticed, but I run a ranch with these hands."

"You can still take better care of them," I maintained, as I began trimming his ragged nails.

"Isn't that sweet of you, fixing me up like that," Jake said, a big, sappy grin on his face.

"Well, somebody ought to do it. I suppose it's the least I can do after all your gracious hospitality. Give me the other one," I said, exchanging one big, nicely trimmed paw for the other scraggly one.

As I worked on his nails, I realized that despite all Jake gave out, he was unaccustomed to receiving much personal attention in return. I was sincerely touched by the way he watched me, his eyes riveted to my face with little interest in his nails. I could have been tattooing each finger, for all he knew or cared.

"Hang on, let me get my file," I said as I let his hand drop. It was clear he had no intention of going anywhere. I filed all the nails that weren't chewed down to the quick, leaving them all in fairly reasonable shape when I had finished.

"So, what's next on the agenda?" I asked, sitting down on the bed to face him.

"We'll start carving the pig and serving the dinner around six, I'm guessing. Hopefully, everyone will still be on their feet by then. There are a few guys who've brought their instruments along, so we'll have some dancing music later on." He fell quiet as he gazed out the window. "Feel like taking a ride?" he asked. "Not a long one, just an hour or so."

"Can you do that?" I asked, caught off guard by the suggestion.

"Sure, why not?"

"Won't you be missed? This is your deal, after all."

"Naw. They've all got plenty to keep them occupied. They'll never know we were gone." I had to give this idea some serious consideration, for although I liked the thought of riding over the countryside again, my legs and butt were sore to the point of near immobility.

"It'll be an easy ride," he coaxed, sensing my equivocation.

"You don't have anything for aching muscles, do you?"

Jake grinned broadly. "Is that what's holding you back? Sure, I've got something that'll fix you right up. You need it before or after the ride?"

"Probably both."

"I'll go get it right now, then we'll sneak out of here before anyone catches us," he said. He glanced down the hallway with exaggerated care as he left the room.

Jake's invitation had filled me with an unexpected burst of joy. I'd never realized until that moment I possessed a dormant desire for sitting atop a four-legged creature as it bore me along through unspoiled terrain. I was downright giddy at the prospect of climbing up on Sabrina and letting Jake navigate us through that ruggedly beautiful landscape. And for some reason, the illicitness of our adventure really appealed to me.

I was beginning to share Jake's naughty attitude when it came to vexing Lavinia, though it bothered me a little to admit it. She and Jake were having a difficult enough time as it was, without added aggravations from uninvolved parties. The more I came to like Jake, the harder it became to wish him happiness with such a domineering, suffocating woman. Surely he could, as he had in the past, do better than that.

What made him go for a woman like her in the first place, I wondered. Or for that matter, what made her so desperate to be with him? Was it some weird trophy thing with her, some flawed ego that compelled her to conquer any man she fixed her sights on? Until embarking on this topic, I had not realized how complex love was for some people.

By comparison, my own experiences with romance appeared tame and pallid. All the mystery seemed to have faded away after the learning curve of school days. I had dated for a few years, then met Elliott. I lived with him for two years prior to deciding that it was the real thing, then we married. Simple, the way it was for millions. So why was love an almost unfathomable riddle to some people?

Jake was hardly the first person I had ever encountered who seemed to lose his heart every time he turned around, although he was likely the most well-adjusted die-hard romantic I had ever seen. With him it wasn't so much that his instincts betrayed him; it was a matter of letting his heart or his imagination be seduced far too often. What he said tickled me, though it had annoyed me greatly at the time: maybe he was just luckier than most, if you took the view that more was better.

Personally, I became exhausted at the thought of so many dalliances that boiled over to the point that only sharing living quarters could satisfy the desire of being together.

This inner debate I found increasingly absorbing was interrupted by Jake's discreet knock on the door.

"Rub this on your…um, sore spots and I guarantee you'll be good as new tomorrow." He handed me a jar, which reeked of medicinal herbs when I opened it.

"Whew, that's strong," I said, coughing as the fumes caught in my throat. "What is it?"

"Can't tell you—secret Indian potion. Now shake a leg before Lavinia tracks us down. I'll wait for you on the front porch."

I did as directed, smearing the gooey mixture on my hindquarters. Instantly, my flesh felt as though I had set it on fire. I washed the potent salve off my hands as well as I could, then waddled gingerly down the hallway to meet Jake for another chance to re-injure myself. I could see Jake smirk as I passed cautiously out the front door.

"Don't worry, in a couple of minutes you won't even know you have a butt," he said, shepherding me down the path. By the time we reached the corrals, I discovered how right he was, though I have to say that not feeling your body's hindmost quarters was not entirely an enjoyable a sensation. But once we were in our saddles and on our way, all corporeal thoughts vanished from my mind, replaced with a renewed awe of outdoor pleasures.

True to his word, Jake led us on a ride that required much less of our animals and was far less hair-raising than the previous day's. Our path took us over gracefully rolling hills, which gave our pace an undulating rhythm I found extremely soothing. It struck me that none of the advice Lavinia or her contemporaries could dispense would ever be more therapeutic or beneficial than one hour spent this way. I imagined a freeway filled with commuters on horseback and decided that incidences of road rage would plummet to zero.

I was a convert, make no mistake, though I had my doubts I'd ever be able to indulge my newfound zeal for riding in downtown San Francisco. I would have to let my memories sustain me and make a beeline for more pastoral locales whenever possible. I also very much doubted I'd be able to persuade Elliott of the soul-cleansing benefits of the equestrian life.

So entranced was I by our muleback excursion, not a peep was heard out of me for the first quarter hour, a fairly remarkable event when you consider my constantly inquisitive mind, or nosiness, as Jake would put it. I wasn't even the one to break the comfortable silence.

"You're awfully quiet back there," Jake said, slowing his pace and allowing me to come up beside him. "It worries me when you're not talking."

"I thought you'd be enjoying the break," I replied.

"Not at all. I like talking with you, even if you are an opinionated know-it-all."

"Ha, ha. It doesn't surprise me to learn you like women with those character-istics," I said, referring of course to his current girlfriend.

"Ha, ha yourself. Maybe I do like it better when I can see you but not hear you," he said with feigned annoyance. I retaliated with a disdainful snort, and we let that vein of conversation die, both of us preferring to take in the scenery ac-companied by our own thoughts. In no time I had lost myself in contemplation again, puzzling once more over the man beside me.

"Jake, do you think you'll ever find the one person you could spend the rest of your life with?" I asked sincerely, for once keeping the cynicism out of my tone.

"I don't know, Ali. I can't say it was ever my agenda to find my perfect mate."

I thought about this for a moment. "Do you think that you would have chosen your mates more carefully if you had been seeking permanence in a relationship?"

Jake scratched his neck reflectively. "Perhaps, but then again, I really can't say I regret any of my relationships."

"Really? Not even Marlena?"

"Nope. If it weren't for my marriage to her, I'd never gotten Rosalinda as my housekeeper. Every phase in our lives brings us something useful, and Rosie's what I got from my Marlena phase."

"You know, for a womanizer, you're awfully philosophical."

Jake grunted. "It's just age. It's hard to go through as much as I have without coming away with a more accepting outlook. Maybe someday you'll be as enlightened as I am."

"If it takes multiple lives to get to that state of enlightenment, I don't think I'll make it," I said.

"I'll tell you one thing for sure, when you get to be as old as I am, you'll understand how hilarious it is to hear younger people talk." I looked at him askance, resenting this vague slight to my sagaciousness.

"What prompted that remark?" I asked, offended.

"What you said about not having multiple lives. I realize you said that figuratively, but even so, it shows your naiveté."

That got my back up. If there is one insult I can't abide, it's being referred to as naïve. "For your edification, Jake, I must tell you that most of the inhabitants of this planet can manage to make it through a single lifetime without having to reinvent their lives through new partners or professions every couple of years." To my chagrin, Jake merely laughed condescendingly. I had expected a more heated response out of him, yet he further vexed me by saying nothing. I stewed while I thought of a comeback to my own assertion.

"So you think I'm some airhead who doesn't even know her own mind?"

"I never said that."

"Well, you seem think that I'm perfectly clueless about my own future."

"That might be a bit harsh," he said.

"How would you clarify what you said then?"

"Let me ask you this: do you see yourself doing the exact same thing in thirty years that you're doing right now?"

"You mean work-wise?"

"I mean everything-wise—same job, same husband, same friends, same desires."

"Yes, actually. I can't complain about my life the way it is, and I'd be thrilled if the rest of my time would play out the same way. Contrary to your way of thinking, I don't see marrying for life as a disadvantage, nor do I think that it is necessary to slough off friends and careers just for a change of pace."

"You don't want much from life, then, do you?"

"Excuse me?" If I'd known how to control the animal I was riding, I'd have stopped her in her tracks. It was that type of inflammatory comment that reminded me of exactly what kind of an arrogant SOB I was dealing with.

"Instead of getting your knickers in a knot, think about it for a minute. You strike me as the type of girl who wants to shake every ounce of truth out of a subject, a person who is constantly on a quest of knowing all there is to know about something or someone, yet you profess to be so meek and mild of temperament, you'd be happy to repeat the few basic steps of your relatively short existence until the party's over. All I'm saying is those two impressions don't jibe."

"Well, I don't know how you came to the conclusion that my life—both at work and at home—is boring. It's not. In fact, that's the thing I love the most about journalism—I'm always pursuing vastly different stories. One month I'm at the Leavenworth Federal Penitentiary interviewing a man on death row for wiping out his entire family, the next I'm in New York to interview a group of young artists who are setting the art world on its ear, and I still have the freedom to chase down rogue mule breeders in Boonieville, Oregon, if I feel like it."

I could see Jake's twisted smile as I belittled him, his profession, his home. "Laughing at every remark you find offensive is a fairly childish tactic for someone your age," I said coldly.

"My dear, I don't find anything you say offensive," he replied calmly. I don't know what threw me more, him calling me dear or the sincerity of his tone. "I love a spirited conversation, and you haven't disappointed me yet."

As aggravating as I found him to be, I had to admire his equilibrium. I doubted it was possible to rattle his cage. Not finding any way to answer, I kept my mouth shut, a policy I probably should have adopted sooner.

The path narrowed as we climbed a more strenuous hill, and I once more fell in behind Jake. After a few minutes we reached a plateau and Jake waited for me to catch up. Resting our mounts, we took in the view, a three-hundred-sixty-degree marvel that sent an electrified current of awe through my whole body.

The angle and quality of light from the low-slung sun cast the most beautiful amber glow and purple shadow onto every tree, slope, and crag in its path. It was more than a stunning sight. It was life distilled to its purest form.

"Still mad at me?" Jake asked.

"I was never mad at you," I said coolly, deliberately not looking at him as I replied.

"That's good," he said and left it at that. We soaked up the view for another minute or two, then put our mules in motion, heading back to the ranch and the party that was still in full swing.

Twelve

Jake had been right about not being missed. Even Lavinia, who was delighted by Jake's sudden reappearance, hadn't seemed to notice his absence. I slipped off to the house as she began to fill him in on the stimulating conversation she had been having with a few of his neighbors.

I let myself in through the front door, bypassing the frenetic atmosphere in the kitchen, where round two of the food preparation was underway. By contrast, the bedroom wing of the house had a tomb-like hush, and once I closed the heavy wooden door to my room, my ears roared with the silence.

I grabbed my laptop, plopped myself on top of the bed, and tried to put my thoughts in order, but I couldn't seem to concentrate. I was experiencing another bout of conflicting emotions, not the least being confusion at the effect Jake had on me.

I ordinarily think of myself as an unshakable pillar of fortitude when it came to going toe-to-toe with anyone about anything. I am naturally prone to debating and often take up the opposing side just for the opportunity of exploring a topic thoroughly. And whether I believed in my position or not, I generally prevailed in my argument.

But not with Jake; I never saw his curveballs coming. He had a way of mixing his free-flowing, benign observations with ones that cut to the quick. In my semi-youthful ignorance, I had never fully valued the potential for wisdom that comes from six or seven decades of living.

I had to acknowledge that he had a point when he referenced age as the reason for his astute reckonings. I suppose to bait and twist me in these little discussions of ours was nothing more than him flexing his hard-won insights.

I had made the mistake of reading too much into his appearance, discounting his intellect due to his clownish façade, and his obviously lousy instincts with the opposite sex. But I was learning. Jake was a man of substance, despite his affectations. And if I carried my new perceptions of the man further, I had to appreciate the compliment he paid me with the nod to my debating skills. Still, after reconciling all these aspects, I felt an odd emptiness deep inside me, the uneasy feeling that comes from being out of one's depth.

I hoisted myself off the bed and headed for the shower. A thorough cleansing was in order, both physically and mentally. I had to settle for a good shampooing; the mental grooming was harder to achieve just then. My head was in a whirl and I wasn't up to any more self-analysis or second-guessing.

A clean body turned out to be sufficient tonic to lighten my mood and I began to entertain thoughts of rejoining the party. But I wasn't quite there yet. Merely passing through the throng now assembled outside, I could tell that the merriment level was at about five cocktails beyond sober. I didn't have a problem being the only stone-sober one in the crowd, but I realized I would find it easier to mix with the locals if I could loosen up and relax a bit first. I decided a quick drink was in order.

I crept down the hallway, reaching the living room unnoticed. I plopped three cubes into a glass and poured a liberal shot of one of Jake's premium scotches, taking it back to my room to drink while I got ready. I could feel the effects of the potent booze from the very first sip. I literally zigzagged back to my room, already feeling too goofy to care who saw me.

It made me laugh to think of my volatile tolerance level, and I had to wonder at what had made me so susceptible this time. I had the handy rationalization of extra exercise—the morning run and the afternoon ride—coupled with too little sleep, plus the hours of slaving away in the kitchen.

I hadn't had anything to eat in hours, either, and that was probably the main factor. But whatever the reason, my inhibitions were vanishing, along with my earlier funk. I was almost ready to mingle with the country set and see what passed for an evening's entertainment so far away from city lights.

While drying my hair, I got a sudden urge to talk to my husband. I curled up in the over-stuffed chair by the window, drink in hand, and speed-dialed our home number. Having gotten the sound of my own voice, I hung up and dialed Elliott's cell phone. This time I was greeted by his recorded voice instructing me to leave a message.

I hung up and stared at the phone. I found myself a tad miffed at not being able to locate him now that I was in the mood to talk. It was quite unlike him to be unreachable at both numbers. He was very predictable in his routines, and he never went out without his cell phone. On a whim, I dialed his work number. He picked up on the first ring.

"Design and Implementation," he answered distractedly.

"Elliott. What are you doing at work on a Saturday night?"

"Oh, hi," he said shyly. He seemed almost guilty at having been caught working after hours. "Where are you?" he asked, coming out of his work-induced trance.

"I'm still at the ranch. I just thought I'd give you a call to see how you were bearing up without me. I tried home first, but I should have known you'd gravitate back to the office if unattended."

"Yeah, we've got a heavy workload right now. We started the big Oakland conversion project on Thursday, and we already see that we've got a bigger job than we had bargained for. We'll probably have to hire more staff. It's going to take a lot more resources than we imagined. We'll all be working overtime for weeks."

"I'm sorry to hear that," I said.

"That's the way it goes in this business. But I don't really mind. I like keeping busy."

"I know you do. So do I." It hit me for the first time that Elliott and I were two workaholics who were destined to find ourselves in middle-age before we realized our youth had been spent on work-related pursuits, the value of which wouldn't amount to much down the road. Someone could set both of us in front of a computer for ten years without complaint, as long as we found the tasks mentally stimulating.

This epiphany made me go cold inside. Sitting in my cozy guestroom, on a ranch hundreds of miles from civilization as I was accustomed to it, I saw my life in a harsh, sterile light. How could Elliott be in his office on a weekend night? But wasn't that our tendency, to retreat into our work if cut off from the tether of one another. In all probability, I would be doing the same thing if Elliott were out of town. I took a swig of my scotch, the ice clanking against the glass.

"What was that noise?" Elliott asked.

"Nothing. Just the ice in my drink," I admitted.

"Oh. What are you up to?"

"I was getting a little work in before I joined the party. Jake invited half the county over for a Western style barbeque and hoedown."

"Oh yeah?"

"Yeah, it's pretty amusing. They dug a pit and roasted a whole pig—"

"*Yuck,*" said my husband, the vegetarian, with great distaste. "You didn't eat any of it, did you?"

"No. There's a ton of other stuff to eat. You wouldn't believe the amount of food we bought—three shopping carts full."

"What's the occasion?"

"Nothing, far as I can tell. Just something to break the tedium of country living."

Elliott laughed appreciatively. "I bet," he said, the city dude with a phobia of all things rural.

"I think there's going to be a square dance later on," I said, mocking the lifestyle I found more appealing at that moment than I did my San Francisco way of life. Elliott was all a twitter now.

"You'll have to do a do-si-do for me," he said.

"I don't think you'll catch me out there," I said, suddenly disgusted by my own hypocrisy.

"Yeah, well, have a good time," he said jovially.

"I'll try. Elliott, do me a favor—don't stay there all night."

"I won't. Jeeze, is it really after six already? Wow."

"What time did you get there?"

"Around nine, I guess."

"God, Elliott—don't you have a life?" I cried out, more passionately than was warranted.

"What does it matter what I do when you're out of town? I might as well work. Besides, what else would I do?" This struck me as a particularly sad and pitiful admission. I couldn't even answer him.

"Elliott, go home, get some dinner. You need a break."

"Are you coming home tomorrow?" he asked.

"Yes, I'll be home tomorrow. I don't know when I'll get in—I'll have to call you from the airport."

"Okay. I'll see you tomorrow, then. Love you."

"I love you, too," I said and disconnected our call, staring at the plaster wall with an abysmal sinking feeling in my stomach. I tossed off the remainder of my drink and dressed in the only halfway appropriate garments I had with me. If this was going to be my last few hours here, I'd better make the most of them.

Thirteen

On my way out, I passed through the kitchen to see if my services were needed. Lowell and Billy were giving Rosalinda a hand, along with a few of the neighbor ladies. Lowell instructed me to get something to eat before it was all gone. I took his advice and headed off to the serving tables.

It had been dark for some time now, the only illumination coming from the strings of carnival lights that had been wound around the trees and crisscrossed overhead. It made me think of a state fair or the saints' days down in Mexico, with the cacophony of excited voices and the dozens of bodies milling about.

I determined from the nearly full trash barrels that I had come at the tail end of the dinner rush. There was still plenty of food, despite Lowell's warning, though I didn't have much of an appetite. I knew I had better eat something or I'd end up reprising Lavinia's performance last evening.

I helped myself to a dollop of potato salad and slaw, and ignoring Elliott's sentiments entirely, let Pico dish me out a sizable hunk of roast pig. Plate loaded, I cruised the picnic tables to find an accommodating spot. I didn't find any familiar faces, so I opted for a vacant table, preferring to be alone over making small talk with strangers. As soon as I sat down, live music started up in Jake's party barn. Little by little, all my fellow diners slipped off to enjoy the entertainment, leaving me to eat by myself.

Even though I hadn't felt hungry, after the first bite I realized how ravenous I really was. I ate every scrap on my plate, especially liking the pork, which was positively divine. Elliott had no idea what he was missing out on. I was on the verge of licking my plate when Billy approached, a bottle of beer in each hand. He extended one to me while taking a long draft of the other.

"Thought you might need something to wash down the grub," he said. I gratefully accepted, relishing the cold bitterness after the salty, smoky pork. "I'll take your plate if you're done with it," he offered.

"Thanks. That was great," I said.

"Didja' have any of the pork?"

"About half a pig's worth," I said, patting my full belly.

"Hope you saved room for something sweet. They're settin' up the dessert table in the barn right now." I didn't think I could even look at dessert after all those cupcakes I had frosted earlier in the day.

"I think I'll just nurse this beer," I replied.

"We got a keg inside, when that runs out," he said, carrying my plate off to the trash.

"Thanks a lot," I called out. After a few more minutes of blissful solitude, I decided to join the party.

The temperature had already dropped about ten degrees in the short time I'd been outside. My contrived outfit of all-purpose black dress, borrowed red cowgirl boots and denim jacket was insufficient to ward off the evening chill. The breeze had turned into a wind, and the chill sent shivers all over my body. I ducked inside the barn just as a huge gust whipped up behind me.

"Evening," one of the men standing inside the entrance greeted me as I slipped in. "Bit on the cool side tonight," he said.

"It sure is," I agreed. I smiled at the group of men, then moved quickly past. As ridiculous as my get-up seemed to me, it apparently fit right in with local customs. Judging by the looks I'd just gotten, the competition didn't have a whole lot better to offer. If I didn't watch myself, I might end up with a new boyfriend by night's end.

All Jake's prize motorcycles had been moved up against the wall to make room for the eighty or so folks now assembled inside. As I made my way through the crowd, I caught a glimpse of the provisional band set up in the barroom. There were a couple dozen people dancing to the country tunes, though it was not the square dance I had predicted. It was more organized than what I usually came across in the city, but it looked fun.

Up by the makeshift stage, I saw Jake's head above the rest as he and Lavinia cut a rug. Old twinkle toes, I thought, as he twirled his partner expertly around the floor. The man was a marvel to me. So far, I hadn't seen him come across anything he didn't know how to do, and do well. I only hoped I'd have half his wealth of knowledge when I reached his age.

I was being buffeted in the general direction of the barroom when I was pushed aside by a more aggressive partygoer. She had two other similarly attired girls in tow, all elbowing past me in their quest to reach the inner sanctum. I was working up a snide remark when the leader turned back to sneer in my direction. I should have recognized the pungent reek of her perfume. Much to my astonishment, Jaylynn pounced on me like a long-lost friend.

"Hey!" she cried out, arresting her petite entourage in their tracks. "Don't you look cute!" she said as she scanned me from top to bottom.

I held my breath as her eyes landed on the blazing red boots; I half expected her to scream and demand that I fork them over, then and there. I was relieved when the only comment she made was "darling boots." Then she yelled over the din, "You seen Jake?" I lifted my eyes in the direction of the dance floor and smiled benignly as she and her pals pushed through the throng. "See ya later," she sang out companionably. I nodded and watched as they were swallowed up by the crowd.

I took a swig of my beer, stashed it on a nearby table and headed to the bar, where I knew I could have a good overview, if I could find an empty barstool. As luck would have it, there was one on the end closest to the dance floor.

From my new vantage point, I observed the awkward interaction as Jaylynn threw her arms possessively around Jake's neck. I saw Jake peel her hands away and attempt to make introductions over the deafening crescendo. The song ended and some dancers left while others awaited more musical offerings. I had to bob and weave to keep sight of Jake and his harem. I laughed to think how cavalierly he had included Jaylynn in his invitations. He was going to pay for it now, one way or the other.

My body temperature had heated up to the point that I was now uncomfortably warm. I wriggled out of my denim jacket and stowed it underneath me. I was trying to locate my host when I was accosted by a tap on the shoulder. A tall, thin cowboy in his late twenties held out a plastic cup full of draft beer.

"No thanks," I said. The music had started up again, and apparently my friend did not hear me over the racket. He thrust the cup at me this time, nearly spilling it on me in the process. I reluctantly took it, more to keep myself dry than to appease him. I nodded my thanks and turned back to relocate Jake.

The floor was packed now, the dancers spilling off the designated dance floor, encroaching on the bar area and blocking my prime view. Another tap on the shoulder. I ignored it, but my new friend persisted. Finally, I turned around and found him sitting on the stool next to me.

"Never seen you around here before," he said, rather lecherously for his age.

"Chet Stocker," he said, eagerly reaching out his hand. I shook it quickly, told him my name, and resumed my search, trying to send a message of disinterest to Mr. Stocker. Neither move proved fruitful. Annoyed, I turned my body around toward the friendly cowboy and stared him down. Far from rebuked, Chet smiled, pleased to have won my attention at last.

"Want to dance?" he asked, sliding off his stool as if it were a foregone conclusion. I shook my head. Taking my refusal in stride, he reseated himself and smiled over at me amiably. I cast my eye around, this time seeking a little assistance from my buddy Jaylynn. I was sure I could shed my unwanted companion if she were to merely walk past us. Her perfume alone would get his attention. But she had disappeared along with Jake and the others. Chet attempted to strike up the conversation again and I hopped off the stool, thanking him quickly for the beer, and hightailing it to the ladies' room.

Can you have déjà vu of something that has only happened inside your head? I guess technically speaking, that would be a premonition. Call it what you will, that was exactly what I saw as I swung open the door of the ladies' bathroom. There, in the anteroom to the stalls stood Jaylynn and her posse, just as I had envisioned before I even knew of her existence.

There she stood, bedecked in a petal pink suede jacket with dyed-to-match rabbit fur trim, pink boots, and a short black denim skirt. Her friends' outfits were brown and blue variations on this classic theme. Their presence dominated the room, as if it were their own private sanctuary, their malevolent glares emanating from their well-camouflaged faces. Two young women slid past me as if anxious to escape the hostile atmosphere. Jaylynn snatched the cigarette out of her friend's hand and took a deep drag before addressing me.

"Who's that woman dancing with Jake?" she demanded to know through narrowed eyes, heavily caked with makeup, as an event of this scale evidently required. I walked over to check my own appearance in the mirror above the sink, relieved to find it was normal by comparison. "Is it his girlfriend or somethin'?"

"You'll have to ask him about that. I barely know the man, and I'm certainly not privy to the details of his love life," I lied, reflecting as the words left my mouth how inaccurate that statement really was. In the short time I had known Jake, I had learned far more about his love affairs—past and present—than I cared to admit. It struck me as somewhat unseemly that I should have so much intimate information, especially on someone I was barely acquainted with, yet it was I who'd been asking the questions.

"She was hanging all over him like she owned him," Jaylynn said resentfully, washing her sentiment down with a manly swig from her bottle of beer. I wasn't stupid enough to tell her that Lavinia had been staying there all weekend. I shrugged at her reflection in the mirror as I touched up my lipstick.

Two girls in their late teens emerged from the restrooms, receiving stony stares from Jaylynn and her friends. The friend whose cigarette Jaylynn had borrowed reclaimed it assertively.

"I want to get back out there," she said through a cloud of exhaled smoke. "I saw one cute guy out there and he was giving me the eye. There just ain't a whole lot to choose from to let the good ones get away."

The friend in electric blue nodded her agreement heartily. They may have been Jaylynn's loyal and devoted followers, but it was evident they had been led to expect a better turnout in the man department. I imagined they were calculating the possibility of hitting their hometown bars before last call, and whom they would go home with if the opportunity presented itself.

Jaylynn, however, didn't seem in a big hurry to leave; she was no doubt weighing her various strategies for dealing with the situation Jake had callously dealt her. I asked her if she was in line for the restroom, and when she shook her head, I seized my chance. Through the walls I could hear the barely muffled questions regarding my identity, which Jaylynn impatiently brushed off.

"She works for some magazine or somethin'," she said. "Come on, let's see if there are any halfway decent dudes out there." As they departed, one of them cried out, *"Watch it!"* eliciting a timid "sorry" as a new group of girls shuffled in.

I should have been thankful to be rid of Jaylynn and her pals, but morbid curiosity got the better of me as I thought through the likely outcome their attendance would cause. I caught up with them and followed at a safe distance. I didn't have to wait long for Jaylynn to spot Jake and make her move.

Lavinia was not with him and Jaylynn succeeded in dragging him onto the dance floor. I wanted to laugh out loud as I watched Jake dance with a trashy tart almost forty years his junior. He wasn't dancing with his ordinary bravado, plainly ill at ease by being made to dance to someone else's tune.

Serves you right, I thought, feeling no sympathy for his predicament. I wouldn't wish Jaylynn on anyone, but it wasn't as if her overtures had come straight out of the blue. He had captured her interest, probably in a fit of romantic lust, and he was solely responsible for her presence. I suddenly found myself pitying Lavinia, though she was an adult and someone who should have known better.

If I really wanted to study the caprices of love, I couldn't have ordered up a more perfect example. Here were three individuals, locked in their private quests for a prize that would never suit any of them. Were all of us guilty of such foolishness at some point in our lives? No, I concluded; that was an indulgence few of us succumbed to.

In any case, I had done enough research for one day. Whatever came of Jake's fickle philandering, it wasn't my problem. Still, it would be a shame if the night culminated in a catfight. The very thought of it made me scan the room for Lavinia's whereabouts. If the fur was going to start flying, then I was going to make it an early night and leave Jake to clean up his own mess.

I moved through the crowd, arcing around the dance floor, keeping a wary eye out for Lavinia. I finally found her, dancing with a rugged rancher type, obviously making his life happier by her proximity. She, too, was clearly enjoying herself, lapping up the attention she was garnering with her performance.

If I hadn't seen her fall apart over Jake the previous evening, I would have thought she actually fancied her current dance partner. But it had to be a ruse, a way of getting back at Jake for Jaylynn, or some other act of spite. Still, she had the rancher fooled. The song ended, and though she tried to flit off gracefully, her new admirer pulled her close for another dance.

I was backing away from the scene, trying to get Jake in my sights again, when my beer purveyor materialized and danced me into the crush of gyrating bodies. I tried to protest, but it was of little use. If he was content to drag someone with absolutely no experience in Western dancing around like a rag doll, then so be it. As soon as the song ended, however, I was off the floor like a shot.

"Hey, hold on there," my dogged pursuer said, latching onto my arm and bringing me to an abrupt stop. There was a directness to these country folk that I was not accustomed to. All this tugging and pushing would not be well received where I came from. I shook my arm free, resisting the urge to smack the guy.

"You're always rushing off," Chet said, hands stuffed in pockets in response to my edgy body language. "We don't have to dance if you don't want to," he said obligingly. A wave of bodies forced him forward, placing him uncomfortably close to me. Pinned in, I decided to be blunt with him.

"You know, you seem like a really nice guy and all, but I'm a married woman," I said, holding up my left hand as proof. Chet took the news unusually hard, as if it never occurred to him before to check for a wedding ring to determine eligibility.

He staggered backward, hand to his brow, apparently crushed by this news. He took another look and recovered rather quickly.

"Is your husband here tonight?" he asked, elated by renewed hope. I stared at him, dumbfounded.

"I'm always married," I said. "Whether my husband is here or on the moon, it makes no difference as far as I'm concerned." I didn't like the look in Chet's eye, a look that suggested I was only playing hard to get.

"See that girl over there?" I said, pivoting him around so he was pointed in the direction of Jaylynn's friend in blue. "I overheard her talking about you in the ladies' room. She said she's dying for you to ask her to dance." Chet warmed to this new prospect instantly.

Without further coaxing, Chet swaggered over to the girl in blue, who had now shed her blue fur-trimmed jacket, revealing a curvaceous figure under her unseasonable tank top. *Bingo,* I thought—a perfect match. Within seconds they were getting down and dirty on the dance floor.

Just as I was free of Chet, Lavinia sidled next to me, friend in tow. She was fanning herself with her hand, perhaps as a signal she was finished with dancing for the time being. Her rancher friend failed to receive the message. He stood there gawking at her as if she had descended straight from heaven, solely for his pleasure.

I have to admit that being hung over all morning must have agreed with her, for she was positively glowing, her big city glamour shining like a beacon in the crowded room. Using me as a foil, she introduced me to her new conquest, though I didn't catch his name. He didn't seem all that interested in me, either.

"Have you seen Jake?" I asked. I was instigating trouble with a question like that, but it didn't bother me. On cue, Lavinia craned her neck trying to locate her errant beau.

"There he is," she said, pointing him out for my benefit. "Looks like he's dancing with one of the local girls." I let this observation slide. Lavinia reassessed the situation, more astutely this time.

"Looks like he needs rescuing," she confided, leaving me alone with her discard. I smiled curtly and turned away, mixing in with the flow of traffic, intent on the exit. Just leaving the barroom made me breathe easier. The air was considerably cooler and fresher in the main part of the barn, and it was nearly deserted. I walked right past Lowell, not even realizing it was him until he addressed me.

"You're not leaving already?" he asked in that soft, calm voice of his. "The fun's just starting."

"Yeah, that's what I'm afraid of," I said. Lowell laughed. I doubled back to where he stood, up against the wall, nearly invisible, which probably suited him just fine. "You guys throw quite the party," I said.

"The boss's motto is 'the more, the better.' It can be fun, once in a while. It's a lot of work, though."

"I hope Rosalinda has retired for the night."

Lowell nodded, puffing on his cigar and diverting the smoke away from me. "She tells me the story you're writing isn't really about mules," he said, looking at me directly.

"That was Jake's idea. I guess he didn't want his employees to know I came out here to dissect his love life."

"Is it his love life in particular or the broader topic of love itself?"

"The broader topic. Specifically, what makes people repeatedly gravitate to the wrong mates. Got any ideas? You've been with Jake long enough to have seen him in action several times. From your male perspective, what do you make of Jake's constant pursuit of women?"

"Hmm, that's a big question. Well, for one thing, the female sex is uncommonly attracted to our friend Jake, in a way like I've never seen before."

"Why do you think that is? I mean, to look at him, you really wouldn't think women would drop like flies at his feet."

Lowell shrugged, obviously not taking the same view of things. "He's a strong, impressively built man. Some ladies are quite attracted to a large physique. I think they find it reassuring, you know, someone who'll take care of them. Maybe it's a leftover primitive instinct." Lowell shrugged again.

"But there's more to him than that. I think he has such an appreciation of living, it can be infectious. Plus, he genuinely loves women. That in itself can be a powerful attractor. He looks at every woman like they're the most delightful creatures he's ever seen, and I'll tell you, I've seen many just melt under that kind of attention." Lowell glanced up, as if looking for the right words. "I guess he makes them feel special."

"But that fascination fades pretty quickly, doesn't it?" I asked.

Lowell smiled wryly. "I suppose it does."

"Any thoughts on the cause of his inevitable disinterest? Do you think it's due to the fact that since everything comes so easy for him, it doesn't mean much to him after he's acquired it?"

"It's possible, I suppose. But to tell you the truth, I don't think he's as cold-blooded as that. Sometimes I think he puts more into a relationship than it could ever be worth. Then, when things fail to be as harmonious as he'd like, he becomes sad and disillusioned. But when the next pretty face comes along, he springs to life with renewed vigor. When you think about it, it's not so hard to understand."

I considered this for a moment. "So, you're of the opinion that Jake has merely made the wrong choices—a couple dozen times, or more?"

Lowell wagged his head equivocally. "Let's just say he's unlucky at love," he said kindly.

"It's rather ironic to hear you say that. Jake considers himself to be exceptionally *lucky* at love."

"Oh well, I guess that only points out his unique perception of life. Most people would view their successive failures at love with a tragic sense of doom, eventually giving up on it altogether."

"Do you think he'll marry again?" I asked. Lowell chuckled.

"I'm not a betting man, but even if I were, I wouldn't dare wager against it." Two couples in full Western party attire passed us on their way out. Lowell called out his farewell and received ample thanks for the wonderful day.

"Honestly, Lowell, doesn't it seem to you that Jake simply lacks the perseverance to make his relationships work? Surely, with all the women he's been with, there was at least one capable of holding Jake's attention who was also compatible enough with him to make it last."

Lowell held his comment; Jake was his good friend and employer, after all, and I was only a snoopy reporter, evidently getting more personal than seemed appropriate. I tried another tactic.

"Can you imagine being in his shoes? After the third or fourth aborted marriage, wouldn't you tell yourself that if the next relationship didn't work out you'd throw in the towel forever?" I stared at him plaintively until he answered.

"I imagine I would. But Jake's not like me. His philosophy is entirely different from mine. He doesn't let setbacks stop him. If the last girl didn't work out, maybe the next one will. What's that saying, that hope springs eternal? Jake's a very hopeful guy," Lowell said, with just a hint of jest.

"Jake admits to being a womanizer, and you see him as a man triumphing over adversity. Now, that's what I call seeing two sides of the same coin," I said cynically. A few more partygoers staggered past, but only for a chance to smooch under the moonlight. I could sense I was pushing Lowell's cooperativeness to the limit. I decided it would not do to alienate him.

"Well, I appreciate your insights," I said, preparing to take my leave.

"Glad to be of assistance," Lowell said graciously, pushing away from the wall. "You heading back to the house?"

"Yeah, I think it's a good time to get some work done."

"I'll walk you back."

"Oh, that's not necessary," I said, but Lowell was too chivalrous to let me walk out on my own.

"It would be my pleasure," he said. For the very first time, I thought I detected a trace of his former English accent. We were just about through the door, when Billy appealed to Lowell for assistance.

"We can't get the keg to work," he said.

"Can't be empty already."

"No, it's got plenty of beer in it still, but I just can't get the tap to work," Billy said. Lowell looked at me, torn. "I'd better have a look at it," he said apologetically.

"No problem. It's only a short walk to the house. Besides, it looks like all the big, bad wolves are inside tonight."

Lowell chuckled and tipped his head in salute. "Sweet dreams," he called over his shoulder.

I stepped out into the chill evening air, and the shock had me scrambling to put my jacket back on. I hurried past the face of the barn and turned sharply at the corner to get away from the icy cold wind. I nearly ran straight into Jake in the process.

"Whoa, little lady," he said a la John Wayne. "Where's the fire?"

"It's certainly not out here," I said, shivering.

"Yeah, a bonfire would have been nice, though it's a little windy. Everyone seems to be having too much fun indoors, anyway."

"Why aren't you in there?" I asked. "Isn't your harem going to get restless?"

"Want this?" he asked, referring to the piece of lemon meringue pie he had been dissecting with a plastic fork.

"It doesn't look particularly appetizing."

Jake gave it a disgusted look and set it on the worktable he was leaning against. The relative quiet was shattered by the sounds of amplified instruments tuning up. "Sounds like a change in the entertainment," I said.

"Most definitely," Jake answered. "Now we're going to get into some real music."

"The first group wasn't so bad, if you like that kind of thing."

"No, they're all right in a pinch, I guess. But these guys are pros." I listened to the first few notes and I could understand what Jake was talking about.

"Blues?"

"That's right, ma'am. *The Crying Shame*, for your musical delight."

"That's a rather dubious moniker, don't you think?"

"Just wait," Jake said, ignoring my skepticism. After a fairly lengthy intro, the singer joined in, his voice heavy with lament. Jake was right; this was no garage band. The haunting unison of vocalist and bass guitar cut straight through me.

"And I ain't never…found a woman again like you, no baby… I ain't ever found a woman…like you…" Before I realized it, Jake had pulled me to him, guiding me through another impromptu dance I didn't remember having signed up for.

"Oh, quit clowning," I complained futilely. Jake had his eyes closed to mere slits, crooning along with the band. "You're a dancing fool, Jake," I said resignedly, trying to make light of this suddenly intimate situation.

"Just a fool, darlin'," he said softly into my ear. I really wasn't ready for this, especially when two jealous females currently on the premises had more than articulately made their claim to him.

"Don't you think you'd better get back to your guests?" I asked, as he whirled me around.

"They're doing fine without me."

"Maybe, but I think Lavinia might appreciate some backup."

"Since when are you so concerned with what Lavinia needs?" Jake said, pulling away in a challenging manner.

"I wouldn't say I was. But it might interest to you to know that she's being followed around by a lovesick country squire." Jake shrugged as if to say "so what?" He pulled me closer and executed two quick turns, nearly whisking me off my feet.

"Jake, you've got that wildcard Jaylynn to consider, also," I said, halting our dance.

Jake reminded me of a spoiled rotten playboy, the kind often depicted in those old fifties movies—the Robert Mitchum or Dean Martin type—who portrayed love as a game only they could win. I wasn't the least bit interested in adding to Jake's Don Juan image. If he wanted to play games with Lavinia and Jaylynn, he was going to have to do it without me.

At that instant, the back door cracked open and two bodies hurled through, preceded by a sharp increase in volume. Jake and I flew apart from each other just as Jaylynn and the young cowboy she had in a ruthless lip lock staggered out of the barn. Engrossed in their new infatuation, they were completely unaware of our presence.

We stood there long enough to determine the lucky hombre was not Dieter, as Jake had predicted. Before either had come up for air, Jake and I had slipped around the corner and back out into the rigid breeze.

"Too bad for Dieter," I said, shivering as we huddled by the side of the barn. I was going to have to make my goodnight brief if I wanted to keep from freezing to death. Jake seemed rather amused by this latest discovery, not the least bit peeved that his young lover had found someone new, nor that his desire to fix up his awkward German employee had been thwarted.

He made a halfhearted attempt to resume our dance, a move I countered with a shaky step backward. It was at this point a passel of revelers burst from the barn's main entrance, headed up by none other than Jake's other lady of the moment, Lavinia. Doggedly at her heels were her admirer and several other folks she had apparently assembled into a ragtag entourage. Because of the way the light emanated from the floodlights, she couldn't make out who we were until she was upon us.

"There you are!" she exclaimed merrily as she recognized us. She seemed too intoxicated to read anything untoward in our being alone together outside.

"Jake, you know George," she said to Jake. "Of course you do, you're neighbors!" she corrected herself.

My heart sank as I realized how gone she was. It would only be a matter of time before she hit the bricks again. I didn't think I could stomach an encore performance of self-flagellation for the sake of love. I congratulated myself for my sound choice in husbands and my distinct lack of emotional imbalance. Life did not have to be so painful or unseemly. I was just about to sneak away from this impending disaster when Lavinia fixed me in her sights.

"Hello!" she sang out. "I'm so glad you're here. I was just telling George and everyone about you. This is the writer I was telling you about," she said, swiveling unsteadily around to address her group. "She's up for a Prescott Award," she told them, oblivious to their ignorance of that particular accolade. "It's a *very big deal* for a journalist," she said confidentially, when the others failed to respond with the proper oohs and ahhs.

"It's damn cold out here," one of the women in their party pointed out. "Let's get back inside 'fore I freeze my tits off," she said, shivering so violently her beer sloshed over the rim of her plastic cup.

"We're almost there," Lavinia said, not wanting her group to break up and abandon her. "We're going to the house for a nightcap," she informed Jake, motioning for her guests to follow her. I couldn't bear to watch, yet I didn't know which way to run, so I stood frozen to the spot. Jake grabbed her by the arm as discreetly as possible, and with thinning patience, told her that wasn't such a great idea.

"I think you've had enough," he whispered hoarsely when she tried to brush him off. Amazingly, the besotted rancher spoke up on her behalf.

"The lady would like to have a drink in quieter surroundings," he said, keeping his voice low so the others wouldn't hear. I saw Jake's back stiffen as he leaned into his neighbor's face.

"You've picked the wrong damsel to protect, George," he said. "This one's hellbent on stirring up trouble—the kind of trouble you don't need." The three of them remained locked in a tense triangle as the men assessed one another.

"Don't be a spoil-sport, Jake. All we want is one little drink," Lavinia taunted. She tried to pull George along with her, yet Jake kept a firm hold on her arm.

"Are we going to get a drink, or what?" one of the men complained, approaching the threesome to see what was holding things up.

"Party's over," Jake said.

"Let go of her, Jake," George demanded.

"When I invite people to my property, I set the boundaries. The party's in the barn. The house is off limits," Jake said. "Let go of him," he said to Lavinia. Obediently, she dropped George's arm and waited sulkily.

"This ain't right, Jake," George said in one last feeble attempt to stick up for his new love.

"You like being a pawn, George? She's only using you to get at me," Jake said, turning his back on his neighbor, escorting a petulant Lavinia down the path, dispersing her drinking pals as he piloted her along. I watched until they were out of sight and followed at a distance. When I saw them enter through the mudroom entrance, I raced to the front door, making it down the hallway to my guestroom well in advance of the warring lovers.

I worked for about an hour, half expecting to be interrupted at any moment by loud arguing, or at least the sound of footfalls in the hallway, but that never occurred. After I had recorded the salient points of my conversation with Lowell, I stretched out on the bed, incapable of working up the initiative for getting ready to retire for the night. The day—and my visit—had come to an unsatisfying end and I was reluctant to put a finality to it by getting in bed and eliminating the possibility of a happier ending.

I drifted off and didn't wake until two-thirty, feeling disoriented and vaguely disappointed. I stripped out of my clothes and crawled between the sheets, finally going back to sleep around four.

When I opened my eyes again, the first rays of dawn were glinting through the sides of the heavy draperies, illuminating the fabric from behind with an incandescent glow. Inspired by my early rising, I washed up and brushed last evening off my teeth, donned my sweats, and set off on an early morning run in an effort to assert control over the rest of my day. I ran hard for forty-five minutes, despite the residual soreness in my posterior.

I walked around and inspected the mules for another ten minutes in order to cool off before returning to the house. I let myself in through the mudroom door, judging that would be the least intrusive way to enter. I planned to get cleaned up and packed and ready to leave before running into anyone. I would check on available flights once I got on the road.

Despite the good time I'd had with Jake, I was anxious to get going. I had grown very fond of him, rascal though he was, but witnessing the deterioration of his latest relationship had tainted my respect for him. It felt no different to me than watching someone you care for drink himself into an early grave. It struck me while on my run that Jake was addicted to bad relationships, and I doubted he would ever break himself of the habit.

As I entered the kitchen, I was startled by the figure standing at the sink with his back to me. I hadn't been expecting to encounter anyone so early on the morning after a big shindig, and I was further thrown by the familiar—and at the same time, the unfamiliar—features of the man who now stood looking at me.

I immediately recognized the build, but his features stumped me. It must have taken me a full thirty seconds to realize the man before me was a freshly shaved and shorn Jake Sorenson. The transformation was shocking, so much so that even after I made the connection, I remained as mute as a stone.

"Coffee?" Jake asked, amused by my dumbfounded state. He handed me a mug, which I took automatically, still unable to take my eyes off him. It was Jake, I could see that now, but a much more refined version.

The unruly gray-blond Neptune-style waves had been shorn into a sleek slivery-gray cut that was surprisingly attractive. The face that had been hidden under the unkempt scruff of beard was well defined, with chiseled cheekbones, well-shaped mouth, a few deep laugh lines, and disarming dimples. The only disconcerting thing about his naked face was the variation in color from forehead to chin, but that would be rectified with a little exposure to the sun.

After all the assumptions and theories I had concocted to explain the attraction he held for the opposite sex, I was flabbergasted to discover the truth: Jake Sorenson was an arrestingly handsome man, a bit weathered, but that only seemed to enhance his charm. Well, no big mystery there. No wonder Lowell didn't endorse my opinion that Jake's looks couldn't possibly be the reason women flocked to him.

I felt totally foolish. So much for my powers of perception. The meager groundwork for my research thus far would have to be dramatically altered, if it were salvageable at all. This revelation shed a completely different light on the subject. No longer would I have to look for ways to justify Jake's magnetism; the dashing gentleman had taken his natural place as heartthrob, replacing the roguish buffoon. It was like finding Brad Pitt's face behind a Bozo the Clown mask. Jake leaned against the far counter, a bemused grin spreading across his features.

"What's wrong? Don't you like my new look?"

"I'm just surprised, that's all. I didn't imagine you could clean up so well."

"Yeah, well, a man's got to look sharp on his wedding day," Jake replied, calmly taking a sip of his coffee. It was a miracle I didn't let my mug crash to the floor. This stunning turn of events threw me completely, setting my head whirling and my heart racing. I was filled with a horrific sense of impending doom. I suddenly felt like I was going to vomit.

"You should see the look on your face," Jake said, callously laughing at my distress. Without his oafish camouflage, his Cheshire grin had a more caustic sting. I blindly reached for a stool to steady myself. I remember thinking, how dare this guy mock me when he is stupidly hurling himself into yet another hopeless marriage. I was so disgusted, I could barely order my thoughts.

"You're going for a record, aren't you? You just want to see your name listed in the Guinness Book of World Records under 'The most often divorced man in the world.'" Incredibly, Jake merely smiled as I railed against him.

"I don't know if it's because you don't have anyone who's willing to be straight with you, or if you're just too pig-headed to listen, but someone's got to say this: you can't go through with this. You can't do this to yourself again. Forget whatever pressure Lavinia's putting on you, it would be as bad for her sake as it is for yours to marry her at this juncture. I know I don't have any right to say this to you, but you need to step away from the situation and think things through more carefully."

The force of my emotions had me back on my feet and pacing. By the time my tirade was finished, Jake's irritating smirk had softened into a shy smile.

"What?" I demanded.

"I'm not getting married today, though I do appreciate your heartfelt concern. It was only a joke. I didn't realize you'd be so gullible." I could feel all the blood rush to my head.

"You're a real bastard, you know that Jake," I said, not knowing if I was more relieved or outraged by his admission. I stared at him, my head reeling with confusion. "I suppose you think you're real cute."

"Honestly, it was a spur of the moment thing. I don't know what made me say it, but it was entirely harmless," he said, laughing despite my acute discomfort. "Believe me, the thought of getting married could only be a joke where I'm concerned."

"Oh really? You seem to thrive on miserable relationships. As far as I can tell, you and Lavinia are made for each other. It seems only natural that you two should tie the knot," I said, indulging a sudden mean-spirited urge. Jake snorted roughly.

"Hate to disappoint you, but the wedding's off," he said, turning his back to me as he scouted through the refrigerator. The way he said this made me almost regret my jibe.

"I'm sorry you two aren't getting along well right now," I said. "I think it will be better when I'm gone and you can settle back into a more private routine."

"There's no routine to settle back into," he said, placing eggs, bread and butter on the butcher-block countertop between us. "It's over. She's gone." I couldn't detect any remorse in his words.

"I'm sorry."

"Don't be. Over's over. There's nothing to regret." He took a bowl out of the cupboard and cracked two eggs into it. I glanced at the clock on the wall; it was only 7:15.

"I didn't see anyone leave. She must have gotten out of here very early," I said, wondering if she was still intoxicated when she got behind the wheel. Then I remembered seeing her car on the driveway when I took my run. I craned my neck to get a glimpse out the kitchen window. Her Jaguar was still parked there. Jake caught my eye as I turned back to him.

"You've always got the reporter's instinct going, don't you?" he asked, his sly smile breaking the somber mood. "She left here last night with George Crenshaw." For a moment, I couldn't fathom what he was talking about. "The guy she was hanging all over last night, or I should say, hanging all over her."

I felt my mouth drop open and my eyes bug out. "You are joking, right?" I asked incredulously.

"Nope. No joking there. He gallantly saved her from the heartless old Jake, and she was so flattered, she ran off with him. It was pretty pathetic, actually."

That answered why I never heard them going down the hallway or shouting at each other. How amazing, I thought, trying to picture Lavinia Houtz with her dandy rancher. They seemed even less suited for each other than she and Jake had been. "She'll be back," I predicted.

"Oh yeah, she'll come back today to get her car and her things, but I don't plan to be here when she does. Regardless of how she feels once she's come to her senses—and I'm sure she'll sorely regret her actions—it's all over with for us. She knows it, too. Any relationship that causes a fairly normal woman to lose control like that can't be good.

"I'm tired of watching her suffer. I guess I've known it wasn't working for some time, but I suppose I have a tendency to let things go too long before I face them properly. Hope you're in the mood for French toast," he said, pouring a dash of cream into his scrambled eggs. I was a little taken aback that he could be concerned about food after what he'd just been through.

"Ah, sure." Jake turned the fire down under the frying pan and threw in a slab of butter.

"We've got real Vermont maple syrup, or we've got Rosalinda's homemade raspberry preserves. You can have one or both"

"I'll have the preserves," I said. He set both up on the counter, along with two placemats and napkins.

"Orange juice is in the fridge," he directed, dredging the thickly sliced bread through the egg batter. I located the juice glasses and filled two. The butter sizzled and snapped while Jake hummed to his own private tune. This domesticated scene was not what I was expecting when I walked through the door ten minutes earlier.

"Can you hand me a couple of plates?" Jake asked over his shoulder. I still couldn't believe this was the same man I had gone riding with, or danced with under his expert guidance. His former disheveled guise had made those events seem so harmless at the time. I wasn't sure how I would have reacted to tangoing with him in his current form.

The change in him was so great, I couldn't help but stare as I struggled to reconcile that face with all that had passed between us. He still behaved with me as he had before, though I had difficulty relating to him the same way. I felt awkward and less inclined to poke fun at him. He just didn't strike me as a big-hearted buffoon anymore.

"So, who's responsible for the transformation?" I asked with feigned ease.

"Lowell cut my hair and I shaved off the beard. It's our little ritual, whenever there's a shake-up in the status quo. Need some more coffee?"

"No, I'm fine. So, what, you've gone shaggy before and then come clean after one of your marriages failed?" I speculated.

"Yeah, I guess that's pretty much how it seems to work. Lavinia said it was my 'passive-aggressive' way of dealing with conflict. I suppose it was rather boneheaded of me to tell her how in the past I had started wearing a beard and letting my hair grow when things got rocky in the love department. Here you go—the world's best French toast," Jake said as he handed me a plate with three savory slices on it. "As soon as I started growing a beard, she started coming unhinged."

"Looks great," I said, sliding onto the barstool. I hadn't realized how hungry I was. "Well, I guess that's understandable. I'd say that's the equivalent of finding lipstick smudges on your husband's collar."

Jake shrugged indifferently. I sure wouldn't want to be in love with the guy, knowing one day I could wake up and find him with a five-day growth of beard, the signal that my time had run out. This new version of Jake looked much more capable of causing heartbreak than the old, shaggy one.

I spooned a generous dollop of jam onto my French toast and smeared it around. That's what I loved about Elliott: if he had a problem with anything, he'd never let it fester. If he were cross about something, you'd hear about it right away. I certainly never needed to wait five days for an indication that something was bugging him. I had barely gotten a bite into my mouth before Jake started fishing for compliments.

"Well, what do you think?"

I had never really identified with the concept of comfort food until that moment.

"Oh my god, it's so good." There was something about that buttery-eggy, piping hot crispiness that just sent me. And the homemade jam—the most intense raspberry flavor I had ever tasted. The combination literally made me feel happy on the inside. Jake beamed like a proud housewife and finally took a bite of his own food.

"Damn, I'm a good cook. I'd make some lucky girl a great wife," he said, pouring on a gluttonous amount of syrup. It was odd how downright jovial he was in light of the fact that his lover had just left him.

"Your heart mends fast," I commented between bites. "Good thing for a man with your kind of…luck."

"What am I going to do, sulk for the rest of my life? There are still many fish in the sea, even for an old codger like me." Jake caught me staring at his profile. "I'm a good looking devil, aren't I?" he said with a wink, grinning that famous grin of his, all the more potent without the bristly whiskers.

"It's an improvement," I allowed, switching my attention to the food in front of me. The truth was, if I ate one more bite, I'd fall face first into my plate. But it was so delicious, I couldn't bear to let it go to waste.

"You going to eat that or just stare at it?" Jake asked. I pushed my plate toward him, knowing I could count on him to help me out. He skewered my half-eaten slice and swabbed the syrup off his plate, cramming the whole piece into his mouth the way only a man can. "You're up early," he said through a mouthful of food.

"I went for a run. I think I'm going to need to go for another one," I lamented as I pushed away from the counter, laying my head on my outstretched arm. I guessed they call it comfort food because all you can think about is getting comfortable after you've eaten it. I would have gladly crawled back into bed and stayed there for the rest of the day, but I needed to get going. Elliott was expecting me home that night, and I didn't even know what flights were available. I sat up and tried to look alert.

"Let's go for a ride—that'll get your blood pumping again."

"I can't," I said, stretching broadly. "I need to be on my way."

"You're not leaving?" He seemed genuinely hurt.

"Weekend's over. I've got to get back. Besides, I've out-stayed my welcome."

"No you haven't. Hey, leave those dishes. I'll get them later."

"It's the least I can do, believe me."

"C'mon. I'm not going to let you spend your last few moments here washing dishes. Let's take a quick ride. This is a perfect opportunity for you to dissect a freshly ruined affair. You can't pass up a chance like this." I shot him a dubious look. "What time does your flight leave?"

"I haven't even booked one yet."

"Then you've got plenty of time." He took the dishrag and plate out of my hand, as if the matter were settled.

"Okay, I'll take a ride with you—a short one—if you let me finish cleaning up."

"Alright, you've got yourself a deal," he said reluctantly. "I'll start saddling the mules and you come out when you're ready." Jake started to leave but couldn't resist tidying up a bit first. "I wouldn't have made such a damn mess if I'd have known you were going to be cleaning up," he said, wiping the wet egg ring off the butcher block.

"Don't worry about that—I'll get it. You better get a move on," I warned him, "you're cutting into our riding time." He dutifully dropped the sponge and begun scraping and bowing his way to the door.

"Yes'm, mistress. I's git right on it. Don' you worry, boss lady. Your mount be ready in a jiffy." I waited until he disappeared out the mudroom entrance before I let out a laugh.

"I's on the job, mistress," he said, popping his head around the corner, causing me to jump a foot. I was doubly startled by his clean-shaven face, for in my mind's eye it was easier to connect the clownish antics with his old appearance. This new look of his was going to take some getting used to.

"Get out of here or I won't go riding with you."

He pantomimed horror and hightailed it out the door. I watched him out the window as he walked down the shaded path and vanished from sight. He was without a doubt one of the most original people I had ever come across, that was for sure. And although I sensed it was unwise of me, I couldn't help but find him endearing.

That sentiment sat uncomfortably with the fact that I knew him to be a cad with women. But I was beginning to believe that was as much their fault as his. He was different than the rest of us, bigger somehow, more alive. No one could own someone like him. I suspected that possessiveness had been a common thread among his lovers, and it had been their misfortune not to realize Jake's aversion to that kind of neediness.

Of course, it was easy for me to cite their shortfalls; I had never been in a situation like theirs. I had to ask myself how I would really feel if I were madly in love with someone who became more indifferent to me as my love grew. That would be hard to take. But I still doubted I would allow myself to succumb to such a lopsided arrangement.

As affairs of the heart were concerned, I held my cards close to my chest, only investing my emotions after a substantial, nonrefundable deposit had been made by the other side. Even with Elliott, I had only felt comfortable enough to marry him because I sensed deep down inside his love for me was stronger than mine for him. As cold and calculating as that may sound, it had taken all the impetus for jealousy out of the equation on my end. Elliott, however, is a different story. But the badgering fueled by insecurity was a small price to pay for guaranteed fidelity.

And lest my admission be misconstrued, I was not putting my husband at a disadvantage; I was the model of a monogamous wife. It was too bad, from my decidedly bourgeois point of view, that Jake had such a difficult time being true to one woman. I was certain he'd be happier if he could.

I wiped down the countertop and went back to my room to change into the only duds I had that qualified as riding gear. I climbed into jeans that were almost stiff from too much wear and inadequate care, and wriggled into my shirt that was ripe with the gamy scent of mule. I laughed when I pictured Elliott's reaction to my foul smelling clothing. I toyed with the idea of wearing this ensemble home, but I decided an airplane was too confined for such a powerful aroma.

I set aside my only halfway decent outfit for the trip home and hastily packed the rest. If I knew Jake, he would conveniently lose track of time once we hit the open trail. Now that he had Lavinia and Jaylynn out of his hair, I got the impression he would be only too happy to have me stick around for company's sake. I'd have to keep an eye on the time if I expected to get home that night.

By the time I reached the barn, both animals had been saddled and tied to a hitching post.

"Good timing," Jake said as I approached. "We're all set. Hop on board and Lucille will take you anywhere you want to go." I noticed he had chosen a different pair of mules for this excursion. I was disappointed that I wouldn't be riding Sabrina, for I gave her full credit for getting me through the last two rides. This one didn't strike me as being nearly as compliant as she was.

"She's not quite as docile as Sabrina, but she's real strong and she's good on the trails," Jake said by way of endorsement.

"I'm not sure I can even get into a saddle after that breakfast," I said, feeling decidedly unathletic after my carb overload. Jake steadied Lucille while I gripped her mane and put my left foot in the stirrup. With considerable effort, I swung my right leg over Lucille's back and I was on. I was very proud of myself, though I tried to act nonchalant about this minor achievement.

Jake handed me the reins and mounted his mule, a large paint named Jupiter. We set off in a different direction this time, down the long entry drive, past the bunkhouse, and through the avenue of sycamores in their fine autumn gold. When we exited the gate, we crossed to the other side of the road and followed a path that ran along the fence line until we came to a gate. Jake unlocked it from his saddle and we passed through.

"It's nice you can ride on your neighbor's land. It makes it feel like you've got the whole county at your disposal," I commented as we rode across a flat meadow, only a scattered herd of cattle and a distant line of trees marking the horizon. Bulging white clouds artfully dotted the pale blue sky. Even a city girl like me could appreciate the unique quality of the lighting that only a fall day can possess.

With every breath I took I felt I was consuming an experience that would stay with me forever. It was my most fervent hope that I'd be able to recall every sensation I had from that snapshot of life with perfect clarity, conjuring it up at will whenever daily stresses made me lose my perspective. I felt contented right down to my toes.

"I like coming over here because it's a great place to run the animals. You wanted a quick ride—you ready? Hold on tight. Pull back on the reins if she gets too fast for you."

With that brief warning, Jake spurred his animal into a full-out run. Without any coaxing from me, Lucille followed chase. Exhilarating would be a good way to describe our breakneck pace, except that terrifying was more accurate. My instinct was to emulate Jake's posture as a guide for surviving this race, but he was well ahead of me and I only caught intermittent and jumbled glances of him as I bounced and rebounded in the saddle.

The sprint lasted probably no more than three or four minutes, yet I felt as though I had just spent half an hour attached to a paint mixer. Once all my loose parts gradually reassembled, I became acutely aware of an overtaxed bladder.

"Any chance of discretely taking a pee once we hit those trees?" I asked when I had caught up with Jake.

"You women really don't have much capacity, do you?" he chided me.

"No, you men have it all over us when it comes to all things urinary," I replied. It seemed like forever, but we finally reached a place where I could crouch unseen. Supposedly out of consideration for me, Jake whistled loudly while I relieved myself. It didn't make my task any easier, having to stave off fits of laughter at his barely recognizable rendition of "Camptown Ladies" punctuated with baritone "do-dah's" in all the appropriate places. This was the kind of scene I should write into my piece, if only to appall my editor.

But the likelihood of rending a story out of this poorly conceived idea was becoming more remote with every passing minute. Sure, I had gotten some useful information during my stay at the Buckin' J Ranch, but all I really had was a partial insight into one man's idiosyncrasies, and that would only be helpful if I intended to write a piece solely about him, which is not what I had been okayed to do.

If I was going to stay with the approved storyline, I would have to implement plan B. I would need to augment the scant pertinent information I had gleaned from my talks with Jake, Rosalinda, and Lowell with interviews from other often-divorced men and women. So far, the only source I could think of for that particular trait was dating services; undoubtedly, the habitually unlucky would gravitate to the hope of improved odds.

It had occurred to me to recruit potential subjects by posting notices on website chat rooms devoted to singles longing to meet their soul mates. I could round up half a dozen veterans of failed marriages and set up a day of interviews at the magazine. Oh boy, Judith would love me for that.

But research was research. And of course, I wasn't going to make her deadline for first draft approval, which she wouldn't appreciate, either. Oh well, maybe I'd get lucky and she'd pull me off this fishing expedition and put me on a real story. Maybe I was one of those writers who did their best work when guided by an insightful editor.

"Hey, did you get lost in there?" Jake called out. He had finished his song and was getting antsy. "If you're late for the airport, it's going to be your fault."

"Hold your…mules, I'm coming," I answered, crunching my way across the fallen leaves in the thicket. Jake was hunkered over his mule, idly taking in the sights when I emerged.

"Now a man could have taken care of that chore ten times faster," he complained as I remounted Lucille.

"I don't want to hear about it. There are far too many differences between men's equipment and women's. I don't think either one of us needs a refresher course in that department." Jake lowered his hat over his eyes, signaling his disdain for feminist tirades. He handed me Lucille's reigns and turned his mule around.

"There's a path up here a ways that cuts through the woods and then down to a creek. It's really beautiful this time of year with all the leaves turning."

I fell in behind him and we were soon so deep into the wooded area, I could only get occasional glimpses of the blue sky through the burnt orange and gold overhead. It was a good ten degrees cooler in the shade. I fumbled with the buttons on my jacket with one hand.

The path began to descend, slowly and unevenly, a thick layer of autumn leaves obscuring the trail underfoot. The mules picked their way down steadily, their dexterity discernible through their undulating haunches. I held onto the saddle horn with one hand and tried to remain as erect as possible, envying Jake's effortless grace in the saddle.

I had been immoderately pleased with my mule riding performance, but the fact that I had gotten on and stayed on a mule during three separate occasions was something I could brag about only in my circle of city friends. Out here, my feat was of no merit. Only when you achieved a perfect seat and command of your animal could you consider yourself a true equestrian, like Jake. I was reminded as I pitched from side to side of his claim that riding a mule was smoother than a horse, due to a lack of withers or something, but you couldn't prove that by me. Then again, I really had nothing to compare it to.

We came to the creek, but instead of crossing it, we followed it for a fair distance, veered right and headed back toward the direction we had come, creating a large loop. The terrain was steeper than where we had dropped down, but the mules had no difficulty bearing us to the summit. From this vantage point we could see over the tops of the trees we had passed through and beyond to the other side of the road and Jake's property.

"It's great being able to see your place from this perspective."

"It's nice because you can get an idea of where we rode the last couple of days. See the water tower over there on the left—if you go straight across and up the fence line—see about halfway up—there's the gate we passed through to Jorgenson's spread. Where we picnicked by the creek is way over on the other side of that hill. And if you look directly across from where we're standing, you can see the trees that line the pathway to my main house."

"Is that a different creek than the one we just passed?"

"No, same creek. It runs down through Jorgenson's land, under the road and then the length of this whole property."

"Does it have a name?"

"Soldier's Creek, but I couldn't tell you why."

I studied the horizon, noticing a formation of pine trees right above where Jake's house sat. "That's interesting how you have just that one clump of pines right by your house," I observed.

"Those are the Christmas trees. Sequoias, actually. Very fast growers."

"You planted those?"

"Yep. It was Connie's idea. She thought it would be lovely to buy a live Christmas tree every year and stick it in the ground. She envisioned having a forest of Christmas trees eventually." I counted five trees of slightly varying heights. "She'd make a big deal about decorating them every year. You wouldn't believe how many boxes of Christmas lights and ornaments and junk I've got stored in the barn."

"I gather you don't share her enthusiasm for that particular holiday." Jake grunted. "Are you an atheist?"

"Darling, I don't know enough about life to believe in anything, including atheism."

"You seem to believe in the institution of marriage, though I can't imagine how you keep your optimism."

Jake snorted at this wisecrack. "Of course I believe in marriage. It's something I happen to do very well."

I croaked in disbelief at this outrageous assertion. "Yes, but you also happen to be a wizard at divorce, so that pretty much negates your success at marrying."

"That's your opinion," he replied smugly.

"Yes, and I'm also of the opinion that the entire problem with your endless cycle of marriage and divorce stems from the fact you don't know how to discriminate."

Jake laughed and shook his head. "You've got me all figured out, don't you? Well, congratulations. You've managed to do in three days what seven wives and countless girlfriends haven't done in almost forty years."

I let the sting of that remark subside before continuing to make my case. "It's fairly obvious, Jake. I can tell you from my own experience, it definitely pays to choose your mate carefully. And if you want to know how I really feel, I think running off with every woman who strikes your fancy is highly indulgent."

"I thought reporters were supposed to keep an open mind. I can see you've forgotten the importance of remaining unbiased."

I chewed on this justifiable assertion for a moment, wondering what exactly about Jake made me so openly critical of him. I decided it was due to some latent feminist tendency that couldn't abide the notion of a man callously discarding one woman after the next in some vague pursuit of an unattainable ideal. Belatedly, the light dawned.

"Your relationship with Lavinia didn't just hit a roadblock, did it? There's someone else, isn't there?" I could see the agitated movement of the muscles in Jake's pretty new face work as he contemplated my accusation.

"Hey, it doesn't hurt my feelings. I don't think you and Lavinia had any business as a couple. But that was a bunch of hooey about her wanting to get married and have kids and you not. That wasn't the story at all, was it? You got tired of her, like all the rest." Jake chewed the inside of his lip, probably to keep from laying into me.

"You're wrong," he said simply as he stared out over the valley.

"I'm wrong about you having a new woman waiting in the wings?"

"You're wrong about why Lavinia and I fell apart. And you're wrong about me growing tired of her, or the rest of them. You really don't have a clue what it's like to fall in love over and over. You may think that you're so superior to me with your tidy little seven-year marriage, but you wouldn't know what to do with a heart-pounding, soul-scorching love, the kind that weakens your knees and sets your head to spinning and makes every fiber of your being yearn for that person.

"I know the power of that kind of love, and though you think I've got some sort of emotional defect, I can tell you I wouldn't trade even one of my 'failed' marriages or affairs for a safe, Milquetoast marriage like yours and what's-his-name's."

The force of his words left me speechless, though I could feel the fire burning in my cheeks.

"And let me tell you something, Ali—until the day you experience the intensity of that kind of love, you won't have the foggiest notion of what makes me tick."

At that point, my heart was pounding, but not for the reason he had just mentioned. His harsh assessment had me nearly quaking with indignation.

"We'd better get back—don't want you to miss your flight." He eyed me coolly for one long second before spurring his mule into a run. I had no choice but to hang on to Lucille for dear life.

We flew down the side of the hill and across the field, sending the lazy cows scattering as we made our thunderous approach. It was wicked of Jake to unleash his revenge for my impertinence that way, and I was sure he'd let up once he had made his point. But no, he wasn't going to show me any mercy.

We galloped all the way to the road, only slowing our pace marginally as we crossed and continued along the trail to his ranch. He brought the mules to a canter, keeping well ahead of me as we followed the long avenue of sycamores to the barn. I was so wrung out by the time Lucille delivered me, I barely had the fortitude to dismount, let alone continue our war of words. I staggered back, trying to catch my breath as Jake removed the saddle from Jupiter.

"Well, I guess I'd better get my things together," I said, backing away. Jake nodded distractedly. I began walking toward the house, my pace quickening as terror wore off and resentment took its place. By the time I closed the guestroom door, I was grumbling epithets under my breath, tempted to march back and give Jake a scathing piece of my mind.

I plopped myself on the bed and tried to bring myself under control. What a son of a bitch! The nerve of him belittling me that way! As if a successful marriage was something to be ashamed of! And besides, what the hell did he know about my life and loves? He had no call to judge me like that!

But as I sat there, I replayed my own words and was forced to acknowledge that

I was the one who had set the tone for his attack on me. Why did I do that with him? I couldn't figure myself out. I had been acting like an aggrieved ex-lover since I had gotten there. But that was the first time Jake had given it right back to me.

I couldn't say that I didn't deserve it; after all, I had flat-out told him that his judgment was hopelessly flawed, that he was pretty much a loser and would probably always be. It was intolerably crass of me, especially in light of the fact he was doing me an incredible favor by not only letting me pry into his personal life but also by showing me such tremendous hospitality. He had been absolutely right in reprimanding my lack of professionalism. It was as if I had forgotten why I was out here, why I had insinuated my way into his home and his life. I had no business insulting him the way I had.

My behavior was even more unfathomable considering what a wonderful time I had had with him. In his eyes, I must have seemed as nutty and irrational as Jaylynn and Lavinia—just another screwball woman trying to paint him into a corner. I wouldn't have been surprised if he changed his mind about our interview.

I was more anxious than ever to get on the road, to get back into my element. Apparently, this country air had negatively affected my brain. I stripped off my smelly garments and wiped myself down with a washcloth. I packed the rest of my things, dressed, and lugged my bags down the path to my rental car.

Jake was unsaddling Lucille when I reached the dust-covered rental. I put the bags on the passenger side and, as Jake had taken the saddle into the barn, I decided to drive rather than walk over to say my goodbyes. Jake had emerged and was bringing Lucille around to the front of the corrals when I pulled up. I cut the engine but did not get out.

"Heading out?" Jake said. He seemed less irritated but still more remote than usual.

"Yep, I've had a great time here, but I've worn out my welcome to the last minute. I bet you had no idea what you were getting yourself into when you asked me to stay the whole weekend. I have the kind of personality that can grate on one's nerves after a while," I said smiling, hoping that my conciliatory tone would bring us back to neutral territory. Jake leaned in toward me, blocking the sun so I wouldn't have to shield my eyes with my hand.

"There's nothing wrong with your personality," he said, a little of his old playfulness seeping back into his voice. "The only thing wrong with you is that you're not fully acquainted with your own mind. But time will change that."

He straightened up and looked down at me with his grey-blue eyes. He was an exceedingly handsome man for his age. The funny thing was I was less comfortable with this new look than with the old. Now as he stared at me I had to turn away, unable to relate to him the same way I had before.

"Well, you better be on your way." He tapped the roof of the car twice and I started the engine. "Drive carefully," he said. I had just shifted into gear when he stopped me.

"Almost forgot," he said, taking a sheet of notepaper out of his shirt pocket. "We never did get around to calling my exes. I wrote down their numbers in case you still want to talk to them, find out what kind of jerk I really am," he said with a smirk.

"Thanks, Jake. And thanks for everything. You've been more than gracious."

"Come back anytime, my door's always open." He stood back and I let off the brake. A sudden cloud of melancholy had descended upon us. The rancor our spirited debate had caused had dissipated and a sadness at parting settled on us both.

I watched him in my side-view mirror as his gaze followed me, until the road bent to the left and he was out of sight. I pointed the car down the road toward Boise, navigating all the country roads without losing my way this time.

Fourteen

I had my laptop set up on the dining room table, ostensibly working on my piece, tentatively titled "Fated Attractions," but it was merely serving as a cover for staring out at the waterfront. From our modest bay window, we had a peek at the bay and the bridge spanning it, a view truncated by the top floor of the building in front of us.

It was a blustery day, the bone-chilling wind out of the north hurling threatening dark clouds across the sky. But in the city, the weather was only an accessory to the day; everyone pushed through their daily routines regardless of rain, wind or heat.

That was one aspect of city living I loved; you could always count on the concerted effort of your fellow city dwellers to prop up your illusion of purpose. In a city, you were guaranteed to find a place to congregate and blend in, accomplish your small tasks, and assure yourself of the validity of your life. Even if you weren't out and about, you felt a part of the whole just by knowing the city was out there waiting for you.

I would be getting my daily dose of the city experience soon enough. I was due at the office in less than two hours to conduct the interviews I had scheduled with numerous casualties of the marriage game. I was in desperate need of getting some work done in advance of those interviews. It was imperative I have something to show my editor; I had already missed my first deadline by a week.

Truthfully, I still didn't have anything resembling an outline to show for all my time spent so far. My only hope was these interviews would yield a more cohesive context for what I hoped would turn into a story. If they did, I'd be able to talk my way to an extension. If they didn't, I'd have to admit my folly and call it quits.

With the considerable will and determination that is the backbone of a good writer, I wrenched my attention away from the window and refocused my mind on the matter at hand. Ploddingly, I reread my notes, cutting, pasting, and deleting until I was left with a few concise statements plus my notes and observations of the seven-times married, mule-breeding womanizer, Jake Sorenson.

I propped my head on the heels of my hands and massaged my forehead. What a mess. What a poor excuse for a literary proposal. I pushed away from the table and went to stand indecisively in front of my closet for a while. It occurred to me I might be faced with what every writer dreads might happen sooner or later: either I was losing my talent for writing, or I was experiencing my very first writer's block. I closed the wardrobe doors and went to draw a bath.

Soaking in the tub led to rehashing the same unfruitful material I had been struggling with since my return from Oregon. Never before had I put such mental effort into a story that had so little real potential. Yet, no matter how frustrated I became, I couldn't let go of the basis of my idea.

I kept thinking there had to be a way to put into words what I was grappling to understand. There had to be a way to convey the essence of a man like Jake and the manner in which he viewed his life and his choices, something that had universal applications for others. I couldn't simply write a piece specifically about Jake, though his life was certainly fascinating enough.

But there was no angle to hang a story on, as he was merely an interesting man, not famous. He may stand out in his field as an expert mule breeder and trainer, but I was working at the wrong publication for that type of article. He would no doubt make a wonderful fictional character, but writing novels is not my vocation.

What kept haunting me was the hope that by talking with men and women who had had similarly tumultuous love lives, I could seize upon the crux of Jake's complex personality, and at the same time, determine what makes some people so vulnerable to the allure of marriage.

Feeling invigorated by renewed optimism, I climbed out of the bath and got myself ready for work. This would be a day of discovery. This would be the day the light started to dawn.

I made it to the magazine at 2:00 on the dot, just in time to conduct the first of eight interviews. I had wisely decided to refer to numbers instead of names, as it was hard enough trying to keep the names of all Jake's wives and lovers straight as it was. Besides, I had no intention of revealing their identities to the public.

It was no accident my arrival left me no time for loitering, and I was lucky enough to avoid Judith until I was escorting volunteer number one to the conference room. I was able to convey the impression of a journalist hot on the trail of another scintillating story, securing a couple hours in which to pan for gold.

Contestant Number One—as I came to view the characters in this charade of mine—was a woman in her late forties, not exactly well-preserved but still attractive, if four-inch heels and mistreated hair does it for you. I asked the questions I had prepared, but I scarcely heard the answers, as I was too busy studying her body language.

Despite the color-abused hair, acrylic nails and revealing outfit, Number One was a soft-spoken, thoughtful woman who had just recently separated from husband number five. It would have been easy for me to probe every aspect of each individual's life if I had been so inclined, as people can be astonishingly forthcoming with total strangers on the flimsiest excuse.

As curious as I became about this woman's story, I had to be mindful of the others waiting to bare their souls to me, simply because I had asked them to do so. I established the essential facts of age when first married, length of each marriage, and a brief description of each husband. Then I asked her to tell me what had first attracted her to these men and what made her decide to marry each of them. Her answers were the ordinary reasons for getting wed—for security, mainly—but with every one, she believed she was marrying primarily for love.

"Starting with your first marriage, what do you feel was the cause of your break up?"

"I caught Jim in our bed with our neighbor," she replied, head down, nervously toying with the purse perched primly on her lap.

"Was there anything that should have prepared you for that type of behavior from him?" Number One took a deep breath and regarded the ceiling before facing me.

"He was always flirting. Everywhere we went, he'd make some kind of flirtatious remark to the waitress or the sales clerk or whoever. It's funny too, because I remember how it made me feel, like by acting that way he was only proving to others how fortunate I was to be married to a guy like him. Does that make any sense? It was like a reflection on my luck and my good judgment, or something. I don't know, I can't really describe it. Like he was a real catch, and I should be proud. But I never once considered these overtures to be a threat to me in any way. Guess I was just totally naïve back then. It never even occurred to me that my husband would cheat on me."

We went down the list of husbands two through five, finding similarities to life with Jim in marriages two and four. Subject Number One impressed me with her continued openness and candor; it was as if she were taking stock of the collective men in her life for the very first time. I ended the interview with one last question.

"Do you think you will ever get married again?" I asked of this woman who was in the process of divorcing her fifth husband.

"Oh, I don't know. I suppose I probably would someday, if I found the right man. Just because I married five stinkers doesn't mean that all men are that way," she said, an unmistakable spark of hope in her eyes. Now, there was a diehard optimist.

I thanked her for her time, handed her a form to fill out for a free twelve-month subscription to *Savoir-Faire*, and led her out to the hallway. I buzzed Elise and told her to bring in the next volunteer, then popped off to the lounge to grab a cup of coffee.

Number Two sprang out of his chair upon my return to the conference room, his overactive gallantry spurred by nervousness. He began to introduce himself, but I cut him off by explaining the anonymous nature of this interview. He apologized and reseated himself across from me.

"I appreciate you coming here today. You understand that the questions I'm about to ask you are strictly for research purposes and no credit or mention of your name will be made, nor is it possible at this point to tell you when or even if the piece will be published." He nodded his assent and I took a sip of my coffee as I sized him up.

He was fifty-five, which was what I would have guessed, with artificially dark hair, offset by startling silver-grey sideburns. If this blatant spot of reality was meant to obscure the fact that he colored the rest of his hair, it wasn't working.

His face was pleasant, slightly weathered, but plainly eager to please. He was of short stature with the kind of build only achieved by regular visits to the gym, and his clothes—chinos and red polo shirt—were meant to show off his efforts. His sitting posture was erect but relaxed, in a way that suggested military training. He had carefully draped his navy baseball jacket over the back of his chair, and all these hints indicated to me that he was a man who liked an orderly world. I consulted my questionnaire and proceeded with the interview.

As Number Two politely answered my questions, I learned that he had been married a total of four times, his last marriage ending over a year ago. He had married his high school girlfriend, who died of cancer at the age of thirty-two. He was left with two young children, for whom he was anxious to find a suitable step-mother. The first two attempts to replace his wife led to miserable but prolonged marriages, the third ending the minute his youngest child moved out on her own.

He married his fourth wife to fill the long void in his heart left by his first wife, yet in the end they divorced, as she could not measure up to his memory of his lost love. He confessed to me that he now knew how wrong it had been to disqualify her for that reason, and he now felt that if he met the right person, he would not make the mistake of comparing her to his first wife.

"So, you would consider marrying again?"

"Yes, I would give marriage another chance, for the right reasons. I don't like the emptiness of single life. I was raised with the belief that you grow up and marry and have a family and stay married for fifty years. In that respect, I feel like I've failed. But I have to remind myself there's a reason behind everything and when it's time, I'll find the right person."

Another optimist. The sincerity of his proclamation touched me, and I had the fleeting idea of arranging a date for him with volunteer Number One. The frank, wistful hopefulness they had both displayed made me want to create an organization to place all these lost souls in good, happy marriages, once and for all. But contestant Number Three dispelled the notion that all divorcées were brokenhearted, deserving creatures with impaired judgment as their only flaw.

"And to tell you the truth, I knew I was in trouble even before the honeymoon was over," Number Three informed me confidentially. "If there's no spark with palms trees, a full moon, and tropical breezes, then there's never going to be one. I'm a very passionate woman, and if the man I married can't see to my needs, then there are plenty of others out there who would jump at the chance. Can you imagine a man being *too tired* to take me dancing on our honeymoon? Just what does he think honeymoons are for?"

She sat back against her chair indignantly. I could sense her right leg swinging furiously beneath the table while she watched me make notes. What I was documenting was her appearance, from haughty, penetrating gaze, to the defensive body language. She professed to be forty-four, but her whole demeanor belonged to an earlier time, to an era in which young women were routinely schooled in the wiles of making a good match.

I had made the mistake of asking her to describe the reason for the breakup of each of her five marriages and had unwittingly unleashed a torrent of complaints that spanned a total of eighteen years of wedded agony.

As she listed her litany of grievances for each husband, I couldn't help but sympathize with the unfortunate spouses. This woman was a witch—that was as obvious as her facelift.

What I couldn't understand was what had prompted any man, let alone five, to marry this woman in the first place. Now that's where the real story would be. If I could speak to those five men, I might uncover some telling clues. Was a pretty face enough to make them overlook the absence of all other qualities essential to a harmonious union?

Maybe she was one of those people who had a real flip side, the kind who batted her false eyelashes and spoke in honeyed tones until the second something displeased her. Even in this thirty-minute interview, I felt her irritation toward me growing, as if she were incensed by having to relive all these unpleasant memories of men who weren't fit to lick her designer shoes.

"One last question," I said, abbreviating her abuse of husband number five. "Do you see yourself ever getting married again?" She snorted harshly, obviously regarding me as a naïve fool.

"Never! There isn't a man out there that deserves a woman like me. Believe me, I've looked. And I can tell you another thing, he'll have to be extremely wealthy and extremely good-looking. There's no way I'll ever settle for less again." She pulled her faux leopard coat tighter around herself, despite the uncomfortable warmth of the room, and lifted her pointed chin at me defiantly. I thanked her for her help and showed her to the door.

By the time I unlocked the front door and bid volunteer Number Eight goodnight, I was thoroughly spent. It was a quarter to six and all the staff had gone home. I switched off all the lights as I made my way back to my office to collect my things.

If I had uncovered any salient truths, any compelling information to justify an article, I couldn't recall them just then. My mind was full to bursting with fragmented echoes from nearly four hours of sob stories, soul-searching catharsis, and ire from eight people, most of whom I'd just as soon never encounter again.

The whole interview process had left me with a gnawing in the pit of my stomach, a sour taste in my mouth, and a growing uncertainty about my fellow man. My head pounded dully and I had a craving to fill my lungs with cold, damp San Francisco air.

I locked my desk and headed out the back exit and down the stairwell, the clank of the release bar giving way to the din of evening traffic. I walked half a block and hailed a cab. I was feeling too tried to cook and too misanthropic to dine in a public establishment. Elliott would be working late, so there was no hope of help on his end.

I had the driver drop me at Fisherman's Wharf, where I picked up a hearty seafood stew, a crusty loaf of sourdough, and a bottle of white wine. I walked the rest of the way to our flat, giving myself plenty of time for critical assessment. Maybe a good angle for a story would be the lengths a formerly discerning journalist was willing to go in search of a story that wasn't jelling. I was certainly more qualified to write about that than compulsive love, which if I could still remember correctly, was the premise that started this wide net-casting process.

Compulsive love—what was that, anyway? Was it only something which affected a small group of individuals past the third grade? Was it simply a symptom of immaturity, an indulgence that had more to do with self-absorption and fantasy, by people who were too lazy to carry out the due diligence required in affairs of the heart? I mean, my God, did they really think it was all a matter of luck when they slipped the ring on their betrothed's finger?

I couldn't imagine placing so much faith and responsibility in another person. Love is far too serious a proposition to approach with a hope and a prayer. Everybody should know that.

I brought the stew to a simmer on the stove and poured myself a glass of wine. I unpacked my laptop on the dining table and began the futile process of documenting the afternoon's interviews. The phone rang and I grabbed it reflexively.

"Hi, it's me." Judith's voice caught me completely off-guard. I had been in the process of coming to grips with the fact that I still had nothing to show her. "What time did you finally get out of there?"

"Gosh, I don't know—around six, I guess." Damn. There was no dodging her this time.

"How'd it go?"

"Well. It went well. I was just in the middle of typing up my notes…"

"I won't keep you, then. I'm anxious to hear what you've got so far. Why don't you come into the office, say around noon, and we'll go have lunch."

"Sounds fine. I'll see you tomorrow."

"Give my love to Elliott."

I replaced the receiver and stared at the phone. The sound of the front door lock giving way tore me from my dismal reverie.

"Hi there. Did I hear you talking to someone?" Elliott asked as he set his computer bag down on the entry table and peeled off his coat.

"Hi. It was Judith. She sends her love."

"That's nice. How is she?" For some odd reason, even though Elliott is indifferent to my choice of career, he and Judith are uncommonly fond of one another.

"Fine, I guess. I haven't talked to her much since I got back." By his distracted "hmm," I could tell he had already stopped listening to me.

"Something sure smells good," he said as he lifted the lid on the stew.

"I had a rather long and tedious day and I didn't much feel like cooking," I said, as Elliott bent down to kiss my cheek.

"That's fine with me," he said taking off his shoes and sprawling across the sofa. "Jesus, what a day." He picked up an inch-thick spiral-bound report and groaned at the effort.

"There's a bottle of wine in the fridge, if you want a glass."

"Maybe later." He threw his head back and kneaded his temples.

"I'll get dinner ready," I said, saving my work and closing my laptop.

"Come and sit with me first," he said, patting the cushion beside him. As usual when I had been away, Elliott had been openly affectionate since my return. I didn't mind it, actually, but I did find it amusing. He hated for me to go out of town, yet the only times he really seemed to notice my presence was on my return. Our reunions were typically sweet, romantic affairs, reminiscent of our early courtship days.

Sadly, the spell generally lost its amorous effect too swiftly. As I had been home for over a week now, I was pleasantly surprised by his overture. I cuddled up next to him, enjoying the fresh whiff of ozone that clung to his skin. He pulled my head toward him with the crook of his arm and kissed the top of it. We sat entwined for five minutes or so, both of us luxuriating in this moment of peace and quiet, before his cell phone broke our tranquility with its annoying jangle.

I remained tucked close to his side as he answered the phone with his right hand. I made a move to get up, but he held me in place as he consulted with the voice on the other end, plainly aggravated by the interruption. As the conversation became more animated, I slipped away and set about putting our dinner together, stopping by the table to fetch my wine glass on my way to the kitchen.

I threw together a salad and heated the bread and set the table while Elliott hashed out a problem with his subordinate. It always irked me the way my business-related calls were treated as avoidable intrusions, whereas his calls were always justifiably important. Still, in this case, I couldn't help but feel a tad sorry for him.

There was no disputing that his job was far more demanding and stressful than mine; I was really only accountable to one person, and the longer I stayed with the magazine, the more my clout and discretionary power grew. Even though Elliott was the head of his department, he had a tower of execs who were forever looming ominously over his shoulder. He also earned the lion's share of our income. His call ended just as I dished the seafood stew into the bowls.

"Trouble?" I asked, as I set the bowls on the table.

"Just a technical glitch," he said, dismissing the topic. Elliott believed his work too complicated for the lay mind to comprehend. In my case, I was sure he was right. I was happy to skirt any shoptalk from his side of the table, as I had plenty of whining of my own to do.

"Want a glass of Sauvignon Blanc?" I asked as I refilled my glass. Elliott shook his head. "I had a weirdly interesting day today," I said. Elliott raised his eyebrows inquiringly as he tasted the stew. "I interviewed eight people, all of whom have been married and divorced at least four times."

"Really? Where'd you find so many people who fit that description?"

"It was amazingly easy. I went online and found a matchmaking chat room and posted a notice for bay area residents. I also ran an ad in the Sunday personals' section."

"That was it?" I nodded.

"I've come to the unscientific conclusion that achieving marital contentment the first time out is a profound oddity these days." Elliott snorted, superiorly proud in his minority status.

"People are too impatient nowadays. They want everything to go perfectly smooth right from the get-go, or they lose interest. It takes a strong commitment and a lot of work to make a marriage succeed," he said, more or less stating my own beliefs. But for some reason, his assertion sounded provincial and overly simplistic. I tore off a hunk of sourdough and dredged it through my broth.

"True, but look at us—we've never had any rough spots to work through. I think we've been extremely lucky in that respect."

"Luck doesn't have anything to do with it," Elliott said with the absolute conviction of a Baptist preacher. "We were smart enough to make a sound choice, that's all. Neither one of us allowed our feelings to cloud our judgment." Again, I had to admit complete agreement with him, yet he made our relationship sound as sterile and unromantic as a math equation.

"Yes, but we've both known couples who seem so well suited who have called it quits. Continual love and compatibility are harder to achieve than I had appreciated before. After all the stories I heard today, I've come to realize there *is* a certain amount of luck involved in any successful marriage. If you really think about it, it was luck—or fate, if you will—that brought us together in the first place. I believe part of the problem with the eight people I interviewed today was the fact that they simply haven't met the right person yet."

"Yeah, but after four or five marriages, do you really think they ever will? Sounds like the sorry souls you talked to have more problems than finding Mister or Missus Right. I doubt any of them would even recognize their perfect mate, anyway. Some people will never know what's good for them. They're just hell-bent on going after the exact wrong thing all their miserable lives," Elliott said, more condescendingly than I thought was warranted. I stopped chewing my salad mid-bite and stared at him.

"That's a little harsh, don't you think?" I said, chasing my words with a sizable swallow of wine. "I mean, I know how you feel—I share your views completely, in the abstract. But you didn't meet these people. Most were as ordinary as you and me."

"As ordinary as you and me? You mean normal? Do you really believe that 'normal' folks get married four or five or six times?" I was surprised by the sudden vehemence in his tone. "Tell me about the fine, sensible, unlucky individuals you met today," he said when I didn't answer his question. I couldn't understand why he was baiting me this way.

"You're right. I'll stop talking. You've obviously had a lousy day and you're just not in the mood to hear about my trivial project," I said as I carried my soup bowl and salad plate to the sink.

"No, come on—I do want to hear about your story. I don't quite understand what exactly you're trying to find out, but I'd like to hear what you've uncovered so far," he said in a more placating tone.

"There's some more cioppino left—do you want it?" I said from the stove, ignoring his sudden interest in my work.

"Sure, I'll have the rest, if you don't want any more. But I still want to hear about your interviews today." I ladled the rest of the stew into his bowl and returned the pot to the kitchen, snagging the bottle of wine from the refrigerator on the way out.

"You sure you don't want a glass?" I asked as I topped up my wine.

"No, I'm fine. You're hitting it kind of hard for a week night, aren't you?" I gave him a stony look and plunked the bottle down beside me. "So, tell me about your interviews. And remind me again, what's this piece about?"

I could feel my jaws clench. "Compulsive love."

Elliott struggled to keep from laughing. "Go on," he said, tittering in spite of my withering glare.

"No, forget it. It wouldn't interest you."

"Now don't get all bent out of shape. I am interested. I find it a little ironic, that's all. Just two minutes ago you were defending your subjects' emotional stability, and yet your premise targets a compulsive tendency, which indicates a behavioral instability." He covered the beginnings of a laughing fit with a phony cough, then resumed a mask of serene sensitivity. "Never mind. I'm dying to hear how it went."

I couldn't tell for sure if he was putting me on or not. He usually took a passive stance where my writing was concerned, offering sympathetic or congratulatory ums and ahs wherever appropriate. Figures he would focus in on the one topic I was about to abandon due to lack of structure and pertinent content.

"Just pretend you're giving Judith your spiel," he said when I hesitated, arranging himself in his most attentive pose. Of course, he didn't know how much I was dreading pitching "my spiel" to my tolerant editor. I drew a deep breath and tried to couch my findings in the most benign manner. "Go ahead, I'm all ears," he urged me.

"Well, to be perfectly honest, I'm not one hundred percent sure where I'm headed with what I've gathered so far. I may end up scrapping most of it—who knows? But what I was hoping to find was some sort of common thread, some sentiment or characteristic or pattern they all shared that I could isolate and make into a theory."

"Any luck?"

"I don't know. I haven't really had enough time to digest the four hours of material I collected. I was working on my notes right before you got home, but I'm not finished."

"Just give me your basic impressions, then."

"Hmm, well…"

"Were they all women?"

"No, five women and three men."

"Are any of them currently married?"

"No, all are divorced or separated right now, though in most cases, they were eager to meet someone new. In fact, one man had misinterpreted the purpose of the interview and had come expecting to be fixed up with a new mate."

"Really?"

"Yes. He was a little bent out of shape by the whole process. I can't say I really blame him. He had waited over three hours to find out he was going to be leaving empty-handed."

"Oops."

"And there was a woman who nearly broke down in tears when she discovered I wasn't going to solve all her problems for her."

"What did she think, that you were a shrink or something?"

"I think she must have figured that we were running some kind of counseling service for repeat offenders. Honestly, I felt sorry for a couple of them, but I wasn't there to sort out their love lives. I didn't tell her that, of course. I said that if I was successful at finding a common denominator among people with multiple marriages, my research might help her and others approach their relationships differently."

"Is that what you're hoping to do?" Elliott asked.

"Well, it wasn't my original intention, but I suppose it could be a natural byproduct."

"So you didn't find any common denominator among the people you interviewed today?" I swirled the wine in my glass while I reviewed my thoughts so far.

"Not really. The only thing all of them have in common is the willingness to remarry again, with caveats, of course. But other than that, it was a mixed bag as far as circumstances are concerned. For instance, one of the women seems perpetually attracted to men who end up physically or emotionally mistreating her. That kind of pattern can only be broken by confronting and eliminating the reasons for wanting to punish herself.

"Then there's the other side of the coin—the man who thinks of himself as the world's greatest catch. He sat across from me the whole time giving me this vibe like he was willing me to drop my pen and crawl over the table to surrender myself to his overpowering magnetism. The guy had an ego like you wouldn't believe. He had been divorced six times, and in every case, he had grown bored with his wives."

"Amazing," Elliott said with a condescending smirk.

"But that's the kind of absence of restraint that initially sparked my interest in this topic. What makes some folks continually retrace steps that never bring them any good results? It seems only logical that if you have three or four failed marriages, you'd give up on the whole idea. So it makes me wonder if some people feel a compulsive need to be married."

"That, or maybe they don't have any respect for the institution itself. Maybe they use it as a vehicle to indulge their momentary illusions of love."

"Oddly enough, I think most of them have a high regard for marriage because of what it symbolizes. I think that they desire it so much they marry for the sake of being married, not taking the time or the effort to decide if the person they are planning to marry is compatible enough to make it last."

"I don't know—I still have a hard time believing someone who values marriage would get divorced over and over again. I think if you really felt marriage was important, you'd find a way to make it work," Elliott said, picking up the rest of the dishes and taking them to the sink.

"Even if there's no way you'll ever work out your differences?" He shrugged his shoulders and filled the sink with hot water and soap. "You don't think it's right to stay in a bad marriage, do you? Would you want to waste your life with the wrong partner?" I asked, handing him the salad bowl to wash.

"No, but if I married someone and it turned out I had chosen unwisely, I would sure as hell be reluctant to trust my judgment a second time around."

I took the clean bowl from his hand, dried it and put it away. I could tell this subject was starting to grate against his sensibilities. I decided to let it drop, not wanting to push my luck. It had been very refreshing to share my work with him. I had enjoyed the chance to kick around ideas, especially in this case where brainstorming was desperately needed.

I returned to his side and began drying the dishes that drained in the rack, neither of us saying anything for a while. I had assumed his mind had returned to his usual preoccupation, when he startled me with another line of questioning.

"What about the mule guy you went to see in Oregon? How does he fit into the equation? Any similarities to the people you saw today? I would imagine you got plenty of material from him. How many times has he been married?"

"Jake? He's been divorced seven times." Elliott shook his head uncomprehendingly.

"Seven times? Unbelievable."

I dried the silverware, suddenly not wanting to take this discussion any further. For some bizarre reason, I had a hard time placing Jake in the same boat with my eight volunteers. It was silly, as there really wasn't anything that distinguished his track record from theirs—except for the fact I had come to know him much better than I expected.

The people I had met at the office seemed like caricatures when compared to Jake. He was not unique because of his long list of former spouses, but because of the gusto and appreciation he brought to his many adventures.

Yet, what did I really know about him? I had shared several intimate moments and been privy to some of his most personal history, but I still barely knew the man. There was an intricacy to his life and his mind I had no hope of becoming acquainted with, especially now that I didn't even have a sound pretext for seeing him again.

"Don't you?" Elliott said, breaking into my thoughts.

"Don't I what?"

"Didn't you hear anything I just said?"

"No, I'm sorry. I was thinking about something else."

"I asked you if your mule breeder was any different than the Don Juan you had in your office today. I met the guy—he seemed pretty full of himself."

"Jake? No, not really. I mean, once you get to know him you see a whole other side of him. He's actually down to earth and quite fascinating, with all the different lives he's had—"

"Not to mention all the wives he's had," Elliott said flippantly. I bit my lip, not keen on the idea of having to defend Jake to Elliott. "What's his outlook on marriage? Does he think he'd do it again after being a seven-time loser?"

"He wouldn't commit to that question one way or the other. But as far as being a seven-time loser, Jake doesn't view his successive divorces in that light."

"Well, that's a novel outlook, I'm sure. So, it's always the woman's fault that the marriages haven't worked?"

"He never said anything like that. He doesn't seem to be caught up in the blame game." I gave Elliott the towel to dry his hands while I wiped down the counters with the sponge.

"So, how does he rationalize his abysmal failures as a husband?"

"He just sees all his marriages as part of the natural progression, each experience bringing something valuable to his life. He doesn't regret anything he's done. He has an almost Zen-like philosophy."

"I wonder if all his exes share his equanimity. Tell me this—if he's so enlightened, how come he keeps doing something he's obviously no good at?" I shrugged and slipped past my indignant husband to rinse out the sponge. "That's definitely something I can't fathom. He doesn't seem to understand that he doesn't have to marry every girl he goes out with, for God's sake. Why would anyone want to go through all the hoopla and legal entanglements when you can just live together?"

"He's done plenty of that, too. Don't you remember him saying at the wedding that he'd lived with dozens of women?" Elliott raised his hand dismissively and walked away.

"Well, good luck with your piece. Sounds like you're going to need it. I don't envy you having to figure out what goes on in some people's heads. This one is beyond my scope of comprehension. I don't know how you're going to make something out of what you've told me so far."

I stood hopelessly at the stove while I watched him unpack his laptop and settle on the sofa, happy to apply his logical mind to problems he understood. He had been right in his assessment of this ill-fated concept, though I doubted he appreciated how accurate he was.

I sat down at my computer and continued to type up my notes, for whatever good I could wring from them. It wasn't until 11:15 that I gave up and called it a night.

I lay in bed with my feet pressed close to Elliott's leg, falling asleep to the soft clack, clack, clack of his fingers hitting the keyboard, trying to will the eight unfortunate volunteers and their various pathetic tales out of my mind, holding up my marital harmony like a cross to ward off similar misfortune.

It was only natural Elliott should find this subject so distasteful; to him, these examples were about as foreign to his way of thinking as they could be. I imagined he would consider the thought of our ever getting divorced inconceivable.

The commitment of marriage was not an idle whim as far as he was concerned. I closed my eyes, comforted by his steadfast allegiance to me, never minding for a moment that he allowed his work to infringe on our limited private time. There was a lot to be said for having a faithful, committed spouse in these times.

I woke in time to share a cup of coffee with Elliott before he piloted himself south for another stimulating day in his isolated universe. I procrastinated as long as I could, finding numerous small tasks to keep me from settling down to work. I trudged through my notes, constantly appealing to the clock for deliverance.

Finally, at 11:00, I closed the file and got ready for my assignation with Judith. Though I may be a pragmatist, I held out the faint hope that I would be struck by a thunderbolt of inspiration and clarity on my way to the magazine. It was foolish, but what else did I have?

Fifteen

"A piece of salmon, broiled, with lots of lemon, no sauce, steamed vegetables, and a pot of oolong tea," Judith said as she handed her unused menu back to the waiter. I could never understand her penchant for dining at fashionable eateries when all she ever ordered was the same unadorned sliver of fish and boring vegetables.

"I'll have the wild mushroom ravioli, and the field greens to start with," I said. The waiter committed our order to memory and vanished, leaving me alone with my editor.

I had managed to avoid any preliminary interrogations by eschewing the office and catching up with her at the restaurant instead. I was plagued by a sense of fraud, for this was the first time in my career that I was meeting my editor empty-handed. I was dreading the inevitable confession that I had absolutely zilch to show her, particularly since I had used the company expense account to finance my excursion to Oregon.

I had concocted a number of excuses for my failure to produce the long awaited outline, but now as I sat face-to-face with her, I couldn't bring myself to use them. Judith was my boss, but she was also my friend. If I told her anything other than the complete truth, she would know it instinctively.

"I'm dying to see how your piece is coming along," she said, never suspecting for a minute that I was about to disappoint her. I had wasted as much time as I could buttering and consuming several slices of bread. I had no recourse but to break the ugly news to her.

"Judith, I don't have anything to show you right now," I blurted out without preamble.

"Nothing at all?"

"No, I'm afraid not. I hate to admit it, but I can't make this story gel. I really thought I was on to something in the beginning, yet the more effort I put into it, the less usable copy I have. I'm not saying I'm giving up on the idea entirely, I'm just saying I'm going to need more time to make it work." Judith kept silent while she poured her tea. "I'd really like to get your gut feeling on the subject before I put any more time into it."

"Well, to be honest, I wasn't sure where you were headed from the outset. I *think* I know what it was you were after, but it struck me as an awfully broad target for a monthly periodical to tackle. It seems more like thesis material for a psychology major, if you really want my opinion." I sighed and nodded weakly, knowing her observation was accurate, as usual.

"Don't get me wrong. If you think you can pull it together, then I'm willing to let you pursue it further. But I'll have to tell you the premise sounded a little too vague to me."

"Yeah, that's the problem in a nutshell. I know there's something to my idea, but at this time I can't figure out how to translate it into a storyline."

"Well, no harm done. You're definitely not the first writer to get stymied by an idea. You got a few days' R & R out of it, at least. I've got something else for you anyway, though I have to say I was looking forward to learning more about the much-married mule man. Did he end up being a dud as an interview?"

"Jake? Hardly. Actually, I've been lamenting the fact that I can't do a story solely about him. He's one of the most fascinating individuals I've ever come across," I said, my mood brightening now that I had this albatross of a story off my neck. "I got a lot of good material from him—I just couldn't find a way to use it."

"Tell me about your trip."

"My big trip to eastern Oregon? Let's see…well, I learned all I'll ever need to know about mules, that's for sure. Jake took me riding three times, on a mule. That was fun. Terrifying, but fun. I got to meet two of his women friends. That was an experience."

"I take it he's not currently hitched," Judith said.

"No, at least not while I was there. But you never know with him—he's a fast worker."

"Did he put the moves on you?"

"Oh no, he was a perfect gentleman with me."

Judith raised her eyebrows challengingly. "Are you telling me he didn't flirt with you, not even a tiny bit?"

"No, not really. I mean, we danced a couple of times—"

"Danced?"

"An impromptu tango and I don't know what else."

"You danced the tango with a lady killer, and you don't think he was flirting with you?" Judith asked, a cynical gleam in her eyes.

"You might have thought he was flirting, but it felt like he thought of me as a kid sister."

"Sorry, I'm not buying the little sister angle. A man who has been married that many times and has lived with countless other women? A man like that never speaks to a woman without flirting."

"Maybe you should have gone to interview him, then. I know what a hopeless flirt you are," I said sarcastically. "I'm sure the two of you could have had a ball," I said, spearing a baby lettuce leaf with my fork.

"Now you're talking. I bet we would have hit it off famously," she said.

I had to laugh; Judith was a petite, unassuming brunette in her early forties, never married, and as plain as white bread. She had occasionally intimated to me that underneath her prim exterior, she had an intense hankering for the kind of whirlwind romance she would never allow herself to have.

The only two men that she had ever dated seriously were beyond conservative, with their Brooks Brothers button-down shirts and their right-wing politics. She had confided to me that both eerily possessed the trait of laying out the next day's garments before retiring for the evening. If there was one thing she had in common with them, it was her love of order and consistency. It was pure fantasy for her to act as though a man like Jake would ever appeal to her.

"I'm sorry, Judith. A seven-times-divorced mule trainer hardly strikes me as your type."

"Don't be silly. You can't deny there's a mystique to a man who has attracted so many women. There's got to be something phenomenal about him or he'd have never had that kind of success with the opposite sex," she said, a flush of excitement coloring her cheeks. "Besides, I think my taste in men has changed."

"Really? And what exactly has brought about this unexpected change?"

"I don't know, maybe the sudden realization that we've been given only a certain amount of time on this earth and there's no reason to limit our experiences."

"Judith, you're not ill, are you?" I asked, alarmed by her cavalier attitude.

"Don't be a twit—of course not. But you intrigued me with your description of this Jake character. Just imagining someone like him made me aware how safe and unadventurous my life has been so far. It's time for me to do some living," she reflected over a sip of her tea. "And this Jake guy sounds like just the ticket—someone who could add some color and excitement to my life. I'm tired of doing the same old boring things."

"Try ordering the ravioli next time, that's safer," I cautioned her.

She gave me a dirty look over her broiled salmon. "You may be flip if you wish, but I'm serious. I want to meet someone wild and full of life."

"Here, try a ravioli—they're out of this world," I said, sliding one onto her bread plate.

"I don't want a ravioli," she said, pushing it away, "I want you to introduce me to Jake," she said, rendering me totally speechless. I don't know if it was the rich food or the thought of leading yet another victim to Jake to be wooed and disposed of, but I felt my heart fluttering unsteadily in my chest.

"You have to be joking," I told her, once I regained control of my tongue. "Jake is not your type."

"I told you, my type has changed," she insisted.

"I must have inadvertently given you a lofty impression of this man. Believe me, he's not what you may think. He's… he's a womanizer. He comes on strong, then boom, without warning, he's tired of you." A peculiar look settled upon Judith's face.

"I think you've got a crush on the man yourself," she said to my astonishment. "That's why you're afraid to introduce me."

"Judith, that couldn't be further from the truth," I croaked with a voice I hardly recognized. "The man is like a machine—he's compulsive in his efforts to attract women. But I can tell you from witnessing it firsthand that his women soon find out how fickle his intentions really are. Look, I think you've let your brilliant imagination get out of hand on this one," I said, reaching into my bag for my notebook.

I flipped impatiently through the pages until I found what I was looking for. "Does this look like the kind of guy you want toying with your love and affection?" I asked as I showed her a picture of Jake from his sister's wedding. It was Jake in his most bedraggled form, the beard and hair gone wild as his feelings for Lavinia dwindled.

"Jesus H. Christ on a raft. This is the man you went to Oregon to see?" I nodded pleasantly. "This is the man that has been married seven times? I can't believe it," she stammered. She took one last look and passed the photo back to me.

I buried my head in my bag so she couldn't see the grin spreading across my face. I took a quick glance at my shaggy friend before slipping him back into the pages of my notebook. If she knew what lay beneath that preposterous disguise, she'd have insisted on an introduction. But there was no way I could tell her the truth. I was tricking her for her own good.

"Okay, so much for that. I guess I'll have to stick to my own crowd for a while longer." She dabbed her lips, mentally dismissing the wily mule breeder.

"Now that's out of the way, let me tell you about your new assignment. I think you're going to be blown away when I tell you who I've gotten you an interview with." Judith enjoyed keeping me in suspense for a moment before dazzling me with her astounding coup. "Are you ready for this?" she asked, leaning in toward me theatrically.

"You've got me on pins and needles," I said rather insincerely.

"I've gotten you an exclusive interview with Malcolm Gray," she said triumphantly, sitting back to bask in my dumbfounded awe.

Malcolm Gray ranked as the second richest American—a steely, entrepreneurial genius turned philanthropist in the last five or so years, making tremendous contributions in an exceedingly low-profile manner. He was nearly as fanatical about his privacy as Howard Hughes had been. But unlike Mr. Hughes, Mr. Gray had apparently not lost touch with the world around him.

"He hasn't given an interview in a decade, at least," I said, marveling at the thought. Judith nodded serenely. Wow, that was impressive. Even more so when you consider all the big league publications that would have done anything for an opportunity like this.

Savoir-Faire was a mere pipsqueak in terms of revenue and name recognition. Our strength was due to our dedication to providing top-drawer journalism on a shoestring budget. We perversely prided ourselves on our slim stable of advertisers, smug in the knowledge that our periodical sold to the discriminating few solely because of the articles, and not for dozens of glossy ads.

"You have the distinct privilege of being the only reporter in twelve years he feels is worthy of his time."

"No kidding?" I said, tittering with pleasure at this improbable honor.

"No kidding."

"So, what's the timeline on this? I imagine he wants me to travel to him."

"With him," Judith said.

"With him? Where?"

"Here's the topper—you're going to be flying with his personal entourage to Afghanistan."

"Why Afghanistan?" I asked. Judith stared at me as in disbelief.

"This was only the biggest story in world politics when it was announced. Where the hell have you been? Oh, I forgot—you must have been hanging out in Oregon with the Cro-Magnon Man when it was all over the news. I'll have to get you the releases.

"It was revealed by his spokesperson less than two weeks ago that Mr. Gray had received approval from the U.S. and Afghanistan governments to proceed with a plan to export to Afghanistan five billion dollars of equipment and personnel—computers, builders, teachers, medical personnel—everything needed to build a new Western-style education facility, a test city, if you will.

"His plan is to create a highly skilled Afghan workforce comparable to India's. It's a wildly optimistic long-range goal, and apparently Mr. Gray is committed to making it work, however long it takes to get results. If his vision comes to fruition, it will be the most positive institutional change ever brought to a third world country.

"Imagine, training kids and adults alike, most of whom have never even seen a computer, to be leaders in the world of technology. It's a ballsy gamble, but hey, the same idea has transformed India into the hottest recruitment market in the world.

"In any event, this is the most money any individual has pledged to an under-privileged country. This is a very exciting story," she concluded, justifiably proud of herself. I sat back in my chair, my head swimming with this incredible news.

"That's absolutely amazing. I still can't believe you managed to secure an interview with Malcolm Gray. How did you do it?" I asked, my admiration and respect for my fearless editor swelling to new heights.

"Hey," Judith said lightly, "it's what they pay me the big bucks for."

I laughed. The pay is not what kept us at *Savoir-Faire*. "Yeah, but why us, and why me? Of all the big names at his disposal, I can't imagine how you swung him our way."

"It took every bit of conniving and back-scratching and favor-collecting I could conjure up, but it eventually paid off. I've been working on getting him for quite some time. It was just terrific luck that he needed someone to record this venture at the same time I was softening him up. But it wasn't luck that sold him on you. It was your dazzling work that ultimately won him over."

I was tingly from head to toe. I couldn't remember feeling this special since the surprise party on my sixteenth birthday. Same emotional high, much better reward this time around.

"He knows my work? Isn't it unbelievable that he reads our little rag?" I gushed, giddy at our small fame.

"I don't think he's ever read *S-F*. I emailed him your best articles and your nomination for the Prescott Award. Just a little properly placed PR," Judith said modestly.

"You are awesome," I said, lifting my glass of mineral water to her in salute. "Oh God, I feel like my face is going to crack from smiling so hard! This is…just… unreal! Afghanistan—didn't think I'd ever be headed to that country. Tell me, when is this scheduled for?"

"You've got a 6:00 flight tomorrow that will put you in Chicago by noon. An aide will be there to meet you and take you to Malcolm's private jet. Here," she said, as she reached for her briefcase and pulled out a manila package, "this has your itinerary and a complete bio on him, plus some questions that might be good lead-ins. Something to keep you occupied on the plane."

"Tomorrow? Six, as in six a.m.? Why didn't you just phone me tomorrow morning to break the news?"

"Hey, don't be a sore winner. It wasn't like I hadn't been trying to nail you down for a week now. You're the one who's been putting me off, not the other way around."

"I'm sorry. I don't mean to sound ungrateful. This is almost too much to comprehend at once. You know how much this means to me. I just don't want to embarrass or disappoint you or myself. Or Malcolm Gray," I said. The weight of what I was about to embark on finally settled on my shoulders.

"Well, this doesn't give me much time to get my act together, does it?" I asked rhetorically as I stuffed the manila envelope inside my bag. I exhaled deeply, and looked across the table for reassurance. "I'm starting to feel nervous."

"As long as you're up to your usual terrific form, I know you'll do a bang-up job. I wouldn't have worked so hard on your behalf if I had thought otherwise," she said. "See, if I had told you sooner, you would have only fretted and worried yourself sick for longer. This way, you'll be fresh, sharp, and alert."

"Alert, for sure," I said, knowing I'd be relying heavily on coffee to make it through the next few days. There was no chance of getting any sleep that night. "How long will I be gone?"

"It's really up to him and you. I would count on at least three or four days out of the country, but it could be a week or more. I would imagine it depends on how long he wants to stay."

I got queasy thinking of how to break the news to Elliott that I'd be in war-torn Afghanistan for an indeterminate length of time. I cheered up slightly upon remembering that Malcolm Gray was one of the grandfathers of modern technology, making him Elliott's hero.

"Why don't you get going? I'll take care of the check and I'll call you later to see if you need anything. I've got the travel department looking into what kind of cell phone reception is possible from there. We'll get something to you as soon as we know."

All of the sudden, I felt like I was on the verge of having a full-scale panic attack. I was anxious to get myself and my gear in order, but at the same time, I was reluctant to leave the protective comfort of my trusting editor.

"Go," she said. I stood up, turned to go, thought of something I wanted to say, turned back to her, but the words wouldn't leave my mouth. "I'll call you later. Get going—you've got a lot to do. And be sure to pack warm clothes—it's very cold over there right now." I nodded, my marching orders giving me the incentive I needed to put one foot in front of the other.

As soon as I was enveloped in the cold autumn air, the reality of my current situation hit me. Excitement welled up inside me and I could barely stifle a scream of delight. Me, Allison Tyler-Wilcox, having an exclusive interview with MALCOLM GRAY! I was so thrilled, I couldn't wait to tell someone. The logical choice would be Elliott, but I wanted to handle that in person. Putting the right spin on this assignment would be important. I thought of calling several friends, but the jitters got the best of me and sent me scurrying down Post Street.

There were no taxis in front of the St. Francis, so I impulsively hopped on a passing streetcar, jumping off a block from the Fairmont, where several cabs were awaiting fares. I could scarcely think as the driver spirited me down the cascading streets, my mind full of the dozens of tiny details I needed to put in order before dawn.

I started by packing a bag—only one, in deference to the limited storage available on most private jets. The thrill at what I was about to do washed over me in intermittent waves, leaving me simultaneously thrilled and petrified. I had momentary heart failure when I couldn't find my passport. I spent half an hour tearing the place apart before discovering I had already packed it in my shoulder bag.

It was at this point that I fixed myself a scotch and soda to calm my nerves. Meditation might have been helpful at this juncture, if I had known how to do it. I hopped in the shower instead, shampooing my hair extra thoroughly, for who knew the next time I'd see a shower.

By the time I had made as many physical preparations as I could think of, I was completely exhausted. Sensibly, I lay down and began skimming Malcolm Gray's bio, my mind still flitting around too much for proper reading. I started a list of notes and questions, but didn't get very far before falling sound asleep. At 4:30, I awoke with a start, the traces of a traveling nightmare dispersing in wisps, leaving me with a vague sense of dread.

I was shaky after my brief nap, but my adrenaline kicked in, and soon I was darting around our condo, gathering this and that as memories of various trips inspired me to be adequately prepared. I began cramming various necessary articles into my already full bag: a thick sweater; another pair of socks; my smallest camera; an extra eight-hour battery for my laptop; an extra pair of underwear; pulled the camera out of my bag, thinking they would never allow me to take my own photos; sifted through all my electrical adapters, and not finding anything exotic enough, removed my hairdryer from my bag; called Judith; and put my smallest camera back in the bag. No photographer would be traveling with me, so she told me to go ahead and take the chance.

I shoved four lined note pads into my computer bag, just in case I wasn't able to recharge my batteries. I stashed an extra lipstick, one tube of mascara and one compact of pressed powder into the side pocket, and I was done. I ordered Chinese food to be delivered and called my parents.

I broke the news to my father first—he was the one who answered the phone. I could tell he was pleased; he had always felt I was "hiding my light" by staying with such a low-profile periodical, when fame and fortune and prestige were surely waiting for me at one of the more established magazines. There was no mistaking the pride and amazement in his light laugh.

But breaking the news to my mother was a different story; she was certain I would be walking straight into a hostage situation, or at minimum, a shoot-out with the Taliban.

By the time she had finished with me, I almost regretted not waiting to tell them until I got back. The Chinese delivery boy arrived in the middle of our conversation, and I hastily stashed the cartons in the oven to keep the food warm. In my distracted state, I had failed to check the temperature, only noticing my mistake when smoke began to escape out the sides of the oven. The smoke detector started to shriek.

"Mom, Mom—I'll call you when I can—I've got to run now." I tossed the phone and grabbed the nearest potholder, seizing the flaming carton and flinging it into the sink, smoke billowing up as I drowned it in water.

"What the hell's happening?" Elliott exclaimed as he dashed through the door.

"I'm afraid I over-fried the fried rice," I said, dumping the soggy contents of the carton down the garbage disposal.

Elliot wrenched the smoke detector off the wall and popped the battery out of the back to stop the deafening noise. "How'd this happen?" Elliott asked, as he opened windows and fanned the smoke out with his coat.

"I was talking to my mother when the food arrived, and I was so preoccupied, I forgot to check to see what the oven was set on," I said, choking on the dense cloud of smoke. "God, that was a close call. Oh well, at least we still have the white rice, spicy tofu and Szechwan eggplant."

"Is your mother all right?"

"Oh yeah, she's fine. I called her because I had something I needed to tell her."

Elliott stopped fanning and looked at me, a funny expression on his face. "Are you… pregnant?" His question was so far out of left field, I didn't know what to make of it.

"God, no! And if I were, I wouldn't be telling my parents before I told you, silly." There was a momentary flash of disappointment on his face, very fleeting, but it took me by surprise. "No, I'm not pregnant, but I do have something to tell you, something pretty exciting."

"What is it?" Elliott asked, a hint of apprehension seeping into his voice. He was standing in the middle of the living room, still clutching his trench coat in both hands. He looked as if he were bracing himself for the worst.

"Don't worry, it's not bad news. Why don't you hang up your coat and get comfortable, and I'll tell you over dinner. Oh shoot, I meant to put a bottle of champagne in the fridge. I guess it's too late now."

"Champagne? Now I'm intrigued. It must be awfully good news if it calls for a celebration," he said, reluctantly walking away, his eyes on me as long as I was in sight.

"So, after he read my articles Judith sent him, Malcolm Gray consented to letting us have an exclusive interview. It turns out Judith's timing couldn't have been better. I guess it occurred to him it would be perfect to have a journalist record his trip to Afghanistan for history's sake. Is that lucky, or what?" I had just given Elliott the condensed version of my thrilling news, carefully emphasizing the honor of the assignment and downplaying the travel aspect of it.

"Jeeze, that's incredible," he said, clearly bowled over by the thought of his wife having an interview with a man he idolized. "Wow."

"I know, I still can't quite believe it, either. And the weird thing is, I hadn't even heard about his remarkable plan for bringing Afghanistan into the technology era. What a gutsy idea."

"I know, the man is a genius," Elliott said reverently. "If anybody can pull this off, it would be him." I nodded respectfully and spooned some more white rice onto my plate, topping it with the spicy eggplant.

"I'm afraid Judith didn't give me much time to prepare. I'm going to have to leave a lot earlier than I would have liked," I said, trying to break the news of my imminent departure to him gently.

"When do you have to leave?" he asked through a mouthful of spicy tofu.

"Six a.m., tomorrow."

He swallowed hard. "You're kidding." I shook my head. "And Judith just told you about this today?"

"At *lunch*. Yeah, I've been running around like a maniac, trying to get myself in order."

"This is a great break for you," Elliott said. "It could be the highlight of your career. It sure is a hell of a lot better than hanging out with death row inmates or a bunch of prostitutes. This is the caliber of person you should've always been writing about. This is the kind of thing that gets a journalist noticed," he said knowingly.

I didn't want to argue, but I had already received a nomination for the most prestigious award in journalism, three times, in fact. All I cared about at this juncture was getting out of there without any static from him.

"Yeah, this kind of interview is impressive on any reporter's resume. It's a big score, but it's also a lot of responsibility. My only hope is that I can do it justice," I said.

"You're the perfect one for the job because you're insightful, intelligent, clever, and unbiased, and more importantly, because you're my wife," he said, pulling me closer to give me a kiss on the lips. "Um, that eggplant tastes good. Is there any left?" he teased me. I handed him the carton.

"The other thing that irked me was Judith couldn't tell me how long I'll be gone. Because I'm flying aboard the same jet with the big chief himself, my return will be dependent upon his schedule—unless, of course, other arrangements can be made. But considering where we'll be, an alternate plan seems unlikely." Elliott had listened quietly, thoughtfully digesting this unwelcome bit of information.

"My hope is we'll be there two or three days, then head back. I guess we'll have to wait and see. Judith is looking into cell phone availability. I was expecting to hear from her already about that," I said. I was not comforted to discover it was already 7:15. I would be in the sky in less than twelve hours. Elliott must have picked up on my anxiety, for he seemed to be on the same wavelength.

"Where's your laptop?" he asked, scooting away from the table.

"I've already packed it—it's in the other room."

"Get it. I want to install something in it," he said, bringing his laptop to the table. I cleared away the empty cartons and fetched my computer bag.

"I'm going to load something onto your computer that will allow you to send and receive e-mail, no matter where you are, without needing a connection. I've been meaning to do this for a while, but now it's essential that you have it."

I stood by and watched as he worked his magic, thereby giving me a tremendous sense of security. No matter what kind of situation I got into, I'd now be able to SOS from anywhere in the world. What a great comfort having a technology wiz for a husband.

"Do you have backup power?"

"Yeah, I have another eight-hour battery in addition to the one in my computer. Both have a full charge."

"Here, take this one, too," he said, removing the battery from his computer bag. "How about backing up your data?"

"I've just got one disc."

"Take these," he said, handing me two flash drives, more capacity than I could ever need. I was going to be loaded down with paraphernalia, but it was reassuring to know I was as prepared as I could be on such short notice.

By the time I got everything situated for my early morning departure, I was too keyed up to go to sleep. The closer it got to 4 a.m. the more wide-awake I became. I had phoned a few friends and given them the quick scoop, canceled a dentist appointment scheduled for the following Monday, and made a list of everything I should have packed. I realized this was backward logic, but it did help to calm my jitters.

I sat with Elliott, curled up next to him while he worked, until his soft snoring alerted me that he had fallen asleep. I shut down his computer and helped him to bed. After completing my pre-bed rituals, I set my alarm for 4:00, arranged for a taxi pickup, and crawled in beside my sleeping husband. I couldn't take anything to help me sleep, for I was terrified of sleeping past the alarm or of being too groggy to function properly.

Instead, I lay awake and listened as the nighttime sounds dwindled to silence, and eventually drifted into a type of sleep that was merely a rehashing of events past or still to come.

I tiptoed out the front door at a quarter to five, just as the taxi pulled up to our building. I had enough time at the airport before the flight left to grab a cup of coffee and a few power bars, then I was off—off to what was to be the most challenging assignment of my career.

Sixteen

I sat on my cot in the tiny room that served as my quarters during our stay in the outskirts of Kabul. It was the end of my second full day in Afghanistan, the third day in the company of Mr. Malcolm Gray.

We had stayed our first night in Zurich, a good halfway point for refueling and stocking up on perishables. We had arrived around noon in Kabul the following day, and I had been at Mr. Gray's side virtually every waking hour since then. I was drop-dead tired, more physically and mentally exhausted than I could ever remember feeling. But I had work to do before I could avail myself of the limited comforts my cot provided.

I had been given the privilege of sitting in on every meeting that transpired between Malcolm—as he insisted I call him—and his cadre, as well as every tête-à-tête with the government liaisons and representatives from other interested nations. I was his constant shadow. Whenever there was a brief pause between powwows, Malcolm used the time to answer my questions.

This was an incredible opportunity for me to witness a titan of industry in action, but it left me very little time to properly record my observations. So far, I only had from the time I left him at night—usually around ten—until we reconvened at half-past six in the morning, which left me with a mere eight-and-a-half hours for sleeping, personal grooming—which, because of our living situation, was extremely minimal—and doing the job I was there to do.

I had learned many fascinating details about the man, and one fact that couldn't be disputed was he never wasted a single moment of any day.

It was already 10:00 and I hadn't transcribed one-tenth of the scribble I had made of the day's events. If I had trouble deciphering my hieroglyphics now, it would be an impossible task at a later date. I wrapped my wool scarf higher to engulf my chin and persevered.

I was able to last only another ten minutes before I became so stiff from the cold that I couldn't make my fingers work anymore. With tremendous effort, I unbent my legs and did fifty sloppy jumping-jacks. It did little more than make my heart beat brutally.

I pulled my bag out from under the cot and rummaged around for more warm clothing. I unearthed my leather jacket and gratefully pulled it on. I shivered as my scant body heat transferred to the cold acetate lining, shivered until the jacket warmed slightly and radiated heat back to me.

I checked my pockets in the vain hope of finding a pair of gloves, one oversight in my rushed packing efforts that I was truly regretting. What I found instead was my tape recorder—another item I forgot to inventory, something that would be an invaluable help to me when it wasn't possible to take notes.

Delighted by this unexpected stroke of luck, I sat down to see if I was fortunate enough to have a tape as well. There was a ninety-minute cassette inside—wonder of wonders—but as I couldn't remember what I had last used it for, I wasn't sure if it was safe to tape over it or not. I rewound it a pinch and listened:

"Funny, Ricard doesn't have that effect on me." The sound of my own recorded voice threw me. When was this taped?

"Yeah, well, I guess I have a lot of fond memories attached to this drink." Jake's voice sent a fresh wave of shivers all through my body.

"Don't tell me one of your wives was French."

"No, but I spent one of my honeymoons in Europe."

"One of your honeymoons? I don't know how you keep everything straight. So tell me, which honeymoon was it, then?"

"That was wife number…three…Pami, nee Pamela Westerly. We took a three-month honeymoon. How do you like that?"

"Maybe you're in it for the honeymoons."

"We spent a whole month in Paris, and we toyed with the idea of setting up house there, but we didn't."

"Tell me about Pamela, Pami."

"Pami was a pretty nice girl. She and I were married for—"

The tape stopped. For a long moment, I couldn't move. I was stunned by this discovery. The past two-and-a-half weeks had been so action-packed, I had completely forgotten I had secretly recorded the first evening with Jake. I pushed the rewind button and let it go until it stopped.

"Let me rephrase that—do you find you tend to get bored in your relationships

with women?" My voice again. I stopped the tape and racked my brain. Slowly, the memory of that evening revived and I could picture the two of us sitting on the bench, marveling at the star-filled sky. The recorder had been in my pocket the whole time, but so far the sound was slightly muffled but still audible. I pushed play again.

"I guess that would be an obvious conclusion. I'd say I've become bored by certain traits or habits or maybe attitudes, but I don't think I can say I left any of my wives out of boredom. Now, it's true that in most cases—with girlfriends as well as wives—my eye wandered, but not because I had tired of I was with."

"What was it that caused your eye to wander?"

"Oh, a beautiful face, or a certain light in a girl's eyes that made me want to get to know her better. I don't know, just the classic reasons that make anyone stray."

I stopped the tape again. I had been holding my breath, afraid to do anything that would break the spell. Hearing Jake's voice had affected me in a way I hadn't thought possible. I set the recorder down and stared at it. All this time I had had a piece of Jake with me, a conversation with him from that first night together, a preserved and tangible keepsake of a man who defied containment.

I jumped up and grabbed my computer bag and emptied the contents out on the cot. I opened every pocket and hidden compartment, desperately hoping to find another cassette. Nothing. Dispiritedly, I returned every item to its proper storage place.

Before I replaced the bag under the cot, I ejected the tape and put the recorder in with everything else. If I couldn't find a clean tape, I had no use for the recorder. There was no way I was going to risk losing a perfectly preserved glimpse of that man. I stashed the tape in the inside pocket of my jacket for safekeeping.

"And what provoked an interest in Calvin Himes?" Malcolm asked me. We had just finished dinner and were still seated at the rickety camp table with two of his key advisors. This had become the accustomed time for the subject to change positions with the interrogator. It was now his turn to ask the questions and my turn to answer them.

This constituted his daily entertainment on this regimented junket, a time for him to lose himself in something outside the scope of his duty and expertise. Playing the interviewee is not my favorite pastime, but in this case, I was only too happy to oblige, taking into account how fortunate I was to be in the great man's presence and the trouble he had taken to accommodate me.

Malcolm's questions were always respectful and his interest seemed genuine. To be honest, it was quite flattering to have such a powerful and dynamic man take what I had to say so seriously. It was impressive enough that he even remembered my name, when you consider how many important issues the man had on his plate.

"I heard about his arrest while in Arizona working on a piece about the Navajo Nation. He was captured in Tucson and it was a big deal in all the news media. The thing that intrigued me was the fact he had blended so seamlessly into his new life. He had married, had twin sons, and was carrying on as if he had been able to shed his former life as easily as a snake sheds its skin.

"I had heard of other fugitives doing the same thing over the years, so it wasn't the novelty of his actions that caught my attention. I remember seeing his face as they hauled him out of the squad car in front of the county jail. There was a look in his eyes as he faced the cameras that seemed to say he was so hurt by the charges against him. I wanted to know how a man who had killed his wife of ten years, their three children and his mother-in-law could view himself as the victim when apprehended four years later."

"I would imagine most criminals play innocent at the time of arrest, and continue to plead so during trial. It seems that very few criminals ever admit their guilt and waive their right to a trial. What you're describing seems to me to be the signs of a classic sociopath," Malcolm said.

"That's true, of course, but with Calvin I got this feeling I could learn something about the human psyche if I could hear his whole story," I said.

"I don't know why, but I had this feeling from the very first time I saw him that he wasn't merely lacking a conscience. It was because I believed he had committed the crimes and was carrying his guilt somewhere in his psyche that I wanted to speak with him and find out what his life was like after he had killed everyone close to him.

"It was my conclusion that some people have a coping mechanism that can propel them through the most hideous of situations, almost as though they have no awareness of what transpired. I think it is the same for a person who has been victimized by violence or loss. They find a way to detach for the sake of self-preservation, not through a conscious decision to survive and go forward, but through an innate force that can't be controlled."

"I'm sure most of us would see that as an act of free will. Your theory seems awfully convenient where the criminal mind is concerned," Malcolm said.

"I would agree that's the case most of the time, especially when the perpetrator pleads innocent. But when a person acknowledges his guilt upon apprehension and never makes an attempt later to justify or deny his crimes, one would expect to see a look of contrition, not victimization."

"But you never made a case in your article for insanity or emotional instability, which, by the way, I was grateful to see." I had to smile at this comment. "When I first began reading it, I was afraid you were mounting a case for his release, or transfer to a mental facility, which would be as bad as setting him free."

"No, I was never interested in his story because I believed him to be innocent or misunderstood or mentally imbalanced—or even a psychopath, for that matter. I saw him as a man who deliberately killed his family, for whatever reason, and then went off to create a new identity and a new life for himself, as if he had never shot five of his loved ones. How could that innate force be so great, so obscuring that it blocked out the memory of what he had done to his family? How could he not be plagued by those horrific scenes, day in and day out? To me that was inconceivable."

"What specifically did you learn about his behavior that led you to your theory of this 'coping mechanism'?" asked Bill Havers, the man Malcolm had chosen to oversee the construction of his pilot university.

"Well, as is fairly common with family homicides, Calvin, after shooting his mother-in-law—who had the ultimate misfortune of arriving at exactly the wrong time—turned the gun on himself, intending to end his own life as well. The gun misfired, severely injuring his hand.

"He became distraught at his failure to kill himself, and as every minute alone with his dead family made his anguish and self-loathing more intolerable, Calvin ran from his house, frantic to do himself in. He climbed the fence at the end of his street and ran down the embankment to the highway, and straight into oncoming traffic.

"Several motorists managed to swerve and avoid hitting him, but a semi truck hit him straight on. The force of the impact landed him back up on the embankment. The driver of the semi immediately radioed in for help, but it was late at night, pitch black, with very little traffic, and no one was able to find the body."

"You mean, this guy just walked away from being hit by a semi truck?" Douglas Martin asked. He was the man charged with recruiting staff for the university complex, and the fourth member of our dinner party.

"Yes, believe it or not, he did. By this time, Calvin was deranged with guilt and the fear of having to live with the consequences of what he had done. I don't know if that explains how he was able to survive the impact of his collision with the truck, but there had to be some force within him that impelled him forward."

"That's incredible. So what happened after he walked away from the accident?" Bill asked.

"He walked for three days, without stopping to eat or sleep. His home was in McCook, Nebraska, about fifty miles from the Kansas state line. By the time he collapsed, he was in rural northern Kansas. He was found by a farmer, who took him back to his home and cared for him. The farmer, a widower himself, lived all alone in that remote part of the state—no television, newspapers, or anything to keep him informed of news events, except for the weekly arrival of *The Saturday Evening Post.*

"This farmer, John Henderson, let Calvin stay with him until his hand and cracked ribs healed. When Calvin left the farm several weeks later, he was sporting overalls and a beard. From there, he walked and hitchhiked southward, eventually reaching Tucson, where he found work as a janitor at Mercy Hospital. It was there that he met Lonnie Davis, a night-shift nurse, the woman he later married." I took a sip of water while they digested this implausible but true tale.

"You're sure about all his wild claims?" Douglas asked.

"Yes, I verified the incident on the highway with the McCook sheriff's office. There were three calls altogether reporting the man running in traffic and the hit. I tracked down John Henderson, who confirmed that he had found a man on his property in pretty bad shape, who he nursed back to health."

"This farmer didn't think there was anything strange about finding this battered stranger on his land?" Malcolm asked.

"Calvin told Mr. Henderson he had just lost his family and was so overcome with grief, he walked away from his home and his job and never looked back. He told him he had sustained his injuries from a hit-and-run accident while walking along the highway."

"He just tweaked the truth a bit here and there, but I suppose the farmer could relate to his loss," Bill correctly surmised.

"I guess so. To answer your original question in a rather roundabout fashion, what I learned about the natural impulse to press on is this: Calvin had desperately wanted to kill himself after what he had done to his family. After his two failed attempts and three days of continuous walking, he had ended up in a pattern of actions that made having to take responsibility for his deeds unnecessary.

"After enduring mental and emotional exhaustion, not to mention the injuries, he had passed into a realm where his own physical needs dictated his moves. And because the farmer believed him when he said his whole family had died and then had tended to his wounds, it effectively took choosing his future out of his own hands.

"From then on, he allowed himself to be buffeted along, until a new life conveniently fell into place. As long as he focused on what was in front of him and not behind him, he was able to disconnect from his past. When his past knocked on his door in Tucson, the nightmare he had literally walked away from rose up and destroyed his new world."

"That is a bizarre tale. It reminds me of a story by Albert Camus," Douglas said. "Is that the article that garnered your nomination for the Prescott Award?"

"No, she was recognized for her story about a woman infected with AIDS. Her children also have it," Malcolm told him before I could reply.

"Sounds like another fascinating saga," Bill prompted.

"It is," Malcolm answered. "But unfortunately, it will have to wait for another night." He consulted his watch and stood up. "Time to hit the sleeping bags," he said as he stood back and waited for us to file out of the cramped room that served as our mess hall.

"I can't say I'll be sorry to crawl between freshly laundered sheets and lay my weary head on a nice fluffy pillow again," Douglas said fondly.

"Oh, you've gone soft, Doug. You needed this job to make a man out of you again." The three men laughed at this rough witticism, then looked at me in unison. "I'm sorry dear; I'm certainly not implying that we're trying to make a man out of you. How are you holding up under these rustic conditions?" Malcolm asked as the four of us headed down the hall toward the dormitory-style rooms.

"I'm doing fine, although a good bathing is definitely in order. But the cat baths are better than nothing."

"Are you able to sleep all right?"

"I'm so darn tired by the time I lie down, I could have a rock for a pillow and I'd never know the difference." Apparently, Malcolm found this claim amusing. He smiled warmly and patted me gently on the back, as a kind father would do with a favorite child. The two other men smiled and said their goodnights, and the three of them deposited me at my door and continued on to their respective quarters.

I worked steadily for two solid hours, the writing coming easily and well. I could have written much longer, as I had seen and heard so much during the day that I wanted to preserve while it was still clear in my head. But I had reached the point where my body was too fatigued to function properly. I obstinately pressed on until I caught myself nodding off with my fingers still on the keys. I backed up my work and prepared myself for bed.

Maddeningly, though I was so tired it hurt, I couldn't fall asleep once I crawled inside the sleeping bag. My brain was far too wound up to make the switch to sleep. I lay there, staring at the dingy ceiling above me in the glow of the pale moonlight, for thirty minutes or more. I switched on my book light and checked my watch: ten after one.

Nearly panicked by the thought of going the whole night without sleep, I willed my mind to think of sweet, dreamy thoughts that I hoped would lull me into slumber. I flipped through a whole catalog of experiences and feelings before finding anything that gave me the sense of comfort I was craving.

To my surprise, flashbacks of my visit to Oregon were what I envisioned in my mind's eye: scenes of bouncing around in Jake's ramshackle Jeep, of watching him from behind as we covered miles of trails on muleback on his and his neighbors' land, of dancing with him under protest, but secretly enjoying every moment of it.

I scrambled out of the mummy bag and employed the book light as I scavenged for my tape recorder and the cassette I had stashed in my jacket pocket. Securing both, I crawled back into the sleeping bag and turned on the tape where I had left off. I positioned the recorder close to my ear with the volume down low and listened:

"I think of myself as a romantic because it is so easy for me to imagine being with nearly every attractive female I meet. I see her, I look into her eyes, and I immediately find myself thinking 'I want to know this person.' Next thing I know, I'm trying to win her over, even if I've got a wife or girlfriend waiting for me at home. I can't help it—I'm just fascinated by women. It's like a curse, almost."

"A curse? You're cursed because you are unavoidably susceptible to every pretty face that comes along? Oh, that's a good one!"

"You make a good show of being The Ice Princess, but my guess is you've had your share of weak moments when your libido got the best of you." My laugh is harsh and defensive.

"How did you come to that conclusion?"

"You don't much care for it when the tables are turned, do you?"

"So, you're suggesting my momentary lapses are no different than yours, yet you've actually ended marriages over mere temptations, and I'd never do that."

"Then you do know what it's like to be hit by a thunderbolt of lust."

"I don't know about a 'thunderbolt of lust,' but yes, I know what it's like to meet someone and wonder what it would be like to be in his world. But I think it's different with you."

Whether the tape ended or I fell asleep first, I couldn't say. But when I awoke in the gloomy predawn, I was enveloped by the wisps of memories of the last morning at the Buckin' J Ranch. The strong olfactory remembrance of buttery French toast topped with homemade preserves soon gave way to the peculiar aroma of instant eggs mixed with the acrid smell of what passed for coffee in our makeshift camp.

I reluctantly left my cozy thoughts and re-hid my treasures. I washed, in a manner of speaking, dressed and returned to the mess hall for another action-packed day with the world's most ambitious philanthropist.

I was sitting at the dining room table, furiously working on my Malcolm Gray story, when the phone rang. I had been home for a week now, but I was still a long way from being finished with this piece.

Instead of tapering it down into a nice, easily readable article, it seemed all my efforts only made it grow more rangy. I was now crossing out whole paragraphs with a red marker. Having to stop and answer the phone gave me a handy excuse for taking a break.

"Hello?" I said, my eyes still obstinately glued to a pile of papers on my desk.

"Allison!" a cheery voice sang out. I raised my head and stared blankly out the window while my mind tried to put a name to the voice on the line.

"Miriam," I managed to say with comparable enthusiasm as my memory bank of voices and names and names came to my rescue. "How are you? How are you enjoying married life?" I asked.

"I absolutely adore it," she crooned into the phone. "This is by far the most wonderful chapter in my life, that's for sure. We are both just idiotically happy these days. My only regret is that we didn't do it sooner."

"That's great to hear. How was the honeymoon?" I asked as I stood up and stretched, and walked over to our living room window for a change of scenery.

"Oh, Fiji was fantastic! I swear, all either one of us can think about is going back there on our anniversary. It was pure paradise. All we did was eat, drink, and have sex. I think it should be mandatory that all newlyweds honeymoon on a tropical island. I don't think there is a better way to begin married life," she waxed rhapsodically.

I had to chuckle; I had never heard her sound so deliriously happy. I chalked up another one for Happy Marriages. Now there were at least two in the world that I knew of for sure.

"Well, it sounds like the honeymoon is still on," I said. Miriam laughed.

"It is, believe me honey, it is. In fact that's why I'm calling. In the spirit of romance, Bob and I are planning a party to celebrate life and love. It's going to be this Sunday, starting around four. Just good food, good booze, and good friends. Please tell me you and Elliott can make it," she said. I assessed the pile of jumbled papers and wavered.

"Oh Miriam, I don't know about this Sunday. Monday is the deadline for an article I've been beating my brains out over. I honestly can't say at this point if I'll be finished with it by the time of your party."

"Well, it's only Tuesday. You've got five full days to whip it into shape. Knowing you, it's probably much further along than you give yourself credit for. Tell you what—I'll let you get your nose back into your computer, and I'll check in with you on Sunday. How's that?" I started to answer, but she talked right over me.

"I can't wait to see you—we've got so much to catch up on." And with that proclamation, the line went dead.

I shook my head and walked the phone back to its cradle. Miriam Sorenson— excuse me, Miriam Hodges—intoxicated by love. Who would've thought? I had known her for fourteen years and, in my mind, Miriam seemed like the kind of person who was destined to forever bitch about the undeserving louts who continually populated her existence. She was about the most cynical person I had ever met, too hardboiled and distrusting to fall prey to love.

Yet here she was, rambling on about marriage and romance, even throwing a party for "life and love,"—if that didn't beat all. I'd have to be sure to tell Elliott about it. I knew he'd get a kick out of the idea. He'd probably be too involved in his project to want to attend a party, so I didn't have to worry about any pressure on his end.

I would have to remember to screen all calls on Sunday, in order to avoid her aggressive form of persuasion. The woman was positively allergic to the word "no." I poured my fourth cup of coffee for the day and settled back at my makeshift desk and tried to refocus my energy on the task at hand.

The days passed, and at 3:15 a.m. on Sunday, November 16, I finished the final paragraph on *Malcolm Gray: Technology Pioneer Turned World Benefactor*. I was so stiff from having sat there for over six hours straight, I felt like an eighty-year-old woman as I hobbled off to bed. Having unburdened myself of that demanding assignment, I slept like a rock till half-past noon.

When I woke, I felt as though I was coming out of ether or some powerful narcotic. After fifteen minutes of trying to adjust my eyes to the bright sunlight flooding through our bedroom window, I wriggled out of the covers and lurched to the kitchen to make coffee.

Elliott was gone; I knew that would be the case. He was under such intense pressure at work that the only way to keep his sanity was to keep his nose to the grindstone every waking hour.

I had felt enormous stress just trying to write one lousy article, yet he was answerable to an entire city. And now it looked as though this project was going to take anywhere from six months to a year. I was going to have to get used to the idea of spending my Sundays with the funny papers or a good movie.

I had slept so hard it took me a few minutes to fully recall that I was now liberated from my latest professional burden. Slowly I began to smile and even giggle as I realized not only had I finished the article *and* it was good, but I had a whole afternoon of *not* writing ahead of me. I felt like I had been given an incredible gift, as though someone had flung open the door to my cage.

I looked out the window at the lovely cloud-speckled sky, and gauging the chilly temperature by the fiercely undulating patterns of whitecaps on the bay, was thrilled to be basking in the sun's warming rays without the intrusion of the cold, relentless wind. It made me feel as lazy and contented as a cat. I could stretch out right there on the rug and nap all day, if I wished. The day was mine.

After the first cup of strong coffee with plenty of cream, I toasted a bagel and slathered it with cream cheese and jam. After the second cup of coffee with cream and sugar, I worked up enough motivation to take a shower and wash my hair. Oddly rejuvenated and inspired by this fit of grooming, I had a third cup of coffee—black—while I polished my toenails.

By the time I drank a fourth cup of slightly burnt-tasting coffee, I had finished the final proofreading. After a few minor changes, it was as done as it was going to get, and I was wired to the teeth. There was no way I'd be able to lounge around the apartment until Elliott found his way home. I had to get out before I started crawling the walls.

Once again, I had underestimated the effect of too much coffee on the heels of a full-throttle work-a-thon. I had not sufficiently come off my highly regimented routine of nonstop writing, and was far too wound up to sit still for long.

While figuring out what to wear on this windswept day punctuated with moments of intense sunshine, I fell into a full-scale overhaul of my closet. I had just completed the reorganization of my shoes, when the phone rang. Without thinking, I picked it up.

"Hey, did you make the deadline?" Miriam asked, in a rush of words that caught me completely off-guard.

"Yes," I admitted without thinking.

"Great! I can't wait to see you. Elliott's coming too, right?"

"Um, no. Elliott's working"

"Working on a Sunday? That's horrible! Well look, we'll just have to have fun without him. And anytime after four is fine. Hell, you could come over now, if you want. Everything's pretty much done. We'll have a pre-party cocktail and we can catch up. What time is it, anyway? Two-thirty. Yeah, come over now, and we can have a proper chat before everyone else gets here."

"I can't, Miriam," I blurted out.

"You can't what?" she said. Miriam was one of two people in the world who could bend me to their will with a minor change in the inflection of their voice. My mother's maiden aunt was the other.

"I can't come earlier. I'm not ready yet. I just got out of the shower," I lied for emphasis.

"All right, just get here when you can. But don't make us wait for long," she said. I agreed and was about to hang up the phone when I heard her call out.

"I almost forgot to tell you—it's a fancy dress party," she said.

"Fancy dress?"

"Yes, everyone's been told to dress to the nines to show what gorgeous, lucky creatures we are. Wear your prettiest, sexiest outfit. See you in a jiff."

I stood there holding the phone, dumbfounded. By forgetting my previous decision to screen my calls, I had not only been roped into going to a party without Elliott, but I had to run around in broad daylight in formal wear as well. I stared at the contents of my closet and wondered how I had let my beautiful day get away from me.

After trying and rejecting various ensembles for being too dressy or too austere or just plain dull, I came across the outrageously expensive designer blouse I had bought on a whim. I had never worn it, nor could I ever imagine wearing it. In fact, the tag bearing the fifty percent markdown still hung from its haute couture label.

It had been purely an indulgence to purchase it in the first place, and as I held it up in front of me, I wondered if it was too late to return it. But as I turned this way and that in front of the mirror, it once again took my breath away.

It was by far the most gorgeous article of clothing I had ever owned in my life, with the fine lace work embellishing the front of the sheer ivory silk, the long sleeves ending in elaborate cuffs of the same intricate lace, the high collar dipping down to a deep V above the tiny pearl buttons.

What on earth possessed me to buy something I would never be brave enough to wear in public? I asked myself, as I reluctantly hung it back in the closet and resumed the futile search for a more appropriate garment.

On the second pass through, I stopped again at the blouse, this time going as far as trying it on. Instant glamour, drop-dead sex appeal. I had been afraid of that. Wow, no wonder the original price had been as much as a month's take-home pay. It was worth every single cent for the effect it could create on the wearer. But what effect would it have on others? Only one way to find out for sure.

I stared at my reflection in the mirror, asking myself if I could really do this. My answer was yes, and my multi-layer justification was this: I had just finished what was probably the most important piece of writing of my career, my husband would be working the whole day, I had been invited to a fancy dress cocktail party in the middle of a Sunday afternoon, and I had nothing better to do or to wear.

Besides, I deserved some sort of reward for schlepping off to Afghanistan to watch a man spend billions in the bombed-out rock pile. That type of journalistic sacrifice had to be worth something as simple as wearing an extravagant and risqué blouse for a few hours. I undid the buttons and removed my bra. Now I was committed.

After the decisive act of wearing the blouse as it was meant to be worn, the rest of the outfit came together easily. It culminated in plain black skirt, ending a few inches above the knee, black stockings and spiky-heeled pumps. It couldn't have been simpler, or more dramatic.

I marveled at the chic woman in the looking glass as long as I could stand it, then turned my attention to practical matters. I chose my most elegant black coat as an antidote to the cold ride to Miriam's, and arranged for a cab to pick me up.

I scribbled a note for Elliott, in the unlikely event he should make it home before me, stole one more glance at Cinderella in the mirror, and practiced sexy walking as I made my way downstairs to await the cab.

I stayed inside the vestibule as I waited for the taxi, avoiding the howling wind for as long as I could. A gust blew my buttonless coat open as I flew down the steps, and by the way the cab driver was eyeing me in the rearview mirror, I could tell my unexpected attire had made an impression on him.

I covered my exposed legs as best I could and sat back and stared out the window. Let him imagine I'm a high-dollar hooker en route from one john to the next; it wouldn't hurt my feelings any.

This improbable scenario made me laugh and think about the language of clothing. Our world had become so relaxed in its dress standards that to wear anything pretty and elegant was as eye catching as walking around with one's naval exposed would have been in the 1950s. The compulsory uniform of gloves and hats and stockings and ties had been discarded and replaced with flip flops, baggy pants and T-shirts.

Yet look how easy it was to attract attention with an ordinary black skirt, high heels, and a peek of lace. With all the effort that went into body piercing and tattoos, elaborately bad combinations of garments, freaky hair color, and garish makeup, it seemed ironic that it took so little effort to really capture someone's attention.

I smiled smugly at this notion and pondered executing a series of experiments to judge the effect of wearing common finery out in a world full of slobs. What could be learned by the reactions generated by this subtle surprise? There could be an idea here, I thought. Probably as good as my last one, I amended as the cab crossed Steiner and pulled over in the 2500 block of Vallejo.

I could hear the music and gay laughter as soon as I stepped out of the cab, and it intensified as I climbed the stairs and pushed through the front door. I was forced to admit that, as with most of her peculiar notions, Miriam's directive to dress up was uncannily effective.

All around me stood happy, smiling people, decked to the teeth, exuberant in their own splendor, thrilled to death to be attending a matinee party, for no special reason at all. I returned smiles and greetings as I waited for my hostess to come welcome me.

"Here you are, finally!" she cried out as she swept toward me in a swoosh of taffeta and velvet. "Give me your coat," she said as I let her liberate me of my only safeguard. She gasped as I turned around to face her. She stood appraising me head to toe, before dragging me over to her beloved.

"Isn't she divine? Understated, yet totally glamorous," she said to her husband Bob, her gushing remarks creating a fresh wave of attention from those immediately around us.

"Stunning, positively stunning," he concurred, bussing my cheeks affectionately.

"Champagne, darling—or would you like something stronger? Bob's concocted some vile but potent brew. Personally, I'm not man enough to try it. Do you dare?"

"I think I'd better stick with the fizzy stuff," I said, which set Miriam swooshing off. She returned in a flash with my drink and many questions.

"So, what's this I hear about you being nominated for a Prescott? How fabulous! But Sharon tells me you've also just returned from Iran or Pakistan or someplace," Miriam grilled me over the champagne.

"Afghanistan," I corrected her.

"What were you doing in Afghanistan, of all places?" I was about to give her the bare-bones version of my latest assignment when she was called away on an official hostess duty.

Now standing alone and feeling conspicuous, I edged my way over to the fireplace, and not only for the safe haven it provided. From this vantage point, I could scan the living room on one side, and the dining room and kitchen beyond on the other.

As I stood warming my backside and casually observing my fellow partygoers, my eye wandered off to the far corner of the dining room, where a tall man stood conversing with a comely young woman with long blond hair that covered the length of her bare back. My attention was so abstractly focused on her that I had failed to notice the man she was talking to, until, that is, I became aware his stare was fixed on me.

I nearly dropped my glass when I realized it was Jake Sorenson, Miriam's brother, who was now staring at me with his customary ear-to-ear grin. Much to my amazement, my heart flailed rudely in my chest while the room became uncomfortably warm.

It hadn't occurred to me I'd run into Jake again, let alone in my own backyard. He had been on my mind ever since I left Oregon, even when I had been preoccupied with work. Yet, I had not connected a party at Miriam's and a chance encounter with her brother from Oregon.

The crowd shifted and I was relieved of his penetrating gaze. I racked my brain trying to come up with a possible reason for the freshly-shorn Jake to travel to San Francisco. The girl, of course.

Bodies shifted again and my straight view across the dining table was restored, but Jake and the girl were gone. Oddly alarmed, my eyes darted about in a vain attempt to locate him. I was pivoting to scan the living room when Jake appeared behind me.

"Fancy meeting you here."

I spun around slowly, his infectious grin putting me instantly at ease. "Yes, imagine running into a rogue mule breeder in this neighborhood," I said. Jake chuckled and I received another distress message from my heart, though I couldn't make out the exact cause.

"You look extra ravishing today," he said. I barely suppressed the urge to cover my blouse with my arms. I had absolutely no business running around in such a flimsy garment.

"Thank you. You're looking quite ravishing yourself," I said with a weak laugh, then became horribly self-conscious again.

"I've missed you," Jake said.

I looked up at him hesitantly. "Somehow I doubt that."

"It's true. With you gone, I have no one to argue with anymore and the house is so quiet and peaceful," he teased.

"Wouldn't that have more to do with the recent decamping of Lavinia and Jaylynn?" I asked.

"They were minor distractions, not at all major league like you," Jake said.

I couldn't tell if his comments were meant to be insulting or complimentary. "That's because it takes years of training to become as pesky and bothersome as I am." Someone bumped into me and I was forced to move in tighter to Jake. I smiled uncomfortably up at him and he chuckled happily at my unease.

"What brings you down to the big city?" I asked, once the ebb of passing guests retreated and I was able to put a reasonable space between us again. I was half afraid to hear his answer.

"I felt like a change of scene. I had some business to attend to in L.A., and decided to drop in on the newlyweds on the way through."

"So it's only a coincidence you happen to be here today? That explains why you're not all duded up like all the rest of the men." Jake looked around at all the tuxedos and suits.

"No, I'm afraid I've developed an allergy to tuxedos. I seem to break out in a rash of 'I do's' whenever I put one on."

"You'd better be careful—we don't want to get me started on the 'M' word again," I warned him.

"Hey, that reminds me—am I famous yet?"

"Not due to any efforts on my part. I've had to sideline that piece for the time being. I've been out of the country on assignment."

"Well, how about you? Are you famous yet?" I looked at him quizzically.

"The Prescott Award," he reminded me.

"Oh, that. The winners haven't been announced yet, but I won't exactly be famous, even if I do get it," I said.

"I thought there was a lot of prestige attached to that award."

"There is, but that kind of fame is fleeting. It would be a nice thing to print on a jacket cover, if I ever get around to writing a book." Our conversation hit a lull, leaving us standing there awkwardly, neither one of us knowing what else to say.

"Where's…your husband?" Jake asked as he glanced around for sight of him.

"Elliott had to work today."

"On a Sunday?"

"He's got a big project in the works—upgrading the entire ERS telephone linking system for the city of Oakland. He's working nonstop," I said.

Jake started to say something when the blond appeared. I was secretly pleased to find out that she wasn't as young as I had first suspected, or quite as pretty.

"Here you are, Jake—one Jack Daniels on the rocks," the youngish woman said. Jake accepted the cocktail and clinked his glass with her outstretched champagne glass.

"Janna, do you know Allison?" Jake asked her. Janna was so unaware of my existence she had to be prompted to take notice of me.

"How do you do," she said briefly and turned her attention back to Jake.

"Allison's a famous writer and an expert mule rider," Jake informed her. I started to protest, but it wasn't necessary. I was the last person she was interested in.

"Do you really have to leave the city tomorrow?" she asked Jake as Miriam joined us.

"Oh Allison, I'm so glad you had a chance to meet my big brother," she said as she wrapped her arm around Jake.

"We met at your wedding," I reminded her.

"Well, I'm surprised you recognized him after that introduction. Jake showed up at our wedding looking like a Neanderthal," Miriam said for Janna's benefit. "It was quite a shock, I can tell you. You wouldn't have known there was such a handsome face hiding under that scraggly overgrowth," she said as she held his clean-shaven face in her hand.

Jake and I stared at each other. I had never mentioned anything to Miriam about my trip to Oregon, and apparently, neither had he.

I suddenly had the overwhelming urge to flee the party. I didn't know what was making me feel so incredibly edgy, but whatever it was, it made me want to crawl out of my skin. I opened my mouth to make some sort of excuse, but as usual, Miriam cut me off.

"Ann and Andre Alexander have been looking all over for you," she said as she dragged me away to find our mutual friends. "They've been awarded a grant to study the penal system and they'd love to hear about what you observed at Leavenworth." I glanced back at Jake, who was watching me as his new lady friend droned on.

My anxiety died somewhat once I was away from Jake, and I was able to make light conversation without too much difficulty. But when my protective enclave splintered off and left me alone again, I found myself pining for the front door. I was about to slip off to reclaim my coat and sneak away from the party when Bob and Miriam signaled for everyone's attention.

"We want to thank you all for coming here today to help us celebrate our two most important blessings—life and love," Miriam said, holding up her glass in a toast. "To my wonderful husband, Bob, who has shown me how much I was missing before he came into my life," she said, looking at her spouse with such love and devotion in her eyes, I nearly gagged.

They treated us to a nauseatingly convincing kiss, which was more than I could stand. I wove my way through the applause, cheers, and whistles, letting myself out onto the deck and out of earshot of the host and hostess.

Fortunately, the deck was sheltered from the wind and the cool evening air was a refreshing tonic after the thick, syrupy-sweet environment inside. It also boasted great views of the bay and Sausalito beyond, though all that was visible at this hour was a tracery of lights. I drank in the cold air until I felt calm again.

As my head began to clear, I wondered at the instant transformation of my stalwart friend. Was marriage really responsible for the drastic change in Miriam? If so, I hoped for an annulment.

I had a deep fondness for the old Miriam, the crusty, headstrong character who would rather eat nails than trust a man with her affections. There is something fishy about a sudden and dramatic shift in someone's personality, and in this case, I wasn't convinced of the vigorous claims of happiness. It just wasn't natural to lose one's innate cynicism overnight in favor of drippy sentimentality.

I heard the sounds from the interior grow louder and turned around in time to see Jake quietly close the door behind him.

"Mind if I join you?" he asked. I offered him a spot at the railing next to me. "It's not that I don't like your outfit, but I don't think you're adequately dressed to stand out here. If you don't want to go in, will you at least take my jacket?" he asked, slipping it off and putting it around my shoulders before I could answer him.

"I needed some air," I said, pulling the suede jacket closer. "It was getting a little stuffy in there."

"That's one way to put it," Jake said. "I would have said that it was getting a little too surreal in there."

"Does she seem changed to you, too?" I asked as I turned to look at him.

"Only a hundred percent," he confirmed.

"Oh good," I said with relief, "I was beginning to think I was the only one who didn't appreciate the new and improved Miriam."

"I'm not saying I don't like the change in her," Jake hedged, "I'm just saying she's definitely sporting a new attitude."

"Well, just between you and me, I prefer the old, unimproved Miriam."

"Oh really? I thought that you, of all people, would be dancing a jig over her newfound marital bliss," he said.

"Why do you say that?" I replied defensively.

"You're the big 'until death do us part' advocate, aren't you?"

"Do you really want to pick up those swords again?" I asked.

"Hey, I always thought of our talks as friendly debates," he said. I could tell by his sly smile he was trying to egg me on.

"I thought about you the other day," I said, rejecting his bait and offering him some of my own.

"Really? I'm flattered."

"I met a woman on a flight from Hong Kong who had recently left her fifth husband. She had to be my age, give or take a few years. I'd say that in less than a decade she'll be on her way to beating your record for the most often divorced."

"I doubt that I hold the record for divorces," he said.

"Oh, don't be so modest," I said. Jake turned around and braced his elbows on the railing.

"Still very touchy about the subject, I see. But if you're so offended by divorce, why are you so negative about Miriam's happy marriage?" he asked. "Seems like you are as contemptuous of good marriages as you are of the bad ones," he said.

"I am not," I said strongly. "I'm thrilled to death for Miriam and Bob. I just happen to find that kind of early optimism a tad artificial and maybe a little desperate, that's all. It makes me worry they might feel as though they have to keep up all the positive rhetoric or the harsh reality will start to set in."

"What harsh reality would that be?"

"Uh…" I tried to backpedal, but I couldn't think what it was I had been re-ferring to.

"You mean the reality that they only have a fifty percent chance of making a go of it?" Jake asked, delighted to have trapped me with my own words. "How's your marriage, by the way?"

I laughed at his amusing tactic. "My marriage is perfect, thank you."

"Isn't that lovely," he said. "I have to say I'm surprised to hear you say that."

"Why, pray tell?"

"Oh nothing. I'm sure two workaholics can happily cohabitate, though I would imagine there's not much room for anything else."

I bit my lip to keep from smiling at this jab. "Elliott and I couldn't be more in love," I told him.

"Don't sell yourself so short," he replied.

"How 'bout we change the subject," I suggested as my temper threat-ened to erupt.

"Fine with me. Ridden any good mules lately?" he asked after a meaningful pause. I laughed despite myself.

"No, not many mules around these parts."

"That's too bad," he said. "I suppose you'll have to make the trek back up to my place whenever you get a hankering to ride a good animal."

"That would be fun," I said, softening as I recalled our trail rides together. "I think about that experience all the time, especially when I'm stuck doing something I'd rather not. Those memories are like an escape for me."

"You're welcome up there anytime. *Mis mulas son tus mulas.*"

"Thank you. I guess I better let you have your jacket back so you don't freeze to death," I said, deciding it was time to go rejoin the party. As we reached the door, Jake stopped me before I went in.

"Ali, I meant what I said earlier."

"What was that?" I asked warily.

"I really have missed you." The sincerity of his words stopped me short. I scanned his face for any signs that he was putting me on and found none. Sud-denly, the door flew open and out popped Rapunzel, breaking whatever mood had left us speechless.

"There you are! I've been looking all over for you," she exclaimed. "Why are you out here—it's freezing!"

"We were just coming in," I said, slipping off Jake's jacket and handing it back to him. "Thanks for the loan. I hope I run into you again sometime," I said, leaving Jake and his new friend before he could say or do anything.

Luckily, Miriam was too blissed-out to take offense at my early departure, though she absolutely insisted I share a cab with another couple who had to get home to relieve their sitter. We rode together to their place on Leavenworth, between Pine and California, then instead of having the cabbie take me home, I had him drop me off in North Beach, in front of one of the many Italian cafés.

I still felt conspicuous in my attire, but at least night had fallen and I didn't look so out of place now. The truth was, I wasn't ready to go home and sit by myself. At the risk of looking like either an on-duty call girl or an eager woman who had been stood up by her date, I chose one of the restaurants that had a separate bar and perched myself on a stool.

As I waited for the bartender, I tried to figure out what sort of drink to order when one doesn't really want to be drinking in the first place. I spied a bottle of Ricard just as the bartender approached, but stopped myself just in the nick of time.

"I'll have a glass of red wine," I said.

"Merlot, Sangiovese, Pinot Noir, Cabernet…?"

"Pinot's fine."

"Sanford, Babcock, Whitcraft, Au Bon Climat?"

"Uh… Sanford sounds fine." The bartender filled a glass halfway and placed it in front of me. I had a sip and cautiously took in the sights around me. It was warm in the bar, but I was reluctant to take off my coat. It really wouldn't do to be sitting in a hip nightspot all by myself wearing a wisp of a blouse. I could just about imagine what my friends would think if any of them saw me like that.

No, it was all wrong to be alone in a bar on a Sunday night while Elliot slaved away at the office. I slid a twenty-dollar bill under my glass and made my exit.

The wind slapped me square in the face as I pushed through the front door. I received this rude greeting as a commentary on my strange behavior. I turned my back on it and proceeded down Columbus, veering to the right at Green. I stayed on the right side of the street, the two-and-three story housing structures acting as a windbreaker as I zigzagged my way up toward Coit Tower, the landmark that loomed over our building like a protective beacon.

By the time I reached the top, I had become impervious to the brutal wind, walking with my coat brazenly open to enjoy its refreshing effects. I paused at the summit only long enough to catch my breath before descending the two blocks to our street, slowly mincing my way downhill in my downhill shoes.

I had a split-second hope as I unlocked our front door that Elliott would already be there waiting for me, but I was quickly disabused of that notion. I had left in the afternoon as Cinderella and that was how I returned, minus the hope of the glass slipper to change my future.

I slipped out of my party finery, wistfully tucking the sublimely beautiful blouse out of sight. I pulled on sweats and made a halfhearted attempt to find something worth eating in the fridge. Failing there, I searched the pantry and settled for a jar of applesauce, of which I ate three-quarters.

At nine-thirty, I forfeited the idea of waiting up for Elliott and got ready for bed. I was reading when I heard him unlock the front door, but instead of getting out of bed to greet him, I switched off the light and feigned sleep when he entered the room.

He came over to my side of the bed and sat down next to me for a couple of minutes before slowly removing his clothes. Part of me wanted to get up and listen to him recount the trials of his day, to say encouraging words and share in his angst, but I remained stubbornly still until he switched off his light.

When I could tell by his rhythmic breathing he was safely asleep, I peeled back the covers and crept into the living room to stare out the window. I knew somewhere up there the sky was littered with stars, but I couldn't see them over our own urban glow. I wondered how Jake felt about abandoning his celestial wonderland whenever he ventured away from the ranch. And I wondered at the change in myself since my visit there.

How ironic it seemed that the man who I had once treated as a joker was now the only soul I cared to confide in. Yet, when I had an unexpected opportunity, I preferred to hide my real thoughts behind a mask.

But that was all right, I told myself, for really, what would I have said to him, anyway? That I was so proud of my article on Malcolm Gray and nervous about the announcement of the Prescott Award winners? That Elliott had not come home before seven-thirty even one night since I got back from Oregon, and I wasn't sure what being happily married meant anymore? That I had played our secretly-recorded conversation over and over to the point that I knew it by heart?

No, I wouldn't have said any of it. Instead, Jake would travel on to L.A. or wherever, thinking of me—if he did at all—as a snot-nosed brat, blind to her own faults and acutely aware of other's. If I had known he would be there today, would I have been able to show him a better side of myself? Or would I have avoided our meeting altogether? Did speculating make any difference?

I drew the drapes and sat in the dark for an hour or so, until my neck sagged under the weight of my head and my thoughts took on the scrambled consistency of a dream. Only then could I bring myself to get back under the covers and lie next to my sleeping husband.

Eighteen

I sat across the desk from Judith as she read my completed article on Malcolm Gray for a second time. I could tell by her expression she was pleased with my work, and I was able to guess which passages she liked particularly well.

"Excellent. Very astute and insightful," she said as she tapped the pages together on her desk. "I think you did a good job challenging the altruistic tone of his investment in Afghanistan without coming across as critical."

"I liked his answer, too—that if he could get computers from his rivals below his own costs, he'd be happy to use them instead," I paraphrased for her.

"Yeah, that's a good line. I also liked the way he answered your hypothetical question regarding training America's underprivileged for jobs in technical support," Judith said, flipping through the pages to find that remark.

"'There are already many social programs at work in a country where capitalism and democracy have flourished for over two centuries. Americans of all economic backgrounds have greater freedoms and opportunities from the day they are born than most Afghans will have in a lifetime. If the people of Afghanistan can cope with war, famine, and oppression as their daily routine and still remain hopeful, think of how inherently easier it should be for any American to persevere and succeed.'" Judith looked at me over the top of her glasses. "Pretty forthright statement," she said.

"Yep, that ought to draw some fire from his detractors, and heaps of mail to us," I agreed.

"I guess he doesn't care."

"No, and why should he? Who does he have to answer to? He has put more money back into the system than he's currently worth, and as long as Ensign Technologies continues to produce the world's most sought after computers, I imagine he'll continue to do so. He's the greatest philanthropist in history and his stockholders love him. That's no easy trick."

"You're right about that. Well, let me e-mail this to Jerome so he can get started on it," Judith was saying when her assistant, Jonathan Doyle, poked his head in the door.

"They're about to announce the award for journalism."

"Oh, thanks for reminding me, Jonathan. What channel?"

"Twenty-three." Judith turned on the small television sitting on the credenza behind her and scooted out of the way so we could see it too.

"They just announced the winner for the children's lit prize," Jonathan said. "Our category is coming up next, I think."

The three of us stared at the TV, willing the speaker to get on with it. I think I was probably less hopeful than the other two, since it was my third nomination for this honor. After the first two losses, I had convinced myself it was redundant to win, as there seemed nearly as much hoopla on the day nominations were announced as on the day they broadcast the winners.

Besides, the public at large lost sight of these acknowledgments remarkably fast. Frankly, losing twice was plenty humiliation for one lifetime. I think I would have preferred that *Savoir-Faire* nominate someone else if they were so gung-ho on winning acclaim that way.

"And the Prescott Award for Highest Journalistic Achievement goes to Allison Tyler-Wilcox for her article entitled *One Mother's Love*."

Judith jumped out of her chair, hands clapping furiously like an overjoyed child. Jonathan, all a-twitter, awkwardly embraced me as I sat rigid as a stone, before throwing his arms around his boss.

"I knew you were going to win this one," Judith claimed as she wagged a knowing finger at me. "How could you not? Everybody knows you should have won for the Calvin Himes story. If they had passed you up for this, everyone would've known for sure the whole thing is a farce," she said.

"Does that mean my competition figures I won only because I lost twice before? Everyone who loses must feel like it's all a political charade," I said.

Judith looked at me as if I had lost my mind. "You just won the Prescott Award, for God's sake! Don't act like a sore winner. This is the biggest moment of your career, so far. Wait till the January issue hits the stands! Talk about a one-two punch. The timing on this couldn't have been better. This is amazing!"

The way Judith was carrying on, you would have thought she were the recipient. She stopped her excited ranting and fixed me with a puzzled gaze.

"Jonathan, let me know who calls for interviews. We'll need to cover as many bases as we can before the awards ceremony," she said, signaling for her assistant to make himself scarce. Jonathan took the hint.

"What is it?" Judith asked as she seated herself on the corner of her desk. "Are you in shock?" I stared at her blankly. "Don't tell me you've taken on some cockeyed notion that awards of this nature are bogus. Let me make it perfectly clear that no such stance will be taken by a *Savoir-Faire* staffer," she threatened unnecessarily. I let out a deep sigh and stood up.

"Don't worry, Judith. I'm not harboring any communistic ideals. I suppose I am in shock. I hadn't really prepared myself for winning. I've been so busy with everything that's been happening lately, I guess I sort of lost track of the whole thing." I leaned against the back of the chair and regarded her as she tried to discern what my problem was.

"What's bothering you?"

"Nothing," I said, as I turned away from her to scrutinize the photos on her wall.

"Hogwash. I want to know what it is—as your friend, not your editor."

I faced her and shook my head. "I don't know what's wrong with me. I should be floating on a cloud right now. I've just won the biggest prize for my field and have completed the piece that will probably be my greatest credit, and yet I feel like I'm not in control of myself anymore."

"How do you mean?" Judith asked, concern showing itself on her crinkled brow. I shrugged and began to pace.

"I know this is going to sound ludicrous, but I don't know if my judgment is reliable enough to allow me to continue on as a journalist."

Judith stared at me open-mouthed before braying disdainfully. "You're putting me on, right? You're so deliriously happy, you're trying to give me a heart attack, is that it? The magazine we've slaved for years to bring into the mainstream just got a huge injection of positive publicity—thanks to your writing and my expert guidance—so I don't need you developing some sort of complex on me. This is an important time for us. We've got to seize the momentum and take it as far as we can," she raved as she worried a groove into her carpet.

"What part of winning the Prescott Award makes you doubt your...your judgment? Didn't I just finish reading the best piece you've written so far? Allison, what the hell are you talking about?"

I twisted a loose thread on the back of the chair and avoided looking at her. "I'm feeling confused by the simplest things these days," I said.

"Like what, for example?"

"Like the idea for an article on marriage and divorce that I couldn't manage to get a handle on."

"So what? So one idea in ten doesn't pan out—big deal. Most of your hunches are dead on. This time you got attracted to something that lacked any real potential as a story. I personally never understood what you were so intrigued by. The world's full of failed marriages—it's just a byproduct of our disposable society. But hey, no harm done. On to the next story," Judith said encouragingly.

"But that's the problem, Judith. I'm still stuck on the belief that there's some-thing important to be learned by dissecting the motives of these people who gladly sail from one doomed marriage to the next. I can't get the concept out of my head," I confessed. Judith leveled her eyes at me.

"Okay," she said. "That's fine. Has this idea taken on a more specific definition, by any chance?"

"Actually, I think I've got a different angle on it."

"Okay, good. Let's hear it," she said as she reseated herself cautiously be-hind her desk.

"I met this woman on the flight from Hong Kong," I began as I took a seat across from her, "who was fleeing her fifth marriage. This woman couldn't have been much older than me. But the thing that struck me about her was her methodology. She marries men as a way to advance her way through the various stages of her life," I said with emphasis. Judith looked at me expectantly.

"Some women do," Judith stated calmly. "But go on. I assume you're going to tie this in with something."

"I was thinking we could profile four or five different individuals and the distinct patterns their successive marriages create, explore the specific reasons they have for getting married and what type of mates they seek out, and then contrast their stories with each other.

"We could use this Helen Chamberlain as the woman who plans to amass a lifetime of experiences and wealth through a long parade of willing spouses, and the guy I interviewed here who thought himself such a prize, he felt compelled to ration out the privilege of being married to him, one woman at a time.

"Then we could pair those with the woman who went from one abusive marriage after the other in the desperate hope of finding someone who would love her forever.

And then there's the mule breeder in Oregon, who's hooked on romance and gets so carried away, he's rushed into seven marriages that had no chance of working."

I sat back, satisfied I had made my case. Unfortunately, I could tell Judith didn't share my vision. She remained silent while she carefully chose her words.

"Unlike you, I trust your judgment. So much so, I'm willing to let you pursue this new angle, for what it's worth, with the proviso that should I need to put you on another story, you'll table your piece, like you did when I assigned you the Malcolm Gray interview.

"But I want you to agree that, if at the end of six months you haven't made a reasonable, compelling case for this idea, you'll give it up." After her pledge of trusting my judgment, I was rather taken aback by the limitations she was placing on me.

"Alright, fine. I appreciate it," I said.

"Be warned—I'm in hot pursuit of another interview that'll be even more of a coup than Malcolm Gray."

"Really?"

"Yes, but I can't say any more right now. But until I have it all firmed up, put your best spin on this idea of yours and we'll see what you come up with. In fact, consider yourself on holiday for the next couple of weeks. Don't even come in to the office during that time. Just throw yourself into writing, sleeping, or getting away for a while. You've more than earned a nice break."

"Thanks, Judith."

She nodded and took a checkbook out of her drawer. "And while you're off duty, I want you to find yourself something dazzling to wear to the award's ceremony next month." She tore out a check and handed it to me.

"You can't be serious," I said as I read the amount. "This rag can't afford to spend this kind of money on a dress."

"It can this time out. Hey, the board of directors is going to be beside themselves over this award. They've been tickled to be backing a magazine that has the elitist appeal of mostly being read by their fellow highbrows. But now they're going to have a taste of worldwide recognition, which I guarantee they're going to eat up.

"So, you certainly don't want to tarnish their glory by showing up in New York in something off the sales rack at Nordstrom, do you?" I smiled at her outlandish logic and tucked the check for twenty-five hundred dollars into my shoulder bag.

"Thanks. I'll try to make the directors proud," I said, standing up to take my leave.

"You've made us all proud. Try not to act like a Gloomy Gus on your way out. I don't want you to confuse the rest of the staff."

As soon as I hit the daylight, the reality of winning the Prescott Award hit me like an electrical shock. I was so thrilled by this delayed realization I ducked into the St. Francis lobby and scurried off to a seldom-used ladies' room, where I allowed myself a full-scale fit.

Gratefully, I had the place to myself, so there was no one to witness my celebratory dance. I hollered at myself in the mirror, breaking into a fit of giggles while I tried to decide who to call first.

I hit the speed dial number for Elliott's private line and got his voicemail. I hung up and dialed his cell phone, with the same result. I then tried CenCon's main number and had him paged. After waiting impatiently for three or four minutes, one of his assistants got on the phone and told me Elliott was in a meeting.

I told the assistant to interrupt him as I had an urgent message to give him. Reluctantly, he agreed and I listened to the entire loop of CenCon's promotional spiel while I waited for Elliott to get on the line.

"Is something wrong?" he asked without preamble.

"No, nothing's wrong—"

"I was in a very important conference—"

"I know. But I have some news I couldn't wait to tell you."

"Are you pregnant?" he asked after a brief pause. This was the second time in recent weeks he had asked that question. It only goes to show how distracted I was by winning the Prescott that I failed to place any significance on this seemingly incongruent inquiry.

"No, I'm not pregnant. I just wanted you to be the first to know that the Prescott Awards have been announced and your wife is now the latest recipient for the Award for Outstanding Journalism," I said, barely able to contain my excitement.

"Wow. That's fantastic. Looks like they finally figured out how talented you are. Well, good news. Um, I've got to get back to the meeting. I'm glad you called me. Congratulations!" he said.

"Elliott—" I called out before he hung up.

"Yeah?"

"Maybe we could go out and celebrate tonight."

"Sure, you bet. Okay, got to go. Love you."

"I love you, too," I said to the dial tone.

Only momentarily thrown off kilter by the abbreviated conversation with Elliott, I dialed my parents' number and told them the good news. I repeated this telephonic news flash five or six times, until I was satisfied all my key friends and family would get the word and pass it along.

By the time I finished, I was spent by excitement and calm enough to sit and plot my next move. I was right on Union Square, but I couldn't concentrate sufficiently to undertake the arduous task of finding the perfect garment for the awards banquet.

Instead, I settled for meandering aimlessly down Post to Kearny, where I hailed a cab and was dropped off at the Fog City Diner. I had a seat at the counter and ate a dozen oysters and silently toasted my triumph with a glass of champagne. After this modest indulgence, I walked the four uphill blocks home.

After about an hour, the great anticlimax began to set in. In an effort to ward off the trepidation of facing two weeks without office or husband to distract me, I diligently put all my notes in order for my unofficial assignment. I knew what Judith was actually telling me when she gave me carte blanche with caveats: I had only two weeks to make something of this nonstarter idea of mine, or I should just forget about it.

That six-month deal was merely for show; I had no doubt Judith would have another assignment waiting for me when I showed up at the office on December 10th, and she would continue to bombard me with work so I'd never have a chance to revisit this colossal waste of time. The thought of defying her by creating a piece even she would have to applaud sent a new wave of enthusiasm and determination coursing through my veins.

I worked straight through till 6:00 before calling it quits for the day. What I had to show for my efforts was a fairly enthralling snapshot of the sanguine husband hunter I had met on the plane.

Now, if I could only flesh out three or four more portraits as vivid as Helen Chamberlain's, and then link them with a theme that applied to all of them, I would have something. I felt sure of it.

But now it was time to rest on my laurels, at least for one evening. Elliott had agreed to take me out to celebrate, so I didn't need to think about making or procuring dinner. But I was antsy to get out and do something.

I was contemplating popping out for a quick walk around the neighborhood when the phone rang. It was my brother. Having heard of my honor through the family grapevine, he called with his congratulations.

As soon as I hung up with him, the phone rang again, and it continued as friends and relatives retrieved my excited messages and called to congratulate me. I got off the last call around seven-thirty and it belatedly occurred to me I hadn't heard a peep out of Elliott yet. I dialed his cell phone and reached him as he crept along the freeway toward home.

"Hey there—I haven't forgotten," he said as he answered the phone. "I think there must be an accident up ahead somewhere."

"I knew you hadn't forgotten. I was only wondering if I should meet you someplace so you don't have to come all the way home first."

"No, I'd really like to take a shower and maybe relax for a bit before we go out. I feel thrashed."

"Well, if you'd rather stay home—"

"No, no. We're definitely going out to celebrate in style. My wife's just been awarded the Prescott—you can't do much better than that. I'll be there in twenty minutes, at the very most. You decide where you want to go. The sky's the limit."

Since it was my choice, I decided to book a table at a place we had always wanted to try, The Mandarin Garden. I knew it was fancy and expensive, and that appealed to my desire for indulgence. I also imagined its interior to be exotic and its food to be uncommonly good. I made the reservation for 9:00, giving Elliott plenty of time to gear up for a little fun.

Before we arrived at the restaurant, I could already sense the evening was too forced to legitimately be considered fun. Even though Elliott was trying his best to be lively and vivacious, I knew he would have much preferred to be face down in his pillow. Because of the late hour and the night of the week, the restaurant was nearly deserted when we arrived, which didn't exactly bode for a scintillating experience.

The atmosphere at our table became increasingly stifled as the few remaining diners dwindled to one other couple besides us. Whether it was due to a desire to impress us with their attentive service or because the staff was trying to get us out of there as soon as possible, we seemed to be continually surrounded by waiters pouring water or wine, serving courses or removing plates, or simply checking on our needs.

Because of the constant interruptions, Elliott and I parceled out our conversations in small doses that could be easily abandoned when someone drew near. It wasn't like us to act so reserved, but we could hear every word the other couple uttered; we were careful to keep our voices down and our topics general. After our final courses were served and the other couple departed, we finally felt more inclined to speak openly.

"A toast to the best journalist alive today," Elliott proposed grandly.

"That's a gross overstatement, but I'll accept your toast anyway," I said, tapping my glass against his.

"I'm very proud of you," he said. I was touched.

"Thank you, Elliott. I'm a little proud of me, too." Feeling more relaxed, we began to honestly enjoy ourselves and the food, which was really good. It was starting to feel more like a celebration.

"Another rough day at the office today?" I asked, helping myself to second minced quail-stuffed lettuce leaf.

"Challenging, as usual. I swear, not a day goes by without some new wrinkle emerging."

"What was it today?"

"Oh, it had to do with the specs for the routing cables we planned to use for wiring the new system. We naturally assumed we'd be using the standard coaxial cables, but we found out the new switching units we ordered take a much wider cable."

"Oh no," I sympathized. "Can you use some kind of fitting to bridge the two?"

"I wish it were that easy. It's just too technical to explain." I could feel Elliott tense as he relived the aggravation.

"Hey, I should've never mentioned work. This is supposed to be a night of celebration," I said.

"It's alright, I don't mind. The way I look at this project is no matter how much I have to sacrifice, it's going to be worth it. I may have to work like a dog for the next ten or twelve months, but the only way they can reward me for executing a project this big—besides a fat bonus—is to make me a vice president."

"Really? I didn't realize you were in line for that kind of move up."

"Oh yeah. It's the only reason I'm doing this. A year from now, I'll be working regular hours, bringing in three times what I'm making now, and you'll be able to quit work and start raising our family."

I blinked hard and wondered if there was something wrong with the acoustics. The way he was smiling at me while cheerfully chomping on his food convinced me I hadn't heard him wrong.

So, that's why he'd been so quick to jump to the assumption I was pregnant every time I had something important to tell him. I tried to smile back with the same heartfelt joy, but my efforts fell short.

"Something wrong?" he asked.

"No…nothing's wrong…"

"What is it?" he asked, wiping hoisin sauce from the corners of his mouth.

"I didn't realize you were mentally gearing up for this huge lifestyle change. I mean, if you're all of a sudden in such a big hurry to have kids, you should clue me in on it, especially since I'm the one whose job it'll be to pop 'em out," I said, reaching for my wine glass in a jerky, anxious lunge.

"Where the hell did that attitude come from? You act as though we've never discussed this—"

"I'm racking my brain trying to remember saying I'm ready to have children."

"We've always said that once we were well established in our careers and making enough to live comfortably—"

"Yeah, but—"

"Well, that time is fast approaching. *I'm* paving the way so you can quit work and take care of our kids."

"But Elliott, I love my work. I'm not ready to stop. I'm not ready to cut short a career that is finally taking off after thirteen years of beating down doors and wrangling interviews and working for nearly nothing. I'm finally on the brink of having the type of career I've always dreamed of. Why would you think I'd want to pull out right after winning the Prescott? My career is just beginning."

Elliott paused mid-bite to glare at me. "So, when do you'll think you'll be ready to start a family?"

"I—"

"Five or ten years from now? You seem to be forgetting that the years are creeping up on you. You can keep telling yourself 'one more year, then I'll be ready,' but what if by the time you get your head around the idea, your body says, 'Sorry, time's up'? Look at the kind of crap John and Rebecca Standish have put themselves through trying to conceive, and she's only forty-one," Elliott said. I wiped my mouth and laid the napkin on the table.

"We don't know that the reason she can't get pregnant has anything to do with waiting too long," I maintained, allowing myself to be sidetracked from the main issue. Elliott gave me a condescending snort.

"Look, if you're really knocking yourself out, working seven days a week, fourteen hours a day just so we can start producing children, then we need to talk. You may be ready, but if you've been assuming I'm ready to stop working and stay home to change diapers, then you've assumed wrong."

The waiters approached and we clammed up as they gathered all the plates and cleared away the remnants of our meal. Elliott asked for the check and we didn't dare speak to each other until we were back in the car.

The ride home consisted of retracing the same turf, with Elliott steadfastly insisting I could resume my job when the kids (plural) were old enough, and me telling him I simply wasn't ready for that kind of change in my life. This was one thing I was abundantly sure of, now that the issue had been forced on me.

Had Elliott and I approached the subject on a less combative, hypothetical basis, I may have hemmed and hawed and admitted to wanting to start a family in a year or two. But having it decided for me, without my input, made me realize I was nowhere near the point of wanting to abandon my career and my freedom, nor was I likely to be anytime soon.

I won't recount every ugly argument presented by either side; suffice it to say I put the brakes on the conversation when Elliott began to cite testimonials from my own parents regarding their fond wish of having a little Allison or Elliott to bounce on their knees.

The anger and resentment I felt by the end of the evening caused me to drag a pillow and blanket out to the sofa, where I spent a miserable night grinding my teeth, thoroughly put out that my triumphant day had been spoiled, broadsided by something I hadn't even seen coming.

Nineteen

When I awoke the next morning, I was alone. After our divergent views regarding family planning had made themselves known, I was glad not to face Elliott. I had my own bruised feelings to attend to, and I was still in no mood to consider that he had any justifiable arguments. I made it through mid-morning nursing the belief I was the injured party in the previous night's war of words, and the only possible solution was for him to come to his senses and apologize.

It was around ten-thirty when I started to be plagued by doubts. Was I being the unreasonable one here? Was I conveniently forgetting our pledge to start a family just as soon as we were financially stable? I couldn't for the life of me remember making such a vow.

I could imagine a conversation wherein I agreed to start *thinking* about having children once we reached a certain level of comfort. I could also imagine how in Elliott's mind that might translate to what he now claimed was our agreed upon agenda of dual child car seats in the back of the family Volvo.

By noon, I had given up trying to work while my brain stubbornly played the "he said, she said" game. I grabbed a jacket and scarf and headed downtown. It didn't much matter how I occupied my time, so long as I was able to forget about our stalemate. I was up for anything that might stave off a full-scale panic attack. I still had thirteen of my vacation days remaining, so I could waste my time any way I saw fit.

It was a clear, sunny day, cool when the wind and shade combined. I walked over the hill and back down into North Beach, stopping at Luigi's for a salad and pizza.

Fortified, I cruised up Columbus, detouring to City Lights Bookstore before cutting over to Grant, taking the shortcut to Union Square through Chinatown. The change of scenery had done wonders for my state of mind, and before long I had completely put the incident out of my head.

I stopped in at the French coffee house on Sutter and had an espresso before continuing on. I poked my head in some of the expensive boutiques along the way, idly sifting through the wares with nothing particular in mind.

It was as I was nearing Saks that I remembered my charge to find something fitting for the awards ceremony. With the amount of money Judith had given me, I could afford to shop almost anywhere.

Curious about what about I might find, I pushed through the heavy glass doors and rode the escalators to the third floor, where one dazzling designer label mingled with the next, all inviting the shopper to try them on and be transformed, let the price tag be damned.

It was an overwhelming experience, at first, and I ended up circling the floor twice before venturing to try on a few things. I had found some gorgeous pieces, but none made it past the fitting rooms.

Slightly discouraged but still hopeful, I left Saks and angled around the square to Neiman-Marcus.

It turned out to be a good day for shopping. I found a dress that was perfect for almost any occasion, and certainly suitable for a stuffy awards banquet. I swore to myself I wouldn't buy anything black, but it was one of those resolutions that simply couldn't stand up to the argument that black is slimming, elegant, timeless, and happens to look good on almost all of us.

I tucked the alterations stub for the long-sleeved gown with the deep V in the back into my wallet and went across the street to Macy's to find some appropriate footwear. No one would be looking at my feet, and if they did, they weren't going to care that I spent one hundred dollars instead of five on a pair of shoes.

If I worked this right, I would have plenty left over to buy something really fun, like the evening bag that Helen had admired and put back on the counter. If I was going to spend this much money, I was going to do it where it would get the most notice.

By the time I made it back home, I had acquired new shoes, bag, and silk wrap to go with my new dress, and I still had money left over. Unfortunately, that kind of thrill only carries so far when there are more serious matters weighing on one's mind. In this situation, concerns about the future of my marriage and career needled me almost as soon as I put my new spoils away for safekeeping.

Of course, the irony was not lost on me that I was suffering doubts about my marriage, after making such a big deal out of other people's failures. Added to that was the fear my career should be in question because, one, my husband wanted me to give it up and, two, my own headstrong notions of probing the conundrum of marriage and divorce had led both my editor and me to question my instincts. Why should it be that I was suddenly so conflicted when on the surface everything was going so well?

It was easy to tell myself I was indulging in worry and the only solution was to bury my head in work. But after three days of steady progress, I had once again hit a roadblock. Interestingly, neither Elliott nor I dared broach the topic of children and forced retirement during the brief intervals that we actually saw one another, so it no longer seemed a pressing problem.

The immediate issue I faced was how to profile Jake. I had sorted out the other three subjects to my satisfaction, but when it came to boiling Jake down to an essence, I found the fact he had been divorced seven times simply a footnote to his bigger-than-life personality.

If I focused on his successive failures in the marriage arena, I was left with a profile that was more of a caricature than an actual portrait of the man. Whereas it had been possible to create reasonable thumbnail sketches of Helen Chamberlain, Volunteer Number One, and Volunteer Number Five without digging past the superficial layer, Jake seemed to defy pigeonholing.

When I thought of Jake, I envisioned the way he handled his adoring mules and the ruggedly beautiful ranch that had become a reflection of his life, and of the long rides we had taken on it together. I thought of tangoing and exotic cocktails and how freely he lived; of the stars in the heavens and his philosophy honed by six decades of living and loving, however unwisely. Ultimately, what I remembered about Jake was how challenged yet happy I had felt in his company.

I suppose for all of us there comes a time when we discover the truth about our own feelings. In my case, it had become impossible to hide behind the façade of my 'perfect' marriage anymore now that Elliott was rocking the boat with his bothersome assumptions. And without that belief to blind me to the truth, what was staring me in the face in the most unrelenting fashion was my feelings for Jake.

Of all the people I had come across in my lifetime, Jake was the one person who most captivated me. I found myself carrying on imaginary conversations with him, or debates, as was usually the case. Without my realizing it, he had become the one person I would most prefer to spend time with. I honestly enjoyed being me more when I was with him.

So, where did this leave Elliott? It was a question I now pondered, with less than reassuring results. Then again, I was talking about real feelings, and shocking revelations are best absorbed gradually, or shoved under the carpet and ignored altogether.

Besides, I knew this was simply a knee-jerk reaction to our disagreement over children. Jake seemed more appealing because he was not the one who wanted me to give up my career—my identity, essentially.

But I loved Elliott; he was my husband, for better or for worse. And Jake was a wild, unpredictable man, decades older than me. A friend. He was a favorite friend, someone I could look forward to having a long, fulfilling acquaintance with for years to come. Oh sure. That was nothing but a lovely dream. How would I ever wangle a trip to eastern Oregon if I had babies to take care of?

While lying awake that night, a solution to one of my various conundrums occurred to me that had a two-fold benefit. I had yet to make contact with the two ex-wives Jake suggested I call. By doing so, I could bring the focus of my profile of him back to the subject at hand, and at the same time I could reacquaint myself with all the reasons a woman with any brains would put up a barrier against Jake's questionable charms. I proceeded with this plan first thing the next morning.

With the background Jake had given me on these two women, I decided Katherine, wife number two, would be the most approachable. I had only to mention Jake's name and she became instantly accommodating. Since she lived less than an hour from the city, she suggested that we meet in person. I was delighted and grateful for the offer.

The following morning I rented a car and drove to Walnut Creek. I had no trouble locating the café Katherine chose for our assignation, nor was it difficult to spot her in the crowded restaurant.

She was close to Jake's age, making her late fifties, early sixties, yet like Jake, the years had left her remarkably unscathed. I doubted anyone in the café would guess she was older than forty-five, at most. She had a delicate beauty, a flawless complexion, finely sculpted features and large luminous eyes. She had the kind of face and figure that would catch almost anyone's eye, beautiful and graceful, soft and appealing.

She spotted me as I walked the narrow aisle to where she was seated. She smiled and stood up to greet me. She was wearing a soft pink hooded sweater over a beige workout suit, her blond, shoulder-length hair loosely held back by her sunglasses.

"Allison? It's a pleasure to meet you. You look just the way Jake described you. Please excuse my appearance. I came straight from my dance class. An hour-and-a-half workout is the only way I can justify my mid-morning treat," she said with a light, lilting laugh.

"I really appreciate you taking the time to meet with me," I said, as I took the seat across from her.

"It's my pleasure. I can never resist a request from Jake, and what you're doing sounded so interesting." The waitress appeared and took our order—a latte for me and a decaf cappuccino and chocolate croissant for Katherine. "So, you're writing a book about Jake?" she asked.

"Well, I don't know about that. I imagine I'll have enough background on him when I'm finished to support a book of some length," I said with a chuckle. But actually, I'm looking to profile a specific aspect of Jake's life, along with three other people I've interviewed. I'm writing a comparative piece on four individuals, the one common denominator being they've all been divorced at least four times." Katherine raised her eyebrows at this news. It seemed to me she found the topic a tad unsavory.

"Isn't it funny that Jake gave me the impression the whole story was about him? Well, you certainly picked a good person to interview on that subject. If anyone's an expert on divorce, it's him," she said with a shake of her head. "I don't know how much help I can be to you—I've only been divorced once, thank the Lord."

"Jake suggested I speak with you and Pam, since the two of you have kept in touch with him over the years. I would guess you've witnessed a fair amount of his romantic misadventures. From a safe distance, that is."

"You can say that, for sure. I've probably heard more tales of true love and heartache than Ann Landers and Dear Abby combined."

"I bet, seeing as you were his second wife. He's covered a lot of ground since that time."

"Yes, I've been watching Jake ride the rollercoaster of love for over thirty years now, if you can believe it."

"You don't even look old enough to have known him for thirty years."

Katherine modestly acknowledged the compliment. "You're sweet to say that. But I have an eight-year-old granddaughter, and just saying that makes me feel old sometimes, though I wouldn't trade being a grandmother for anything in the world."

"How many children do you have?" I asked.

"Only one daughter, Laurie. How about you, do you have any children?" she asked.

"Ah…no. My husband and I have careers that demand a great deal of our time."

"I understand." She paused as she digested this excuse. "But you're young. You still have plenty of time." I tried to smile at her supportive comment, though all I managed was a lopsided smirk.

"When you were married to Jake, did either of you want children?" I asked.

"I did, in the beginning. I can't remember if it was something I had ever discussed with him. It was pretty much a given—marry the man you love and start raising a family. That's the way it was in our time. I'm so relieved I never became pregnant during that first year of marriage, as I had assumed I would. And after a certain point, I took steps to insure I wouldn't conceive.

"Underneath it all, I knew there were fissures in our marriage we'd never be able to bridge. But outwardly, I convinced myself we were experiencing the awkward stage every newlywed couple goes through. As time went on, I realized no amount of effort was going to save our marriage. It was then I started pulling away emotionally from Jake."

"Was there any one event that precipitated your detachment?"

Katherine considered this question as she sipped her cappuccino. "I think it struck me one day that our temperaments were too different. We were basically incompatible, despite our sincere attempts to overlook that fact. He was so robust and outgoing. He saw life as a thing to be conquered, and his enthusiasm spilled over into every aspect of his world. He was larger than life, and I began to see that the love of one woman would not be enough to hold him.

"He was so susceptible to the lure of new adventures, and I felt it was only a matter of time before he'd tire of me and want to move on. Believing this, whether rightly or wrongly, made me become insecure and withdrawn, and that insecurity became a cause of worry to Jake. It was a self-fulfilling prophecy, really. The thing I dreaded became a reality, and my fear was the mechanism that brought it into being."

"I would think his infidelity with your best friend was what ruined your marriage," I said, brazenly opening old wounds. Katherine flinched ever so slightly, but she covered her discomfort smoothly.

"Our marriage was already irreparable when that began."

"You seem quite high-minded about it. Most people could never come to terms with a breach of that magnitude. You must have a forgiving nature to have remained on good terms with either of them."

She seemed to consider this for a moment. "I could have hated both of them and let the hate eat me up and prevent me from starting a new life. But even after what the three of us went through, I still love them both. None of us really knew what we were involved in at the time. Only in retrospect could we begin to make sense of it. But that's the way life is. If you started out knowing everything, you'd never have to make any mistakes," she said with a breezy laugh.

"It sure would be nice to avoid mistakes, but at least some of us learn from them. Others never seem to. Look at Jake, for example. He's over sixty, yet it doesn't seem he's ever going to figure out that marriage just isn't for him," I said.

Katherine gave me a sympathetic smile. "I guess he wouldn't be Jake if he gave up on romance," she said.

"Maybe so, but he can still pursue romance without getting legally entangled," I argued.

"I don't know. It seems to be ingrained in him that marriage is the logical next step if you fall in love."

"Even so, I can't understand how he can keep throwing his hat into the ring," I said.

"I think it's because he's never found the right person," Katherine said, as if it were the most obvious answer in the world.

"You really think it's as simple as that?" I asked doubtfully.

"I do. I've always thought Jake would make an excellent husband if he could figure out what's right for him." I had to study her face to make sure she wasn't having me on. "Believe me, I've been privy to more details of his love life than I care to admit, and I know what makes him tick. That's why I can still be friends with him after all that's happened between us."

"So you think he's just a misguided optimist?" I asked, still not convinced.

"That's one way to put it, I guess."

"But what about all those women he claims to have lived with who he didn't take to the altar?'

"I couldn't say. Something must have happened to save him from that fateful course, at least a few times," she said. "Or maybe he wasn't in love with them. Maybe he caved in to their demands, but only to a point. Or maybe he's just someone who can't live alone. Who knows?"

"Do you really think he's had as many live-in girlfriends as he claims?"

Katherine laughed. "There's been a least a dozen that I can vouch for personally."

"Does Jake call you every time he loses his head over a woman?"

"It sure seems that way."

"I'd say Jake is awfully lucky to have an understanding friend like you," I said. "What does your husband think of all this communication with your ex?"

"Walker isn't the least bit threatened by Jake, thank heavens. Jake has been a part of my life for so long after our divorce that Walker views him more like a wayward brother-in-law than my ex-husband."

"That's interesting."

"Jake and Walker couldn't be more different. The funny thing is that Jake wholeheartedly supports my marriage to Walker. He considers him to be a perfect husband for me—safe and even-keeled. He also thinks Walker's boring, but apparently that's part of what makes him an ideal mate for me," Katherine said with a chuckle.

"Do you think Jake will ever find the kind of happiness you've found with your husband?" I asked.

"I'm not sure Jake's even looking for the kind of relationship I have with Walker. We have a deep, loving marriage, but it's hardly the electrifying, pyrotechnic type of love that Jake craves. I think part of his problem is he's hooked on the thrill that only comes with fresh encounters. That's the way some people are, I guess," she said, gently peeling a layer off her croissant.

"Jake told me that he has two grown children. What kind of father would you say he is?"

"Well, I've never met either one of them, but I think considering he was late coming to the game, he's made a strong effort to get involved in their lives. He's in business with both of them. I think they run his clubs, or something."

"When you say he was late coming to the game, what do you mean?"

"For whatever the reasons, he wasn't involved with either of his kids while they were growing up. I don't recall exactly how old Ben was the first time Jake met him, but he and Eliza didn't have anything to do with each other until she was in her late teens."

"Do you think it had anything to do with selfishness on Jake's part? Maybe he was too caught up in his own life to have time for parenting?"

"Oh no, Jake is the most generous person I've ever met. I don't know how well you know him, but surely you've seen how big-hearted he is. It was Eliza's mother who wanted to keep her daughter away from Jake, probably out of spite.

"Jake's actually generous to a fault. In fact, I think a lot of his entanglements grow out of his almost indiscriminant generosity. He gets bitten by the love bug then makes some extravagant gesture, and before he figures out the girl isn't right for him after all, she's fallen head over heels in love with him."

I nodded in agreement, as I had personally seen the scenario played out with Jaylynn. Jake bought her a horse and offered to board it for her, and then he couldn't shake her loose.

"What was your impression of Jake?" she asked. "I understand you went to see him in Oregon."

"Oh, Jake was the perfect host. I had a wonderful time with him. When I asked about Jake being selfish, I was just playing devil's advocate. He couldn't have been more gracious or accommodating toward me and my endless questions."

"He sure thinks highly of you. He couldn't say enough nice things about you."

"Really?" I said, wondering for the first time how Jake would describe me to someone else. It made me a little edgy as I reviewed my stay with him. I had a hard time believing I'd made such a favorable impression on him.

"Oh yes. If I didn't know better, I would have sworn he was developing a crush on you," she said with a teasing laugh. I joined her with a weak titter of my own.

"Well, I've taken up enough of your time," I said, taking a twenty dollar bill out of my wallet and laying it on the check. Katherine tried to take the check away from me, but I held her off. "It's the least I can do."

"Thank you. It was a genuine pleasure to meet you, Allison."

"And for me, too. Jake told me I should also speak to Pam. Do you think she'll be as receptive to the idea of talking to me about Jake?"

"I would imagine so. She and Jake aren't quite as close as he and I are, but Pam's the kind of person who doesn't mind giving her opinions, especially where Jake is concerned."

"Does that mean she doesn't take the same open-minded view of his life as you do? Perhaps she harbors some resentment toward him?"

"It's more that she gets frustrated by the fact he can't ever seem to get his house in order, emotionally speaking. But definitely make contact with her. I'd be more than happy to call her and pave the way, if you'd like me to."

"I appreciate the offer, but I don't have any qualms about pestering people I don't know," I said facetiously. I left a tip and collected the rest of the change, exchanging small talk with Katherine as we both got ready to leave.

"You're welcome to call me if you think I can be of any further help," she said before we parted in the parking lot. "I know I'm not privy to everything that goes on in his head, but I'm probably the closest thing he's got to a best friend."

I thanked her again and watched as she got into her Mercedes and cautiously exited the parking lot. The thought of her once being married to Jake left me utterly baffled.

When I returned home, I immediately dialed Pamela's number, and was secretly relieved to get her voicemail. I left a fairly detailed message explaining who I was and what I was doing, and asked her to give me a call at her convenience. I preferred handling our introduction that way, for I was slightly intimidated by the prospect of talking with her.

I had gotten the impression from both Jake and Katherine that Pam didn't suffer fools or mince words. While I awaited her call, I sat down and made a quick list of questions. After putting my thoughts in order, I typed up my notes from my conversation with Katherine. I was just getting up to make some coffee when the phone rang. It was Pam.

"Thanks for returning my call," I said.

"No problem," she replied.

"I met with Katherine Clarkson this morning. She said to give you her regards." This wasn't true, but I needed some way to break the ice. Even over the phone I could tell Pam was not inclined to offer information without receiving something first.

"That's sweet. How's Kathy doing?"

"She's doing well. I understand you two stay in contact." It was more of a question than a statement of fact.

"We do, but not as much as before. About every six months or so one of us will pick up the phone and we'll spend an hour or two getting caught up."

"Katherine told me she hears quite often from Jake. I guess he calls her whenever he's having women trouble."

Pam laughed. "Yep, that's about the only time I hear from him, too. But understand, with the way Jake operates, it means we're in almost constant contact with him." She laughed again.

"He's quite the ladies' man, I gather. I went to visit him at his ranch in Oregon, and in the three days I was there he had visits from two of his not-so-happy girlfriends."

"That sounds about right. Jake's number one problem is he can't say no to himself. I used to tell him his head was going to snap off at the neck one day from too much whipsawing back and forth. He's one of these guys who's attracted to almost any female who crosses his path. I think he needs to send himself to Females Anonymous." I had to laugh at that one.

"You think he's capable of ever breaking his unfortunate habit?"

"Jake? Not a chance. It's too much a part of his nature. It's been the pattern of his whole life." For some reason, this pronouncement wasn't exactly what I wanted to hear.

"Katherine believes Jake would settle down and be monogamous if he ever found the right person," I argued hopefully. Pam barked out a sarcastic laugh.

"Kathy is one of the sweetest people I have ever known, but I swear, sometimes she makes Pollyanna look like Scrooge." This interview was starting to have an unsettling effect on me.

"Is it hard to remain friendly with Jake, feeling the way you do about him?" I asked. Pam sighed heavily.

"I've known Jake Sorenson so long, I can't imagine not having him in my life, no matter how limited our involvement. I love the guy, but I can't help seeing him for the way he really is."

"Do you think he'll marry again?"

"Oh sure, he's got plenty of years ahead of him and he hasn't slowed down a bit since I was married to him."

"Why do you suppose that is?"

"I don't know. He's just hell-bent on making the same mistakes over and over. And he happens to have more energy than anyone I've ever known."

"Do you mind if I ask you what attracted you to him?" She was silent for a moment, and I wondered if she resented my prying.

"His natural exuberance, I guess. Even when he and Kathy were so miserable, he had this irrepressible enthusiasm for life. He was always upbeat and on the watch for every little joy that came his way. And I guess I was envious of the way he treated Kathy.

"It must seem pretty low to you that I could have cheated with my best friend's husband, then turn around and marry her ex as soon as the ink on their divorce was dry." I didn't comment. "The reality was they were never going to last as a couple. I realize that sounds extremely self-serving, but our affair made one of them happy, and that was a fifty percent improvement."

I was glad this interview was taking place on the phone. I would have found it hard to disguise my reaction to her cavalier sentiments.

Do you think the fact that he had been unfaithful to Katherine with you put a strain on your marriage?" I asked.

Pam treated me to another harsh bark. "Let me guess—Jake told you I was compulsively possessive and irrationally jealous."

"Well, I don't think he phrased it precisely that way," I hedged. I was relieved to hear her laughter soften.

"To answer your question, yes. It's true, however Jake sugarcoated it for public consumption. I *was* compulsively possessive and irrationally jealous. When you consider the circumstances, it would have been difficult to be otherwise. Not only had he snuck behind Katherine's back with me, but there had been at least two other affairs prior to that."

Now that was a newsflash. "Did Katherine know about those affairs?" I asked, my mind racing to recall exactly what Jake had told me about his second marriage. The way I remembered it, he had only strayed with Pam because of his misery and her proximity.

"No. At least she never let on if she did. You'd have to ask her about that," Pam said.

I wasn't sure I wanted to know the answer.

"Do you think your fears and jealousies were justified?" I asked.

"Ultimately, yes. Of course, Jake's version probably makes it sound like I drove him away with my unfounded suspicions."

That did sound more familiar, but I didn't want to be the one to confirm it. "I have to say I find it remarkable the three of you managed to put all this behind you," I said.

"I know. It's not the way your usual love triangle evolves."

"Who presented the first olive branch?"

"Jake. After our marriage broke up, he had a fit of remorse for the way he had treated Kathy. He went to her and poured his heart out and somehow she forgave him. And me. Hurting her the way I did had been a tremendous burden to carry, believe it or not, and I was very relieved when she came to me offering reconciliation."

"That was awfully magnanimous of her," I said. I thought I detected a catch in her throat when she answered.

"You're not kidding. I know I'd never be able to do what she did, but I don't think many others would either."

"And the reason you both forgave him is what?" I wondered out loud.

Pam thought about this for a moment. "For me, I guess it was because I honestly don't believe Jake has a malicious bone in his body. Even after all these years and all his relationships, I see him as a guy who can't figure out what's right for himself. It's kind of sad, actually," she said with the first note of compassion I had heard out of her so far.

"But he's an old man—you'd think he'd have gotten it by now."

"He's only two years older than me."

Ouch. "You know what I mean," I said, trying to gloss over my faux pas. "How many people do you know who have been married seven times?" I asked rhetorically.

"I know. It's pretty hard for most of us to relate to the way Jake operates. But if you think about it, every new love interest manages to overlook that aspect of his life. I guess the new ones find a way to diminish the significance of the women in his past."

She had to be right about that, or how else would anyone preserve the hope that they might be his one true love? "Well, I appreciate you taking the time to talk to me," I said, winding up our interview.

"Anytime. I'd be curious to see the finished product. You might be able to shed new light on an old dog." I took this as a vote of confidence.

I thanked her and told her I would send her a copy of the magazine when the article came out. I didn't bother to tell her Chinese might become our national language first. I hung up the phone and stared out the window without noticing a thing. The more I learned about Jake, the more confused I became. At this point, I wasn't sure I knew the faintest thing about the man.

y conversation with Pam signaled an end to my working spurt. The enthusiasm I managed to summon had been stymied by the conflicting observations I had gathered from ex-wives two and three. More than ever I suspected my
instincts were playing tricks on me.

But instead of pronouncing the subject dead, I simply relegated it to the at-
tic of my mind, hoping rather unrealistically that my subconscious juices would
transform a weak premise into something of merit. In the meantime, I turned my
energies toward more practical matters, like an all-out cleaning binge and an indifferent attempt at writing my Prescott acceptance speech.

By the seventh day of my exile from the office, desperation caused me to pick
up the phone and call Judith's cell number. I hung up before she could answer,
forgetting that my number would display on her phone. In less than a minute,
the house phone rang. I wasn't going to answer it, but I grabbed it right before it
went to voicemail.

"Hey—did you call?" she asked.

"Uh, I think I hit your number by mistake," I lied feebly.

"It just so happens I was about to call you." My heart sped up. I found myself
simultaneously dreading and pining for a new assignment, something that would
save me from having to crawl into the hole I had dug for myself.

"Oh…"

"I'm holding your tickets to New York in my hand this very moment. They
arrived from the travel agent two minutes ago. Would you like me to have someone drop them off at your place, or do you want to come down and get them?"
It would have been one way to occupy my time with a constructive task, but for
some reason I passed on the errand.

"If you can spare someone, send them over," I said. "I'd rather not break my concentration just now." I was turning into quite the fibber.

"No problem. How's it going?"

"Good, good," I said with a distracted air.

"Well, I won't keep you."

"Okay. Thanks for the tickets."

"De nada."

I hung up. This was not normal behavior for me, and I didn't like it at all. If I were older, I would have suspected a mid-life crisis. But there seemed no plausible explanation for anything I was doing these days, unless you considered the pressure my husband was putting on me to give up my career and have babies. Or that I was unreasonably preoccupied with a man many years older than me—a seven-time loser with a wandering eye.

I had to find a way to shut my mind to those conflicts and concentrate on something else altogether. But what? I had four more days until I left for New York, and then after that I'd be at Judith's mercy, per our agreement. That wouldn't really be so bad. The trick would be to occupy my time until then.

As I had already cleaned our condo from stem to stern and had purchased a complete ensemble for the awards banquet, the only recourse I really had was to spend time with family and friends. The problem was many of my friends were overachieving fiends like me. I was afraid the few who weren't had tired of failed attempts to connect with me and would be lukewarm to my sudden desire to get together.

As for family, they were scattered hither and thither and to spend time with any of them would mean travel and planning, neither of which was feasible at the moment. I could make a few calls and entertain myself that way for a couple of hours, send out a few e-mails, make enough attempts at contact to preserve my relationships for another year or so.

Since I couldn't think of anything more constructive to do, I made a list of those to call and those to e-mail, and set about the process of elimination.

Though I tend to be aloof when working, lack of purpose combined with two major accomplishments worth bragging about made me quite verbose once I got rolling. I did such a good job of getting caught up with friends, I didn't get off the phone until almost 1:00. I was in the midst of searching our nearly bare cupboards for food when the phone rang. It was Miriam Hodges, returning my call.

"Darling, so good to hear from you!" she exclaimed. "I've been meaning to call you, sweetie, but I'm afraid I've been so involved with work and whatnot since our honeymoon that I've lost touch with people."

"I know the feeling."

"Well, we need to get together."

"Yes, we do."

"I've got an idea," she said excitedly. "Have you had lunch?"

"No, as a matter of—"

"Good. How soon can you get to Jack's at the Embarcadero?"

"Um…twenty or thirty minutes, I guess," I answered, running my hand through my uncombed hair. I had done little that morning to prepare myself for public appearance.

"Fabulous. I'll call and get a table. I've been eating lunch there almost every day for the last two weeks," she said.

"We don't have to go there, we can go somewhere else," I suggested.

"No, no, no—that's a perfect place for me," she insisted. "I'm on that protein diet—just fish, meat, and veggies. Got to stay slim and trim for my lover man. Okay sugar, see you in a bit."

I replaced the phone and wondered how I could've been desperate enough to be roped into lunch with a nauseatingly happy Miriam, so delusional in her bliss that she imagined herself slim and trim.

I reached the restaurant fifteen minutes late and then had to wait another twenty for Miriam to show up. She strutted to the table in the wake of the patient host, talking into her cell phone for another two minutes after she had been seated. I tore off my third helping of bread and chewed on it as my irritation grew.

"Okay, my love—got to go. Yes, I'm here with her now. Okay darling, I'll tell her. Ciao." She made kissing noises into the phone, making my jaws clench. "That was Bob. He sends his love," she said unnecessarily.

Finally turning her focus to me, she reached over and gave me a modified bear hug, reminiscent of the kind her brother would give if confined to a chair. It was weird how I continually lost sight of the fact that the two of them were siblings. There were similarities, but too few worth noting. And certainly not when it came to marriage; Miriam had barely managed one to his seven, and it had taken her almost fifty years.

I couldn't help but feel a pang of loss for the good old curmudgeonly Miriam who had been unsuitably replaced by this effusive, love-struck version. If I ever needed that sharp, unsentimental sounding board, it was now. I would never think of trotting out my troubles to this Miriam, especially the one about my husband wanting me to sacrifice all for future Tyler-Wilcoxes.

"You look fabulous, as always," she said, though rather insincerely, as she wasn't even looking at me. Her attention had already strayed to the menu, a list she had surely memorized by now. And even if she hadn't, her agenda was the same as Judith's: broiled fish, steamed vegetables, and NO potatoes.

"This is so nice," Miriam said as the waiter relieved us of our menus. "Seems like there's never enough time to do the really important things, like catching up on all the good gossip."

She gave me one of her old ornery smiles, generating the slim hope that the old Miriam wasn't dead, only hibernating. Once she settled into the reality of having to share control of her life with another person, she'd surely snap back into her "take no prisoners" outlook.

"I'm afraid you asked the wrong person to lunch, if it's gossip you're looking for. I've been out of the loop lately," I told her. I took a sip of Sauvignon Blanc and noticed how she watched me enviously. I motioned for her to have a sip, but she declined with a distracted shake of her head.

"Too many carbs," she said. "Well, I don't mean gossip-gossip—I was referring to personal news, like your trip to Afghanistan, or your trip to Oregon." So Jake had told her, eventually. "I can't believe neither one of you told me you'd been to his ranch," she admonished.

I merely shrugged. "I didn't withhold that information intentionally. You were away in Fiji, and then I was away again, then it sort of slipped my mind." That was a laugh. I had thought of nothing so much as my time with Jake, and I had a half worn-out tape of our conversation to prove it.

"Well, I'm glad you two hit it off. He's a character, isn't he? I know I'm biased, but I get such a kick out of him. I think he's the greatest. I just wish he could find the right person and settle down."

That sounded so comical coming from her, I nearly choked on my wine. "You honestly think that would be possible? At this point, I'd say the guy's incorrigible." Miriam looked almost hurt. "Come on—he's sixty-two and he's struck out more times than Jose Canseco."

Miriam got downright offended. "He's got a very good heart," she said defensively, sounding way too much like the reformed Miriam for my taste.

"Good heart, sure. But he's also got terrible judgment," I countered.

"You don't know what it's been like for Jake. He's too kind-hearted for his own good."

"Are we talking about the same Jake?" I asked out of sheer meanness. It hadn't escaped me that the sweeter and more understanding Miriam became, the more intolerant and cynical I sounded. She narrowed her eyes at me, probably wrestling with her old self for control of her tongue.

"You know, it's curious that he had nothing but good things to say about you," she said, trying to shame me into being nicer where her big brother was concerned, "yet you sound like you're repulsed by the man."

"Not at all. I'm very fond of your brother. He's one of the most interesting men I've ever met. But I'm talking as one girlfriend to another. You said yourself you're biased. You can't see him the way an uninvolved party can."

"Well, biased or not, I know that all his life, women have thrown themselves at him. You've seen him—he's gorgeous. And he's always been successful and rich. And I don't care how old he gets—he'll always have to fight off the admirers. No matter where he goes, there's some woman trailing behind him. You can't blame a guy for getting caught up in all that. And to make matters worse, he's a soft touch himself. He sees a pretty face and bam, he thinks he's in love. Believe me, it hasn't been easy for him. What?" she asked as I tittered to myself.

"It's so funny the way both of you characterize his love life. To hear him tell it, *he's* cursed because he falls in love every other day, and you think the women are totally responsible for his string of marital disasters," I said, shaking my head dubiously.

I could feel Miriam's ire rising, despite her best efforts to control it. The waiter set my crab cake appetizer in front of me, producing more feelings of ill will from my dining partner.

"One of these days you're going to pay for eating like a teenage boy," she warned with a disapproving scowl. I cut off a piece, dredged it through the red pepper sauce, and held my fork aloft.

"Want a bite?" I offered cruelly. She waved my fork away as if she'd never dream of such a breach of diet. I made a silent bet with myself that she'd stop off at the first French bakery on her way back to the office.

"Well, since we're on the subject of Jake, it might interest you to know I had very enlightening conversations with two of your brother's former wives this week."

Miriam stared at me uncomprehendingly. "Why would you do that?" she asked.

"Did Jake happen to tell you why I went all the way out to Boonieville, Oregon?" She never did have much tolerance for mysteries. I sensed the old Miriam was on the verge of unseating Miss Sweetness and Light once and for all.

"When I met your brother at your wedding, I became professionally intrigued by his dismal matrimonial record, and I started wondering about all the people who have gotten married over and over and over and never seem to get it right. Jake was kind enough to allow me to dissect his love life, one wife at a time."

Miriam was so disconcerted by this admission, she stared mutely at me, only looking down blankly when the waiter set her broiled snapper in front of her.

"Anyway, when I was visiting him, Jake suggested I speak with his second and third wives to get their sides of the stories. It turned out to be quite helpful." Miriam was still in a state of confusion and was unable to put her disbelief into words.

"Something wrong?" I asked, looking inquiringly at her fish. She shook her head. I set my empty appetizer plate aside and assessed the platter of steaming hot sand dabs, French fries, and coleslaw.

"Katherine told me—"

"Wait a second—are you saying Jake allowed you to call his former wives to ask them what kind of husband he had been?" she asked, exasperation making her voice shrill and her face tense.

"Yes. Anyway—"

"But why are you doing this? You're writing about my brother, making him look like some kind of oddity, aren't you?"

"No, I just want to understand what makes some people say 'I do' when they don't stand a chance. And it's not only him—I've got three other fascinating cases for comparison. Don't worry, I'll change his name to protect the guilty. We wouldn't want to inflame the hearts of all those women out there with similar vulnerabilities to marriage," I said sarcastically, then immediately regretted it when I saw the genuine look of alarm on Miriam's face.

"Honestly, I'm only trying to find out what makes some people tick, that's all. Despite my personal feelings, I don't plan to make a mockery of Jake or any of the unfortunate souls out there who haven't been blessed with good marriages," I said. The thought of "good marriages" eased her anxiety to the point that she was able to look at the subject with a more detached perspective.

"So, exactly what secrets about Jake's life are you planning to use?" she asked, helping herself to one of my fries.

"Oh, I don't know. I'm still in the process of whittling down his data into a semi-manageable format. He's a hard one to condense into a thousand words."

"You're nuts for even trying," she said with a trace of feisty glee in her voice. I pushed my plate closer to her and watched as she attacked my haystack of fried potatoes. "So, what were his ex-wives like?"

"Well, I met with Katherine face to face, and spoke to Pam via phone," I said, snagging a fry between Miriam's greedy lunges.

"What was Katherine like? Jake always said she was stunningly beautiful."

"You never met her?" I asked, caught off-guard.

"No. I was only a kid when he married her. Remember, he's almost fourteen years older than I am, and I was living with my folks in New Jersey while he was tearing it up in L.A." Yes, the age difference; that was probably why I couldn't connect the two of them in my mind.

"The new you would have liked Katherine. The old you would have hated her," I said.

"What do you mean the 'old me' and the 'new me'? I haven't changed." I snorted. "How am I different?"

"Forget it. Let's just say that Katherine is very sweet and has an unbelievable capacity for forgiveness. She's the polar opposite of Pam, wife number three, who happened to be Katherine's best friend until she married your brother. You didn't know that either?" Miriam shook her head, dismayed but intrigued.

"Yeah, well, apparently it was one of those rare triangles that had a happy ending. The three of them kissed and made up after he and Pam split, and they've stayed in touch for over three decades now. Pretty crazy, huh? See why I find the subject so fascinating? You and I can count on one hand how many times we've fallen in love, and Jake's done it so many times, he can't remember them all."

"I can't believe he told you all this. I've never heard any of these stories," Miriam said. By the expression on her face, I gathered her mind was reeling as she tried to imagine what Jake's life had really been like. "What were the other wives like?" she asked.

"I don't know. I've only talked to those two."

"What did Jake tell you about the others?"

"You must have known some of them," I said.

"I remember a couple of them, but honestly, my head blurs when I think of Jake's women. So, tell me—what were they like?"

"You don't want to know. Besides, I can't keep them straight without my notes in front of me. You'd better eat your fish—it'll be inedible when it's cold," I warned her.

"It's already inedible," she said, looking at her less than appetizing snapper and wilted vegetables. "Give me one of your sand dabs," she said, seizing a filet before I could assist her. "I guess I do have a blind spot where Jake is concerned. I've never even considered any of his wives or girlfriends as tangible beings before. They seemed more like phases he was going through."

"That might be a fairly accurate way of looking at it, though I met two of his current conquests, and I can assure you they're for real. Different, but definitely tangible."

"Jake told me he wasn't seeing anyone right now."

"Yeah, well, they don't last long, do they?" We both fell silent as we privately lamented this sad truth. The waiter came and collected our plates and returned with dessert menus. I was about to turn him away before he could hand them to us, and Miriam beat him to the punch by blurting out her order.

"One crème brûlée," she announced. "For you. I'll just have a bite."

Now that Miriam had let down her guard, the rest of our lunch passed in much the same fashion as all our previous lunches. We gossiped, groused, and supported each other's battles with blind loyalty, though I was careful to skirt my problems with Elliott.

I suppose deep down inside, I was hoping his pressing need for children would pass without any more wrangling. Miriam's phone began ringing before the dessert arrived, and on the third call she simply turned it off without answering it.

"Guess they can't live without you," I said, knowing how demanding her business associates could be of her time.

"They're going to have to," she said, polishing off the last of the crème brûlée. The waiter offered more coffee, but I declined and asked for the check.

"Good idea you had. It would have taken us weeks to get our schedules coordinated if you hadn't been spontaneous. I'm going to pay the bill so you can get going," I said.

"No you're not, and no I'm not," she said flatly, snatching the check from my hand before I could even look at it. "It was my invitation, so I'm paying. And I'm not going back to the office—screw it. I've got some Christmas shopping to do, mostly for me, of course. And you're coming along to keep me company."

That's my girl, I thought, happy to aid and abet in the undoing of Miriam Goody-Two-Shoes. Bob had to find out sooner or later what his wife was really like, and it might as well be sooner. Miriam signed her credit card slip and we headed for downtown and a little harmless fun.

Twenty-One

The old Miriam and I had so much harmless fun that Elliott actually made it home before I did. Somehow, both of us managed to forget entirely that we had spouses to answer to and we carried on as if time were of no importance.

We flitted all around Union Square and its immediate environs for hours, stopping around five-thirty for cosmopolitans and appetizers at Postrio. It wasn't until Miriam finally turned her cell phone back on and discovered she had thirteen new messages that it occurred to us the rest of the world considered us AWOL. I didn't dare turn on mine.

When I arrived home at ten minutes after seven, I did my best imitation of someone who had accomplished many tasks in one day. I had wisely stopped at the market to pick up dinner fixings, extravagantly paying the cabbie to wait while I shopped. I had many props to back up my harried appearance as I burst through our front door and found Elliott sitting on the sofa, a bottle of beer in his hand.

My first thought was I opened the wrong front door; my second thought was something horrible had happened. I stood in the entry, letting the bags slide out of my hands to land where they would.

"Elliott?"

He had been so deep in thought, he hadn't heard me come in. "Oh, hi there. Let me give you a hand with the bags." He stood up, unsteadily, and came to help me put away the groceries.

"Have you been home long?" I asked, searching his face for clues to his uncharacteristic behavior. All I could find were signs of deep fatigue.

"Since about six-thirty," he said. I felt a pang of guilt for gallivanting around town while he sat at home by himself.

"Wow, that's early for you. Sorry I didn't get back sooner—I figured I wouldn't see you till seven-thirty or so," I said, careful to keep enough distance between us so he couldn't smell any alcohol on my breath. I then realized it wouldn't matter because he was drinking too. It was hard for me to imagine that Elliott would have consumed enough booze to put him in such a state, and his zombie-like attitude was starting to concern me.

"Elliott, are you feeling all right?"

"Yeah. I'm really whipped, that's all."

"You look like it. Why don't you have a seat and I'll get started on dinner. We can have either the swordfish I bought or this spinach ravioli, whichever sounds the best to you."

Elliott wandered back to the sofa and sat down heavily, pressing his palms against his eyes. He was actually beginning to scare me. I went over and sat next to him and he put his arm around me, pulling me close, the way a small child would clutch her favorite dolly.

I didn't say anything for a while because I didn't want to disturb him, but after about five minutes in his stranglehold, I had to straighten up. His eyes were closed and his mouth was open. I feared he was on the verge of falling asleep and I'd be trapped like that for the duration of the evening. He snapped out of it when I eased up his arm, jumping to attention as I pulled away. I could see in his eyes how disoriented he was.

"Honey, you're working way too hard," I said as gently as I could. I'm sure it sounded like nagging to his ears, but I had to say something. He leaned over and picked up his beer and took a swig.

"It won't last forever," he replied.

"Neither will you." I could feel him tense up and I decided to try a different approach. I stood behind the sofa and began to massage his shoulders.

"That feels good," he said, his voice melting as I attempted to unknot his twisted muscles.

"I think you need to hire a team of massage therapists to come around to the office every day and unkink everyone. I'm sure your whole staff is as tight as you are." I kneaded the golf ball size lumps on his shoulders with my knuckles, feeling the muscles yield gradually as I sawed back and forth over them.

Elliott groaned at the pain and relief, his head bobbing more and more as I turned his back from cement to something more pliable. When I had used up all my strength and his muscles had pretty much returned to normal, he grabbed my hand and kissed it, pulling me around to him and plopping me down on his lap. It was so good to see him smile again.

"Hi there," I said.

"Hi there." He tickled me and I squirmed to get away. It struck me it had been a long time since we had laughed together. "Do we have time for a quick romp before dinner?" he whispered in my ear.

"I can romp if you can," I whispered back.

"I can."

"Are you sure?"

"Yeah, I'm sure."

After nearly nine years with the same man, you'd think I'd know everything there was to know about him sexually. Elliott surprised me that night. It wasn't until much later I figured out he must have been operating on a different level, a state of consciousness produced by extreme exhaustion combined with an obsession to carry out his will, at all costs. Elliott was at his physical limit, yet there was a yearning inside him I interpreted as unchecked passion for me.

Only in hindsight did I realize it was part of his concerted effort to execute his master plan. Poor Elliott. It wasn't his fault that the companionable paths we were on suddenly diverged. His future hopes were so far removed from my desires that I completely misjudged his tenderness.

Afterward, when we showered together, and stood drying off in front of the mirror, how was I to know he was trying to picture me with distended belly, pregnant with our first child? Ironically, I got the impression everything was fine between us and this act only proved he had dropped his intentions of turning our life on its ear.

After we had eaten the pan-seared swordfish with cherry tomatoes, green onions, and garlic on top of creamy polenta, Elliott started to look like his old self again. I made a silent pledge to make a nice dinner for him every night, if he could only manage to get home at a reasonable hour. He might be able to sustain this insane pace if he modified it just enough to allow for a proper dinner and an hour or so to unwind before bed.

I succeeded, much to my amazement, in convincing him not to do any work on his computer, to relax and listen to music instead. He sat in our one comfortable chair, his shortwave radio on his lap, picking up stations as far away as Mozambique.

It was while I was cleaning the dinner dishes that Elliott remembered he had found a package outside our door when he got home.

"I think I put it on the hall table. It's addressed to you."

I found the white envelope with the turquoise logo on it, and it belatedly registered that these were the plane tickets for New York. "Judith had our tickets sent over. That was sweet of her. Let's see here…one for Mrs. Allison Tyler-Wilcox and one for Mr. Elliott Wilcox. Wait a second…they both have a departure date of this Thursday. That can't be right," I said, picking up the phone to call Judith at home. "That's less than three days from now."

"Tickets for what?"

"The airplane tickets for New York," I said, slightly irked by his forgetfulness.

"I can't go," he said.

"I know. There must have been a mix up. Hi there, it's me. Sorry to bother you at home. I got the tickets, but there seems to be a mistake. They have us departing at 8:45 a.m. on *Thursday*, returning on Sunday at 4:50 p.m."

"Yeah, that's right. You're booked at the Empire for four nights," Judith replied in a groggy voice.

"But why are we getting there so soon? The awards dinner isn't till Saturday night."

"I know, but you've got two interviews set up for Saturday morning, back to back, and I thought it would be nice for you and Elliott to have at least one whole day to yourselves. It was a little bonus gift from me," she said.

"Oh. That was really sweet of you. I appreciate that."

"I didn't want you to show up at the awards ceremony all jetlagged."

"I can't go," Elliott said again.

"I see. Well the problem is Elliott can't be away from his work for that length of time right now. Maybe we can arrive on Friday instead, and…uh, maybe catch an earlier flight on Sunday?" I said for both Judith's and Elliott's benefit.

"Why do you want to make it such a rushed trip?"

"I can't go, at all."

"Wait, hold on—you're both talking to me at once. Hang on a second," I said to Judith, putting my hand over the receiver. "I'm going to get her to change the departure to Friday and get an earlier flight on Sunday, that way you'll only miss two full days and you can even head straight to the office when we get back on Sunday." Elliott got out of his seat and walked over to me.

"I can't get away at all this week. It's completely impossible—"

"But you're only going to miss Friday—you shouldn't have to work on Saturdays anyway, and then you'll make up for that by being there on Sunday," I said in an exasperated whisper. Elliott further infuriated me by standing there, arms across his chest, eyes closed, head shaking stubbornly. I felt like hitting him over the head with the phone.

"Uh…Judith, I'm going to have to call you back. Seems there's a scheduling conflict with Elliott's job. I'll call you tomorrow at the office."

"Okie dokie, but don't wait too late. I don't know how hard it's going to be to change those tickets," she warned. I assured her I'd get back to her first thing, and hung up the phone.

"You want to tell me what this is all about?" I said, hands on hips, toes tapping.

"Why are you getting so bent out of shape? We never discussed my going to New York with you."

"Well, how stupid of me! I naturally assumed that my *husband* would *want* to accompany his wife during the most important moment of her career." My tone was one notch below a rant now. I could sense that any second this was going to turn into a full-scale shouting match.

"Hang on a minute here. You can hardly claim that my need to be at the office virtually all my waking hours is something you hadn't noticed. What makes you think I can drop everything and jump on a plane to New York for four days, just so I can be sitting by your side for two hours at some silly awards banquet?" That was the first official punch of a fight that would only get uglier.

"Again, it was the stupid notion I've been harboring, that it's supposed to mean something to one spouse when the other achieves the highest honor in her profession. So I guess you're saying that if there were any awards for the type of thankless slave work you do, you wouldn't expect me to accompany you to the rubber chicken tasting in your honor? Is that what you're trying to tell me?

"Don't you have even a tiny clue how important this is for my career? You could at least *pretend* to be proud of me. A normal person would be excited by this kind of thing," I hissed. We were squared off now, sleeves pushed back, anger burning in our eyes.

"I *am* proud of you, but you shouldn't think the world can stop spinning while you thank whoever one thanks for a Prescott."

"I'm not asking for the world to stop," I said through gritted teeth, "I'd simply like my husband to share in this very special night."

"But it's not one night, is it? No, it takes a minimum of two nights and two days of travel for this thing. If it were held anywhere in the bay area, then no problem—of course I'd be by your side. But you've got to have some consideration for my situation.

"You don't have any idea how much stress I'm under these days. You have absolutely no way to relate to how tough my job is. It's completely different for you—you pound out a few thousand words, if that, and give it to your editor to polish up for you. And if you're real lucky, all the literary types make a big fuss about your little article and give you an award—whew, that was tough."

I've been told that hate and love are so close, it's possible to trip back and forth over the imaginary line without notice, without the blare of horns or flashing lights to warn you to step back.

I had never experienced the phenomenon until that very instant when Elliott wadded up thirteen years of hard work and dedication and threw it in my face. Kill. Hurt. Maim. Hate. That's all I could think as I glared at him, tears of resentment stinging my eyes. Leave.

I pivoted around and stormed off in the direction of our bedroom, which was not a very long walk. I suddenly felt so claustrophobic, I thought I'd hyperventilate. Despite the short route, I didn't make it to our bedroom door before Elliott grabbed me by the arm.

"Hey, hold on," he said. I swung around, ready to sock him one.

The fierceness of my anger made him drop my arm. "Come on, let's sit down and talk about this like adults. This doesn't have to turn into a brawl—" I stepped inside the bedroom and slammed the door and locked it. "Allison, open this door. You're behaving like a spoiled brat."

"Drop dead!" I screamed, bursting into tears. I wanted to strangle him, hurt him, make him take back his nasty words. I wanted him to appreciate the significance of winning a Prescott Award and how talented I must be to have won that honor.

Surely that was the crux of the problem; he simply didn't realize how important I was in other people's eyes. If only he could act like…like a normal husband, whatever that was. He should be jumping up and down with enthusiasm for what I had done. Was he so fixated on his esoteric profession that he was oblivious to how many lives my writing touched?

I felt my resentment for Elliott's appalling indifference surge through my veins, filling me until I was like a rabid dog, dying to bite someone. I performed a mad dance as I pulled open drawers, threw myself on the bed with fists pummeling the pillows, charged into the bathroom to stare at the hideousness of my distorted, tear-soaked face.

I sank onto the toilet lid, melting like the wicked witch. I couldn't stand this; how could something that was supposed to be one of the highlights of my life turn into a hateful melodrama? Why couldn't Elliott support me? Why couldn't he just this once put me first?

Hadn't I been flexible enough to make the dinners and do the shopping, even though I had my own deadlines to worry about? I laughed at my absurd pride in having a marriage of equality! I had only been kidding myself.

The minutes ticked by slowly as the climax of my anger evaporated, leaving everything as it was before—almost. I blew my nose and wiped away the theatrical smears of mascara and wondered what our next moves would be. I didn't have long to guess before I heard Elliott knocking softly on our bedroom door. I crept closer so I could make out what he was saying.

"Allison, please. Open the door. We need to talk. Come on, we can't leave things like this." I debated for a moment then opened the door about a foot. He was standing there in the darkened hallway, holding something in his hand.

"I made some coffee. Do you want some?" I shook my head and opened the door to let him in. Coffee? Who has a fight like that and turns around to make coffee? Seeing the beer in his hand earlier made me feel like I was finally witnessing Elliott with all his rules and self-imposed restrictions stripped away. I found it oddly comforting to walk in and find him sitting like that, once I had gotten over my initial shock. It had made him seem more human.

But that brief unguarded moment had passed, and Elliott the Impervious was safely at the helm again, bringing order and coffee to my wretched soul. He arranged himself on the bed and consulted his coffee before speaking.

"I think we need to back up and start all over again. We both said some ugly things and I think it would be best to avoid all derogatory remarks in the future. Let's both air our sides of the situation and see if we can't come to an understanding."

I stared at him, feeling utterly deflated. Talk about anticlimactic; his sterile approach to solving our differences made me want to forget the whole thing. What was there to talk about, anyway?

I was going to New York to receive a Prescott in front of my peers and all the major publishers and editors in this country and my husband wasn't going to be with me. We had already established that—what more was there to say? I didn't even have the heart to tell him he'd won.

"As I said earlier, it's simply not possible for me to take any time off this week."

"I know."

"If it were next week, I could've maybe squeezed a day out somehow." I looked up at the ceiling and prayed for patience.

"But as it is, I'm already a month behind—"

"Elliott, I know. You can't go, and that's the end of it. I should've never assumed you could," I said, defeated. I flopped listlessly into our armchair and picked up a pillow and hugged it to my chest. I wanted to cover my ears to ward off any more of Elliott's redundant haranguing, but I restrained myself.

Fortunately, my glumness seemed to take the starch out of his sanctimonious monologue. He sipped his coffee while he hunted up any overlooked grievances he might make examples of. I twisted slightly in my seat and stared out into the static glow of the city at night.

"I know this means a lot to you, Allison, and I really am proud of you. And I'm so glad you were able to have your career and achieve so much." The words sounded right, but I couldn't help but feel he was merely massaging my hurt feelings, or softening me up for the next blow.

He said nothing more, and I began to relax my guard, my mind already wandering off to practical matters, such as the departure date for New York. Now that I was going by myself, I might as well take advantage of an extended break. As I glanced around me I realized how confining these walls had become recently.

"And you know, we should be thankful things worked out this way, you achieving this kind of recognition when you did. Now you won't have to deal with any remorse for not having pursued your dream." I hadn't been listening, but he'd caught my attention with that comment.

"You had your career and you made it to the top of your profession. You'll never be like some women who suddenly wake up when their kids are in high school and lament the fact that they sacrificed their prime years for their children, but never did anything that was intellectually stimulating or personally rewarding for themselves.

"Of course, being a mother has to be one of the most rewarding experiences a woman can have—I'm not discounting that. But you're way ahead of that game. You can bow out of journalism knowing you've worked your way to the pinnacle and been rewarded for your efforts, and who knows, maybe when the kids are grown you can get back into it. Having a Prescott Award on your resume is like having money in the bank, I'm sure."

I stared at Elliott, and my spirits, poised for a rebound, plummeted further. Elliott, so certain of his world and his place in it. This was not a revelation, of course; he had been that way ever since I'd met him, must have been that way his entire life.

Ironically, his conviction that a successful life came from careful planning was one of the reasons I had been attracted to him in the first place. Two sensible, like-minded persons like us had only to imagine our goals in order to achieve them. That was the doctrine we had both bought into; how were we to know that our goals would one day vary so dramatically?

At least I was willing to admit we weren't as finely attuned to one another as we liked to assume. I was finally ready to accept that there came a point where that nasty device *compromise* had its usefulness. But would I ever get Elliott to fairly participate in the relinquishing of one desire in favor of another?

I looked into his eyes, all a-twinkle from his philosophical reckoning, and realized it would never occur to him his wife was not ready for midnight feedings and endless piles of dirty diapers. He may be fired up to start a family, but I was in no hurry to alter my life in such a profound and irrevocable way.

I suppose I had imagined one day I'd wake up and want nothing more than to hear the sound of our infant child crying for me to pick it up. But that day had not come, and the more I tried to conjure up enthusiasm for such a dawning, the more panicky I became.

"Elliott?"

"Hmm?"

"What if I were to tell you that I'm not emotionally ready for motherhood yet?" He regarded me warily. I fidgeted with the frayed end of the pillow while I worked up my courage.

"I'm just not ready to give up my freedom yet. I love my work and I love our lifestyle, and besides, I don't think I have what it takes to be a parent." Elliott set his coffee mug on the floor and crossed one leg over the other knee while he contemplated this inconvenient admission. "Say something," I said at last.

"Well, I don't think what you're feeling is uncommon. In fact, I think in the vast majority of cases, most couples feel like the decision is one that is forced upon them. I think more people spend time trying to avoid pregnancy rather than achieving it."

There was a comforting note to his reasoning that allowed me to hope for one fleeting moment he was willing to let me decide when the time was right to have a child. His next words blew that hope to smithereens.

"The point is, you have to let nature take its course. You may not *ever* think you're ready, if it were left up to you. I know what a procrastinator you are. If I had never brought the subject up, I don't think having kids would have occurred to you until you hit your fifties." I sensed a note of levity in his comment, but under the circumstances, I didn't find it all that amusing.

"It's best to put it out of your mind for the time being and just deal with it as it happens," Elliott continued in his former seriousness, "that way you don't have to feel like you're responsible for making the decision. I'm sure that's how most couples deal with it," he said matter-of-factly.

Of course, it couldn't be simpler. I pinched the bridge of my nose to stop the onset of more tears. I was suddenly overcome by nausea, and the very thought of having nausea for two or three months—on top of everything else—made my heart pound with fear.

"Are you all right?" Elliott asked as I bounded out of the chair.

"I can't do it!" I cried. "Elliott…I'm just not ready," I croaked, shaking all over. I was on the brink of hysteria. He put his arms around me and held me close to him. My sobs came in fast, shallow fits and starts.

"It's okay, sweetheart. You will be when it's time," he said, stroking my hair. I pushed away and looked him straight in the eye.

"No, Elliott. What I'm saying is I don't know if I'll ever be ready. The truth is I'm not sure anymore that I want to have children." The look on his face made me regret telling him the cold, unvarnished truth. His whole body went rigid and he backed away slowly.

"Look, all I'm saying is I'm so unready to have children at this particular point, the very idea of having another being to take care of scares me to death. Elliott," I said, taking a step toward him, "I'm not saying that I don't want to have kids. I always have thought I'd be a mother someday. And believe me, I completely understand how important starting a family is to you right now, but the timing has to be right for both of us."

It was hard to tell if my backpedaling was getting me anywhere. It was my turn to wrap my arms around him and give him reassurances that everything would work out the way it was supposed to, in time, just as he had said.

It took a little persuading, but in the end Elliott seemed to let go of his doubts about his wife's priorities. I think he was willing to believe my consoling words because hearing me say I didn't ever want to have children had been an ugly shock that he'd just as soon forget about.

So, the night ended in armistice; yet as we lay there side by side, I realized that if I had been hoping to use compromise to resolve our differences, I had given myself too large a dose. I was still traveling to New York by myself, and more importantly, I had unequivocally relented on the issue of children. I replayed all of Elliott's reasonable assertions in hopes of convincing myself he was right, but every point he had made was countered with a new objection of my own.

As I tossed and turned and commanded myself to sleep, I was forced to acknowledge my crime. I had been dishonest to my husband by making him believe I wanted children, too. If there was one thing I was becoming absolutely sure about myself, it was the fact that I no more wanted to have children than I wanted to run a daycare facility.

What about me would even suggest I was cut out for motherhood? Was it the fact that my career was the backbone of my identity, and without it I would fade away to nothing? Or was it the fact that I hastily return a baby to its rightful owner at the first hint of trouble? Or was it because I had so little room in my life I'd never had so much as a goldfish for a pet? Even the houseplants had to be tended to by a traveling horticulturist.

I was one-dimensional and self-involved, if you wanted to be realistic about it, and Elliott was no better. I laughed out loud to think of him pledging to help out more with the kids while at the same time hiding behind his work as an excuse for unavailability.

Who was he trying to kid? He may like the notion of having the nuclear family, but I seriously doubted that he had any idea how much a baby would impact his daily life.

I popped my head up to see if my laughter had disturbed Elliott's sleep, but he was out for the count, his mouth ajar, his breathing coming in rhythmic rasps. I carefully pulled back the covers and crept out of the bedroom, closing the door quietly behind me.

I wandered around our condo with the lights out, letting the filtered external gloom guide my way. It felt nice to have this time to myself. It felt almost illicit to carouse around my own premises without anyone's knowledge. And since I was free to do as I pleased, I rooted around in the back of the pantry where I kept a bottle of scotch stashed. I poured an inch or so into a rocks glass and carried it with me as I cruised from room to room.

I was slightly disadvantaged by the smallness of our place, ending up all too soon in our study, the last room I was at liberty to explore in the quasi-dark. I sipped my drink and let my hands run over each of our desks and assorted office equipment. I sat down in my old-fashioned desk chair, rocking and swiveling while my eyes surveyed the contents of the room, trying to identify objects I could just barely see, but had lived with so long, I could name from memory.

This was where Elliott and I had come together as our true selves. How many nights and weekends had we spent in this room, working back to back on our separate occupations, occasionally breaking each other's concentration with companionable questions or with interesting facts we found worthy of sharing. Just a couple of nerdy brainiacs with nothing more exciting or stimulating to offer one another than the fruits of their professional endeavors.

As I sat there, it struck me that I wasn't sure I'd be interested in spending the rest of my days cooped up in these confines chasing intellectual pursuits. I loved my work, it was true, but at least in my job I had different faces and stories and environs to keep me stimulated.

That was what really kept me from wanting to give it all up. I needed the flux of new challenges and fresh thoughts to give me the sense my life wasn't stagnant.

I took another sip of scotch and swung my seat around like a child, spinning myself like a wheel of fortune. I coasted to a stop slowly, the last inch of my ride depositing me smack in front of my tape recorder.

Well, wasn't that a handy twist of fate? No one could accompany my rebellious mood better than the wily Jake Sorenson. I switched on the tape where I had last turned it off:

"How did I know you'd be good at this?" Pause. *"You going to let me play, or is this just an exhibition game? All righty, let me show you how it's done."* Balls clanking loudly. Jake swearing.

"Have you ever been dumped by a woman, or have you always been the one to initiate the breakup?"

"Well, I am impressed. Even when facing a sound thrashing, you still have your reporter's mind going on all cylinders. Nice touch," Pause. Jake's muted kibitzing.

"You never answered my question."

"What question?"

"Have you ever had your heart handed to you on a platter?" The sound of billiard balls clanking. I heard myself groan as Jake finished me off.

"Good shot," Pause—Johnny Cash in the background.

"That was a dandy finale, one that calls for a celebratory drink."

"It's getting late." How typical of me. It was not a nice surprise to find out how uptight and prim I really am.

"Hell, its only 11:15. There's plenty of night left."

"I've been traveling a good part of the day, and I still have some writing to do."

"Oh, don't go all prissy on me. One drink—you can manage that."

"Alright, one drink, but only if you answer the question I've asked you twice already."

"What was that question again?"

"Have any of your wives, girlfriends, lovers, concubines ever given you your walking papers?"

"Once."

"Was it one of your wives?"

"No, this girl was too smart to make that mistake. Annalise was her name. I tried to get her to marry me for five years, but she didn't trust my track record. She would have been the fourth Mrs. Jake Sorenson, but she had more sense than that. She made the right decision, I reckon."

I switched off the recorder more forcibly than I meant to. I held my hand to my mouth, biting my finger to control my emotions, which were mixed, to say the least. Why did this wild man affect me so deeply? Merely listening to the two of us interacting made my skin tingly all over. I could only hope I had not betrayed myself while I was there at his ranch. Or again at Miriam's party.

"Oh, God," I groaned, remembering my discomfort that night. Seeing Jake again, the non-shaggy version, had plainly affected me. There was no doubt about it. It had been one thing to listen to this tape in Afghanistan, where hearing his voice considerably quelled my feelings of loneliness.

Then I had thought of him only as a friend, a kindred spirit, if it's possible to say that about anyone you spar with constantly. I had convinced myself I possessed a secret treasure I could bring out to console myself whenever I needed.

But seeing Jake in the flesh, feeling his eyes on me…oh no…but it was true. I had feelings when I was around Jake that I had never in my life experienced before. I certainly felt more alive and more excited and definitely more stimulated when I was with him than I did with Elliott, but it could have been due to the fact that Jake was still so new to me.

I shook my head. No, even when I compared my courtship days with Elliott to the couple dozen hours I had spent with Jake, I simply couldn't deny that being with Elliott was practical and safe, while being with Jake was exhilarating.

It was his sense of romance. And when I say romance, I mean a romance with life; Jake put as much of his heart into everyday living as he did his affairs. Not that I could personally vouch for that, but judging from all I had heard and seen, I'd venture to say that was the case.

As for the romance between sweethearts, I think I finally understood the message Jake had been trying to convey to me: romance, the type he had experienced repeatedly over a forty-year period, was this powerful undercurrent that snuck up on you and slowly pulled you in, and it wasn't until it was too late that you realized you'd been snared and there was no getting free.

But when the intoxicating first sting began to fade, Jake—like millions of other romance junkies—waded back out into unknown waters in hopes of getting stung again. Romance is like a narcotic; it produces a reflexive action that we are unable to control.

I laughed at myself, the late-bloomer, the naïve one who thought all along I knew everything there was to know about love and romance, and what I didn't know firsthand didn't really exist. What a silly, boastful fool I was.

But now that I finally had it figured out, what was I going to do about the irrational feelings I had for a seven-time divorced, sixty-two-year-old mule breeder who lived out in the middle of nowhere?

I stood up and began to pace. I had to look at this situation logically. If I was experiencing these feelings for Jake, the reason had to be because my relationship with Elliott had hit a temporary snag. If we hadn't been wrangling about New York and babies, I'd be sound asleep next to him, and I wouldn't have been listening to Jake's voice in such a susceptible frame of mind. Good, that was good. I was getting somewhere. I was going to pour water on these unruly feelings and watch them fizzle to nothing.

Okay, if I took the problems with Elliott out of the equation, then I would be impervious to the feelings I had for Jake, right? Yet there was no point denying that, everything else aside, Jake had carved out a place in my heart, no matter how brief our association had been. But I could control how much I thought about him as long as things were going well with Elliott.

Possibly, I hedged, except for the fact that seeing Jake at Miriam's had thrown me into a tailspin, and that had been prior to winning the Prescott and prior to Elliott telling me it was time to retire and start producing children. There went that nice, tidy theory.

I swallowed the last of my scotch and navigated the dark hallway for another splash. It occurred to me, as I felt my way through the condo, that perhaps I could cope with Elliott and his unreasonable demands if I developed an alternative existence for myself, one that allowed me to roam at will like a cat during the night while Elliott slept blissfully unaware of my deviant behavior. I could drink all the booze I wanted and write my articles in secret, then sleep in the daytime while he was beating his brains out at work. I'd wake up in time to shop and make dinner and make sure everything was in perfect apple pie order. How would he ever know the difference?

I chuckled to myself as I carried my drink into the living room and sprawled out on the sofa. Hell, I could even have a kid, then insist on hiring a nanny to help out in the daytime, what with the strain of having to stay up all night with a cranky newborn. I could turn the child over to the nanny, crawl under the covers and manage to keep both of us happy.

I was chuckling over this ingenious but impractical plot when the solution to our dilemma suddenly occurred to me. I sat bolt upright, shocked that I hadn't thought of it sooner.

I was so surprised and delighted by my epiphany, I discarded all caution and went to tell Elliott the good news. It had to be the modest alcohol consumption that convinced me he would welcome this late night bulletin. It was only after I had roused him out of a sound sleep that I got the first inkling I had made a tactical mistake.

"What? What's wrong?" he asked as I jiggled him awake.

"Nothing's wrong. I just want to tell you something important," I said as he scooted up and turned on the light, temporarily blinding me.

"It's almost 1:00," he said with growing annoyance.

"I know, but this couldn't wait." I could have told him forget it, I was only dreaming, go back to sleep, but I was propelled onward by a cockeyed sense of optimism. I pushed his legs over and sat down next to him.

"I figured out a way that we can both get what we want," I said.

"What are you talking about?"

"Kids—I'm talking about having children, and what you said about me having to quit work," I replied enthusiastically. So far, Elliott's reception was hardly encouraging. I plowed on undeterred.

"For me the main stumbling block has been the part about having to give up my career. But it just hit me—I already have the most perfect stay-at-home-mom job there is. When you think about it, how often do I really need to go into the office? Hardly ever, if I didn't want to. So you see, there *is* no problem. You get to be a father and I get to keep my job." I had been so pleased with myself, Elliott's anger took me totally by surprise.

"You woke me up to tell me that? What's the matter with you?" I sat in stunned silence. "First of all, what you seem to be overlooking is the reason for not working for the first few years after we start our family is so that you can devote yourself to our children's care and upbringing, and not solely to deprive you of a job. And secondly," he said, halting mid-sentence to sniff the air.

"Have you been drinking?" he asked, putting on his glasses, as if it would enhance his sense of smell. Startled, I admitted my guilt.

"I couldn't sleep. I just drank a shot of scotch to relax me." It wasn't until after I had gotten the words out that I became incensed by his puritanical outrage.

"Do you make a habit out of that kind of thing?" he asked snidely. "You know, alcohol can cause irreparable damage to an unborn child."

"Don't be so damn controlling," I said, leaping up from the bed. "You tell me when to give up my career, when to get pregnant, what not to drink—I'm sick of it. You do not control my body, okay? This is my life and my body we're talking about here, and I'll decide those things—not you." I stood there, hands on hips, glaring at him, daring him to cross me.

"What has gotten into you lately? You have been completely disagreeable and unyielding."

"Unyielding? Just because I didn't roll over on my back and let you impregnate me at your first command?"

"There's no talking to you when you're like this," Elliott said piously.

"Oh, go to hell," I said, storming out of the room and slamming the door. I marched purposefully for five or six paces before I realized I had nowhere to go. "Well, that was brilliant," I congratulated myself.

I went over to the sofa and sat down, hoping that Elliott would not come out to continue this undignified discourse. Oh God, what was happening to me? Why did I think for one moment that was the smart way to approach Elliott on the subject of children and work? I seemed to be losing all sense of reason.

But as I sat there I was forced to acknowledge the purpose behind my rash act. Deep down, I knew my marriage was headed for the rocks, and I was desperate for a way to bring it back on course.

But confronting him only made things worse. It did tell me one thing, though: Elliott was bound and determined to have his way. I could stop laboring under the delusion that we'd be able find a middle ground where we could both be satisfied.

It also confirmed for me that I was so willing to compromise, I had once again given him the impression I was all for having kids, when in reality, it was the last thing I wanted—at least not right now. Oh, who was I kidding? No matter how hard I tried, I could not picture myself toting around a couple of screaming children.

I picked up my glass and stared at the remaining whiskey, but I didn't have the heart to kill it. I set it down on the coffee table, and slumped against the back of the sofa, where I eventually fell asleep.

I slept hard enough to miss Elliott's departure, waking up at the first sign of dawn, just before seven. I dragged myself into bed where I lay, unsleeping, till nine, trying unsuccessfully to find a solution to the friction between my husband and me.

Twenty-Two

It took me a while to locate Judith. Every office I entered, it turned out I had just missed her. When I finally caught up with her, I realized the last thing she needed to deal with at the moment was my personal life. I followed her into her office, where she tried to make me feel welcome, though she was interrupted every two or three minutes with some new glitch to sort out.

"I wonder every month at this time what makes me stay in this business," she said as she hung up with the production manager.

"I picked a bad time to stop by," I said, standing up.

"No, no, no—sit down. I always whine like a princess the day before we go to press. Besides, I think we've got everything nailed down now. So what's on your mind? Oh, the tickets. What'd you guys decide?" I took Elliott's ticket out of the envelope and slid it toward her. "So, what should I do with it?"

"Cancel it," I said, not meeting her eyes.

"I thought we were going to change the departure to Friday, with an early return on Sunday."

"Yeah, well, that idea didn't fly."

"Well, what does he want to do—catch an early flight on Saturday, returning Sunday? That would be a bitch, but I can see if it's available." Judith's earnest desire to accommodate our scheduling difficulties was starting to make the situation feel even more awkward.

I looked her straight in the eye for emphasis. "No," I said, shaking my head, "Elliott doesn't want to go, at all. Period."

Judith was clearly puzzled. "Why doesn't he want to go to the awards ceremony? This is the big one, as far as journalism goes."

"He's too busy with work right now."

"Let me see if we can do the Saturday departure and the Sunday return. Surely that won't cut into his work schedule. Besides, this time of year in New York is one of the most romantic scenes I know. There's a certain festivity in the air, with all the Christmas hoopla everywhere. Even if it's only for a weekend, it'll be worth the trip," she said, picking up the phone to call the travel agent. I shook my head and motioned for her to hang up.

"Elliott's working seven days a week, practically around the clock."

"But—"

"Judith, believe me, it's no use. He's not going and that's that." I got up and stood by the interior window that divided her modest office from the rest of the operation, gazing at nothing in particular.

"What's going on with you two?" she asked.

"Nothing," I said.

She didn't buy it for a second. "Yeah, I can see that." I made a feeble attempt to laugh, but it came out more like a wheeze. "Tell me. Come on, if you can't trust your editor, who can you trust?"

It was hard to keep anything from Judith. For one thing, she had known me for years prior to my involvement with Elliott. She had enough history on me to gauge my ups and downs without me having to say a word. Resigned, I sank back into the chair, ready for confession. I rubbed my temples, reluctant to pull Judith into our private conflict.

"Elliott wants me to give up my job and start producing children." Judith's face looked like ten flashbulbs had gone off in front of her eyes. She started to laugh, as if this could only be a joke, but swallowed it when she realized the odds of me kidding about something like that were next to nil.

An exasperated *"Why?"* was all she could manage.

I shrugged. "I guess his biological clock just went off, without a hint of warning."

"But why does he want you to quit working for the magazine? What better setup could you have as a working mother?"

"Hey, you're preaching to the choir, and Elliott's not a convert. He has it in his head that I can only be a good mother if I devote every second to child care and rearing. Squeezing a career in on the side would not be allowable."

"That's ridiculous," she said, plainly outraged. I raised my eyebrows in agreement, but didn't comment further. "When did he become so unenlightened?"

"I don't know. I'm beginning to think he's been that way all along and I somehow overlooked it." I chewed on a nail, wondering if this were true.

"Well?" Judith asked, an unmistakable note of panic in her voice. I shrugged.

"We're at an impasse," I said. We sat and regarded each other silently for a moment.

"So, what's the next move?"

"You tell me," I said sarcastically.

"Well unfortunately, this is the kind of issue that doesn't resolve itself. Unless, of course, you get pregnant and crazed hormones change your way of thinking."

I hooted at the idea. "Don't worry, I'm not planning on getting pregnant."

"At least a woman can still decide that one on her own," Judith replied. "But if he wants kids so badly, sooner or later you'll have to come to some kind of agreement."

I let out a deep sigh; I could feel my emotions working themselves to a boil, and I knew any second they might spill over the top. I stood up again, not anxious for Judith to see me on the verge of tears.

"At the risk of offending you, I feel compelled to tell you that in all the years I've known you, I don't recall you ever saying you were looking forward to having children one day. In fact, if I were ever to place a bet on it, I would have wagered that would be the last item on your agenda."

"I don't suppose I really have any secrets from you, do I?" I said, flopping back into the chair.

"I was afraid of that," she said. "Well, this does present a problem. How serious do you think Elliott is about starting a family?"

"Honestly, I think he's got it timed down to the minute. He's working on the Oakland ERS conversion—which is going to take considerably longer than they first estimated. And once it's completed, he'll be in line for a promotion and a hefty pay increase. He's probably got a date in his head for impregnating me that would synchronize with the completion of his project nine months later."

I laughed, but apparently Judith didn't find this prediction humorous. She got up and began slowly pacing back and forth behind her desk.

"It might be a good idea to get some counseling," she suggested hopefully. "Sometimes it's the only way to sort out these differences."

I got a good laugh out of that one. "Can you really envision Elliott dragging himself away from work to meet with me and a marriage counselor? Oh boy, I can just hear his reaction to that. Besides, why should he be inconvenienced when it's his wife who's being the difficult one?"

"Had you agreed to having children?"

I waffled my hand equivocally. "I suppose I agreed that someday we'd have kids, but I never sat down and said 'I want babies and I want them by the time I'm thirty-five' or anything like that. He didn't say anything like that, either. Before we got married we had talked about children in general terms, but we never talked about anything specific.

"To be perfectly honest, I didn't know until Elliott sprang it on me the other night that *he* even wanted children, let alone right away. I had been assuming we were pretty much on the same page as far as that was concerned. I should have realized Elliott's got a timeline and a master plan for everything." I laughed weakly and buried my face in my hands. Judith came over and put her hand on my shoulder.

"What are you going to do, Allison?"

I shook my head. "I don't know. I really don't know what to do. I feel so trapped. Not only is he asking me to give up the one thing I take the most pride in, the very thing that defines who I am, but he also wants to saddle me with the endless responsibility of a child—or two. I just…ugh, I feel like I'm going crazy."

Judith eyed me sympathetically and returned to her chair, assuming the posture of the attentive psychiatrist. "I think it's going to be good for you to get away for a few days. It'll give you time to think and to sort out your feelings. I want you to remember that a career and a marriage are two very different things. They're both important, but it's up to you to prioritize them.

"And just so you know, my life won't end if you choose family life over this nerve-racking business. You and I have put a lot of our souls into getting the magazine to this stage, and it would be a shame if you weren't around to enjoy the glory when we break into the big leagues.

"But in the end, this is just a job. There are more important things in life, or so I've been told." Judith, the uncomplicated, unmarried, and unencumbered workaholic smiled wistfully at the crossroads decision I was up against.

"Thanks. I'll try to keep that in mind," I said, pushing out of the chair.

"And remember to enjoy yourself. My flight is scheduled to arrive at five on Saturday. I know that's cutting it short, but there's really no way I can get away sooner. Worst-case scenario, I'll go straight to the Waldorf. If I land on time, I'll see you at our hotel and we'll ride over together. Keep your chin up, baby. Everything always works out in the end."

I left Judith with this uncharacteristic platitude ringing in my ears. I tried to make it my mantra, but the very first sight I encountered as I left our building was a mother anxiously strapping an infant into a car seat in her Volvo while a toddler pushed the stroller willy-nilly all over the sidewalk. My heart sank.

Tuesday passed without too many hostile communications between Elliott's camp and mine. I rationalized that couples who had as much time together as we did tended to treat ugly blowouts with lesser and lesser importance as the years ticked by. Putting together an evening meal seemed to rate higher than rehashing last night's affronts. But Wednesday was another story.

Oddly enough, both Elliott and I were in fairly decent spirits when we met up on the home front. I'd had a rare inspiration while shopping and had thrown together one of the best meals I had ever created. But it was while we were in the middle of dinner the wave of discontent that had rolled back to sea came crashing down upon us again.

The phone rang. Elliott and I looked at each other; I had nearly finished my food, so I was the one to answer it. It was my mother. After the initial hello, how are you's, I wandered off to our bedroom. There was a sense of detente between Elliott and me, but there was still enough distrust in the air that I wasn't willing to make him privy to my conversations with family members.

"So how is everything? Did you have a nice time when Uncle George was in town?" I asked.

"Oh, yes. We had a lovely time. We went to the aquarium, and we went out to dinner every night. It was fun."

"What did you think of his girlfriend?"

"She was nice." It took me three or four seconds to decipher the hidden meaning in my mother's bland comment.

"You didn't like her," I surmised.

"No, I wouldn't say *that*." This was code for "she's horrible."

"What happened?" I asked, relishing the thought of someone else's problems instead of my own. Silence. Getting indelicacies out of my mother was one of the greatest challenges in life.

"Is she trailer-trash?" I held my hand over the receiver to conceal my laughter.

"No…"

"Is she twenty-five?"

"No, Allison, she's in her early forties, I'd guess."

"Well…?"

"She's…an exotic dancer, if you must know." My eyebrows shot up at that.

My Uncle George with a stripper! I bet that was the last thing my parents were prepared for. I held my hand over the phone while I tittered.

"Allison, the reason I'm calling is because of a phone conversation your father had with Elliott today."

Elliott? That bulletin brought me back to my own troubles in a hurry. Why would Elliott be talking to my parents? I knew at once this was not a good sign. "Who called whom?"

"Elliott called here at the house and your father answered," she said. This revelation seemed all the more bizarre because Elliott had not mentioned a word of this.

"Why did he call?" I asked. I stopped stuffing last minute items into my garment bag and perched on the edge of our bed. Something told me I wasn't going to like what I heard.

"He was hoping that either your father or I could exercise our influence and find out why you're being so adamant about not having children."

I couldn't believe my ears. My mouth dropped and I spent several seconds forming indignant rebuttals geared to shame and wound Elliott before I remembered I was on the phone with my mother.

"Allison?"

"I cannot believe Elliott would call Dad and say something like that to him," I said hotly. I glanced over my shoulder to see if he was lurking in the doorway. Oh boy, the walls would be shaking tonight.

"So it's not true?" my mother asked.

"Is what not true?"

"That you're suddenly against having children." I pinched the bridge of my nose. I'll kill Elliott, I thought. How dare he sneak behind my back and sic my own parents on me.

"I, ah…Mom, I can't imagine why Elliott would drag you and Dad into this," I said, perplexed and irate.

"Then there is a problem," my mother surmised.

"Yes, there is a problem, a much bigger one than I ever realized." I was tempted to march out to Elliott and get a three-way brawl going, but it didn't seem fair to inflict that kind of ugly drama on my mother. Besides, I would have been the big loser in that match.

"Why have you decided you don't want children?" she asked. Now a new element had been interjected into what should have been a private matter: the wounded feelings of the would-be grandparents.

"For one thing, I've never said I don't want children. What I have said is I'm not ready to abandon my career and become a fulltime mommy."

"There's really no such thing as a part-time mommy," my mother reminded me.

"You know what I mean. Housewife and mom, that's all. No job."

"Well, there's a lot to be said for having that luxury. Of course, women didn't really work as much back when I had you kids, and I know how different it is nowadays, with both parents working and the kids shuttled off to daycare or the babysitter—"

At this point I pulled the phone away from my head. I took deep breaths until I felt I could maintain a civil tone of voice. "Yes, Mom, but you weren't asked to give up something that was very important to you. You didn't have a career you'd studied for and put thirteen years into building—"

"I worked at Harrison's department store for three years before your father and I got married."

"That's not really the same thing, is it Mom? You didn't win a Prescott Award for best sales clerk, did you?"

"Why are you being so hostile? I can see what Elliott means when he says there's no talking to you."

An outraged gasp escaped my lips and I was a split second away from hurling the phone at the wall. But there was someone else I needed to vent my anger on. "Mom, I'm sorry—this really isn't a good time to talk," I said sweetly. "I was in the middle of dinner when you called."

"Oh, dear—I wish you would have said something," she said apologetically. "I had no idea—"

"That's okay, Mom. I'll call you later, all right?"

"Of course, dear. And Allison, I hope you know it's not our intention to interfere."

"I know, Mom."

"Remember that Elliott is only trying to do what's best for his family."

Ha! "Goodnight, Mom."

"Goodnight, Allison."

I switched off the phone. "That son of a bitch," I swore under my breath. I was so mad, it was all I could do to walk out to where he was sitting on the sofa without hurling curses at him as I advanced. Instead, I simply walked up and closed the lid on his laptop, trapping his hands inside.

"Jesus! What are you doing?" he exclaimed. He pushed the lid open and hastily logged on to make sure I hadn't screwed anything up. "I could have lost what I was working on," he said with an overdose of righteous indignation. I snorted my lack of concern for his near calamity.

"You *enlisted* my *parents* to gang up on me?"

"I thought—mistakenly, I see—that they might be able to find out why you no longer want to have children. I mean, it's not an insignificant matter—I'm your husband, and all of a sudden you start making noises that your career is more important than starting a family."

"Elliott, when was it ever said that I didn't want kids? Or for that matter, when did I say that I *wanted* to have kids? We've never really discussed this at all, not in any meaningful way. But out of nowhere you decide it's time for me to start pumping out babies and quit the magazine.

"Why can't you understand that this is not entirely your decision? Especially since you're not the one who is most affected by the outcome." Believe it or not, I actually remained fairly even-tempered and rational to this point.

Elliott, on the other hand, shot straight through the roof.

"You've turned into the most self-centered, egotistical person I've ever met. This whole Prescott business has gone right to your head. You think there's nothing more important in this whole world than the measly contributions you make to a magazine that no one reads." He was shouting by this time. I missed half a beat due to shock, then retaliated with both barrels.

"Why do you suddenly feel so threatened by my success? I never hid the fact I was a journalist from you. If it was a baby machine you were looking for, you should have put that demand out front in the very beginning, then neither one of us would have had to settle for something we don't want.

"And another thing—you attack my work as if it were comparable to garbage collection, yet you sacrifice all your waking hours to building a system that will be obsolete in five years. You think that makes you a hero?"

Suffice it to say that once the gloves got tossed aside, things got pretty bloody. We finally called a marginal truce when we were both too emotionally spent and physically exhausted to carry on anymore. I blubbered the whole time I washed my face and brushed my teeth, and thinking of getting up predawn to catch a 7:45 flight made me feel even sorrier for my dismal circumstances.

Elliott stole a blanket and went off to sleep on the sofa, which meant I'd have a hard time sneaking out for something to drown my sorrows. I had scarcely five hours before I had to be up. If I had been in any better shape, I would have left for the airport then and slept a few hours at one of the nearby hotels.

I would have welcomed the anonymity of a generic hotel room, with no personal mementos to tug at my heartstrings. Instead, I marinated my psyche in bruised feelings and a terrible sense of failure. When I awoke to the alarm clock's nerve-grating whine, Elliott was already up and dressed for work.

"I brought you some coffee," he said from the doorway.

"Thanks. You can set it right there."

"I can wait and take you to the airport, if you want me to." I looked at him standing there, hands in his pockets, completely at a loss as to how to forge an accord between us.

"No, that's all right. It'll take me a while to get ready," I said, checking the time.

"Well, I better let you get at it, then."

"Yeah."

"Allison?" I looked up at him. "I think we need to have a serious discussion when you get back." I nodded, my stomach twisting itself into knots. I knew it would only get worse before it got better. "Well, have a good flight," he said. He approached and gave me a stiff hug and a dry peck on the cheek.

"Thanks," I said. Though I wasn't willing to admit it just yet, deep down I knew that what Jake had said was true: over's over.

I slipped into the back seat of the cab and looked up at our condo as we pulled away from the curb. I tried to recall Elliott during the time we purchased it. We were very excited, or I should say that *I* was very excited. Elliott was pragmatic. Buying our first home had been a milestone for me; it was merely a steppingstone for Elliott.

I wondered now what I had ever seen in him. I suppose I had been shopping for someone who was steady and logical and sure of his way, a tower of moral fortitude and personal convictions. I forgot to include on that list empathy and a sense of humor.

I had realized Elliott was a little stiff, but I didn't see how rigid he truly was. It was funny that I had turned him into this strong, unerring protector, when it should have been obvious from the start how controlling and narrow-minded he really was.

But that was it, wasn't it? We project what we want to see onto the person who has caught our eye for one reason or another. Who knew what Elliott saw in me? He apparently saw me as someone who was pliable enough to adjust to life as he envisioned it. Whatever it was, I'd say we both missed getting what we wanted by a mile.

It suddenly occurred to me I had stumbled onto a crucial element that had been missing from my theory about marriages that end in divorce. It became clear as day one reason those marriages hadn't worked was because neither party fully recognized the other for the person they really were. They had simply caught a glimpse of someone and automatically assigned attributes that didn't reflect his or her true nature.

Weren't Elliott and I guilty of doing exactly the same thing, choosing one another for reasons that didn't jibe with reality? There was a key here, somewhere. People who had a series of defunct marriages were unable to accurately assess their potential compatibility with someone because they were relying on a mere snapshot of that person, one flavored by an ideal.

Take Jake, for example. He had misjudged women so often, he had gone all the way to the altar seven times without discovering the unsuitability of his mate. Yet within an hour of our first meeting, he had as much as proposed marriage to me. Why? Because he had liked the way I looked and his imagination took it from there. Somehow he managed to credit me with traits that he had no way of knowing if I actually possessed. If I hadn't been with Elliott, how far would he have pursued those unfounded feelings?

I got out of the cab and snagged an abandoned cart for my garment bag and laptop. Judith had booked first-class tickets—God love her—and I had only to wait behind one fellow traveler to check in. Even though the wait was short, I couldn't keep my mind off my recent revelation. If I applied this one key aspect to all the folks I had interviewed, I might be able to tie the story up in a nice, glossy ribbon.

The man ahead of me picked up his computer bag and I advanced to the counter.

"Good morning, Mrs. Tyler-Wilcox. Are you traveling alone to New York?" the ticket agent asked when I handed her my ticket and identification.

"Yes."

"One first-class seat, nonstop to New York's Kennedy."

I watched the agent as she checked me in. "You know, I…can you tell me when's the next flight out of here to Boise?" The agent barely glanced at me as she accessed the information I had requested. My pulse quickened and I could feel myself begin to sweat. Had I completely lost my mind?

"There's a flight departing at 8:45, nonstop to Boise. The next is flight number 243, leaving at 10:30 with a stop in Portland—"

"Is the 8:45 flight booked?" I asked. Now that I had introduced this insane plan as a possibility, I was nervous I wouldn't be able to pull it off.

"It looks like there are still a few seats available."

"What time does it get in?"

"The arrival time is 11:25." I had no bags to check; I could arrange for a rental car and be on the highway by noon. If I drove like a maniac I could get there in three hours, now that I knew the way there.

"Did you want me to book you on that flight and cancel New York?" the agent asked, her fingers continuing to type away while she awaited further instruction.

"Not yet." I turned around to look at the growing line behind me. "I need to make a quick phone call."

"I'm going to go ahead and put a reserve on flight number 1490, leaving at 8:45. Just walk up to the counter when you're ready," she said kindly. I walked away, jittery and excited, as if I was about to embark on a true adventure. I was nervous and thrilled and certain that I was about to do something I could never adequately justify to anyone, including myself.

I found Jake's number and misdialed twice before hitting all the right digits. I almost disconnected once I heard the phone ring on the other end, but a man answered before I lost my nerve.

"Is this…Lowell?" I asked.

"It is," he replied brightly.

"Hi Lowell, it's Allison Tyler-Wilcox—the reporter who came out there a few weeks ago—"

"Of course, Allison—nice to hear your voice. I suppose you're looking for Jake."

"Is he around?"

"Let me get him for you." I put my hand over the phone and exhaled deeply.

"Now, why would a world famous journalist be calling me at this hour of the morning?" Jake asked as he picked up the phone.

"Hi Jake, it's Allison," I said stupidly. "I'm sorry to bother you—you're probably heading off to the mules right now." Boy, was I regretting this idea. "The reason I'm calling is because I was about to do the craziest thing—"

"You? Something crazy? I don't believe it."

"Well, it's true. I'm at the airport in San Francisco, on my way to New York for an awards ceremony on Saturday—"

"Congratulations, by the way. I heard you won top honors."

"Thank you. Well, anyway, on my way to the airport I had this thought—a breakthrough, of sorts—and, well, I was hoping to talk to you about it. It's about the article I'm doing."

"Shoot."

"Um…actually, I was hoping to do it in person." A moment of awkward silence passed. "Would it be horribly inconvenient for me to drop by the ranch sometime this afternoon?"

Jake laughed. "You're in San Francisco, on your way to New York, and you want to stop by?"

"Crazy, huh?" By the way my face burned, I knew it was beet red. I was so grateful Jake couldn't see me.

"Yeah, especially for you. But sure, come on over. You know you're always welcome."

"Thank you. I promise I won't take up too much of your time. There's a flight getting in a little after eleven, and I'm hoping to be at your place by three, then get back on the road by four-thirty or five."

"Allison, you are more than welcome to come out here and pick my brain and make me feel foolish for all my mistakes, but there's no way in hell that you're going to drive all the way from Boise and back in a single afternoon. Come, but you're staying the night." He sounded absolutely firm about that.

"But—"

"No buts."

I was going to be in New York by myself anyway, so what did it matter? "Alright, if you're sure I won't be imposing."

"Oh, knock off the prissy stuff. We'll expect you by three, and we'll send the posse out by four. Call if you have any trouble finding the place."

"I won't, I mean, I will." I could hear Jake snicker to himself as he hung up the phone. I would have never guessed just twenty-four hours ago that I'd be ditching New York to sneak a trip to Oregon. I couldn't imagine what Elliott would think of my irrational behavior, but it did give me naughty pleasure to try.

Twenty-Three

I pulled into the Buckin' J Ranch at precisely 3:00. The flight was a few minutes late and the car rental experience took longer than I had hoped, but I made up the time by driving like a fiend.

It wasn't necessary for me to break all land speed records to get to Jake's by a specific time, but now that I had set this clandestine assignation into motion, I couldn't wait to get there.

The very act of leaving the tense, claustrophobic atmosphere that our marriage had become made my heart swell with new hope. Merely getting away from Elliott for a few days was bound to improve both our states of mind. If nothing else, it would give me a chance to get a proper perspective on our relationship and sort out exactly what I wanted my future to be.

Jake was out on the porch when I drove up. I was all keyed up from my breakneck drive, but just seeing his lanky, lazy saunter brought my tempo down a few notches. The air was surprisingly cold as I stepped out of the rental car, which was panting and pinging from its laborious journey.

"Got any bags, or did you simply hop a plane with the clothes on your back?" he asked as he approached the car. I gave him a defiant smirk and popped the trunk. I grabbed my purse and caught up with him as he mounted the steps.

"I see that being a Prescott winner agrees with you," he said approvingly as he threw me a sidelong glance.

"Thank you."

He opened the door and stood back for me to pass. The air inside was welcomingly warm and heavy with the trademark aromas of Rosalinda's kitchen. Someone, I would suspect not Jake, had put up garlands of cedar and other tasteful ornaments of the season.

"Would Milady like her usual rooms?" Jake asked in a flawless English butler's accent, something he must have picked up from the early days with Lowell.

"That would be lovely, Jeeves," I said, though not as smoothly as Princess Diana.

The lights were already on in my guest room and it was evident that someone had recently freshened it up. A small pot of narcissus graced the top of the dresser and the drapes were pulled back to display the barren but beautiful early winter landscape. In the near distance I could see Connie's Christmas trees, making me feel as if I had walked into a subtle but authentic holiday greeting card.

"I thought your ranch was beautiful in the fall," I commented as I stood at the window looking out.

"You should see it in the spring. They haven't come up with adjectives to accurately describe how gorgeous it is then." He came over and stood next to me. "Welcome," he said, smiling broadly.

"Thank you, Jake." I gave him a sideways hug that made me feel more self-conscious.

"So, you have some new insights into what compels people like me to make such poor choices? It must be an earth-shaking revelation to make you come so far out of your way to tell me in person," he said as he led the way out of the room.

"Why don't we sit in the living room. Rosalinda's got the whole kitchen filled up with Christmas cookies and cakes and whatnot. I'll tell you, that woman can *cook* when she puts her mind to it. You need paper and pen, or reading glasses, or anything?" he asked facetiously.

"Very funny. Well, at least you haven't forgotten me," I replied. "What with all the women in your life, I'd say that was an achievement."

"Ah, same cheeky ball of fire, I see," Jake said, though he didn't seem terribly annoyed. It was pretty interesting to see the way the two of us naturally fell into playful banter after only a few minutes in each other's company. I suppose it was a sign of our comfort level with one another.

"Can I get you something to drink? I bet you're hungry. I know the kind of piddly junk that passes as airline food these days."

"Actually, I'm fine. They served up a fairly respectable breakfast in first class."

"First class? My, my. You have hit the big leagues, haven't you?"

I shrugged off his sarcasm. "My editor is spoiling me these days. But I could use a glass of water."

"How about some coffee?"

"Water's fine."

Jake disappeared down the hallway and returned with water for me and coffee for himself.

"So, tell me about this brilliant epiphany of yours. I'm dying to know if it will cure me of my shameful ways."

"Who knows, it might."

"The floor's all yours, Madame Journalist."

"Okay, I was thinking about…relationships, and it suddenly occurred to me the reason some marriages are doomed from the very start is because one or more of the parties involved convinces themselves that the person they've fallen in love with possesses characteristics they don't really have.

"What I mean is, they fall for the person based on a favorable first impression, and project a temperament or qualities on them that are in fact wholly missing."

Jake looked at me as if he were waiting for the punch line. "You're saying they don't see the person for who they really are—they have a physical attraction to someone and then make up their own unrealistic version of what they're like?"

"Yes," I agreed emphatically, pleased that he caught my meaning so quickly.

"Yeah, well, that's for certain. God knows I've been guilty of that mistake about a dozen times." His nonchalant manner threw me off balance.

"You're aware that you've repeatedly made the same error in judgment, yet you've done it over and over again?" I asked, perplexed.

"Sure. It's a human foible—we all have them." Jake's facile admission had taken all the wind out of my sails. "Is that the extent of your 'big breakthrough'?" he asked, a hint of condescension in his voice.

"Yes, I suppose it is. It seemed so monumental this morning when it dawned on me," I confessed.

"Must have been the earliness of the hour," Jake suggested.

I laughed weakly. "I guess so." I felt like such a fool sitting there, humiliated by my complete ignorance of simple facts most people take for granted.

"May I make an observation?" Jake asked. I nodded. I had the sinking suspicion that now would be payback time for all the prying inquiries I had made into his personal life. "I'm getting the impression the reason you're so flummoxed with the concept of marriage is because of your inability to understand your own."

I'm sure his effrontery registered on my face immediately, for he hastened to add, "Now think about it. You've spent hours poring over the details of my 'failed marriages,' as you're so fond of calling them, looking for some sort of clues. Now you've spoken with others who are similarly disposed to poor judgment, but so far you've not come up with any one explanation that sufficiently pinpoints the crux of the problem. And you never will.

"There are as many reasons for couples breaking up as there are people. I'd venture to say you're clinging to the totally obsolete notion that humans get one legitimate chance to mate for life, and anything beyond that is somehow immoral or weak." I had to close my mouth, for it was gaping wide from the inaccuracy of his remark.

"You don't know what you're talking about," I said sharply. Jake sat back and casually sipped his coffee, goading me into further defending my position. "You make me sound like some prudish Bible thumper or something, a throwback to the Stone Age, someone completely out of touch with modern times." Jake shrugged his shoulders as if he had nothing more to add. I was so irate with his erroneous assessment of me, I felt on the verge of tears.

"Do you have any idea how many marriages end in divorce these days?" he asked rhetorically. "They estimate over forty percent end in the first five years. Yet, to you divorce is this mysterious affliction only the truly unenlightened have to endure.

"You see someone like me who's done the unthinkable seven times and it shatters your reality. I'm wealthy and successful and relatively intelligent and fairly likable, so what's wrong with me? I think it scares you to realize that divorce can happen to anyone, and that it's not an exclusive curse of the dastardly or the dumb. So I've got to ask you, what is it you're so afraid of?"

With that one simple question, my world tumbled down. It was as if he had knocked down my house of cards with one well-aimed puff. Suddenly, my mind imploded, my heart broke, and my soul shriveled up to nothing. I don't know who was more surprised, Jake or I, when great, hideous sobs broke from my chest.

"Ali, Ali—take it easy, darling. This is all purely for the sake of intellectual debate," he tried to assure me. But he didn't know how on target he had been. Once I got past the outrage, I couldn't help but hear the truth in his words. Judith had tried to point out that my obsession with this topic was way out of proportion; even Elliott had come out of his own self-absorption long enough to voice the same opinion.

Surreptitiously, I had been desperately trying to find evidence divorce was a calamity that could, and should, be avoided at all costs. What I was actually seeking through this journalistic enterprise was assurance my marriage was rock-solid and impervious to such a downfall. And why was this so important to me? Because I knew in my heart-of-hearts our marriage was hollow and unfulfilling, and it always would be.

Add to that dismal assessment the fact that I had thought about giving up my career—the essence of my identity—for offspring I didn't want, all to save a basically unfulfilling marriage I wasn't sure about. I was finally forced to recognize this was nothing but a recipe for disaster.

I gave up the futile attempt to stem the flow of tears and buried my face in my hands. Jake sat beside me and pulled me to his chest, rocking me gently as he tried to console me. When I had exhausted all my pent-up emotions and felt I could cope with this shocking outbreak of self-realization, I pulled away from Jake and tried to regain my composure.

"Do you feel like talking about it?" he asked.

I took a deep breath and asked for a drink. "Whiskey, if you have it." Jake poured out a suitably large portion and handed it to me, pouring one of equal strength for himself. I let the liquor do its job while I went over the scenario in my head.

Elliott and I had both made the honest mistake of assuming the other would be the perfect counterpart to our respective personalities. We had been pretty far off the mark, as it turned out, but both of us were so disciplined and determined, we trudged on in spite of our inherent differences.

At least that's how I saw it now, though I surely couldn't speak for Elliott. One thing I knew without a doubt was how I was clueless as to what went on in his mind, despite all our years together—further proof that we were so ill matched.

Once I started babbling, there seemed no stopping me. The dam had burst and Jake was unfortunate enough to be standing in the flood's path. I told him of feelings I had never disclosed to anyone. I ranted about Elliott's cruelty of insisting I quit my job solely to fulfill his desire for progeny, and how hurt I had been that he valued my professional achievements so little.

Jake continued to listen patiently, never interrupting or criticizing me or giving me a well-deserved taste of my own medicine.

It was after dark by the time I finally wound down, and by then I was thoroughly spent. Jake and I sat in the darkened room, the only illumination coming from the lighting in the hallway, our silence so companionable, one would have thought we had been friends for decades.

The sounds in the public portion of the house grew as Lowell and the others wandered in from their day's work. The sweet smells of baked goods were replaced with the savory aromas of browned beef and simmering vegetables.

"I suspect you could use a little rest before dinner," Jake said, extending a hand to help me up.

"And a shower," I confessed.

"You take your time. Dinner won't be ready for a while yet."

Although I thought myself all cried-out, a fresh wellspring of tears poured out of me while I held my face toward the showerhead. I did feel calmer when I emerged, though the feeling of exhaustion had intensified. The clock read 6:14 when I lay my head on the pillow, and 8:47 the next time I opened my eyes. I sat bolt upright, nearly making myself sick.

In a panicked daze I pulled on my skirt and sweater, brushed powder over my face, ran a comb through my hair, and dashed off to the dining room. My face fell as my fears were confirmed. There, at the far end of the table, sat Jake, all by himself, reading *The Wall Street Journal*.

"Hey, you made it," he said, standing up. "I was afraid you'd gone into your Rip Van Winkle routine again."

"I should've never lay down," I said. My lightheadedness was now accompanied by acute hunger. "Well, it smelled good," I said sadly.

"It was. But don't worry. No guest of mine will ever go hungry, not with Rosalinda in the kitchen." Jake pulled out a chair to seat me and went into his faithful butler mode. "Will Madame be having wine with dinner this evening?" he inquired. I glanced down at the glass in front of his place and said I'd have whatever he was having. He then disappeared, returning promptly with a plate piled high with food.

"Oh, God, I don't think I've ever been so famished," I said as he filled my glass with wine.

I ate like a street dog, barely restraining myself from swallowing every bite whole. I attacked the roast beef, roasted potatoes, buttered Brussels sprouts, parsleyed parsnips, glazed carrots, and creamed onions with equal vigor. I washed down everything with the '82 Saint Emilion, that I later learned was chosen as a special treat for me. All the while, Jake looked on, always the attentive host.

"Why are you so nice to me?" I asked when I had all but licked the plate.

"Hell if I know. You sure don't deserve it."

Although I had been hugely embarrassed by missing dinner as scheduled, it was a relief to not have to put on a false front for the others. Now that I had confided my troubles to Jake, I felt much more relaxed around him. It was self-indulgent to descend on him out of the blue, then unravel before his very eyes, but he was so gracious and understanding that I exploited his good nature to the fullest.

We wandered back to the living room, where earlier I had unceremoniously given up the ghost of my marriage. Even as I acknowledged this watershed experience, I knew the formalities still lay before me. We were just another statistic now as far as I was concerned, but I felt in my bones Elliott would not give up so easily. And then there were my parents.

As Jake poured us snifters of cognac, it hit me that so much of my resistance to admitting my error in judgment was due to their guaranteed disappointment. But none of it mattered at the moment. I had disappeared into the Twilight Zone, a million miles from reality, safe from all my troubles.

It goes to show how cavalier I was in my refuge that I didn't even care if my husband and parents were worried sick about my failure to materialize in New York. The best I could manage was to hope they hadn't bothered to check up on me.

"Cheers," Jake toasted, as he sat down in the chair to my right. We sipped our cognac and stared at the fire.

"Jake, I don't even know how to apologize for dumping all my personal problems on you."

"Don't. That would be an insult. I care about you." This seemed explanation enough for both of us.

"Jake, do you think I'm an idiot? After all, I practically called you a cretin for being married so many times."

"No, I don't think you're an idiot. A foolish, arrogant twit, maybe, but not an idiot." We sipped in silence.

"You're young. That's the only thing wrong with you. When you get to be my age, you'll have a lot more humility and life experiences to your credit. Maybe by the time you hit fifty you'll understand divorce is not the worst thing that can happen to a person. But enduring a bad marriage can be." I'd heard veterans of divorce say this before; I only hoped I'd come to believe it someday.

"Jake?" I asked a few minutes later.

"Yes?"

"How can you stay so optimistic about love after all you've been through? I'm facing my first breakup and it feels like murder. I can't imagine having the courage to put my heart out there again for someone to stomp on. The way I feel right now, I doubt I'll ever trust anyone again, or myself, for that matter.

"To be honest, I can see myself spending the rest of my years solo, only going out when friends take pity on me, and then it will be as the odd woman out at dinner parties, the single old bag they feel compelled to include in their holiday dinners because they feel sorry for me."

Jake laughed out loud at this dire prediction. "You ought to try your hand at fiction. I'd say you have a natural talent for it." He was trying to tease me into a better mood, but the more I thought along those lines, the surer I became that my happy life had ended, with only anxious solitude to replace it.

Maybe I should move to Florida to be close to my brother, I thought gloomily, somehow imagining this might save me from being lonely. But he was married and had children and I'd fall into the same holiday charity category I would be trying to escape.

I'd probably end up teaching journalism at some state college, forging friendships with students who looked up to me for winning a Prescott Award way back when. I would turn into a caricature of an academic, my former short-lived fame my only calling card…

"Looks like I lost you," Jake said, snapping his fingers in front of my face.

"Sorry. Were you saying something?"

"I was saying as hard as it might be for you to imagine right now, I'm willing to wager you'll be in another relationship within two years, quite possibly married by then."

"Oh, please—you must be joking!" I said, nauseated at the mere thought of it. "Care to place a bet on that?" I snorted dismissively. "I guarantee you it won't happen. You can laugh if you want to, but you're still wrong."

"No, I'm not wrong."

"What makes you so certain?" I demanded, feeling a bit provoked by his outlandish assumption.

"Because I know human nature, that's why. You seem to be forgetting I've had more than a little experience in the matter," he said cheerfully.

"Oh, I haven't forgotten. But you're different than I am."

"Thank you for noticing." I let his smart remark pass. "The only difference between your situation and mine is you're a novice at this kind of thing and I'm an old hand. Believe me, I've sworn off marriage half a dozen times, and you've seen what good it's done me."

"Yeah, but I don't fall head-over-heels in love every five minutes, like you do."

"No, I suppose you're too serious and level-headed to do something like that. I'd guess that besides what's-his-name, you've probably only had one or two significant relationships in your whole life. Am I right?"

It irked me that he could make my fidelity sound like a disadvantage, and that he was right once again. "Yes, and that's exactly my point. I don't run around all willy-nilly, ready to throw myself at the first pretty face I see."

Jake chuckled and shook his head. "Ali, Ali, Ali. How old are you—thirty-four, thirty-five?"

"Thirty-six."

"I have to tell you you're awfully naïve for a girl—pardon me, woman your age, especially for one as attractive as you. I suppose that's why you fell for such a stick-in-the-mud," he mused.

"It's funny how you've always taken a dim view of Elliott, yet I got the distinct impression at Miriam's wedding that you hit it off with him. Why are you suddenly so down on him?"

"Why are you suddenly defending him? This is the same repressed control freak who more or less ordered you to quit your job and pop out babies. Are you having second thoughts about leaving him?"

His question sent my system into a state of alarm. "No. It's definitely all over except for the shouting."

"Are you sure? Maybe you'll feel better after your trip to New York. Maybe after you receive your accolades publicly you'll be able to retire gracefully. Or maybe you'll decide you're too afraid to be alone," Jake conjectured.

"And maybe I'll end up married and divorced more times than you," I quipped. Jake laughed.

"Not a chance. You're too sensible." The word "sensible" didn't strike me as particularly flattering coming from him. "Want another one?" he asked as he picked up my snifter.

"No, I'm good. I'll never make my plane in the morning if I keep carrying on like this."

"Would that be such a bad thing? You could stay here and torment me at your leisure." I smiled at the thought. How nice it would be to hang out at the ranch all day, take a ride whenever I felt like it, gorge myself on Rosalinda's good cooking. Jake turned around from the bar to gauge my reaction.

"You giving the idea some thought?" he asked.

"You wouldn't want me around. I'd drive you crazy in under a week," I said.

"Yeah, but it might be a fun kind of crazy."

"You're incorrigible, Jake. You honestly don't know who's right for you and who's not, do you?" There was a smirk on his face I couldn't interpret. "Well, I guess I'd better hit the sack again. If you're up around five, would you mind banging on my door, just in case," I asked.

"Will do."

"Thank you for taking such good care of me," I said from the top step.

"Any time."

Twenty-Four

The minute I landed in New York, I regretted not staying in Oregon another day. The weather was so horrendous, we were almost diverted to Logan Airport. The cab ride into the city was interminable, and when I finally reached the hotel, the torrential rain had turned to sleet.

Being alone in a big city under these circumstances left me few options. I had actually been looking forward to a few days in Manhattan, for a chance to feel the pulse of a true metropolis, to bustle along with the crowds, to be jostled and jangled on the subways, and fight for a cab—just long enough to be grateful I lived on the other coast.

Of course, I had envisioned doing all these things with Elliott, which would have made the experience entirely different. But I was determined to have a good time solo, though at this point it seemed rather doubtful.

It would have been one thing to roam around town, visit any number of fabulous restaurants, comb the museums, take in some music at the Carlisle or one of the other swanky nightspots, if the weather hadn't been so inhospitable. I would have welcomed any diversion that would have helped quell my feelings of loneliness.

Instead, I ordered room service, flipped mindlessly through the TV channels, and moped. By Saturday morning, I was relieved to have two appointments to distract me. The pride I had placed in my professional achievements now struck me as pathetically vain and trifling.

The Prescott Award seemed a hollow victory when it was all I had to show at this stage in my life. Even though I had been trying to convince myself otherwise, the fact I had no messages or voicemail awaiting my reply rapidly quashed any hope I had that starting a new life was going to be a seamless experience.

The temperature dropped overnight and I awoke to find the dismal grey slush of the previous day had been transformed into a perfect white frosting of fresh snow. The world looked better to me as I gingerly picked my way across frozen sidewalks, down the avenues and side streets, passing others intent on shopping or rendezvousing with friends and family.

The Christmas finery in the hotels and department stores did lend a certain sense of jolly festivity, though every couple I passed made my heart sink with regret. By the time I reached my first destination, I was more than ready to be done with this whole Prescott business and flee the isolation that comes from being surrounded by unknown millions.

Though I had originally seen my two interviews as distractions, sitting down face-to-face with fellow journalists was not as diverting a task as I had hoped. I donned a mask of professionalism and tried to answer their questions with the same seriousness with which they were asked, but I had a hard time believing what I had to say was even remotely interesting.

I wondered idly as I rode the elevator down from my second interview how those two writers viewed me. I suspected they both figured I was either uncommonly lucky or remarkably bad at being on the other side of personal questions.

Three o'clock found me in one of the hotel bars, hiding behind *The New York Times* and a glass of sherry. I exercised every bit of will power I possessed to keep from checking every five minutes for any messages that might have been put through to my room. I had left my cell phone on, the excuse being Judith might need to reach me, but even that didn't ring. At ten to four, I gave up and returned to my room.

My heart leapt to my throat as I caught sight of the red light flashing on the telephone. I followed the instructions for retrieving voicemail, conflicting hopes assailing me as I waited for the message to play.

I listened as the concierge confirmed that a limousine would be waiting out front at 6:30 to take me to the Waldorf. I hung up, biting my lip to keep from crying. Here I was, at the pinnacle of my career, and I couldn't have felt more sad or alone.

It wasn't until I was stepping out of the shower that I finally got a call from Judith. The news wasn't good. The weather in the East had turned so treacherous, her plane had been rerouted to Chicago, where she would be forced to remain until conditions improved. My spirits sank to new lows. Not only would I have to attend the stinking awards ceremony alone, there was now the possibility that my return flight to San Francisco might be delayed.

"Worst snowstorm in fifty years is what they're calling it. Damn it! I should have never tried to arrive the same day as the awards," Judith berated herself. "I'm really sorry, Allison. I feel like a heel leaving you there by yourself. Damn, I can't believe this is happening."

"Hey, don't worry about me—I'm fine. I'm in this fabulous hotel room, all of New York at my feet. You're the one I feel sorry for," I lied for her benefit. "Are they going to stick you in some crummy airport hotel?"

"I don't know. So far they're maintaining it's still a possibility our flight will take off again. Personally, I think the worst is yet to come. I think I'm going to call it quits and head for a hotel while I still have a chance. You should see this place—wall-to-wall people, and none of them look too happy." There was a lot of noise on the line and I had trouble hearing her.

"If they're going to insist on holding this damn event in December, they should at least have it somewhere out of the Frost Belt, like Fort Lauderdale. I probably should get on the next flight to California, but frankly, I'm too beat."

The casualness with which she was willing to abandon me did nothing to buoy my mood.

"Sounds like you'd better make other arrangements, then—"

"What? Sorry, I can't hear over the racket here. I'll call you after the dinner to see how it went," she screamed into the phone.

I started to say something, but I was no match for the din that engulfed her. After a final hurried goodbye on her end, the line went dead. I sat staring at my reflection in the mirror as I held the useless receiver in my hand. As soon as I re-placed it, the phone rang again.

"Hello?" I asked, certain that it was Judith, hoping against hope they had just announced her flight was resuming.

"Allison?" It was Elliott.

"Elliott. Hi."

"How are doing? I hear there's a terrible storm out there. Is everything okay?" he asked.

"Yeah, so far, everything's fine. It's actually kind of nice, with the snow falling," I said, looking out the window at the thickening drifts on the ledge. "It feels rather Christmassy," I said.

"That's good," Elliott replied in his usual distracted manner. I could have told him the power was out and we were sure to freeze to death by morning and I would have gotten the same response.

"Well, I just wanted to make sure everything was all right," he said. I didn't know how to respond to that. He was so adept at concealing his feelings, I couldn't

"I was living it up long before I was ranching. What would you like to hear?" he asked as he flipped through his list on his iPod.

"Astor Piazzolla," I replied automatically, remembering the name from our recorded conversation.

"You liked that, huh? Let me see if I have any on here. Yep, here we are." It wasn't the same song he had played in his barn bar, but it had the same characteristic flavor.

"I love this music," I said, the unique instrumentation and melodies striking a chord inside me, likely from the association to happier times. "You'd better get some of this before I eat it all," I warned him.

"Why don't you have a seat and I'll dish up a sampling of everything for both of us."

"Jake, you're going to spoil me irreparably. What am I going to do once I get back to reality?"

"Don't go back to reality—find yourself a new one," he cavalierly suggested.

I barked at the notion. "Easy for you to say. You get to go back to your bucolic paradise. I have to go back to San Francisco and figure out how to get divorced."

"Are you sure you're at that stage? Things might look a whole lot better once you get home."

"No, I don't think so," I said. "I get this horrible knot in my stomach just thinking about seeing Elliott again. It's weird—I've never once thought about living my life without him, but it's like a cloud suddenly lifted and I could see him as he really is for the first time.

"I know now we're not as well matched as I used to think we were. As horrible as it sounds, he honestly gives me the creeps. You wouldn't believe what a one-dimensional bore he can be. I talked to him earlier tonight and it was like I had no connection to him at all. Nothing. Just listening to his voice made me want to scream."

Jake laughed, the tail end of a French fry dangling from his mouth. "I'd say you're done, then," he agreed once he finished chewing.

I shook my head sadly. "I was brought up to believe there was one special person in this world who would fit me like a glove, and once I found him, we'd get married and live together forever—maybe not blissfully, but at least compatibly," I said.

"Yeah, and some people are raised to believe in the Tooth Fairy and Santa Claus," Jake said, spreading mousse de foie gras on a toast point.

"Myths and fairytales, is that what you're saying about the ideal of marriage?" Jake nodded. "So, there's really no such thing as everlasting love?" I asked.

"Oh sure there is. It's happened a million times over. But where some people get caught up is in thinking you have to be that lucky the first time out. And then there are some folks who never get it right." I smiled.

"I'm not sure where the notion started that you only had one chance to make the right choice, but obviously modern standards have righted that misconception. So don't worry, darlin'—if at first you don't succeed…"

"Please, not that. Besides, who in his right mind would want an arrogant, know-it-all twit divorcée?" I asked with rhetorical glumness.

"Oh, I think you'd be surprised. Arrogant yuppie twits are all the rage these days." I wanted to laugh, but couldn't. "Come on, let's dance," he said, pulling me to my feet. "You know I can't sit still to tango music."

"No, no," I protested, uselessly.

"You remember your part—ochos, figure eights. Come on, place your hips against mine—that's the way."

"Jake, I can't dance the tango in this dress."

"You look great in it, by the way."

"Honestly, I'm too tired and too intoxicated to do this," I said.

"You're doing fine," he insisted. "Just lean back and relax and let your feet go where I guide them." His manipulating gestures, geared to make me follow his lead, sent me instead into a fit of giggles which eventually stopped our dance.

"Feel better?" Jake asked as I finally wound down. "It's good to laugh. It's also good to dance," he said, clutching me back into position. I laughed again, but not uncontrollably this time. "And it's even better to laugh and dance together," he said, emitting a long, contrived laugh to go with mine.

"Oh, Jake—I love you. You're so crazy." Our laughter halted abruptly. Jake held me close while he whirled me around, making no further comment. What the hell had I said? Oh, help me, I thought. I studiously concentrated on my footwork until the song ended.

"Well, that was fun," I said, heading straight for my champagne glass, avoiding any eye contact with Jake.

"Let's change the mood here," Jake said as he switched Astor Piazzolla for Old Blue Eyes. I went over to the window and pretended to be absorbed in the view, but in reality I was petrified that I had irrevocably altered our friendship. In a moment, Jake joined me.

"Uh, Jake…what I said—you know I meant that…your friendship means a lot to me—I don't know what I'd do without you right now."

"It's all right, Ali. I know what you meant."

"I just don't want you to feel that you've been cornered by yet another female," I said, flustered by his cool response.

"I can think of worse things than being cornered by you." I looked at him. I was getting conflicting signals, and I wasn't sure what he was saying. "I have to tell you, I really thought an ace reporter like you would be better at sniffing out the truth. But sometimes you can be remarkably slow on the uptake."

"What are you talking about?' I asked, mystified.

"Do I really have to draw you a picture?"

"Yes, I guess you do." Before I knew what hit me, Jake leaned over and gave me a kiss that literally took my breath away. When I regained my wits, I pulled away.

"Jake—"

"Allison. Why do you think I came here? Sure, it was because I knew you'd need a shoulder to cry on. But the only reason that I cared enough to fly all this way for your sake is because I love you." I stood there, astounded.

"I didn't want to lay this on you while you're trying to sort out your marriage. Believe me, that was the last thing I wanted to do. But I hated the thought of you being here all by yourself, especially with what's going on. As you well know, I've been there before. I know what hell it is."

I can't say which startled me most, his admission or his sincerity. Needless to say, I was at a complete loss. Jake gave me a look of expectation, but the best I could manage was an indecisive wobble of my head.

"I…uh…uh…"

"I was hoping for something a tad more enthusiastic," he said, an enigmatically wry smile on his face. He knocked back the rest of his champagne in one swift movement.

"Oops, looks like we need another bottle," he said as he poured the last dribble into his glass. "I'm feeling the sudden need to get plastered," he cracked, as he went in search of reinforcements.

I stared at my reflection in the windowpane and tried to make sense out of what had just happened. I suppose my initial reaction had been one of fright; even though I had come to the same conclusion about my feelings for him, I had never dreamed of him reciprocating in kind.

Thinking of Jake in romantic terms had been more of an acknowledgment of an abstract fantasy than anything else. Admitting he loved me presented me with a reality I was not prepared to deal with. But beyond the initial shock, what did I feel? Blank, I felt utterly blank.

I was too stunned to fully assimilate this drastic change to our simple friendship. And now that he had introduced this new element, would we cease to be friends? The very thought of losing my key ally sent a ragged bolt of anxiety through my chest.

An unusual scent caught my attention, and I turned to find Jake sitting on the arm of the sofa, lighting a cigar, a fresh bottle of bubbly chilling in the ice bucket.

"Bring me your glass. We will have no dry glasses at this party tonight," he said, his mood reflecting his more swashbuckling side. I obligingly handed him my glass.

"Let's see, what shall we drink to now? It's got to be something different—we've already toasted love and marriage…I know—divorce. Here's to your upcoming divorce," he said, lifting his glass in the air. "Come on, Ali—it was just a bad joke. Wait, I've got it—here's to you, the finest journalist in the land." He touched his glass to mine, but it was not a toast I cared to participate in.

"Lighten up, Ali. You're being a regular wet blanket," he said in an oddly jocular tone.

"Jake, I think we need to clear something up here—"

"There's nothing to clear up. Here, have some more of this caviar—there's still a lot left."

"I don't want any caviar. I want to talk," I said, waving his offering away.

"Go ahead, talk away."

"Well, for starters, you first told me you came to New York to give me moral support, then you told me you came here on business. Then you told me you came here because you're in love with me. I think maybe you're just toying with me, trying to get some kind of rise out of me," I postulated. Jake gave me a look over his cigar that suggested not only was I way off base, I was being insulting as well.

"Oh come on, Jake—let's be real for a minute. You become infatuated every time you turn around. You've got a string of ex-wives as long as your arm, and God knows how many others have been the object of your affection." Jake puffed on his cigar as if I were boring him. "I think you've confused the warm, fuzzy feeling of a good friendship with love," I told him.

Jake rolled his eyes heavenward. "I love how you *think* you know how I feel," he said condescendingly.

"So, what then?" I asked, hands on my hips. "You say you love me, sweep me off my feet, and then abandon me a week later when the next love of your life bats her eyes at you? Thanks, but I think I could do without a walk in Lavinia's shoes."

Jake laughed out a large puff of smoke. "Why would you even compare yourself to her?" he asked.

"She was the last one driven witless by your kind of love—that I'm aware of, anyway." He took the insult and smiled. "For all I know, she might have been a perfectly normal person before she met you."

"Ali, what are you going on about? Have a seat, would you please. You're too wound up."

"All I'm trying to do is illustrate the fact that you have lousy judgment when it comes to this sort of thing. In all your sixty-some years, you've never picked a single woman who was right for you."

"Until now," he said, over his cigar.

"Jake, this is no time to be playing with me. I need a good friend now, not someone who merely wants to add me to his collection." My blood was up, and Jake could see it.

Wisely, he opted to be the calm one. "Ali, I meant what I said. I'm not trying to mess with your emotions."

"I don't know how you can say that," I said, suddenly impatient with this new development. Okay, let's suppose for a moment you really do believe you're in love with me. What kind of lunatic would I have to be to consider something other than friendship with you? I would be setting myself up for a major heartbreak if I gave into my feelings for you. I'd probably set the record for the quickest breakup you've ever had, and then where would I be? At this stage, I'm can't even imagine trusting my own instincts again."

"So, you do have feelings for me," Jake concluded. I stared at him, wondering how I managed to let that slip out.

"As a friend. I have feelings for you as a friend." Jake smiled and chuckled lightly to himself. "Look, it's late. I should go," I said, making a start for the door. I didn't make it out of the living room before he grabbed me by the arm.

"Ali, don't leave. We'll drop all this talk about love and just carry on as if I had never brought it up. Stay a while longer. You're in New York City in the middle of a snowstorm, with an endless supply of champagne and a man—a friend—who thinks the world of you. What do you say?" I looked him straight in the eyes and pulled my arm free.

"No, I have to go. I'm afraid I'll do something very stupid that I'll undoubtedly regret."

"Well, you don't have to make it sound so flattering," Jake said. I couldn't tell whether I had really hurt his feelings or not.

"Jake, I will never forget this." I took one last look at his face, gave him a quick peck on the cheek and bolted for the door.

"Ali, wait," he called out down the hallway. I kept moving and didn't look back. He called my name again as I rounded the corner. Once out of sight, I slowed my pace. I heard his door close softly and I increased my speed. Then I thought of what had transpired, and stopped.

He told me that he loved me. Wasn't that what I was secretly hoping for, all those times I had replayed the tape of the first night in Oregon? Didn't I know somewhere deep down inside that the way I felt when I was with him was the way I always wanted to feel? Wasn't feeling slightly off balance and excited and happy and unsure what love was supposed to feel like?

The problem was I didn't have anything to compare it to. I realized now that marrying Elliott had been more akin to a business arrangement than true love. I had loved Elliott—I couldn't have spent seven years with him and not have felt something—but I had never been *in love* with him. I resumed my walk, slowly.

I couldn't think of the word love without receiving a pang to the heart. I did love Jake; I knew I did. At least, it felt like love. But that could have been the alcohol talking. Or the fact that I was so lonely and afraid of my future. Besides, there were more reasons to put plenty of distance between Jake and me than I could list.

For starters, he was obviously jinxed when it came to relationships. And it was absolutely impossible for him to remain faithful. That reason alone was enough to keep me moving. Plus, he was as old as my father.

God, how did I ever let my life get so fouled up? I was perfectly fine before I met Jake. I had a good, solid marriage… But the friction between Elliott and me was not due to knowing Jake. What had blown us apart would have surfaced eventually. So I couldn't blame Jake for that.

But I suppose he could be accused of opening up my mind to a different concept of living. That was what really appealed to me, besides the man himself. There was something so attractive about the manner in which he approached life. He had no rules, no regrets, and he seemed to take every encounter head on.

I thought of my first impression of him at Miriam's wedding; even though he looked like a disheveled eccentric, a happy-go-lucky farce of a man in fancy cowboy duds, I remembered feeling an odd attraction to him.

It must have been his smile. He had been standing there, all six-feet-two of him—six-four with the boots, and he was grinning at me like he had never been happier to meet anyone in his life. It's hard not to fall for a person with that kind of charisma, and I guess that was the reason he had attracted so many women in his life, even during his scraggly periods.

But I couldn't fall for him; I knew way too much about him and the myriad others who had probably heard the very same words he had just told me. Yet…with all those perfect examples of why I should being running for the hills, the thought of him being so close stopped me in my tracks.

How could I let this happen to me? How did I manage to fall in love with a guy who had "Danger—Keep Away!" written all over him? I'm normally far too sensible to make that kind of mistake. I must have become deranged by the death of my marriage.

That was it: Jake had made his move on me when I was at my most vulnerable point, when all my defenses had been used up and I was desperate for anything that would make me feel better about myself.

I heard the elevator open and a man and woman talking. I had been standing there in the hallway for who knows how long and I hastened to look like I wasn't loitering in the halls like a derelict.

I resumed the search for my room, only to find I had passed it several doors back. The man and woman walked passed me, giving me wary looks as I fumbled with the plastic key that refused to admit me to my room. I tried to smile reassuringly, but they turned their heads and kept walking.

When I finally got the lock to cooperate, I pushed open the door only a crack, then closed it again. For some inexplicable reason, I couldn't bring myself to go in. I leaned against the wall, wishing my head would clear and I could make sense of what was happening to my life.

Here I was, the winner of an award I no longer cared about, married to a man I no longer wanted to live with, in love with a man I was too afraid to be with. Why was everything so mixed up these days?

I kneaded my brow with the heels of my hands, then pushed away from the wall, heading in the direction of Jake's room. I just needed someone to talk to. Jake would listen, regardless of what he believed he felt for me.

No, it wouldn't be right to go back there. I turned around.

But maybe he could explain to me how I could have married Elliott for the wrong reasons when I felt certain I was doing it for all the right reasons. I had been too hard on Jake, thinking there was something inherently wrong with him that he had failed to make any of his marriages last. It really wasn't as simple as I had once believed. I stopped.

But still, he was the one who continually made poor choices. Take Lavinia for example—even on the face of it, you could tell they were an impossible mismatch. She was all the things he wasn't, and a control maniac to boot.

But who knew—maybe she had been a perfectly normal person before she met Jake. I considered this and shook my head. No way. She was a psychotherapist, and let's face it, some of them have more quirks and hang-ups than their average patient.

I started toward Jake's room again. But that just made my point—the guy had no judgment. Honestly, what on earth did he see in me? We couldn't be more different. Granted, I wasn't controlling and unyielding, like Lavinia, and though I could be a bit of a know-it-all at times, I couldn't hold a candle to her.

So maybe I was a refreshing twist on his last girlfriend—similar enough in some ways, different enough in the ones that went against his grain the most.

I stopped again. I was going to go crazy. That was it. I was going to set him straight, right then and there, or I'd never get out of the hallway. I marched to his door and knocked, then knocked more forcibly as I recalled the distance from the door to his bedroom.

"Don't beat the door down, I'm coming," I heard him call out. I silently ran through my spiel one last time. "Well, hello again. Did you have a change of heart?" he asked, leaning languidly against the doorframe. He had traded his tuxedo for the hotel bathrobe and a pair of slippers.

"No. I came here to tell you that regardless of what I may feel about you, I've made my mind up that nothing is going to come of it. I won't let it. I may be screwed up in the head right now, but I've still got enough sense to know that giving in to my desires could only lead to disastrous results. So," I said, drawing my first breath, "we'll just have to leave it at that."

I stood resolutely, as if I had been expecting to feel some kind of relief after taking a stand. None came. Jake peered curiously at me, which cast further doubts about this course of action.

"Okay. Well. That's all I wanted to say, so…goodnight."

"You came back here to tell me what you had already told me in so many words?"

I shifted on my feet nervously. "Yes. That was it."

"Why don't you come inside? We certainly don't need to discuss this in the hallway," he said, backing up to let me in.

"There's nothing more to discuss," I insisted.

"Come on, Ali. I'll order you a nice cup of tea—"

"I don't want a cup of tea," I hissed through my teeth. "Look, just tell me you'll get this whole stupid idea about being in love with me out of your head."

"I can't do that," he said.

"Yes you can. You're a love junkie. You live for the thrill of the conquest. You feed off the initial excitement, and when it's gone, you go in search of your next fix. By tomorrow you'll be on to the next girl and you'll have forgotten all about me," I predicted.

"And are you going to forget the way you feel about me?" he asked. He turned the bolt to hold the door ajar and approached me slowly. I backed up as he advanced, until I hit the wall on the other side of the hall.

"Ali, what are you so afraid of?" I swallowed hard, but couldn't answer. "I'll tell you what you're afraid of. You're afraid to let yourself be happy, aren't you? You've tormented yourself by staying in a loveless marriage only because you've dreaded facing the fact you simply made the wrong choice.

"But you've crossed that hurdle. Now you're afraid of being with the man you do love because you find my history with women unpalatable. You fear I'll tire of you and discard you like all the heartbroken wretches before you," he said in a slightly mocking tone.

"It's a valid worry," I maintained. I didn't even bother pretending what he had said wasn't true. His proximity was making it harder to keep my wits about me. I had the sudden vision of a starving man standing in front of a buffet table, unable to bring himself to touch the food because of a sign saying "Eat at your own risk."

I knew everything Jake had said was the truth, but his past was something I couldn't get out of my mind. I remembered wondering how wives four, five, and six managed to overlook all their predecessors, never imagining for a second that I would soon be in their shoes. It was a leap of faith I didn't feel I could make. Jake lifted my chin, forcing me to look into his eyes.

"Allison, I swear that I'm in love with you, and that I honestly and truly believe I will be in love with you for a very long time." I tried to pull away, but Jake held me still.

"I'll do anything you want me to do to prove my sincerity. We'll hop on the next flight to Haiti, get you a quickie divorce, and I'll marry you the minute the ink on your decree is dry—"

"Elliott would never agree to a quickie divorce," I said, still unsure about Jake, but softening against my will. "Besides, I can't even imagine being the eighth Mrs. Jake Sorenson." My head swam at such a bizarre notion.

"Fine, then file the paperwork the normal way and we'll go and hang out in Paris until it's all finalized. Then we'll just live in sin till you can stomach the thought of being married to me," he said, his enthusiasm seeming authentic enough. The thought of running away with Jake until all my problems vanished made me laugh.

"We can't do that," I argued.

"The hell we can't." I bit my lip as my eyes glazed over with tears. I looked away and tried to breathe.

"Ali. Ali—look at me." I couldn't, so he turned my head for me. "Do you love me?" I couldn't answer. "Do you love me?" he repeated. "Tell me you don't and I'll leave you alone, I swear."

Here it was, my big moment of truth. All I had to do was tell him I didn't love him the way he professed to love me and I'd be off the hook, scot-free, able to walk away with my sanity intact. Jake kept his eyes focused on mine, willing me to answer him, but my mouth wouldn't work.

I had another vision, this one of the inside of my head as my brain imploded. I could feel tears welling up in the corners of my eyes and I swallowed hard to keep from crying. Jake smiled ever so slightly and backed away.

Slowly he turned and walked the few short steps to his door. Without looking back, he walked in and began to close the door. Finally, some force welled up inside me, causing my lips to open and my voice to speak.

"I do," I croaked. Jake turned around. I stood there, shaking from the effort of trying to control my emotions. "I do love you, though I wish to God I didn't."

Jake crossed the hall and drew me to him, holding me tightly as uncomfortable spasms broke out in my throat. He held me as I let loose all the fears and regrets that were trying to break free. We stood there, in the hallway, in the middle of the night, in the middle of a terrific snowstorm, and he held me until I was all cried out.

When I had finished and had wiped the remnants of my mascara on the lapels of his white terrycloth robe, he kissed me. That kiss knocked the final stone out of the dam, and there was no stopping what was to follow.

In that one decisive moment, I abandoned all sense of reason and propriety, trusting that whatever the cost of such a rash act, I would have the resources to pay for it. Jake whisked me up and carried me over his threshold, without another word of protest from me.

It's been three years now since I moved into the Buckin' J Ranch. Although we didn't hole up in Paris until my divorce from Elliott was final, we did spend Christmas there, flying directly to the French capital from New York. I like to think of it as having had our honeymoon before my divorce. I had been guilt ridden about such behavior at first, but I'm eternally grateful to Jake for giving me an idyllic refuge during that emotionally draining time.

Being on completely neutral turf gave me the equanimity and resolve to deal with an irate Elliott and my distraught parents without giving in to their demands. It was crazy of me to put so much trust in Jake, and I worried those first several months that my temporary insanity would eventually be my undoing.

But Jake has never given me a reason to regret my decision. Running off with him signaled the beginning of a whole new life for me, one that I wouldn't trade for anything.

I still write for *Savoir-Faire*, though I have fewer assignments than before. Judith generously allows me to accept only the ones that interest me the most. It's no problem to do my job from this remote location, and I travel only when I've taken an assignment that requires me to do so. And when I do leave the ranch to conduct an interview or do research, Jake always accompanies me.

Contrary to my oath, Judith did nominate me for a Prescott last year, and amazingly enough, I was awarded the honor a second time. Unlike the previous awards banquet, I had both Jake and Judith by my side.

It's funny, though, how little any of that means to me these days. I suppose it was all-fire important when I was with Elliott, simply because of how much was missing from our relationship. The irony is that I'd give up my career in a heartbeat if Jake asked me to, though it would never occur to him to do so. He likes the fact I have my own mind and ideas and the ability to use them both.

Despite my initial trepidation regarding all the female ghosts in Jake's closet, things have gone more smoothly than I had expected. We did have a surprise visit from Lavinia and her new husband. She blanched from her head to her toes when she found me in residence, but recovered quickly, being the master of outward control that she is.

I amused myself by wondering how she and Elliott would have hit it off. For all I know, it could have been a perfect match. I'm afraid I can't say the same for her and Lester, but I suspect Lavinia glommed onto him in some contorted effort to torment Jake and reassure herself. I have to say that it did neither.

Their unscheduled visit ended with the familiar sight of Lavinia being escorted out on the arms of a dismayed Lester and a trusty Lowell, while Jake and I stood well out of her path, recovering from our mild shock to her parting remarks. I wanted to feel sorry for her, but it was all her own doing. She never did learn to call before coming.

Jaylynn has remained a fairly constant visitor, though she's no longer fixated on Jake. She has Dieter acting as her devoted slave these days, so everyone is happy. She still lives in the same backwater town, though I have seen her emerge from Dieter's lodgings in the early morning hours on several occasions. She looks after her magnificent horse, gives the German cowboy something to live for, and pretty much stays out of our hair.

As far as keeping Jake on a leash, I don't believe I'm deluding myself when I say it's not necessary. For one reason, we're together practically all the time, so courting another woman would be rather difficult.

But don't think I've got my head in the clouds; I nearly went into a panic when Jake came down with the flu and was unable to shave for several days. But as soon as he was able to get out of bed, those frightening whiskers were removed and he's never had so much as a five o'clock shadow since.

He claims to be more in love with me every day, though he has given up the almost weekly proposals of marriage. Instead, he's taken to hanging certificates redeemable for one wedding, the time and place of my choosing, all around the house.

One day I'm going to take those pledges down and have one framed. That will serve as my marriage certificate, for the foreseeable future at least. Who knows, I may change my mind and make him step up to the plate again. But then again, I might not. After all, what's the big deal about marriage, anyway?